Finding

Hayes

T0321554

Laura Pavlov is the *USA Today* bestselling author of sweet and sexy contemporary romances that will make you both laugh and cry. She is happily married to her college sweetheart, mom to two amazing kids who are now adulting, and dog-whisperer to one temperamental yorkie and one wild bernedoodle. Laura resides in Las Vegas where she is living her own happily ever after.

Also by Laura Pavlov and Published by HQ

The Magnolia Falls Series

Loving Romeo
Wild River
Forbidden King
Beating Heart
Finding Hayes

Finding Hayes

LAURA PAVLOV

ONE PLACE. MANY STORIES

HQ
An imprint of HarperCollins*Publishers* Ltd
1 London Bridge Street
London SE1 9GF

www.harpercollins.co.uk

HarperCollins*Publishers*
Macken House, 39/40 Mayor Street Upper,
Dublin 1, D01 C9W8, Ireland

This edition 2025

1
First published in Great Britain by HQ,
an imprint of HarperCollins*Publishers* Ltd 2024

This book contains FSC™ certified paper and other controlled sources to ensure responsible forest management.

For more information visit: www.harpercollins.co.uk/green

Typeset in Sabon Lt Pro by HarperCollins*Publishers* India

Printed and bound in the UK using 100%
Renewable Electricity at CPI Group (UK) Ltd

To anyone who has ever felt judged,
misunderstood, alone or not seen.
This one is for you.
I see you.

XO

1

Hayes

I pulled on my boots and glanced out the window to see the snow falling, hiding the grass outside the firehouse, which was covered in a layer of white powder. I was happy to be done with my three-day shift and ready to get out of here and get some sleep. We'd been slammed every day with several medical emergencies due to the cold temperatures. There'd been a bad car accident, and my paramedic training had come in handy when we'd received the call, but thankfully, everyone was going to be all right.

This afternoon, we'd gone over to the elementary school because, of course, I'd volunteered to talk about fire safety for my godson Cutler's second-grade class. He was my best friend's son and my boy in every way imaginable, and there was nothing I wouldn't do for him, even if it meant calling him by his favorite handle, Beefcake, in public.

I was tired and ready to call it a night.

"Hey, Rambo, you heading out?" Beebs asked, as he dropped his backpack onto the bed across from me.

We all had nicknames, aside from Lenny Davis, who was just a dick by nature, and I knew calling him "asshole" wouldn't fly, so he was the only dude who went by his given name here.

I'd been granted "Rambo" my first year on the job when I'd gone into a fire and came out covered in soot, carrying a three-year-old little girl. The local newspaper had run a story about it with my photo on the front page, saying I looked like Rambo charging out of that fire. The little girl had been okay after a short hospital stay, and the name had stuck because the guys at the firehouse wouldn't let it go.

I'd hated the attention at the time, but it had been worth it to be able to place that little girl in her mama's arms.

Priscilla Larson was a thirteen-year-old teenager now, and she still brought me cookies every single year on the anniversary of that fire.

These were the things that I loved about my job.

"Yep. I'm ready to sleep for a week." I pushed to stand and grabbed my coat. The snow had been coming down hard all day, which meant it was cold as hell outside.

"Yeah, it's not letting up out there, so drive carefully. I actually walked here, and I stopped in at Whiskey Falls for a quick bite on my way in. The hottest chick I've ever seen was in there talking to Ruby. Damn, I was pissed that I had to leave for work," Beebs said. He'd gotten the nickname because his long hair was styled to swoop across his forehead, and it was no secret that he spent a shit ton of time on it every morning. So, he'd started out as "Bieber," and somewhere along the way, he became "Beebs."

"Who was she? A tourist?" I asked, pulling the zipper up on my coat.

"Nope. She said she grew up here. She's here for Abe's funeral," he said, and my hand froze on the zipper.

"Was her name Savannah?"

"Probably to you," he said, as he barked out a laugh. "But she told me that I could call her Savvy because I think she was feeling the Beebs, if you know what I mean."

"Sure, she was." I rolled my eyes. "She must be into that young boy-band look, then."

Savannah Abbott was in town.

I knew she'd come.

She'd loved Abe Wilson like he was her own grandfather.

But I was surprised to hear that she was hanging out at Whiskey Falls bar, because the few times she'd ever come back to town, she'd only gone to see Abe.

She'd avoided me, or at least it felt that way.

"I'm all man, baby," Beebs said, as he pounded his chest before turning to see Lenny walk through the door, his face straightening.

"Beebs, get downstairs. We've got a meeting in five." Lenny was the other lieutenant on our crew, and we always worked opposite shifts.

There was no love there.

Long before he'd fucked my fiancée, I hadn't cared for the dude. He'd always been a whiney little bitch, even back in high school when I was quarterback and he sat on the bench. Instead of working harder to be better, he just complained about the injustice of not getting play time.

Maybe you should suck less, dickhead.

"Yeah, got it. I'll see you later, Rambo." Beebs clapped me on the shoulder, and I nodded before making my way toward the door.

Lenny just stared at me as I moved in his direction, and then he held a piece of paper out to me. "Hey, Woodson. Kimber is hosting a fundraiser this weekend for the firehouse. It would be nice if you showed up, because the guys tend to go if you go." He hadn't ended up with my ex, because apparently, she'd cheated on him shortly after I'd found them together. And the asshole had the gall to come try to discuss it with me and bond over the situation.

We weren't friends. Never would be.

I snatched the paper out of his hand. Another fucking fundraiser. Just in time for Cap to retire in three months.

How fucking convenient.

"And what exactly are we raising money for this weekend, Lenny?" I said, not hiding my disdain for the man.

He quirked a brow. "Kimber thought we could get some new bedding and window coverings in here and spruce the place up."

Spruce the place up? It's a fucking firehouse.

He had no interest in fixing this place up. She'd never hosted so many events as she had these last few months when word got out that Cap would be announcing his retirement soon.

Which he did announce recently.

And now this fake motherfucker wanted to present this family environment, as if that made him some sort of leader. He wasn't the dude charging into fires anymore. He always sent the younger guys in first.

Lenny Davis did not lead by example. He was good at playing the game.

And I'd always hated that part of my job.

The politics.

I wasn't any good at it. I was all about putting out fires, helping people in distress, and making sure our guys all got home safely.

"Sure." I smirked. "And what did last month's fundraiser get us?"

"Are you referring to the hoedown that Kimber hosted at our place? We raised enough money to get that big-screen TV down in the hangout and the standing popcorn maker."

Like I said, the man doesn't lead by example.

"I don't think the people in this town should be giving their hard-earned money to buy us a TV or new curtains. We have a budget for those things." I stepped closer, leaning in and keeping my voice low. "You could just try doing your job and

4

not acting like a fucking saint to impress Cap. We're here to fight fires, remember?"

He stepped back, the corners of his lips turning up the slightest bit. "It's not about the fires, jackass. You just don't get it, Hayes. The owner of a football team isn't the guy cleaning up the shit in the stadium; he's the one showing up to the party who everyone wants to talk to. I'm the face of this house, and you—you clean up the shit."

I shoved him back against the wall, getting in his face. "This is a fucking firehouse. Those guys need to be led, not attending parties so we can buy stupid shit. Do your fucking job."

I could see the fear there. I was several inches taller than him and probably had forty pounds on the asshole. But he held that annoying smirk on his face and pushed me back, barely moving me. "And why should I do that? I've got you to do my shit work."

"Everything all right in here?" Cap's voice pulled me from my anger.

I nodded slowly as I took a step back. "Yeah. Everything's fine."

"You know Woodson just has a temper sometimes, Cap. But I can handle him." Lenny chuckled, and my hands fisted at my sides. This fucking guy got under my skin.

"How about you go get your meeting started," Cap said to Lenny, turning to me after Lenny walked out of the room. This man had been more of a father to me than my own dad ever had. "You all right, Hayes? Long shift?"

"I'm good. I'll catch up on sleep over the next few days."

"All right, son. Take it easy." He called me that sometimes, and I didn't show it, but it meant something to me. "Get some rest."

"Will do, Cap." I made my way out to the cold, jumped into my truck, and headed through downtown toward my house. But when Whiskey Falls bar came into view, something had me turning the wheel and pulling into the parking lot.

I hadn't seen Savannah in years, and I was curious to see how she was doing.

Hell, the truth was, I'd never understood the way she'd cut me out of her life so abruptly all those years ago.

I pulled the door open, and the place was quiet, aside from Ruby, who was standing behind the bar, which was not the norm, as she didn't work here anymore. Her father owned the place, so maybe she was filling in for someone tonight. But my gaze landed on the woman she was speaking to, sitting across from her, head back in a fit of laughter.

Savannah Abbott had the best laugh.

Always had.

She was the one person who could bring it out of me, because she was funny as hell. At least, she used to be. She also used to be a scrawny little thing, with her hair tied back in a ponytail. But today, long caramel-brown waves ran down her back, and she didn't look like the sixteen-year-old teenager who'd left town in a hurry.

Who'd left me.

She wore a pair of faded jeans and a black turtleneck sweater, and the foot of her cowboy boots rested at the base of the barstool.

"Looky here," Ruby said, when she turned to see me walking in. "I figured you'd head home after your long shift."

"I didn't expect to see you here either," I said.

"Dad's got the stomach bug, so I'm covering for him tonight. What's your story?" She arched a brow.

"I guess I was craving a burger," I lied. I'd come to see if Savannah was here, but instead, I feigned surprise when my gaze met her honey-brown eyes. "Hey, Sav."

"Long time, no see, Hayes."

"That's a fucking understatement," I said, my words coming out harsher than I'd meant them to.

"I'm sure you survived just fine." She shrugged, reaching for her wineglass and taking a sip.

"Let me get that burger going for you." Ruby set a beer in front of me and disappeared into the kitchen, and I dropped onto the stool beside Savannah.

Damn, she was pretty. Always had been, but she looked different now.

She was gorgeous and sexy and all grown up.

But I'd be cautious where this woman was concerned. She was probably going to be gone as quickly as she came.

"I'm guessing you're here for Abe's funeral?" I asked, as her gaze moved along every inch of my face, making no effort to hide it.

"Yep," she said, letting out a long breath. "You look good."

"You need to get out more, then. I just got off a three-day shift, and I feel like shit."

"Always the optimist." She chuckled.

Damn. I'd missed her laugh.

"You look good, Shortcake."

I was surprised at how easily her nickname rolled off my tongue.

Like no time had passed at all.

2

Savannah

Hot damn. Forgetting about Hayes while I'd been away was a lot easier than seeing him after all these years. He was even sexier than I'd remembered.

Hayes Woodson, aka my best friend from as early as I could remember. We'd been neighbors, classmates, pals, buds, besties, and all that good stuff.

We'd both had a lot of drama in the homes we'd grown up in, and we'd always been there for one another.

Until we weren't.

Until he showed me his true colors.

And when people showed me who they were, I believed them.

Well, that's not entirely true. Sometimes it took a couple of punches to the gut before I fully believed them. But eventually, I got there.

I was a strange mix of irrationally positive and upbeat and happy, yet there was also this dark cloud that hung over me, reminding me that every time I let my guard down, I got bitch slapped.

So, I'd remain irrationally positive and upbeat and happy, but I wouldn't let my guard down.

Definitely not around this man.

Even if he was ridiculously good-looking.

I sighed, remembering how many fantasies I'd had about my best friend back when we were teenagers. Even when he'd started dating the ice queen from hell, Hayes was the only boy I'd ever fantasized about back then.

He'd managed to break my heart and crush me—yet we'd never even had a romantic relationship.

Well, not outside of my fantasies, at least.

"I hate that nickname," I said, trying to feign irritation even though I'd missed the sound of his voice.

"Well, I was never a fan of you calling me Woody, so I guess we can call it even." He smirked when Ruby came out of the kitchen carrying two burgers and set one in front of me.

"What's this?" I asked.

"I figured you could use a meal after the day you've had."

Hayes glanced over at me. "Funeral's tomorrow, right? What happened today?"

I thanked Ruby before reaching for my burger and taking a big bite. I thought about how much I wanted to share with him. But this was Hayes. Whether I ever spoke to him again didn't really matter; he'd always been the best listener I'd ever known.

Probably because he didn't talk all that much.

Ruby's brothers, Rico and Zane, who I hadn't seen since we were all kids, walked into the bar and called her over. She said she'd be back, and I looked up to see the large man beside me just staring at me.

Like he was waiting.

He'd always been a big guy, but he seemed larger now.

"Did you get taller?"

He raised a brow. "No. Maybe you got shorter."

It had always been our joke. He stood a foot taller than my five-feet-four-inch frame.

"I'm not shorter."

"I'm not taller. Tell me what happened today."

"Why? We haven't seen one another in more than a decade. Why do you want to know?" I asked, as he took a bite of his burger. He pushed up, leaned over the bar, and reached for a glass before filling it with ice. He grabbed the soda gun and poured himself what looked like a Coke, acting like he owned the place.

"Maybe I'm just bored and feel like being entertained," he said.

"I always was the best entertainment you ever had."

"I wouldn't argue that. I survived your tap-dancing phase, your stint playing the violin, and then the piano. Then there were those years when you thought your voice was a perfect mix of Taylor Swift and Adele."

I arched a brow and recalled the lyrics I'd written when I was certain I was going to try out for *American Idol*, and I belted out the chorus. "He's the luckiest guy around, and he's pretty sporty. He likes to watch me laugh and call me shorty. He puts on his cowboy boots. Sometimes he has the toots." I continued singing over my laughter as the corners of his lips turned up. "He's my partner in crime till the end of time, and he's my very best friend, but that doesn't rhyme. Even when I'm lost and in a daze, I can always find my . . . Hayes." I threw my hands in the air and shook them around, celebrating my grand finale, and both of Ruby's brothers applauded and whistled from the other side of the bar.

Hayes barked out a laugh.

I'd always loved the sound of his laugh. This gruff, foreign sound from a guy who didn't let himself go there often. I had a hunch not much had changed, just by the grumpy disposition he still carried himself with now.

"That one was a winner. What was it called?" he asked.

"'Finding Hayes.' Had I known you were going to become

10

a firefighter, I could have played on that—you know, like the smoky haze. My lyrical genius would have had a heyday with that. I believe it's called a heterography."

"I see you haven't lost your charm for knowing random shit." He took another bite of his burger. "Are you going to tell me what happened today or not?"

I thought it over. "Why should I? We don't even know each other anymore."

His shoulders stiffened, and I didn't know why he'd be offended, because it was the truth.

He'd betrayed me.

Hurt me when I was at my lowest.

We'd obviously grown apart, and I hadn't been able to see it when it was happening.

"Fine, let's catch up. I know how much you love to ask questions. What do you want to know?" he asked, wiping his hands on his napkin.

"What happened to that she-devil you used to date?"

"Kate?" he asked, his gaze hard now.

"The one and only. I heard you got engaged to her?" I did not hide my disdain.

"I did. It was a dumb move."

"You can say that again." I rolled my eyes. "She was the worst. Clearly, you just saw the big boobs and the pretty face."

The girl had a black heart. She was mean and manipulative, and I'd never liked her.

"I think I was just with her for so long, and I didn't want to see who she was. I don't know." He scrubbed a hand down his face, and for a second, I felt bad for him.

And then I remembered what he'd done.

"You were always blinded by that girl. So, why'd you call off the engagement?"

He narrowed his gaze. "How do you know I called off the engagement?"

11

"I don't see a ring on your finger. There's no way Kate would wait this long to get married. She had the patience of a petulant child." I paused for dramatic effect before continuing. "On a sugar high. After days of no napping."

"I get it. You never did like her." He chuckled. "After we got engaged, she fucked Lenny Davis, who also happens to be my coworker at the firehouse. Obviously, I called things off after that."

"One would hope that would do it. Every man has his limits." I smirked, because I knew that girl would eventually show her true colors.

"Okay, so now you know my story. Tell me what happened today."

"Always so nosy," I said, sinking my teeth into my bottom lip because being around Hayes felt . . . comfortable. Easy. I wanted to hate him, but so much time had passed it was hard to tap into all that anger I used to carry. I'd be cautious, but having a conversation with Hayes felt like a gift I could allow myself. We had a history, after all.

"For fuck's sake, Shortcake, I just told you my shit story. Just say it."

"Fine." I pursed my lips and pushed my plate away. "I got a call from Abe's probate attorney in San Francisco, and I met with him this morning before coming here. Abe left me his farmhouse."

"Holy shit. That place is huge. Who did he leave all the land to?"

"Also me," I said, as I cleared my throat.

His eyes widened. "Wow. That land is on the water. It's got to be worth a couple million dollars."

"Correct. I'm a little stunned." I reached for a french fry and popped it into my mouth, because I was still processing what the probate attorney had shared with me.

"Well, you two were always close. You kept in touch with

him all these years?" he asked, as if he couldn't believe that Abe had left me more money than one could imagine.

"Of course."

"How often did you talk to him?"

"What's with all the questions?" I crossed my arms over my chest.

"I'm just saying . . . you left this town in your rearview, and the man left you a fucking fortune. From what I've heard, you only visited a couple of times in all the years since you left, and one of those times was for Lily's funeral."

"That doesn't make you a rocket scientist. Of course, I came for her funeral. They were family to me. And for the record, *ole judgy one* . . . I spoke to Abe every single day after Lily passed away. I used to talk to them both twice a week up until she went into the hospital. I taught them how to FaceTime."

He looked stunned, as if it were unimaginable to believe that I'd make that effort. For someone I loved.

"You talked to him every single day?" he asked, his voice harsh and laced with doubt.

"I don't know if it's more offensive that you didn't seem to believe me at first, or that you seem like you're angry now that you believe it's true. Who the hell do you think you are?"

He just shook his head. "I guess I'm just stunned, seeing as you made zero effort to keep in touch with me."

"Well, I had my reasons, right? I don't know why you're surprised that I didn't make an effort to keep in touch with you."

"I just assumed you left everyone from your past behind. Apparently, I was wrong."

Was he seriously trying to guilt me?

He had some nerve. "Anyhow, there you go. I inherited more money than I'll ever know what to do with. Are you done with your questions?"

"So, what's the problem? You made it sound like a bad day. Seems like a pretty epic day to me."

"Oh, really? I lost a man who meant the world to me, and you think I'm happy about it?"

"For fuck's sake, Sav. That's not what I meant. He passed away over a week ago. You and Ruby were acting like the sky was falling down when I walked in. I thought something bad happened today."

I sighed. "Well, there's a loophole in this inheritance, and it's sort of a big one."

"Let me guess. You have to stick around for a week to get everything listed for sale, so you can get the hell out of town and go roll around naked in your millions?"

Well, this is an interesting plot twist.

"Funny, you should take it there. Clearly, that one time you saw me naked really made an impression." I waggled my brows because I couldn't help myself.

"I never saw you naked."

"You did, too."

"Savannah."

"Hayes."

"I never saw you naked."

"Why are you so hung up on this? It's okay that you forgot."

"You obviously still have a way of derailing a conversation. Why the hell are you upset about inheriting millions of dollars, and when the fuck do you think I saw you naked?"

"Well, my mom said we bathed together once when your mom asked if you could spend the night, when Saylor was just a baby."

"If my sister was a baby, then we were not even three years old." He huffed. "We were toddlers."

"Still. It happened."

"You're ridiculous."

"I've been called worse." I reached for my wineglass. I'd purposely only allowed myself half a glass of wine because I needed to drive out to the farmhouse, where I'd be staying tonight.

Home sweet home.

I couldn't wrap my head around any of this.

"Fine. I saw you naked, long before you looked like…" he paused, looking away as if he couldn't stand the sight of me.

"Looked like what, Woody?" I snarled, mad that I'd let the nickname I used to call him slip out.

"Like . . . this." He waved his hand in front of me. "All womanly and shit."

Now it was my turn to laugh. And I laughed hysterically. Irrationally.

My life was a mess right now, and Abe had just thrown a giant wrench into the middle of my shit show. But Hayes gaping at me lightened my mood.

"Thanks for noticing," I said, oozing sarcasm, even though I loved the way his heated gaze moved down my body as the words left his mouth.

I couldn't help myself. Even if the man had caused me a lot of heartache, I could still find him attractive.

"What's the other secret you're holding out on? You have to wait for the money and stay in this town for a few days? You can't leave right after the funeral?" His voice was all tease, and I hated that I found him so charming.

I was long over my crush on Hayes Woodson.

Long. Over.

"Very funny. But that's not it." I reached over and grabbed his Coke. I needed a little sugar boost. He just raised a brow while I took a sip.

"So, what is it?"

"I have thirty days to find a husband."

Hayes narrowed his gaze. "You're joking."

"Nope. That's what the will said."

"That can't be right."

"Oh, it's definitely right. Abe wants me to get hitched and live in that house like he and Lily did. He left a note for me to renovate the place because that's what I do for a living. He and I had always talked about me spending a few months here and renovating the place, but he never wanted to spend the money. That house is massive. And, yes, it's a project that I can handle. But I've never been required to get married as part of a renovation."

"There has to be a loophole. There's no way that it's legal to require someone to get married in order to receive an inheritance. I'm sure you can get out of it," he said, his tongue dipping out and sliding along his bottom lip.

Was he intentionally messing with me? Or was he literally just that sexy and didn't even realize what he was doing?

His dark hair was still cut short, just like it was when we were young. His mossy green eyes had a gold ring around them with pops of amber. He wore a gray hoodie and a pair of jeans, and he managed to look like he'd just stepped off of a modeling photo shoot.

"Maybe. The probate lawyer had no time to discuss things with me after he read the will, and he told me I could seek outside legal advice if I chose not to respect Abe's wishes." I was suddenly overwhelmed again. This trip down memory lane had been fun, but I needed to remember that there'd been a reason we hadn't spoken in all these years.

Hayes Woodson was not my best friend anymore.

He hadn't been for a very long time.

I'd shared way too much with him already. I knew better.

I needed to end this conversation right now.

I dropped a twenty-dollar bill on the bar and reached for my coat on the back of my barstool.

"It's been nice catching up with you, Woody. Maybe I'll see you around."

His jaw ticked, and he looked a little startled that I was leaving so abruptly. "Yeah. I'll be at the funeral tomorrow. I'll see you there."

I nodded as I pulled my beanie over my head and slipped my mittens on my hands before making my way past him toward the exit.

Tonight had been a lot.

This whole day has been a lot.

Ruby came around the bar and hugged me. "I'll see you at the funeral tomorrow, and I'll have River get you on his schedule Monday morning so he can take a look at the paperwork for you."

"Thank you." I held up a hand and made my way out to the blizzardy cold. My car was covered in snow, and I groaned. I used my gloved hand to clear the driver's side of the windshield before sliding into my cherry red 1995 Honda. She was old, but she'd been good to me. I turned the ignition, and nothing happened.

"Come on, Big Red. Don't fail me now." I pumped the gas and tried again.

And again.

My head fell forward against the steering wheel, and I fought back the tears.

I will not cry. I will not cry.

Money was extremely tight at the moment—well, aside from the check that the probate attorney said I'd be receiving in the next few days. He said Abe had granted me a small advance until I was officially married in thirty days, when I'd receive the full inheritance he'd left me. Then he'd handed me the keys to the farmhouse, so I'd canceled my hotel reservation in town, which was one less expense that I'd have at the moment. The last thing I needed was a huge price tag to fix my crappy car. But apparently, Abe had thought of everything. He'd noted that he wanted the keys to the farmhouse given to me the day I'd be called in for the reading of the will, because he knew I'd be heading to Magnolia Falls for his funeral and that I'd need a place to stay.

His heart was so big, and every time I thought about him being gone, I couldn't keep the tears away.

So, I let it out.

I cried because I was back in a place that held a lot of memories for me.

Both good and bad.

I cried for the loss of both Abe and Lily. Two people who had been a constant in my life. Two people who had treated me like family when I'd needed it most.

I cried for the loss of my best friend. A man I still felt a connection to, but desperately wanted to hate.

Wanted to forget.

I cried for my father, who was sick and didn't have the financial resources to get the help he needed.

I cried for my piece-of-shit car that had failed me once again.

I cried because I was tired of being failed by everyone and everything, and I still woke up every day and put a smile on my face and tried to live my best life.

There was a knock on my car window, and I sucked in a breath and swiped at my tear-streaked face.

I could see him through the falling snow.

I was overwhelmed, so I let the tears fall, making no effort to stop them this time.

3

Hayes

"Open the goddamn door, Sav," I said for the third time.

Seeing her upset had always done strange things to me.

I heard the click of the lock, and I pulled the door open. It was cold as hell outside, and she'd left twenty minutes ago, so she must be freezing if she'd been sitting out here in a car with no heat.

Crying.

Savannah Abbott was crying.

I could count on one hand how many times she'd cried in all the years I'd known her.

She was always a bright light, even when shit was raining down on her. That's why I'd been so surprised that she'd walked away from me so easily. I hadn't expected it. Not in a million years.

Maybe I didn't know her at all.

I bent down, because the sound of her sobs was too much. I placed a hand on her back and moved close to her ear so she could hear me.

"Let me give you a ride, Shortcake. It's cold out here."

She gasped a few times before wiping her face and turning

to look at me. Honey-brown eyes locked with mine. They were puffy and wounded, and she just shrugged. "It's just been a day. And now my car broke down. I'm just—"

She didn't finish the statement.

She didn't need to.

She was sad and tired, and I understood it.

Without thinking, I shifted forward, sliding one hand beneath her knees and one behind her neck, and I pulled her out of the car.

I expected her to freak out.

Slap me. Yell at me.

But she did none of that. Instead, she just buried her face in the crook of my neck as I carried her to my truck. I set her on the passenger seat, pulled the seat belt across her body, and buckled her in.

She didn't fight me.

"I need to get my keys and my purse and my suitcase," she said, her words shaky.

I nodded before moving to the driver's seat and turning on my truck and cranking the heat.

I jogged over to her car and grabbed everything she needed. I noticed her bumper was barely holding on when I opened her trunk, and I knew this car was old as shit and on its last legs. By the condition of it, I guessed she didn't have the finances to put into it yet. This money from Abe would help her, and I was glad he'd left it to her.

I placed her suitcase in the back seat of my truck and climbed into the driver's seat, handing over her keys and purse.

I drove out toward Abe's place, and she was quiet as I turned down the dirt road and glanced out at the water on my right, just as I saw her swipe at fresh tears.

"It's all right to be sad. You were close to him. I'm sure it's a lot to process." I pulled into the long driveway and made my way toward the old farmhouse.

"His dream was to renovate this place someday. He wanted me to come do it, and we talked about how we'd do it together one day."

I put the truck in park and turned to look at her. "Did you say that's what you do for a living?"

"Yes. I'm an interior designer. I've flipped a few homes on the side for myself. But my day job is designing for clients. Or at least, it was. I was working for a big firm in the city. But I lost my job a few weeks ago. So, yeah," she said, her voice starting to quake again. "My life is a mess. I'm jobless, and I just agreed to let my apartment go at the end of the month because I'm broke."

"Well, you've got a home here now and an inheritance worth plenty of money to cover your expenses in the city," I said, reaching into the center console for some napkins and handing them to her.

"Yeah, sure. I've got it for thirty days, and then they'll take it all away." She shrugged.

"Remember the words you painted on your bedroom wall in high school? One day at a time. Isn't that your mantra?"

She ignored me, staring out the window.

"Come on, Sav. It's me. You can talk to me. Peas and carrots, remember?"

"Some days are harder than others. And yes, it's permanently on my skin, so of course, I remember." She tugged off her pink mitten and held up her wrist for me to see the tiniest tattoo of a carrot there.

I traced my thumb along the ink before she pulled away quickly, sliding her mitten back in place.

"Why'd you lose your job?"

"Because this client was inappropriate with me. He was much older than I was. The guy was married and very wealthy," she said, as she glanced out the window, watching the falling snow. "I told my boss that I wasn't comfortable working with him, and a week later, I was fired."

21

"That's fucked up. What did the guy do? And why didn't you sue the asshole for firing you?"

She looked back at me. "I'm tired, Hayes. I don't want to talk about everything that has gone wrong in my life with a man I barely know anymore. Thank you for the ride."

Shots fired.

I wasn't going to remind her that she'd been the one to walk away from me. I'd tried to reach out to her many times after she'd left—an embarrassing number of times. She'd clearly wanted nothing to do with me.

But now wasn't the time or the place to bring that up. She was grieving the loss of a man she loved.

I pushed out of the truck and grabbed her suitcase from the back seat, just as she was coming around to get her luggage.

"Here, I can take that."

"I've got it," I said.

"I don't need your help, Woody!" she shouted. "I'm a big girl. I can take care of myself."

"Stop being a stubborn ass. Your car broke down. You have no job. You just inherited millions of dollars and found out that you need to find a husband in the next few weeks. A man you loved is being buried tomorrow." White snow covered the top of her head, and I leaned forward. "You. Need. Help. Let me carry your goddamn bag inside and make sure the heat is working, and then I'll leave."

She whipped around and huffed toward the front door.

"The driveway hasn't been shoveled, so it's probably pure ice," I grumped, just as she lost her footing and started skidding toward the front porch.

But in typical Savannah fashion, she righted herself, did some sort of spin, and then threw her hands in the air like she was saluting the judges after a skating routine. "Remember that time I wanted to be a professional ice skater?"

I chuckled as she made her way up the steps and paused

when she got to the door, searching for the right key. It was dark and difficult to see, so I pulled my phone out and turned on the flashlight.

"Thank you," she said, as she put the key in the door and pushed it open.

She flipped on the lights, and I was surprised that it was warm inside, but the place was a mess. Her eyes widened as she took it in. The old wallpaper throughout the entry was faded and peeling, and several wood floorboards had been pulled up. I followed her deeper into the house, and when she turned the lights on in the kitchen, she groaned. There were dirty dishes piled in the sink, the oven was old and rusted, and the whole place appeared to be in a time warp. Renovating would be a huge undertaking.

"Well, at least it's sort of a blank canvas. Everything needs to be redone."

"Are you sure you're okay staying out here alone?"

"In this mansion?" She quirked a brow and chuckled. "Yeah. It's warm, and the electricity works, which is more than I can say about my apartment in the city at the moment. I'll be fine. Thank you for the ride."

I nodded, feeling uncomfortable about her staying out here alone. It might be grand, but it was a fucking mess.

"All right. Let me just walk through the house and check all the rooms, okay?"

She sighed. "Fine. Let's go together."

We made our way through the formal dining room that was as dated as the rest of the place. The living room had no furniture in it anymore, as Abe was clearly only using the small den off the kitchen to watch TV. The rest of the house was similar. Seven of the eight bedrooms were practically bare. Like he'd gotten rid of the furniture, but never got around to replacing it.

"Looks like me and my future hubby will have our work

cut out for us fixing this place up," she said, as she turned around and waggled her brows at me with a laugh.

That was Sav. She'd just lost it in the car, and her world was crumbling around her, but she was cracking jokes now and making the best of the fact that she was staying in this scary-as-fuck house alone.

Some people were glass-half-full people. Others were glass-half-empty.

Savannah Abbott's glass had always been overflowing.

But I didn't know her anymore, and I'd seen cracks in that exterior already tonight.

She was trying to hold it together. And she didn't need to do that on my account.

"You've got my number if you need anything. Just text me. Unless you deleted me, seeing as you haven't used it in a long time."

"I'm fairly certain you're still blocked." She smirked. "But if someone tries to murder me during the night, I'll unblock you if I'm desperate."

She did fucking block me.

"Good to know that you're willing to unblock me if you're being murdered." I walked toward the front door, still trying to wrap my head around the fact that she'd really wanted to be done with me when she left all those years ago.

"Desperate times and all that," she said, pausing at the front door. "Thank you for the ride. I really do appreciate it."

"How will you get your car in the morning?"

"I'm a very resourceful girl, remember?" She shrugged, and then her gaze softened. "I'll Uber to the funeral and deal with the car after."

I wanted to offer her a ride, but I stopped myself. She'd made it clear she didn't want my help, or maybe she just didn't want to be around me at all.

I nodded. "All right. I'll see you there."

"Sure. Thanks for the ride. Get home safely." She pulled the door open and nearly bumped into me, trying to get me to leave.

My God. She couldn't get me out of here fast enough. I leaned down and took a little whiff near my armpit. Maybe I stunk.

Her head fell back in laughter. "You don't have BO, Woody."

"What? I know."

"I know what you're doing. You used to do that all the time. That little sniff test. And trust me, during your football years, you smelled rancid. I hated getting in the car with you."

I barked out a laugh as a memory flashed through my mind of the way I used to grab her and shove her head toward my armpit when she'd gripe about my stench after practice.

"I remember. You were very dramatic." I walked backward out of the house and into the cold. "Lock the doors."

"Thank you, caveman. I will."

I turned around and jogged to my truck after she closed the door.

Tonight had been a blast from the past.

Seeing Savannah had brought back a lot of memories. Good and bad.

I turned on the engine and cranked up the heat, rubbing my hands together when my phone vibrated in my pocket for the millionth time.

My best friends and I had an ongoing group chat, and someone was always texting something.

ROMEO

I heard Savvy is back in town. Have you seen her, Hayes?

KING

That's who you should have dated all those years ago, instead of that evil, cheating hellion.

RIVER

She's back for the funeral. Ruby called and asked me to look over the will. Abe left her everything but has some requirements in there that are a little . . . unusual.

NASH

He left her everything? That's pretty amazing. It's great when the good guy wins, you know?

ROMEO

Savvy was always nice to everyone. What kind of unusual requirements could he put in the will?

KING

Does she have to share the land with the Mexican cartel to bring drugs across the border? Provide a safe house for homeless alpacas? Start a cannabis farm and keep the whole town high as a kite?

NASH

Where do you come up with this shit?

KING

The inside of my head is a beautiful place.

RIVER

Well, it's also a crazy place. None of those things are correct, you crazy fucker. I don't have the details, so I'm waiting to look over the paperwork on Monday.

ROMEO

Have you seen her yet, Hayes? I know it's been a long time. But you two were tight back in the day.

KING

You never once hooked up? All those sleepovers and all that time you spent together?

NASH

He has no reason to lie. He was with Kate. He and Savvy were always just friends.

ROMEO

Demi said Savvy stopped into Magnolia Beans, and she went on and on about how stunning Sav is. And she said that she's just as nice as she always was.

What the fuck is this? An episode of The Bachelor? Why are we talking about this? We were friends, and then we weren't. I saw her. She seems like she's doing well. Still hates me for no fucking reason. I'm glad you're going to help her out, River. She deserves to keep that inheritance.

RIVER

Yeah. I'll do what I can to help her. It's not my area of expertise, but I'll read it over and hopefully, I can help.

Thanks. Nash, do you think you can get your friend, Warner, to help out with a car that needs to be towed and fixed?

NASH

Yes. The dude never sleeps. He's always working. I'll send you his info now and you can text him.

Thanks.

KING

So . . . we're dying to know if Beans is right. Young Savvy was cute back in the day. Is grown-up Savvy hot?

Beans was the nickname we used for Romeo's wife, Demi. There was a long pause, and I refused to answer his dumbass question.

NASH

He isn't answering, which means she's definitely hot.

ROMEO

He sure as hell isn't denying it.

RIVER

Oh, he's using emojis. She's definitely hot.

KING

The one who got away is all grown up now. And she's hot. Our boy doesn't know what to do with himself.

Your boy is going to kick your ass the next time he sees you. I'm heading home. I'll see you at Abe's funeral tomorrow.

KING

You sure will. And we'll all be seeing Savvy there, as well. 😍

I sent a quick text to Warner about getting Savannah's car towed from Whiskey Falls bar. She may not want to see me, but I was fairly certain she didn't have the money to fix that piece-of-shit car of hers right now. We had a history. She was going through a hard time. The least I could do was help her out with her car.

We were friends once, after all.

And that's what friends do.

4

Savannah

A lot of people had come out for the funeral to say their goodbyes to Abe. One notable person that was missing today was Sheana, a woman he'd married after Lily had passed away. Their union was brief, as she'd clearly been after his money, and she'd preyed on the goodness of a lonely man who was much older than her. I'd struggled with his decision to marry her, but she'd gotten what she wanted and managed to leave with a large sum of money. In the end, Abe realized he'd been scammed, and he'd said it was worth the money to be rid of her. Of course, she hadn't bothered to show up to his funeral.

But he'd told me what he wanted for his service, and he'd set the money aside so it would all be taken care of.

He had prepared me for everything, aside from the fact that he was leaving me his estate.

Oh, and also the fact that he was giving me one month to find a husband.

It was ridiculous. Ludicrous. But it was also a very Abe thing to do.

He never stood on ceremony.

He was a straight shooter and an honest man.

A good man.

A few of his friends had gotten up and spoken, and I was the last one to go up there and say a few words. It had been a long time since I'd been back here in Magnolia Falls, and I no longer cared if everyone was gossiping about my family.

When I was a teenager, I cared.

When people whispered in my presence back then, I cared.

When I saw the hurt on my father's face, I cared.

But today was about Abe. And he was loved by everyone who knew him.

I'd already hugged everyone who'd shown up, and it was good to see so many familiar faces. Faces that I'd missed. Faces that were part of my childhood.

One face in particular that was staring at me right now.

Hayes sat between his group of friends, and they'd all been really sweet when they'd come to say hello. I'd grown up with most of them. River, King, Romeo, and Nash were always with Hayes when we were young, and they'd welcomed me into their group with open arms back then. Saylor had been my neighbor, just like her brother, and she was like a little sister to me. We hadn't kept in touch after I'd left because I'd needed to walk away from her brother. But I knew that she and Hayes had gone through their own hard times, just like I had. I was happy to see that she and King were married, because they were two of the nicest people I'd ever known, and they appeared to be ridiculously happy. And Romeo and Demi were adorable. I didn't see that as a possibility when we were young, as they were from two different worlds. But they were really cute together, and I was glad they'd found their way to one another. They'd both always been really kind to me and never judged me, even when everyone else in town did. This group had been different. And River and Ruby . . . I should have predicted it. They were both strong and fierce, so seeing them together seemed like the world made sense. Nash seemed very happy with his fiancée, Emerson, whom I'd met today and liked immediately. She was the local pediatrician and had been the one to introduce me to Nash's son, Cutler.

Beefcake.

I mean, how cool is a kid who can pull off a handle like that? It made me emotional to meet his son. I'd known Nash since preschool, and seeing him as a dad had me a little choked up.

Every time I looked up, I found Hayes watching me.

I wondered if he felt bad about the way our friendship had ended. If he'd had any idea how badly he'd hurt me.

I took to the podium just as Midge Longhorn squeezed my hand and stepped away. Her speech had been inappropriate and hilarious, and Abe would have loved it.

I set my note cards down and cleared my throat.

"Thank you all for being here today. I'm grateful, and I know that Abe would be, too. I'm sure Lily's looking down on all of us, smiling because everyone in town came out to say goodbye to the love of her life." I reached for my water and took a sip, my gaze locking with Hayes's, and he gave me the slightest nod of reassurance. I quickly looked away, my attention back on my note cards.

"I was ten years old when Abe and Lily invited me to come help out at their ranch. It was during the brief time that I wanted to be a professional horse racer," I said, pausing as everyone chuckled. "I'd never even been on a horse, but I knew they were beautiful, and I wanted to see what it would be like to run through a field and let the wind blow in my hair and just, I don't know, be free, I guess."

I let out a long breath. "Abe and Lily never made fun of my dreams. They encouraged me. They were like the grandparents I never had. They offered me a job, and I'd go every day after school and clean the stalls and help feed all the animals on the weekends. Abe taught me how to ride, and Lily taught me about home décor, which turned into a profession for me. They both believed that I could be anything I wanted to be, and for a young girl with big dreams—" I pushed the lump in the back of my throat away. "It meant everything."

I took another sip from my water bottle. I wanted to be upbeat. Make this more of a celebration of life than a sad occasion. But I was struggling at the moment.

"After Lily passed, I spoke to Abe every single day. Even if either of us were sick, we found a way to check in. Abe Wilson became my safe place over the years, and I hope I was that for him, too. He was a good man. A hard worker. He had the kindest heart, and when I went through difficult times in my life, he never left me. He never judged me." My gaze locked with Hayes's, and it was clear that he was listening intently. "He is the reason that I continue to chase my dreams every single day. And I miss him so much. I hope I can help keep his legacy alive by renovating the home he and Lily shared, just the way he'd always wanted it to be. But we can all keep his legacy alive by remembering to be kind to one another. To offer a shoulder or a hand to someone in need. Because that's who Abe was. And whenever I'm out on a horse, running through an open field with the wind blowing around me, I'll think of Abe. Because he taught me how to live and how to love and how to let go of things." I took another sip of water, trying hard not to cry.

"People come into your life for a reason, and my world was always a better place with Lily and Abe in it. The last time I spoke to Abe, which was on the morning of the day that he passed—" I paused, needing a minute to pull myself together. The entire church was packed, but it was so quiet you could hear a pin drop, aside from a few sniffles. "He knew his time was coming to an end. We talked about it often. And our joke was that even if we couldn't talk every day on FaceTime, I'd still be talking to him wherever he was. He laughed and said he had no doubt that I'd find a way to talk his ear off in the afterlife." The room erupted in laughter at that, and I smiled. "Rest in peace, sweet Abe. I'll love you forever."

34

I smiled before gathering my note cards. "Thank you all for coming. Abe didn't want a reception or for me to throw a luncheon after. He said to tell everyone to go to The Golden Goose and to go out and live their lives. No sulking. No tears. Just happy thoughts about a man who had a very happy life. Thank you."

People applauded, which caught me off guard, and I made my way down the steps as they started to exit the church. Pastor Joseph gave me a hug and thanked me for sharing my story.

I looked up and was surprised to see Scotty waving at me from where he stood near the exit. What are the chances that my Uber driver would be my ex-boyfriend?

Apparently, the odds were high because, according to Scotty, there were only two Uber drivers in Magnolia Falls.

Wonderful.

"I can't believe you stayed. I could have walked home," I said when I made my way to him.

"I liked Abe. He was always so good to you. I didn't mind hanging out and waiting for you. And that's a long walk back to the farmhouse from here," Scotty said. He'd filled out since I'd last seen him, but I guess that was to be expected when more than a decade had passed. His hair was still shaggy and long, and he wore the grunge look well. He was the lead singer of a band called The Disasters, and he'd talked incessantly about it on the way to the funeral.

But my mind was elsewhere.

I was actually looking forward to walking home and being alone. But I couldn't very well turn down the ride since he'd waited two hours for me.

"Well, thank you. I appreciate it," I lied.

As we stepped outside, Hayes was standing there, and his gaze moved from me to Scotty and back to me. "Hey, do you need a ride?"

"She's got a ride," Scotty said, before I could respond.

"Just making sure she wants to take that ride." Hayes

squared his shoulders, and I rolled my eyes, because they were both ridiculous.

They'd never cared for one another.

Maybe I'd let Hayes's dislike of Scotty sway me back in the day. But today, I could make decisions for myself. I certainly didn't rely on Hayes Woodson anymore.

"I'm all set. Thanks for the offer, and thanks for coming," I said, and he nodded. I brushed past him and found my stride beside Scotty as we made our way to his car.

I was emotionally drained.

I wanted to be alone.

Cry it out.

But the minute Scotty slipped into the driver's seat, he started talking. "You two didn't keep in touch after you moved away?"

"Me and Hayes?"

"Yeah. You were so tight growing up."

"Well, people change. No, we didn't keep in touch." I could taste the bitterness on my tongue as the words left my mouth.

They say friendship breakups can be as tough as romantic breakups. I'm here to say, the ending of my friendship with Hayes Woodson was the greatest loss of my life—as far as a person who was still living.

I'd grieved, and I'd hurt, and it had taken a long time to get over the betrayal.

I'd been blindsided by the person I'd trusted most.

"I always thought he was the reason that you broke up with me," he said, turning to look at me when he approached the stop sign.

Are we really doing this on the day I just said goodbye to Abe?

Scotty and I had dated for six months. It was high school. It just didn't work out.

And sure, Hayes hadn't liked him, but that wasn't the reason I'd ended it.

It wasn't the only reason, at least.

Scotty was a narcissist at its finest. He was all about himself, and it had been entertaining at first, but it wore on me over time.

"Nope. I think the relationship just ran its course." I stared out the window, looking at the field where Abe had taught me to ride a horse all those years ago.

My head was pounding. My heart felt like a gigantic elephant had copped a squat there.

"I don't think so, babe. I think that dude was jealous." He turned down the final street, and relief flooded me that this was almost over.

Did he seriously just call me babe?

And is this driveway the longest driveway known to man?

"It was my choice, Scotty." I made no attempt to hide my irritation. He had zero self-awareness. We'd dated more than a decade ago, and today was not the day to have this conversation. Hell, there wasn't even a reason to have the conversation. We'd remained friendly after we broke up.

But today I was grieving, and he was completely unaware.

"I think it was hard for you to share me back then. But I'm more balanced now," he said, as he put his yellow Camaro in park.

I sighed. He wasn't going to let it go. "Hard for me to share you with who?"

"My fans. The music industry." He shrugged. "I couldn't give you what you needed because of my craft, my people—they came first back then."

I did what I could to stop my jaw from hitting the floor. The Disasters only performed once, from what I remembered from back then. And it had been in the garage of Scotty's parents' house. Me and four other people attended the show—I'm not judging, because I was proud of him for chasing his dreams, but I hardly had to share him with his fans and his "people".

"I promise you that I did not break up with you because

of your musical aspirations. You know I support chasing your dreams. I've had many, and I would never have a problem with someone pursuing what they love."

"So what was it, then?" He reached for my hand, and I startled.

What in the absolute loving hell is happening?

I was in some sort of Magnolia Falls twilight zone.

We hadn't talked in years. I thought this would be a faint memory for him.

"Scotty, I don't know what's going on here, but I'm just not up for it today. I'm sad, and I just want to go inside and be in my feels, okay?"

"Can I come inside with you?" He waggled his brows. "Remember all those good times we had?"

Actually, no. I can't recall a single good time at the moment.

"I need to be alone. But it was good to see you. Take care." I tugged my hand away and unbuckled my seat belt.

"I miss you, babe. Let me take you to dinner tonight."

"I can't tonight." I pushed out of the car.

"I'll call you, okay?" he shouted, but I just kept walking, relieved when I heard him pull down the driveway.

Just as I put the key in the door, the sound of crunching gravel came from behind me. I turned around to see Big Red driving toward me.

With a man I didn't recognize behind the wheel.

I truly was in a Magnolia Falls twilight zone today.

I marched toward the car, as the guy put it in park and stepped out.

"Who are you?" I demanded, arms crossed over my chest. "And how do you have my car?"

"I'm Carter. I work for Warner."

Is that supposed to be helpful?

"I don't know who Warner is."

He tossed me my key and pointed at the blue truck now

coming up the driveway. "That's Warner. He owns the mechanic shop. He followed me here so we could drop your car off."

Warner got out of the blue truck and walked toward me. "Engine's fixed. You needed an oil change, too, so we got it all fixed up."

"First of all, I didn't call you. Do you just pick up random cars left in bars' parking lots and fix them?" I shook my head in disbelief.

Carter chuckled, and Warner looked confused. "No. Hayes reached out and asked me to take care of it and drop it off here for you."

Hayes.

Of course he did.

Maybe it was guilt from the way our friendship had ended.

I sighed. "Where did you get a key?"

"He said you always kept your spare in your glove box, and I'll be damned if he wasn't right." Warner laughed. "But in the future, it's not the best idea to leave a key in the car. It's an easy way to get it stolen."

"No one is exactly trying to steal Big Red," I said, trying to hide my laughter and feign irritation. They'd fixed my car and that meant I wouldn't need to call Uber for a ride and risk another awkward drive with Scotty.

"Fair point." He chuckled.

"How much do I owe you?"

"It's already been taken care of," Warner said as he and Carter climbed into his blue pickup and waved.

Of course it was. This was such a Hayes move. He didn't ask; he just did it.

And yes, it was nice that he'd had my car fixed.

The problem was, I didn't want Hayes Woodson to do me any favors.

That hadn't been helpful to me in the past.

And I'd learned that lesson the hard way.

5

Hayes

I stirred the chili on the stovetop and peeked out to see Cutler working on a puzzle, with a large glass of chocolate milk beside him. Cutler Heart was the coolest little dude I'd ever known. His father had all these rules about chocolate milk and when he was allowed to have it, but that's what uncles are for. Today it would be chocolate milk, and in high school, I'm sure we'd be buying him his first beer.

"You good, buddy? Dinner's almost ready."

"I love your house, Uncle Hayes. And you make the best chocolate milk."

I chuckled. "It's all about the chocolate, Beefcake. I double it up. I know how my boy likes his milk."

He glanced over when the flames in the fireplace crackled. It was cold as hell outside, and the snow was still coming down hard. I was grateful for a night off to hang with Cutler. Nash and Emerson were having a date night, so he'd be sleeping over here tonight.

We'd already built a snowman out back, and I'd taken him cross-country skiing before it got dark.

There was a knock on my door, and I told Cutler to keep working on his puzzle.

I pulled the door open to see Savannah Abbott standing on my front porch with snow falling down all around her, looking like she wanted to murder me.

"Hey, Shortcake. What brings you out in this lovely weather?" I smirked. I'd gotten a call from Warner letting me know she wasn't happy that I'd had her car fixed and delivered to her. I figured as much.

I just didn't care.

She needed a car to live out there by herself.

She could be pissed if she wanted to. She wasn't speaking to me anyway, so this wouldn't really change anything.

"I came to see how much I owe you. You really shouldn't have had my car fixed without talking to me." There were puffs of white steam coming from her mouth when she spoke.

"Would you like to come inside and have this conversation? It's much warmer in here."

"Stop telling me what to do. I'm fine out here." Her lips trembled as the lie left her mouth. She wore a white hat with an oversized pom-pom on the top of her head. Her white coat and white mittens matched, and she looked cute as hell, even if she was being a stubborn ass.

"Okay. Well, I'm cold standing by the door, so either you come in or you can call me—if you want to unblock me." My voice was all tease, because damn, I was enjoying myself.

There was a peace that came over me, knowing that Savannah was here.

Home.

My world had always been better with her in it.

Maybe hers was worse with me in it.

"Unblock you? That's your big concern?"

"Well, if you want to discuss the car, and you won't come

inside, yeah, that's my concern." My tongue slid across my bottom lip as she started bouncing up and down and rubbing her hands together.

"Look who's here, Uncle Hayes." Beefcake sauntered over from behind me.

I had to bite back a laugh when I turned around to see him standing there in his gray joggers, but he was no longer wearing his hoodie. He had a bare chest, which he didn't have five minutes ago, so clearly, he'd heard a woman's voice and decided to take off his sweatshirt.

It was a very Beefcake move to do that.

The kid had more swagger than all of us put together.

"Hey, Beefcake." Savannah's entire disposition changed as she took him in. They'd met at the funeral this morning, and of course, she was already putty in his hands.

Cutler moved forward, took her hand, and led her inside.

Just like that.

He walked her straight toward the family room, where the fire was blazing, and motioned for her to sit down.

Which she did.

This kid was everybody's kryptonite.

"Let's get you warmed up. How about some hot cocoa for our girl, Uncle Hayes?"

Was he for real?

She chuckled and then glanced over at me. "I could go for some cocoa."

For fuck's sake.

I moved to the kitchen and heated the milk before adding in the chocolate and listened to Beefcake fill her in on the dangers of being outside in this cold weather for too long.

I could barely drag the kid inside after we built that snowman. But he knew what to say, and I admired his game.

I came out with the mug and set it on the coffee table. "We're about to eat. Do you want a bowl of chili?"

"Uncle Hayes makes the best chili. And we don't even have to eat at a table like I do at home. We eat down here, and we talk shop."

"I guess you can twist my arm into a bowl of chili." She raised her brows as she tugged her mittens, hat, and coat off and set them beside her. "You talk shop? Like firefighter stuff?"

I continued to listen as I moved to the kitchen and ladled us each a bowl of chili and carried them out and set them on the coffee table, before grabbing the cornbread that Emerson had sent over for us to have tonight. I was thankful that Nash's fiancée loved to bake, because she was always sending treats over.

"Yep. But my uncle does lots of medical stuff, too, just like my Sunny. She's a doctor. Uncle Hayes has to take care of sick people, too. When I grow up, I want to be like all my uncles."

I dropped onto the couch beside Cutler, while Savannah sat on the other side of him. We all reached for our bowls and started eating.

"I think that's nice that you love your uncles so much."

"Yep. I think it's how you loved Abe, right? I could tell you loved him when you talked about him today," Cutler said, over a mouthful of beefy goodness.

I chuckled and handed him a napkin.

She studied him for a long moment. "Yeah. I bet you're right."

"How come you seemed mad at Uncle Hayes when you got here? Did he do something to your car?" he asked, and I just sat back, enjoying the show. I'd let Cutler speak for me all day long. She didn't seem to get as annoyed with him as she did with me.

"My car broke down, and he had it fixed without talking to me." She shrugged, before taking a bite of the cornbread.

"What? That was so nice of you, Uncle Hayes." Cutler beamed up at me, a little dribble of chili on his chest. I leaned forward and cleaned him up with my napkin and winked. "My pops does that for Sunny all the time. He gets her car cleaned, or he brings her her favorite drink from Aunt Demi's coffee shop. She calls that acts of kindness."

Savannah leaned back against the couch and processed his words. "I see your point, Beefcake. I normally love acts of kindness. But me and your uncle, we haven't seen each other in a long time, so it just caught me off guard, I guess."

"But Pops told me you two were best friends, like me and J.T. are best friends. So even if you don't see each other, you're still best friends."

Let's go, Beefcake!

"Well, a lot has changed. But you're right. It was a nice thing for him to do. I'd just like to pay the bill. I don't like owing anyone, you know?"

"How come? Friends do things for their friends. Me and J.T. always help each other. You worry too much, Savvy. Uncle Hayes, do you want her to pay you back?"

"Nope."

"But it's my car," she said, her honey-brown eyes glowing in the firelight as they locked with mine. "I can pay my own way."

"Listen, I know money's tight right now until you get your inheritance. So how about you agree to let me just do this for you right now."

"Why?"

"Because I can, Shortcake."

Cutler's head fell back in laughter after he set his bowl down on the coffee table. "I love that my uncle calls you Shortcake."

"I'm not even short. He just happens to be a freaking giant." Savannah covered her mouth and stared at me with wide eyes. "Oh, wait, can I say freaking around him?"

I barked out a laugh. "Yes. Freaking isn't a bad word. Relax, Sav."

"I say freaking all the freaking time!" Cutler shouted, and they both burst out into hysterical laughter.

"Okay. Anyway, you're a giant. I'm normal-sized."

"To me, you're a shortcake."

"Well, thanks for the chili. Just tell me how much the car was, and when I have the money, I'll get it back to you," she said.

"How about this? When I need a favor, I'll let you know." I arched a brow.

"You're ridiculous," she said.

"And you're stubborn. It wasn't a big deal. He owed me a favor."

"Fine. You fixed my car, and you fed me." She reached for her hot chocolate. "Thank you."

"Was that so hard?" I asked. Cutler had made his way back to his puzzle and was calling Savannah over to look at it.

"It was pretty hard, Woody," she said, before hysterical laughter escaped her. "Oh, my gosh. *That's what she said!*"

That had always been our inside joke when we were in high school. It used to bug the hell out of Kate that Savannah and I had this language that was all our own. I guess it should have been a big red flag that my girlfriend didn't have a sense of humor at all.

"You nailed it." I arched a brow and then followed it with the same joke. "*That's what she said.*"

"Well played." She pushed to her feet. "Okay, I'm going to check out this puzzle and head home."

She walked over to where Cutler was intently working on his puzzle. Savannah ended up sitting beside him and helping him for the next hour.

I stayed out of their way and cleaned up the dishes and just listened to them talk and laugh.

"Okay, I'm going to get out of your hair. Thanks for dinner and for the car. I will pay you back when I get this money from Abe." She shrugged as she slipped her coat on.

"River said he was going to meet with you on Monday morning. You sent the paperwork over to him?" I asked.

"Yep. Ruby made a copy and gave it to him. Hopefully, he

can get me out of that whole marriage thing." She pulled her hat onto her head.

"Why do you think Abe put that in there?" I asked, as I walked her to the door.

She thought about the question. "Well, you remember how I used to always say I was going to get married someday and have lots of babies?"

"Yes. You definitely knew what you wanted, even when we were young." I'd always admired that about her. The confidence and faith she had in others. In this grand plan for having the life she'd pictured for herself.

"Well, he knew that I wanted to be married and to have kids. That I always knew what I wanted for my life. But I haven't had a lot of luck lately. He thought I was wasting time on dating apps and that I should do it the old-fashioned way and go out there and meet someone." I shrugged. "He and Lily had that rare kind of love, and he didn't want me to give up on that. But come on, putting that in the contract and forcing me to marry someone? That's madness."

"Yeah. It's pretty crazy. Are you dating someone now? Is that why he thought he could speed things up?"

She studied me for the longest time before she spoke. "Are you curious about my life now, Woody?"

I'd always been honest with this girl. I wouldn't start lying now.

"Yeah. Of course, I am. Just because you moved away, doesn't mean I don't care what happens to you."

And with those words, her gaze hardened. "Well, you need not worry. I don't plan on marrying some random guy in the next thirty days. I'll find a way out of it."

She made her way out into the snowy night and climbed into her car.

I didn't like her driving that piece of shit, especially in this weather.

But Savannah didn't want my help, and she'd made that clear.

What I couldn't figure out was why I couldn't just stay the fuck out of her business.

That was my specialty.

I didn't get involved.

I kept to myself.

I liked it that way.

But now that she was back in town, I couldn't seem to stop thinking about her.

Maybe it was just our history or the shitty way things had ended.

Maybe it was the fact that I'd missed my best friend.

I'd definitely missed her.

6

Savannah

There were things that I'd missed about Magnolia Falls.

Abe and Lily.

The people that lived here.

The quaint downtown.

My childhood home, before I'd found out my entire childhood was a sham.

But this relentless snow was not something that I'd missed. Not even a little bit. My car was not equipped for it, and I was sliding all over the place as I took side streets toward downtown to meet with River.

I could barely see out the windshield because the snow was coming down hard, and my wipers were not strong enough to handle the falling snow. I squinted through the bit of opening that I could see and turned the music down so that I could concentrate on the road.

"Don't fail me, Big Red. We can stay home the rest of the day if you just get me there and back in one piece." I was grateful that I'd left early, because I was driving slow. I pumped my brakes as I took a left turn, but I was already starting to slide, and I whipped the wheel around to try to stop it, but I was spinning.

Completely out of control.

The next thing I knew, I was sliding off the road. I screamed and tried desperately to correct myself, but it was too late.

Please don't let the car flip.

My hands were still gripping the steering wheel, even when the car came to a stop.

I glanced out the window and was relieved that I was upright, even though I was in a ditch.

It was fitting for the current state of my life, in a way.

I groaned and attempted to open my door, but it wasn't moving. I shook the handle harder, and nothing was happening.

Damn it.

I climbed over the seat and pushed as hard as I could on the passenger side door, so hard that when it flew open, my momentum had me tumbling out into the snow.

This day just keeps getting better.

The sound of a car pulling up had me rolling onto my stomach so I could try to push to my feet, but the snow was deep, and I wasn't making any progress.

Before I could process what was happening, I was being lifted upright as I blinked a couple of times against the falling snow to see Hayes standing in front of me.

He looked—pissed.

"What the fuck are you doing out here?" he hissed, brushing the snow off me.

"Don't you dare yell at me!" I shouted, shoving him back. "I hit black ice and slid off the road."

"Because your car is a piece of shit."

"Don't bad-mouth Big Red!" I yelled before storming around him to get my purse and keys.

"What the hell do you think you're doing now?" he asked, when I started walking past him.

"I've got a meeting in ten minutes. I need to find out how I can hold onto the house that Abe loved and get it renovated like I promised him I'd do someday, without having to get married!" I whipped around so I was facing him.

Before I knew what was happening, he moved forward, throwing me over his shoulder, fireman-style, as he marched toward his truck. I pounded my fists against his lower back.

"Stop fighting me. You're acting like a child." He tossed me into his truck and bent down to meet my gaze. "This ends here."

"What ends here?" I said, my breaths coming hard now because I was fuming.

"This. This anger. I don't know what the fuck I did to you, Sav. But you left me and cut me out of your life. So stop acting like I'm the enemy and let me drive you to your goddamn appointment." He grabbed my purse, opened it up, and pulled out my phone. Of course, he didn't ask first, because Hayes just did whatever the hell he wanted to do. He typed something into it and then turned the screen, holding it right in front of my face. "I have unblocked my number from your phone. Do not block me while you're here. You roll into a ditch, you call me, and I'll come. Do you understand?"

I nodded, because I didn't have any fight left in me. I was cold and wet and tired.

He tugged my seat belt across my body and snapped it into place, before slamming the door and storming around to the driver's side.

We didn't speak as we drove to River's office, and he cranked the heat in the truck.

"You can drop me off, and I'll find a ride home," I said, keeping my voice low.

He came to a stop in front of River's law office and backed into a parking spot right in front. He turned to face me. "I'm coming in with you, and then I'll take you home."

I shook my head. "Why are you being so nice to me?"

"Why wouldn't I?" he hissed.

I can think of a few reasons, but it doesn't seem like the time or the place.

He climbed out of the truck and hurried around to the passenger side, but I was already out of the truck. I tossed my hands in the air like I was doing some sort of gymnast dismount, and he rolled his eyes.

He always was chivalrous.

Until he wasn't.

My phone vibrated, and I pulled it out of my back pocket and narrowed my gaze when I saw the text.

SCOTTY

> Hey, babe. Drinks tonight? The band is playing at Whiskey Falls, and I can bring you up on stage if you want.

I sighed and glanced over my shoulder to see Hayes reading the text.

"Nosy much?"

"Whatever. You're short. You make it easy." He brushed past me. "I can't believe you're starting things back up with that dude. For the record, he isn't playing at Whiskey Falls. It's karaoke night. It's anyone's stage." He raised a brow as he held the door open, and I stepped inside.

"Perhaps I should perform there tonight. I never did get a chance to sing that song the way I should have."

He cleared his throat, but it sounded like he was covering a chuckle, which made me laugh.

I didn't know how it was possible to know someone the way I knew this man, and then find out you didn't know him at all.

Why was he so familiar? So easy? This connection was something that was just a part of us.

Or maybe this is what sociopathic serial killers do?

They spend years pretending to be someone they're not, only to get their prey to fall under their spell, and then they slowly suck the life from them.

Hayes Woodson would never suck the life from me again.

Been there. Done that.

"Hello, Hayes," Cassie said. I recognized her right away, as she used to take riding lessons from Abe out on his ranch. She turned toward me and then gasped. She threw her arms around me. "Oh, my gosh, Savannah, it's so good to see you. I didn't know you were coming in today."

"I put her name on the calendar," River said, as he quirked a brow and made no attempt to hide his irritation.

"I don't really use your calendar. I prefer my own system," she said. "Anyway, I didn't want to bother you at the funeral, but I was hoping to run into you while you were home. Hey, why don't you meet me at Whiskey Falls tonight for karaoke? I'm old enough to drink now!" she squealed, and Hayes and River both glared in her direction. "I'd love to catch up."

"How about you catch up when you aren't on the clock," River snipped, and I laughed because I couldn't help it. She was completely unfazed, and I turned my attention toward her.

"I'd love to catch up. I'm having car problems at the moment, but if I can get it fixed, I'll text you." I smiled before Hayes placed his hand on my lower back and guided me into his best friend's office.

"I didn't know you were coming," River said to the man beside me as he closed the door and settled across the desk from where Hayes and I sat.

"Her car broke down, so I'm here. What did you find out?" he asked.

"Obviously, inheritance law is not my specialty, but after researching this over the weekend, it appears that you can make up the rules for your own will."

"Meaning?" I said, leaning forward and tugging off my hat and mittens. I welcomed the warmth after freezing my ass off outside.

"Meaning, exactly what Abe's probate lawyer, Bert Lovell, told you when you met him in the city. Abe gave you the keys to the house as he wanted you to stay there while you were in town. He made it clear that his hope is for you to renovate the home and make it what it once was. He'd like you to raise your family there, but he didn't make that a requirement. He doesn't want to be the one to decide where you live." River reached for his coffee. Bert Lovell had told me this the day he'd beckoned me to his office. And then he'd handed me the keys, and I'd driven straight to Magnolia Falls. The place I'd grown up in. The place I'd avoided for many years.

"I see. He just wants to decide when I get married?" I asked, shaking my head in disbelief. "There must be a loophole."

"That's the thing about wills. There are no loopholes. You can leave your money to whoever you want, however you want. You make the rules." He shrugged from the other side of the desk.

"That's ridiculous. You can't demand someone get married," Hayes hissed.

And for the first time since I'd arrived in town, I agreed with him.

"Actually, you can. I researched it quite a bit this weekend, and there have been countless cases that were very similar to this. People who have a lot of money do some crazy things. And Abe isn't demanding she get married. He's giving her a choice. She gets the keys to the farmhouse and twenty-five thousand dollars to hold her over financially while she begins renovations. If she chooses to get married within thirty days, she meets the first requirement. She'll receive fifty thousand dollars as a second payment. After she's been married for three months, everything will be signed over to her, in her name.

Savannah, you will receive a million-dollar check at that time, as well as the deed to the house. I had some numbers run on the land, and you'd be inheriting somewhere in the vicinity of six million dollars in total."

"Fuck, that's a lot of money." Hayes raised a brow at me.

"And if I stay married for three months and then the marriage comes to an end?" I asked, my voice shaky, because six million dollars would solve a whole lot of problems for me, as well as providing everything my father needs at the moment.

"He didn't make any rules after the three months. If you separate, divorce, or never speak to the dude again, the money is yours. The house is yours. You can sell the house and the land after the three months, but he made a special note in here that he would prefer that you kept the house in your family, because it meant something to him. But the option is yours."

It didn't feel like the option was mine. Abe was stuck in his ways, and he wanted me to have everything he and Lily had. But forcing me to marry someone was not going to bring me my soul mate. It would be a business deal, and I couldn't fathom why he'd put me in that position.

"So where does one get a husband for three months?" I asked with a laugh, because obviously, this deal was going to die right here.

Did I need the money? Yes.

Did I see a way to meet a man and fall in love, all in the next thirty days? Hell no. I'd spent years dating every type of man out there. Businessmen. Artists. Cowboys. Playboys. Scientists.

And not a single one had kept my attention for three months.

I always found something wrong with them. Every single time.

Clearly I had trust issues, because I was always trying to figure out what their game was. How the hell would I find someone I liked enough to marry?

"I have some ideas," River said, clearing his throat.

"Hold up, brother." Hayes leaned forward, his elbows on his knees, and my gaze scanned his thick thighs before I forced myself not to stare and turned my attention back to River. "She has to get married within thirty days, *or what*?"

"That land is considered a gold mine. The state has been trying to purchase it from Abe for the last three years. If she chooses to pass on getting married, it's her right. She keeps the twenty-five thousand dollars, and she can stay in the house for thirty days. Then the land is sold off, and Savannah will donate the money to the charity of her choosing."

"This is fucked up," Hayes grumped.

I couldn't agree more. It was fucked up, but I didn't know why he was so pissed off about it. No one was asking him to find a bride and get hitched.

"Listen, I never expected anything from Abe. Obviously, I'd love to renovate that farmhouse and make it what he always dreamed it should be. But the bigger struggle is the money, because it would help tremendously." I cleared my throat. "I found this cancer trial that I really want my father to try, but it's a fortune to get in on a trial, and his insurance only goes so far," I said, because it was difficult to hold it in anymore. "But I don't see a way that I can marry someone in thirty days. I just don't have any options right now."

I'd lost my job and my ability to help my father.

I was at a loss, and this offer from Abe felt cruel at the moment. But he wasn't a cruel man. There must be a reason he was doing this, but right now, I couldn't see it.

Hayes whipped his head in my direction, gaze narrowed and laced with question.

He knew about my father. I'd told him. Could he have possibly forgotten something so devastating? Was he that cold of a man?

"I didn't know your father had cancer," Hayes said, and it only made me angrier.

"I'm sorry to hear about your father," River said, as the man beside me just sat there gaping at me like he was in shock by the news.

"Thank you. Me, too." I pushed to my feet. "I think we're done here. Do you have someone who can help me negotiate the land and the house with the city?"

River looked between me and Hayes before he held his hands up. "Hear me out. I have an idea."

"Are you going to rewrite the will and take out the ridiculous stipulation and let her inherit that money?" Hayes asked, pushing to his feet and crossing his arms over his chest.

"That would be illegal," he said. "But what if you found a husband and just agreed to be married for three months? It's a short time in the big picture of your life, and everybody wins."

"What am I going to do? Offer a stranger money to marry me?" I shook my head at the ridiculous idea.

"No. That would look suspicious." River chuckled, like this was a perfectly normal conversation. "And they could blackmail you and turn you in. It can't be a stranger."

"What are you suggesting?" Hayes asked.

"What I'm about to say never leaves this office."

Nothing good ever came from a statement like that.

7

Hayes

I dropped back down in my seat because we may as well hear him out. River was a smart fucking dude, and I knew he'd do what he could to help Savannah. Whether or not she believed me, she meant a lot to me.

There were very few people that fell into that category, but she'd always been one of them. Even though her leaving hurt like hell, I'd still walk through fire for her.

"Sit." I looked over at her, and she huffed back to her seat.

"What's this grand idea?" she asked.

"If you marry a stranger, it's going to look suspicious. You aren't dating anyone at the moment, right? Were there any recent serious relationships?" River asked.

"Nope. I just found out that my last boyfriend, who I broke up with over a year ago, is currently serving time for stealing a car," she said.

"That's a dumbshit thing to do." I leaned back in my chair.

"I haven't even told you the best part. It was a cop car. And there was a suspect handcuffed in the back seat."

Savannah had always enjoyed fixing broken things. Nothing about this surprised me. But she was too smart for her own damn good, and once she got people on their feet, she moved on.

That's what she'd done with me. But I hadn't been standing on my own two feet at the time. I'd been at my lowest point.

"So, he's not going to be a possibility," River said as he barked out a laugh.

"Definitely not. But he wrote to me and told me that he passed the bar exam from prison, so if you need an assistant when he gets out, I'm sure he'd love the opportunity." She smirked. The beauty of Savannah Abbott was her heart. She wasn't kidding. She'd probably call River the minute the dude was released and try to help him out.

She'd always been that girl who showed up for everyone.

Until I needed her most.

And I was fine with it, because needing people had never paid off for me. We'd been too close. I preferred keeping most people at a distance.

Life was easier that way.

"I'll keep that in mind." River chuckled. "So here's what I'm suggesting."

He folded his hands together slowly and leaned back in his chair, as his eyes moved from me to the woman beside me.

Slowly.

What the fuck is he up to?

"I can't advise you to break the law. I can simply make some suggestions that could help your situation." His lips turned up in the corners.

"Okay," she said.

"So you came back to town for a funeral, and you ran into some old friends. One old friend in particular." River arched a brow, his gaze locking with mine.

Why the fuck is he looking at me like that?

"Sure. It's been great seeing Ruby and Saylor and Demi." She smiled.

"I'm not talking about the girls. I'm talking about a certain best friend you haven't seen in years," he said.

"This guy?" Savannah flicked her thumb in my direction, and I glared at her. "We can barely stand one another anymore."

"That's even better," River said. "That way, no one gets hurt."

"What the fuck are you talking about?" I hissed.

"I'm talking about something that's easy to believe. Two old friends who everyone in town knew were inseparable back in the day. They haven't seen one another in years, and now Savvy's back in town, and they reconnect. They pick up right where they left off. Things progress. A few weeks later, they realize they can't live without one another, and they tie the knot."

"You've got to be kidding me," I said, as a sarcastic laugh left my mouth. "I can barely get her to let me help her out of a snowbank. There's no reconnecting going on here."

"Hey!" She whipped around to look at me. "You have shit taste in women. I'd be a freaking score for you. You should be so lucky to marry me, you grumpy bastard."

River's head fell back in laughter, and I flipped him the bird.

"This is what I mean. You already seem like an old married couple," River said, waggling his brows like the dickhead he was.

"You're the one who rolled into town acting like I'm the enemy. This is an insane idea. You can't be seriously considering this?"

"I never said I was considering it. I just didn't appreciate the way you acted like fake marrying me was so appalling." She crossed her arms over her chest, and I couldn't stop staring at her full lips. Did she always have those plump lips?

"Right. You get to be appalled by the idea, but I should be honored?" I shook my head in disbelief. "I've got news for you, Shortcake. I'm not the marrying type. Maybe you should consider your Uber driver. You seemed awfully cozy with him yesterday."

"Were you always a jackass, and I just didn't see it when we were young?" She arched a brow, the corners of her lips turning up the slightest bit.

"I've always been this way. It just took you a while to catch on, I guess," I said. "But you sure caught on, didn't you?"

"I'm disengaging from this conversation. It's a ridiculous idea anyway." She clapped her hands back and forth twice, letting us know she was washing her hands of the idea.

"Is it? Obviously, as an attorney, I can't recommend anything that doesn't fall within the constraints of the law. But I'm just pointing out, as a friend, this arrangement does benefit both of you."

Of course, that comment got her attention, and she slowly turned toward me, curiosity dancing in her honey-brown eyes. "How does it benefit you?"

"It doesn't," I said, zero emotion in my voice.

"Hayes," the jackass on the other side of the desk said.

"River." I mimicked his self-righteous tone.

"Hayes. River." Savannah tried to cover her laugh. "Please tell me what I'm missing."

"It's nothing," I said.

"Oh, so you invited yourself here, and you get to hear my whole messed-up story, but I get—nothing. Typical, Woody. You give nothing."

She may as well have slapped me across the face. I'd never shared half the shit that I'd shared with her with anyone else. It was our shtick. Sharing and confiding in the other. I'd trusted her.

I ground my teeth hard before I responded. "That's an asshole thing to say, and you know it."

"Takes one to know one." She smirked.

Such a fucking smartass.

"Fine. I'm an asshole. You hate me. I get it." I shook my head. "I don't know why the fuck I'm even here trying to help you."

That had her eyes softening. "I don't hate you. And for what it's worth, if I were going to fake marry anyone, I would choose you."

"There we go. But let's not use the word *fake marry* in this office." River chuckled. "So why would you choose him?"

I am definitely going to beat his ass later.

"He'd be the safe bet. It would never go anywhere because we aren't friends anymore. So there would be no risk of anyone catching feelings."

"Unlike Scotty, the Uber driver who invited you to karaoke night with his band?" I said, feeling good about reminding her what a douchebag that guy was.

"Well, yes. Scotty tends to fall easily. It would be messy to enter a—er," she paused to look at River, trying to choose her words carefully, "arrangement with someone who might not understand the situation."

"So, let me get this straight . . . I'm a safe bet because I'm an asshole, and I don't have feelings?"

"Exactly. There would be no confusion." Her lips turned up in the corners.

"This is good progress. We know all the reasons why it would work." River took a sip of his coffee. "You both get something out of it, and then you go your separate ways. It's a regular marriage; you just go in knowing that there is an end game."

I barked out a laugh. This was the most ridiculous thing he'd ever come up with, and he'd come up with plenty of batshit crazy ideas over the years.

"I know how this benefits me. Clearly, we all know. And helping my father is the only reason I'm going to ask this." She cleared her throat. "How does it benefit Hayes?" She directed her question at River, knowing I wasn't going to answer her.

"Well, Hayes won't admit that it would help him, but it wouldn't hurt, that's for sure. He's up for a promotion at the firehouse. John Cook is retiring in a few months. He and Lenny are both candidates in the running. Lenny is playing the game a little better than our boy, Hayes. He's got his wife throwing events and presenting this family atmosphere, which looks good on paper."

"Lenny Davis? The guy who banged your evil fiancée?"

I let out a long breath with half a nod. "I think Cap sees through it. But I've never been good at the social side of the business. The politics and the bullshit."

Her gaze filled with empathy as she took me in. "You just want to save lives and put out fires."

There were little moments where she put her guard down and let me see her. Vulnerable moments that she didn't want me to see. But when she did, it was so familiar that all I wanted to do was pull her onto my lap and wrap my arms around her and keep her here with me.

My father had left me and my sister when we were young. My mother had failed us time and time again, as well. My fiancée had faked a pregnancy and fucked my coworker.

And none of those losses compared to the loss of Savannah Abbott in my life.

"If I don't get the job, then I don't get the job."

"But then you'd be working for Lenny, which we both know won't work. So what you're not saying, that we all know to be true, is that you'll leave. You won't stay here and work for a man that you despise. I know it, and you know it. So play the fucking game," River hissed.

He was right. Working for Lenny would never be an option for me. One of us would be leaving that station, and that meant leaving Magnolia Falls.

I was at peace with it.

Saylor was with Kingston now, and she'd be fine if I left. I wouldn't go far, and I could come home often to visit. Everyone would get over it.

"I remember Kimber from high school. She was nice enough, but the girl had zero style," Savannah said, interrupting my thoughts.

"And that matters because?" I didn't hide my irritation. I didn't want to talk about this anymore. I'd come here to sit in on the meeting and make sure she'd be okay. I didn't need anyone dissecting my life.

"Because I could put her to shame with my wifely skills. Hell, I could throw a party for my man that would be the talk of the town."

River's head fell back in laughter before he sat forward and rubbed his hands together. "I like the sound of that."

"Throw a party for your man?" I quipped. "The same one you can't stand most of the time?"

"It's a short-term"—she glanced at River—"*arrangement*. I know my role. You know your role. It's a couple of weeks, and we both get what we want before our marriage starts to crumble, and I need my space."

"You're serious right now?" I asked, shaking my head in disbelief.

"I want to help my dad, Woody." Her voice was soft, another glimpse of my old best friend being exposed. "And honor Abe's wishes for the house. I could restore it and sell it to a nice family. I could help you get your promotion, and I think you should get a settlement from the inheritance for agreeing to marry me."

That had my blood boiling. "You think I want your money?"

"Why not? It would only be right that you should get something when this all falls apart," she said, glancing at River and then looking at me mischievously. "I mean, if things don't work out for us the way we hope they do, then you shouldn't walk away empty-handed."

"If I did this, which I'm far from convinced is a good idea, it would only be to help you. If it meant I got the promotion and didn't have to see that kiss-ass piece of shit get promoted, that would sweeten the pot. But the only way I will consider this is if we have it in writing that I don't leave this— arrangement or marriage or whatever the fuck this is—with any financial gain."

I'd had a father who had a shit ton of money, and he never took care of me or my sister. I'd worked hard to provide for both of us. I did not want or need handouts from anyone.

It was a hard line for me.

"We could write up a prenup. That looks honorable," River said.

"I don't care how it looks. I'm not doing this for the money. That's my point."

"So you're considering it," Savannah said, her teeth sinking into her juicy bottom lip.

"I want you to be able to help your dad."

"That's very generous of you," she said, but I could see she was struggling with this, too. She directed her question to River. "How would this work? Would we have to live together?"

"Yeah. If you two were to suddenly reconnect and fall in love, you'd get married within the next month and live together for three months."

"We cannot live together for three months," Savannah gasped.

This marriage is already off to a great start.

"You could live in different parts of the house. I don't think anyone will be paying attention, so if you realize it was a mistake in a couple of weeks…" River smirked, as he tapped his pen against the desk. "You separate, but you're still working on the marriage, right? And then in three months, you just call it quits. Everyone wins. Put on a united front starting now, and then things can fall apart a few weeks after you're married."

This had all the makings of a disaster.

"We can be a married couple living separate lives. No one will be the wiser." She shrugged. "Where would we live?"

"My house. That farmhouse is a fucking disaster right now, and it needs to be renovated. You can work on that while we're living at my place. My house is large, and I'm gone three nights a week at the firehouse anyway. You'll barely have to see me."

"I like the sound of that." She smirked.

"I don't think it will be that complicated. Who's going to be paying attention?" River asked. "But you just can't tell anyone what we've discussed here. It would have to stay between the three of us."

"I can live with that." Savannah turned to look at me. "So, are you in? Do you want me to be your ball and chain for the next few months? I promise to be the best girlfriend and then fiancée and then wife before I leave you high and dry and file for divorce." She extended her hand in offering to seal the deal.

"Sounds like a match made in heaven." I oozed sarcasm and wrapped my large hand around hers.

It was probably the worst idea I'd ever agreed to.

But for whatever reason, I couldn't say no. "I'm in."

8

Savannah

I followed Hayes out to his truck, and my head was spinning. River gave us a boatload of things we'd need to do, starting now.

First, we were not to tell anyone what was discussed in the office today. He wouldn't even say it aloud.

Second, we needed to start being seen together. Take our romance public immediately. The first time would be tonight at Whiskey Falls.

Third, when we're in public, we would need to pour on the PDA. Things were going to be moving quickly, and it would need to be believable.

When Hayes pulled open the passenger door, I climbed in, and he reached over to grab my seat belt. I slapped his hand away. "I can buckle myself. I only let you do that earlier because I was a mess."

He raised a brow. "We're in public. I thought it was a boyfriend thing to do."

Damn this man. I tossed my hands in the air. "Fine. Spoil me."

He pulled the seat belt across my body, and his hand grazed my thigh as he did it.

How was I going to pretend to date him?

Here I was, trying to avoid him, and now I'd agreed to marry him?

How did this even happen?

Once he was in the driver's seat, he cranked the heat and started driving toward the farmhouse.

"Are we making a huge mistake?" I whispered.

"Probably," he grumped, before glancing over at me when he came to a stop sign. "But it will get your dad the treatment he needs. And it'll give you a break in life. One I think you could use."

I wanted to be offended, but it was sweet. And I had much more to gain from this arrangement than he did.

"Thank you for doing this. I promise I'll pour it on thick in front of your boss," I said.

"Don't worry about that. I'm not sure I'm the right guy for the job anyway."

"Why do you say that?" I asked, as he pulled down the long driveway toward the farmhouse.

"Because I have no desire to play the game. Maybe I'm not meant to lead if I can't get on board with the politics side of things."

"Don't you dare say that about my future husband," I said, as I waggled my brows. "We're going to get you that promotion, Woody."

"How about you just focus on figuring out how we're going to pull this off."

"Well, tonight's our big debut, right? We'll put on a show and have everyone talking. It'll be easy."

"All right. I'll pick you up in a few hours." He put the truck in park and jumped out in the snow to come open my door.

I'd yet to date a man who did this. I'd been fine with it because I wasn't some damsel in distress. But I'd be lying if I didn't think it was sweet that he did it every time. Always had.

"I can meet you there," I said.

"You don't have a car, remember?"

Shit. I forgot about that. "I'll get it towed, and hopefully, they can fix it soon."

"I'll call Warner; don't worry about it," he said, placing his hand on my lower back as I walked up the icy steps.

"I can call Warner." I pulled out my keys.

"He owes me a favor. And it might look good that I'm taking care of your car, for the sake of appearances."

"You're proving to be a very impressive boyfriend, Woody." I pushed the door open.

He walked backward down the steps and held up a hand. "See you in a few hours, Shortcake."

I stepped inside, taking in the monstrosity before me. I'd gotten the kitchen cleaned up, and I'd washed the linens and remade the bed at least. But there was so much work to do here that I didn't know where to start.

I didn't know if I should even start.

Would we seriously pull this off? Would anyone believe that Hayes and I were actually in love?

My phone vibrated in my pocket, and I pulled it out to see my favorite picture of my dad and me filling the screen.

"Hey, Dad. How are you feeling?"

"I'm doing okay, sweetheart. Missing my girl, that's for sure. How was the funeral?" he asked.

"It was sad, but I knew it would be."

"You loved him. That's to be expected, honey."

I went to sit in the only chair that wasn't falling apart in the kitchen. I didn't know how to approach the conversation. "Abe left me his farmhouse and some money."

"That's amazing. He and Lily loved you like you were their own. I'm not surprised."

"I think it would be enough money to get you into that trial that Nadia and I have been looking into," I said.

My father had hepatoblastoma, a rare liver cancer that not many doctors were familiar with. That's why it would be so valuable to be able to fly him to Texas where they were doing this particular trial, which was having huge success.

The last decade had been brutal for my father. His marriage to my mother had fallen apart in the worst way. He'd survived his first bout with liver cancer and celebrated remission, only to find out the cancer had come back with a vengeance.

He was too sick to work anymore, so he was living on disability. His self-esteem had taken a hit so many times that it had become difficult for him to stay positive. He'd always been this big force in life, but the illness and the heartache had taken a toll on him physically and mentally.

"Savvy, I don't need you worrying about me. I'm just fine."

He was anything but fine. He was rail thin and could barely keep food down. I was so grateful for his girlfriend, Nadia, who'd been the best support system for him. I was doing my best to help him, as I lived in the same apartment building as they did, just in a different unit. Now that she was living with him, it had taken a lot of pressure off of me, and it was the only reason I could be here. I knew he was in good hands.

"Did Nadia talk to you about the trial?"

"You know Nadia. She's always researching that stuff. I don't want either of you to worry about that. I've been feeling good lately. I finally painted those bookshelves she's been after me about for six months. They look great."

My chest squeezed at the sound of his voice.

He sounded good.

But cancer could be a wicked asshole most of the time. Every time I was hopeful, it seemed like something happened.

I knew he needed to try something different because nothing had been working thus far.

"I'm so happy you did that. I'm sure it felt good to get your creative juices back," I said.

My father had been a successful journalist before his world got flipped on its ass. His wife had a very public affair right around the same time that he got diagnosed with liver cancer. We moved away, and he never quite found his footing after that. I resented my mother for the role she played in the deterioration of his life.

Yes, we still had a relationship.

She and Mr. Jones, the theater teacher at Magnolia Falls High School, moved to the city shortly after my father and I did. They had a son, my brother Harry, who I happened to adore.

They lived just a few miles from my apartment in the city, and my parents had actually repaired their relationship a bit over the last few years since his second diagnosis. My mother and her husband, Ben, checked in on my father often.

Dad had moved past the anger and the hurt somehow, so I'd tried to do the same.

But I still held a lot of resentment toward her for what she'd done to his life. To my life, and that was something I was trying to let go of.

My brother, Harry, played a huge role in me moving forward with my mother.

"Yes. I actually started writing a few months ago. I just hadn't told you yet because I didn't know if it would amount to anything. But it's coming along. I'm writing a novel."

"Dad," I said, feeling the lump form in my throat. It was the first time I'd heard him truly excited about something that didn't involve me or Nadia in a very long time. "That's amazing. I can't wait to read it."

"It'll be a while, but you'll be the first. I promise." He paused, and I could tell he was drinking something. He worked hard to stay hydrated most days, as this latest round of chemo depleted him so much. "Enough about me. Tell me about Magnolia Falls. Have you run into anyone?"

We both knew what he was asking. He and Hayes had always been close. My father had taken him under his wing, as Hayes's father had left them and cut off all contact.

"Yes. I've seen Hayes several times. In fact, we're going to have dinner tonight." I had to start selling the idea of Hayes and me as a couple. My father would never support me fake marrying someone for money. Hell, I didn't even support the idea, but it was for the greater good, so I'd get over it.

"It's always bothered me that your friendship ended after we moved away. I truly thought that friendship was one that would last forever. You two were so close. Hayes was part of our family. I always blamed myself for moving away and coming between you two."

I tried to push away the heaviness that was settling on my chest. I'd never shared with my father what had happened. He'd been dealing with a hell of a lot more than learning that your best friend didn't want to be bothered with you anymore.

I was certainly not going to add to his burden.

So, I dealt with it alone.

I dealt with everything alone.

The brutal divorce my parents went through.

My mother having a torrid affair with one of my high school teachers and the whole town finding out.

My father's cancer.

Completely uprooting our lives and moving away with no notice.

Leaving Abe and Lily and a part-time job that I'd loved.

And the loss of my best friend.

"It's part of life, Dad. People move on. But it's really nice seeing him again." How was I going to explain that I'd married him in such a short time? "He looks really good. I think he's actually flirting with me."

I knew my dad would love this juicy tidbit.

"Oh. I always thought he liked you as more than a friend, if I'm being honest. And he never seemed happy with that girl he dated the last few months before we left."

The devil.

The ice queen.

The bane of my teenage existence.

"Kate? Yeah, I think they broke up a long time ago. I never cared for her," I admitted, as I had good reason besides her cheating on Hayes.

"Someone sounds a little jealous. I always thought you had a crush on him, as well," Dad said with a laugh.

Normally, I would insist that he was crazy, but I just laughed. I needed to set this up like some sort of long-lost love affair. My father would be crushed when it all got blown to pieces, but hopefully, he'd be in better health and on his way to a full recovery.

It would all be worth it.

"Maybe I did, and I just didn't realize it," I said, rolling my eyes because this was far from a crush.

I'd survived without Hayes for a long time, and I sure as hell wasn't some giddy schoolgirl with stars in my eyes now.

"Anyway, if we can afford to get you into this trial program, I just need to know that you won't fight me on it."

"Fine. I'll agree to go if it's not too outrageously expensive," he said. My father was completely disconnected from reality with the financial side of his illness. His disability covered the minimum to keep him alive. Nadia and I handled everything else. We'd fought hard to get him into several different trials over the last eighteen months, and we'd been denied every time.

Every. Single. Time.

So, yeah, I'd marry my ex-best friend and live with him for a few months, if it meant I'd have the resources to help my father. And I'd even do what I could to help Hayes get his promotion, because he was doing me a huge favor by agreeing to this.

Although, I wouldn't get my hopes up. He could easily change his mind and bail on me.

It wouldn't be the first time.

9

Hayes

"You good, dude?" Romeo asked, as my gaze tracked Savannah out on the dance floor with the girls.

"Yeah. Of course."

"So you came with Savvy tonight, huh?" King smirked.

River shot me a warning look. The fewer people that knew, the better. It wasn't a full-on lie. I'd known her most of my life. Even though we hadn't talked in years, it didn't feel that way. It felt like I'd just seen her yesterday. We'd always had a connection. So whether she hated me or liked me, it didn't really matter.

I knew this girl.

I knew her well.

I may not have understood her choices, but I knew who she was.

Good to her core.

Maybe she'd just outgrown me. I could understand that. She was always destined for big things. For more. I'd known it early on.

I wouldn't fault her for that. My life was a shit show, and it was easy to get pulled down in all that drama back then.

"Yeah. We've been spending some time together, and I'm not going to lie—it's nice." That was true. I'd never lied to my boys, and I'd find a way to do this without lying now.

At least, I'd try.

River, Romeo, Nash, and King were family. They were more like brothers to me.

"She doesn't seem to hate you, that's for sure. She walked in here with you and looked like she was having a good time," Nash said.

"And you did, too," Kingston added, raising a brow as if he were testing me.

"Hey, our boy is happy. Let him be. He'd missed her, and we all knew that. They've got a history, and clearly, they're picking up where they left off." River took a pull from his beer. He was setting things up.

Always the lawyer.

The song stopped, and Ruby, Demi, Peyton, Saylor, Emerson, and Savannah came walking toward us with big smiles on their faces.

My gaze locked with Savannah's, and she held it this time.

She'd had a few drinks, so maybe she was more relaxed.

Her guard was definitely down, and I didn't mind it.

"Hey there, friends and fans." Scotty's voice pulled my attention to the stage. "We're getting ready to take the stage, and I know a lot of you are here tonight to hear The Disasters perform, so I want to let you know that we plan to give the crowd what they want." There were very few cheers and a few groans, and I glanced over at Savannah, giving her a knowing look.

She surprised me when she smiled so big it had my chest squeezing. How long had it been since she'd smiled at me like that?

Too long.

"Does anyone else think that naming your band The

Disasters is sort of like setting yourself up for failure?" Romeo asked.

Everyone chuckled.

"Yeah, not the wisest choice," Kingston said, his eyes on me as Savannah took the stool beside me.

Scotty was back at the mic because the dude couldn't help himself. "All right, we're going to kick this off with an oldie. This one is for the girl that got away. She knows who she is."

His eyes were staring right at the woman beside me, and her shoulders tensed. "Dear God, what is he doing?" she whisper-hissed, leaning close so only I could hear.

I leaned down, my lips grazing her ear as the smell of vanilla and lavender flooded my senses. "I don't know, but maybe it's time we make sure he realizes you aren't available. Well, that's pending how you want to pull this off."

Her eyes widened when she pulled back, and she gave me the slightest nod. She leaned against me, and I wrapped an arm around her on instinct.

It was so easy.

Far too easy.

I'd never been an affectionate guy. I believe that was Kate's big complaint after I'd found her riding my coworker like she was a professional jockey.

She'd blamed me.

"You're cold, Hayes. You have zero emotion. You give me nothing."

It was easy to believe, because I was closed off. I wasn't looking to let anyone in more than necessary, and I'd always been that way.

With the exception of Savannah Abbott. She was the one person I'd always let in.

I was surprised how easy it was to fall back into that comfort, especially after the way she'd left. Maybe I was just playing along, doing my part to make it believable.

Hell, I didn't know.

My thumb ran up and down her arm over her sweater, and I kissed her cheek, lingering there a little longer than necessary.

I noted everyone at the table watching us, but I forced my attention back to the dickhead on stage singing about how his woman left him, and he wanted her back.

Irritation seeped in because I'd never liked the dude.

He'd been possessive of her back in high school. He'd tried like hell to come between our friendship, and it had pissed me the fuck off.

Clearly, that hadn't changed.

He finished his song and had the audacity to walk toward our table. My hand moved to Savannah's waist, and I tugged her closer, pulling the whole barstool with her. Her hand rested on top of mine, and I relaxed. She wasn't going to bail on me. At least not tonight.

"Hey, Savvy, you're looking fire tonight."

Yeah, I'd like to pull out a hose and blast your ass the hell out of here.

"Thank you," she said, stroking her hand over mine, and his eyes tracked there.

Good. Take the hint, asshole. She's with me.

At least for the next few months.

"I wanted to see if you'd like to get dinner tomorrow night?" he asked, completely ignoring the fact that she was clearly here with me.

I leaned forward, ready to teach this guy some manners. Whether this was real or not, she was leaning against me. Our hands were intertwined. And him hitting on her right now was a dick thing to do.

She must have noticed, because she turned slowly, her hand moving to the side of my face and catching me off guard. "Hey. Give me a minute, okay?"

I nodded, and she pushed off the stool and walked away,

with dickhead Scotty on her heels. I followed them with my gaze. I didn't trust the dude, and I sure as hell wouldn't let him out of my sight with her. They stood a few feet away, and she was talking to him, and he didn't look happy.

Good. He needed to back the fuck off so I could give this fake marriage a try.

"What in the holy hotness is going on here, Hayes Woodson?" Peyton asked, and everyone laughed. She was sitting on Slade's lap, as apparently, she and Demi's brother were a full-on couple now. Slade reached for his water and chuckled at his girlfriend.

"We're just having fun. It's good to see her again," I said. And it was all true, so I didn't have to feel bad about a damn thing. I needed everyone to believe we were falling for each other, but I had to ease them into the idea of me with a girlfriend before I could sell them on the idea of me with a wife.

"I always thought you two liked each other when we were in high school," Demi said.

"But then you dated that bitch on wheels, Kate." Ruby raised a knowing brow at me. "And trust me. I like a badass bitch. But that girl, she was the worst. She put on this show like she was sweet and kind, but then you'd watch her actions, and she was a mean girl to her core."

Yeah, Kate had been a very layered person, showing me different sides of herself over the years we'd spent together. Ruby was not wrong about her.

"Well, sometimes you don't think you deserve better than that, you know?" Saylor said, her gaze locking with mine. My sister had a heart of gold, and she knew me well.

"How about we don't psychoanalyze me tonight and just have a good time, yeah?" I reached for my beer and took a pull. I'd driven here, so I wouldn't have more than one.

And then Savannah made her way back to the table, with a tray of shot glasses on it, all clear, while one had dark liquid in it.

"I wanted to celebrate being back in town, so the tequila shots are on me. And I got you a Cherry Coke shot, Demi." She chuckled as she passed out the shot glasses. Everyone else had walked here, but I'd picked up Savvy, as the farmhouse would be a long walk, especially in these cold temperatures.

She handed me mine, her fingers grazing my hand.

"I'm your ride, remember? And I'm sure as hell not letting you get in an Uber with Scotty after you've had so much to drink."

She leaned closer. "Don't overthink it, Woody. Take the shot. We'll walk home. You can come get your car tomorrow."

"It's a far walk to your place, Shortcake," I reminded her.

"Then I guess I'm spending the night at your place." She winked, and I reached for my glass.

"Cheers to old times and good friends!" Kingston shouted, and we all tipped our heads back before grabbing a lime.

"Damn, that first shot always hits a little different," Romeo said, and we all laughed.

The girls went on stage together and sang a few songs, and it was entertaining as hell.

And we drank and laughed and stayed out way later than I'd planned. Demi dragged Romeo out of there, as she was pregnant and exhausted. I was fairly sober now, as I'd stopped drinking after that shot, but I still wouldn't get behind the wheel, so we'd be walking home.

Savannah sauntered over to me, where I sat on my barstool, her cheeks flush, hair a wild mess of long waves flowing down her back, her jeans hugging her curves in all the right places.

She wrapped her hands around my neck, her nose brushing against mine, lips close enough to kiss. "Take me home, Woody."

Her words slurred, and I nodded. I reached for her coat on the back of the barstool and helped her into it, before zipping it up and taking her hat from her coat pocket and pulling it over her ears. I found her mittens next, and she held her hands up. "You like taking care of me, Hayes?"

Her voice was all tease, but my dick jumped to attention at the tone of her voice. At the heat in her honey-brown eyes. I slipped the mittens over each hand and nodded.

"Always, Shortcake."

We walked outside and said our goodbyes as we made our way home. Once it was just me and Savannah heading toward my house, she groaned. "These damn boots were not a good idea."

I looked down at her heeled boots and chuckled before bending my knees and patting my back. "Hop on."

"You're going to give me a piggyback ride all the way home?" She laughed. Her words made it clear that she was still very tipsy.

"A whole block and a half, yeah. I'm a fucking firefighter. I've carried a lot more than a lightweight like you. Get on."

She jumped up, and her arms wrapped around my neck, her legs around my waist, and I started walking.

"Do you think everyone noticed us acting sort of like a couple tonight?" she asked, her lips grazing my earlobe just beneath my beanie.

"They definitely noticed. What did you say to Scotty?" I'd been dying to ask since she'd come back to the table.

"I told him that we'd hung out the last few days, and those old feelings had returned," she said, before nipping at my earlobe and shocking the shit out of me.

I yelped. "Hey. What was that for?"

"You always had sensitive lobes, remember?" she said, over a fit of laughter. "I used to love tugging on them and messing with you."

"Yeah, you sure did." I turned down my street and headed toward my house.

"Sometimes that feels like a hundred years ago." I could hear the sadness in her voice.

I put the key in the door and walked inside, making my way to the couch and setting her down. I tugged off my coat and tossed it on the couch, before dropping to my knees as she gaped down at me.

"What are you doing?" She tugged her mittens off and tossed them on the couch.

"I'm taking off your boots. You said your feet hurt."

"Wow. You do know I'm a sure thing on this whole fake marriage thing, right? You don't need to pamper me behind closed doors." She chuckled as I tugged the first boot off and wrapped my hand around her socked foot and gave it a squeeze before doing the same to her other foot.

"Everything I do isn't for something, Sav." The words came out harsher than I meant them to.

She looked down at me, and her hand moved to the top of my head as her fingers scraped along my short hair. "It's easier to hate you when I'm not around you."

The admission hit me like a punch to the gut.

She'd blocked me. She was admitting that she hated me.

It was one thing to think it and another to hear her say the words.

"Why in the fuck would you hate me after everything we've been through?"

Her eyes welled with emotion, and she shook her head. "You left me, Hayes. When I needed you most. You crushed me, and it took me a long time to get over it."

"I don't know what the fuck you're talking about." Her being drunk worked in my favor because at least she was opening up to me.

"Oh, God," she said, as she jumped to her feet before sprinting around the couch toward the bathroom. "I'm going to be sick."

I made my way down the hall and heard her heaving. I pushed the door open and stood there as she hung her head over the toilet. I waited for her to finish vomiting before reaching around her body and unzipping her coat and carefully slipping it off her shoulders.

She groaned, and I moved to the sink and turned on the water, wetting a washcloth and wringing it out. I handed it to her and flushed the toilet before helping her sit back so that her back was pressed against the wall. "Sorry about that. I'm not used to drinking so much."

I sat beside her. "So, how about you tell me why you drank so much, then?"

"Since when do you ask so many questions?" She wiped her mouth and forehead with the damp cloth.

She was right. I wasn't usually this inquisitive because I didn't normally give a shit.

But I gave a shit about Savannah.

"Since when are you someone who deflects every question that's asked?"

"Fine. I'm fake marrying a man I have worked hard to hate for a very long time, and I'm lying to everyone in my life about it. And it's all so that I can help my father who is dying before my eyes. And let's not forget that I just had to say goodbye to Abe, a man who was like a grandfather to me, who also left me the money to help my father, but with all these crazy conditions. That's reason enough to drink tequila, isn't it?"

I chuckled. "I've known you a long time, Sav. Fake marrying a man you've worked hard to hate is not the craziest thing you've ever done."

"That's your answer? That I've done worse than being deceptive to everyone I know?"

"Just saying. I'm the only living witness who knows it was you who pulled that fire alarm our freshman year in high school."

"You are such an asshole for bringing that up," she groaned. "I did that for you."

"I know you did."

I still remembered it like it was yesterday. I'd had a late night because my fucked-up stepfather, Barry, had come home drunk and was breaking furniture and going crazy. I'd had a chemistry test that morning and knew I'd fail since I hadn't studied the night before because I was dealing with family drama, per usual. And if I failed that class, I'd be yanked from the football team because Coach did not mess around. I'd thought it would cost me my future. But it turned out that football wasn't my future anyway.

"And you didn't end up taking that football scholarship, did you?" she asked, but she made it clear she already knew the answer.

"I did not. But that's not the point."

"What's the point?" she asked, her voice sleepy now as she fell against my shoulder.

"The point is, as a firefighter, I could have you arrested, knowing what you did," I said over my laughter. "A fake marriage is nothing for a hardcore criminal like you."

She laughed, her eyes were closed now, and she whispered four little words that I hadn't expected to hear from her.

"I missed you, Hayes."

I missed you, too, Shortcake.

10

Savannah

Sunlight flooded the room, and I tried to lick my lips, but it appeared my tongue was superglued to the roof of my mouth. It felt like someone was banging their drums inside my head, and I covered my eyes with my hands and rubbed them several times before attempting to open them.

After I blinked a few times, I sat forward.

Where the hell am I?

Tequila. Puking. Hayes.

"Oh, God," I groaned.

"You beckoned, Shortcake?" Hayes's voice called out from somewhere outside the room, before he appeared in the doorway.

I glanced around. "Is this your room?"

"It is."

"Did something happen between us?" I asked, panic coursing through my veins. I would know if I slept with someone, especially Hayes, wouldn't I? But what was I doing in his bed?

"Relax, Sav." He came around my side of the bed and handed me a mug of coffee. "I carried you in here after you puked more than any human ever should, because it's the only room with a bathroom attached. I slept in the guest room."

"Oh."

"Oh? That's your apology for basically asking if I took advantage of you?" he grumped, before making his way back toward the door.

"Where are you going?"

"I have to get to work. I left a spare key on the counter for you. You're going to need it when you move in here in a few weeks anyway. Your car is in my driveway, and the keys are on the table."

He'd thought of everything. He'd taken care of me, and I was being rude.

"I'm an awful human being, and if you want to make a citizen's arrest and tell the whole town that I pulled that fire alarm back in the day, I wouldn't blame you."

"Nah. That would hurt my chances of getting promoted to captain, if my fake wife was a fire-alarm-pulling criminal. I'll be working for the next three days, and then it'll be showtime again. River thinks we should do this whole dating thing for three weeks and then get hitched. We don't want to do it on the day of the cutoff because that'll look a little too obvious. So, we take it to the next level this week."

"Okay. I can do that. I'm going to get dressed and head out to the farmhouse now," I said, taking a sip of coffee as he started to leave the room, and I climbed out of bed. "Hey, Hayes."

"Yep." He glanced over his shoulder at me.

"Thank you for taking care of me last night."

He didn't answer. He just nodded and walked away. I heard the door close behind him, and I had a flashback of me telling him how I'd hated him all these years.

Why do I feel guilty about that now?

I had every reason to despise Hayes Woodson. Just because

he was being nice now didn't mean that what happened in the past didn't happen.

We were just two people with a history, that were helping one another out right now.

I pushed out of bed, looking down to see I was fully clothed, and I remembered him taking my boots off.

I remembered him rubbing my back while I puked.

I had a flashback of him carrying me to his bed.

Why did he have to be so damn sexy, too?

It only made me want to hate him more.

I made my way to the bathroom and splashed water on my face. I glanced over at the bathtub and stared at it for a long moment. The hot water wasn't working at the farmhouse, so I'd been taking really fast ice-cold showers the last few days. The thought of a hot bath sounded really nice, especially considering I had a hell of a migraine. I ran the bath, turning the water on extra hot.

He wouldn't care, would he? He let me sleep here. I would be living here soon.

I let the tub fill, and I walked out to the kitchen and refilled my coffee. Hayes's house was not a typical bachelor pad, but that didn't shock me.

He'd always been very clean. His house was decorated with minimal décor, but there was thought behind it. He took pride in it. He'd always hated the chaos in his childhood home, so I wasn't surprised that he'd made a comfortable one for himself.

I moseyed down the hall, smiling when I took in one of the guest rooms that was clearly for Cutler. It had a bookshelf, a few puzzles, and some stuffed animals.

Hayes was always adamant that he didn't want kids after the way he'd grown up, and I wondered if that had changed. As his future fake wife, I could probably ask. The way he was with Cutler made me think he may have changed his mind.

Just seeing them together made it clear how much he loved that little boy.

It was a side of Hayes I didn't know. A softer side.

I hurried down to the bathroom just in time to turn off the water, and I set my coffee on the ledge surrounding the large tub. I pulled off my jeans and sweater from yesterday before unstrapping my bra, because who in the world wants to sleep in a bra? I pushed my panties down my legs and glanced out the small window to see the snow falling once again.

This was exactly what I needed. I dipped my toe in the water and a loud shrieking yelp escaped, and I stumbled back.

My God. This man must have his hot water heater cranked up.

I leaned over to turn on the cold water just as a loud voice startled me from the doorway.

"Are you okay? What happened?"

I whipped around to see Hayes standing there gaping at me, and he wasn't looking away.

"Oh, my gosh! What are you doing?" I covered my parts with my hands and reached for the only thing I could find, which was a small hand towel. I frantically tried to cover anything I could, as he moved past me like this was no big deal. He opened the cabinet across from me and pulled out a towel and held it up, with a deviously sexy smirk on his face.

I quickly wrapped it around myself and glared at him. "Why are you so calm?"

"Because it's my bathroom." His lips turned up in the corners. "And I've seen you naked before, remember?"

"You are the one who doesn't remember," I said, my heart racing because he'd just seen every inch of me.

When was the last time I shaved?

My God, this was so bad.

I liked to prepare before someone saw me naked.

And especially before Hayes saw me naked.

"Well, I can promise you this, Shortcake. I will not forget it this time."

"What are you even doing here?" I snarled, tightening the towel between my breasts. "I thought you left fifteen minutes ago."

Why am I breathing so heavily?

He was fully clothed, but it was the way his eyes trailed up my legs as he took in every inch of me that had my body betraying me.

"I live here." He pulled out another towel and set it on the counter.

"You could have knocked."

"Why would I knock? The door wasn't closed. I heard a shriek, and I thought your hungover ass fell down or something."

"That's because I thought you were long gone."

"I came back in here to tell you that I drove your car around the block, and it's running great. I can't have my little woman driving an unsafe car," he said, as he leaned against the wall and crossed his arms over his chest like he didn't have a care in the world.

"Thank you?" I said, sarcasm pouring from my almost naked body.

Why was he still in here?

"You're welcome. I thought you were leaving. That's why I started up your car."

Damn it. His reasoning made complete sense.

Once again, I was the asshole. How was that possible?

I sighed. "The hot water heater isn't working at Abe's place, so I saw the tub, and I thought you were gone…"

"Hey. You don't have to ask to take a bath, Sav. I'll turn your car off and leave the keys on the counter. Take your time."

"Thank you. And, er, sorry about the little show."

"Don't apologize for that. Great way to start the day." He

winked and pulled the door closed after he stepped out of the bathroom.

I buried my face in my hands and groaned. I dropped the towel and mimicked the pose I'd been in when he'd walked in and then looked in the mirror.

He'd definitely seen a lot. Especially when I whipped around.

I tied my hair up in a pile on top of my head with the hair tie on my wrist, before dipping my toe back into the water. It wasn't as hot as it had been a few minutes ago, before I'd embarrassed myself. I climbed in and sank beneath the hot water, allowing it to cover my shoulders.

I closed my eyes and forced myself to relax.

So much had happened since I'd arrived in Magnolia Falls.

I'd let my guard down with Hayes because it was so easy to do.

But I needed to remember that this was a business deal, nothing more.

* * *

I'd spent the last few days placing calls to the hospital in Texas and gathering all the information we'd need to get my father admitted into this trial. Insurance would pay a portion, and all that was required up front was ten thousand dollars cash, which I currently had on hand. It felt damn good to be able to go forward with the application process, because normally, this was where everything came to a stop. But I had the money, and we could keep pushing now. Obviously, it would cost much more once he was in, but the initial deposit after insurance was covered. I no longer felt guilty about lying to everyone about what I was about to do. Because if this worked, it would be totally worth it. I'd spoken to Nadia about it, and she felt confident it could be the difference between buying him several more years of life or throwing in the towel now. I was not giving up on my father.

I'd also started coming up with renovation plans for the farmhouse. I'd met with Nash and Kingston, who owned RoD Construction, and all I would need was a deposit to get things started here, and the rest of the money would be released in a couple of weeks.

After I become a married woman.

Hayes and I had been texting while he was at the firehouse because we had to come up with some plans for this week. Maybe we texted about other things, too, but I didn't have many people here that I talked to, and he was probably bored at work.

So, yeah, we texted often when he was at the firehouse.

I wasn't going to overthink it.

It would be hard to prove that we were in a real marriage if we didn't speak when he was away for days at the firehouse.

Saylor had reached out and asked me to meet her at The Golden Goose for lunch today. I pulled the door open, and she waved me over.

"What's going on with you and Grumpy-hot-fireman?" Midge asked as she greeted me at the door. I'd always liked her, even though most people found her abrasive. I clearly had a type that I was drawn to.

Grumpy.

Moody.

Annoyed most of the time.

I was about to say that nothing was going on, and I stopped myself. We needed people to think something was happening.

"What do you mean?" My voice was all tease as she led me toward the table in the back where Saylor was sitting.

"I heard you two were quite the spectacle at Whiskey Falls the other night. And he carried you home?"

I laughed. "How do you possibly know that?"

"I've got eyes everywhere, Savvy." She waggled her brows. "That is one sexy, fire-blazing, unattainable man. If you can harness that, more power to you."

Saylor shook her head in disbelief as she caught the tail end of the conversation. "Ew. That's my brother, Midge."

I batted my lashes at the older woman beside me. "A lady never tells her secrets."

Where the hell did that come from?

I slid into the booth beside Saylor, and our server, Letty, came over and took our orders before we even got a word out.

"Thanks for meeting me here," Saylor said. "I just wanted to see how you're doing with everything. I know Abe's passing was hard on you."

"Yeah. Most days, I still can't believe he's gone. It's a huge loss. I miss our chats. I miss his laugh. How stubborn he was when I told him to go to the doctor or eat better," I said, feeling the ache in my chest that I'd felt since the day I'd heard the news.

"Yeah. He and Lily loved you. They missed you so much after you moved away." Saylor reached for her soda after our drinks were set down on the table. "I'd go out there and ride, and they'd talk about you the whole time. We all missed you, you know?"

Saylor had been like a little sister to me growing up. But when I left, I cut off all ties to this town, aside from Abe and Lily.

"I missed you, too. I was just dealing with a lot back then. It was almost too much, between my mom's affair and my father finding out he had cancer."

"I hadn't known about your dad, and I don't think Hayes knew either, because he would have told me. He was shocked when you left. But that's when everything went down here, too. I guess in Magnolia Falls, when it rains, it pours, huh?"

"Hayes knew. I told him." I reached for my water and

took a sip before setting it back down. "And I'm sorry for everything that happened with your mom and that I wasn't there for you."

Lily had filled me in that Hayes and Saylor had been removed from their home due to an altercation with their stepfather. They'd gone to live with friends for a while, and eventually, Hayes took custody of his sister when he turned eighteen. I didn't know the details, but I knew they'd gone through a lot.

I guess we all had.

Saylor waved her hand around. "Don't be silly. We all had things we were dealing with. Mine led me to this place, right here, right now, and it's exactly where I want to be. Maybe yours led you back here for a reason, too."

I chuckled. "I don't know about that, but I'm happy to be here now."

I wasn't staying. Magnolia Falls was not my home anymore. And with Abe and Lily gone, that meant there was nothing here for me anymore. But I couldn't say that to her. To anyone. I was about to marry her brother, and it needed to appear like I would be staying. This whole plan was already more complicated than I'd expected. And lying to people I cared about was not something that I felt good about. I needed to get this renovation started, get hitched, and then get divorced, sell the farm, and leave town.

"Oh my gosh, is that Savannah Abbott?" Kimber's high-pitched voice had my head turning. She'd always been ridiculously bubbly and over the top. She'd been a bit pretentious back in the day, and I wondered if she'd outgrown that now.

"Hi, Kimber," I said.

"I heard you were back. So sorry to hear about Abe. I was sad we weren't able to make it to the funeral, but Lenny and I were out of town for my cousin's wedding."

"He wouldn't have wanted you to miss that," I said, because it was true.

She held up the bags in her hands. "I've been out shopping like crazy for the fundraiser Lenny and I are throwing for the firehouse. I've never met a credit card I didn't love." She chuckled.

"Yes, Hayes mentioned the fundraiser. He and I will be there," I said, and Saylor coughed a little over the sip she'd just taken from her soda. Hayes had actually mentioned the fundraiser, but he'd made fun of it. He didn't want to go, but I'd just found the next place to debut our new relationship.

Kimber arched a brow. "You're coming with Hayes?"

"Yeah. We've been spending a lot of time together since I've been back home. I guess we're picking up where we left off."

"Interesting." She eyed me suspiciously. "He's Magnolia Falls' most unattainable bachelor."

"I don't find him unattainable at all." I reached for a french fry and smiled.

"Well, you two were always close."

"And we're even closer now," I said, smiling up at her with all the confidence in the world.

"Really? How serious is this with you and Hayes?" Her eyes were wide, and she tapped her chin with her finger anxiously.

This was my moment.

I kept my face perfectly unaffected. "I'd say things are going really well. We plan on throwing a big Valentine's bash for everyone at the firehouse, so we'll get that invite over to you as soon as we have all the details."

She didn't hide her surprise. "Oh. Throwing parties together already? That was fast."

"Nothing fast about it. It's always been there; the timing just wasn't right. But when you know, you know. You know?" I chuckled at my repetitive words, and Saylor's head fell back in laughter.

"She's right. It was always there," Saylor said.

"Good for you. I'll try not to make my party too over the top, because that would be no fun to have to follow one of my shindigs." She snorted.

"Don't hold back at all. I'm guessing we can both throw a good party."

"Well, you haven't seen the parties that Lenny and I throw. Everyone in town talks about how fabulous they are." She quirked her brow.

"I'm looking forward to it."

Thankfully, she walked away, and I turned to find Saylor gaping at me.

"So, what exactly is going on with you and my brother?"

I couldn't lie to her face, but I also couldn't tell her the truth.

"It's complicated." I shrugged.

"Nothing would surprise me with you two." She picked up her grilled cheese and took a bite.

I wasn't so sure about that. A fake marriage might surprise her.

Because it surprised the hell out of me.

11

Hayes

"Tell me why you insisted that we come to this horrible event?" I asked for the third time since we'd arrived at Lenny and Kimber's house.

"I need to scope out the competition, Woody. I've got to throw the event of the century and put these two in their place. *I want to make my man proud.*" She waggled her brows playfully as we huddled in the corner. It had been like this for the last week. We'd been seen everywhere together, per River's encouragement.

And I was sick and tired of socializing.

But I'd be lying if I said I didn't look forward to spending my days with Savannah. When I wasn't at the firehouse, I was with her at the farmhouse. I feigned irritation and acted like it was a big inconvenience, but nothing about it bothered me.

She leaned closer to me as if she were sharing some CIA high-level secret. "Kimber thinks hiring a few servers and passing out champagne flutes makes her a top-notch hostess? Look around. Everyone is bored out of their minds. Our party is going to be the talk of the town. This is a total snoozefest."

I barked out a laugh. "Can we be done with the parties after tonight?"

"You never did like people-ing, did you?" she asked, and my eyes scanned down her cream-colored dress that hugged her curves perfectly. Ever since I'd walked in on her naked in my bathroom, I'd thought of nothing else.

I'd fucked my fist too many times to count.

This whole fake relationship was messing with my head. I probably needed to go out and get laid, and that sure as hell wasn't going to happen now. It would be a while until this façade was over.

"No. Enough is enough. How long do we have to stay?" I asked.

Savannah paused when a man in a white coat walked our way and offered us an appetizer. This party was a joke. They'd hired staff and put on this fancy event, and they could have just used the money they'd spent on throwing this party to buy the things they wanted for the firehouse. This was all to impress Cap.

Lenny was playing the game, and I hated to admit that he was damn good at it.

"Thank you," Savannah said, as she reached for one of the little snacks on the tray, and I grabbed a few, popping one into my mouth. She took a bite and then quirked a brow. "I love me some pigs in a blanket, but we can do better than this. Also, River said that everyone is talking about us. Apparently, we're the most adorable couple ever. But I think I need to give you a different nickname. Woody is juvenile. We need to amp things up."

"Amp things up? We've been out every single night that I haven't been at the firehouse. How much more amping do we need to do? Don't some couples just stay home and relax together?" I whispered against her ear.

"Awww . . . that's sweet, you big baby. Once we're married,

we can play up our home life. But right now, it's game time. You need to suck it up, and I need a catchy nickname for the man who managed to steal my heart."

"What are you going to call me, Shortcake?" I smirked because she was taking this whole thing far too seriously.

No one in Magnolia Falls gave a shit if she got the inheritance on false pretenses. Everyone in town loved Savannah Abbott.

I looked up to see Kimber and Lenny walking our way, and I silently groaned.

"Hayes! Savannah!" Kimber was too much on a good day, but throw in a champagne flute and the woman gave annoying a new name. "I'm glad you could make it to this very special soiree."

They were so pretentious, and it bugged the shit out of me.

"Oh, yes. I can't keep this one home. He loves to take his girl out on the town," Savannah said, flicking her thumb over her shoulder at me before pressing her ass against my groin as I wrapped my arms around her on instinct. She startled a bit, and I was guessing she felt my dick spring to life, but that's what happens when you press your perfectly round ass there.

I tightened my grip, my forearm pressed against her chest as I locked her in and chuckled against her ear. She paid me back by wiggling her ass to mess with me.

I nipped at her ear before looking up to see Kimber and Lenny gaping at us.

"I sure do like taking my woman out, but I also like getting her home." I kissed her neck, because we'd really been putting on a show lately.

Over the last week, I'd kissed her neck. Her hair. Her cheeks. Her hands.

Never her lips. That appeared to be off-limits. Though I hadn't actually tried, it was my instinct telling me it was too far.

"Kimber tells me you two are throwing some sort of

Valentine's party for the firehouse. It's not a fundraiser? Seems sort of silly to host for no purpose."

Before I could speak, Savannah was already answering. "Parties shouldn't have any purpose other than to have a good time. We just want to celebrate with our fire family and not invite the whole town over just to beg them for money."

She was messing with them, and I fucking loved it.

"Well, you'd be surprised how generous locals are when it comes to their firefighters. That's why we step up our game the way that we do, you know? The finest champagne served in real crystal flutes. My secret is that I spare no expense, and I spend a lot of time putting on these events, making sure the servers are dressed to the nines and the food is pristine. I hope you know what you're getting yourself into, Savvy."

"Well, pigs in a blanket are a personal favorite of mine, but no one has ever called them pristine," Savannah said, her voice all tease. I took a sip of my champagne to stop from laughing just as she glanced over at me. "We've got big plans for our party. Isn't that right, *Lover*?"

Lover. It was definitely a step up from Woody. Although, the way my dick was straining against the zipper of my jeans, Woody seemed more fitting at the moment.

"*Yes, baby.* I'm looking forward to it," I said, and Lenny stared at me like I had three heads.

"I've never seen you like this," the asshole said.

"Like what?" I narrowed my gaze.

"So . . . not dick-ish." Lenny took a sip of his champagne.

Savannah turned in my arms with a wicked grin on her face. "See, I told you. Love works miracles. It can even make the biggest dick softer."

I thrust forward. "I don't know about that."

Her head fell back in laughter, and Kimber grumbled about something, but we totally ignored them as they stalked away.

"That was brilliant. Hell, even I'm smitten with us. We

could win a freaking Academy Award," she whispered, her hands wrapped around my neck.

My eyes zoned in on her lips, and I wanted to lean down and claim that sweet mouth of hers.

"Hey there, lovebirds," John Cook said, and we both startled.

"Hey, Cap." I extended a hand as Savannah turned around to face him, and my arms came around her waist, my chin resting on top of her head.

"Hi, John. I haven't seen you in forever," Savannah said, leaning forward and giving him a big hug. I hadn't realized they knew one another as more than acquaintances.

"It's great to see you, sweetheart. So, you're the one putting this smile on Rambo's face, huh? He's been a little less grumpy lately."

"I try," she said with a laugh. "He makes it easy."

Wow. We were so convincing, even I was buying our bullshit.

"How is Clara?" Savannah asked.

"She's doing great. She's here, and she'll be thrilled to see you. Let me go find her, and I'll bring her over. She still talks about you all the time. I swear that winter you spent with her was one of her favorites."

I didn't remember Savannah spending a winter with Clara Cook.

"I didn't realize your captain was Clara Cook's husband," she said, after he'd walked away.

"How do you know Clara?"

"She loves to cross-country ski. Remember that little stint where I wanted to be an Olympian, and I decided cross-country skiing was my best chance to get there?"

I just stared at her. "I faintly remember your interest in cross-country skiing, but I didn't realize it was all that serious."

"That's because you had just started dating that heathen,

Kate. You were all sexed up and distracted, and I was out there chasing my Olympic dreams."

"Sophomore year? I was hardly sexed up."

"Well, it was the first time we'd dealt with a third wheel in our relationship, so we didn't spend every waking minute together."

"You were never a third wheel," I said, pushing the hair away from her face.

"Oh, I know. I was referring to Kate. She was definitely the third wheel."

A loud laugh escaped my mouth. Damn, she was funny. "Are you claiming I wasn't present, Shortcake? Because from what I remember, you started dating that boy-band-wannabe, Scotty, shortly after I met Kate, and you were suddenly busy all the time."

"First off, that's incorrect. You lost your virginity and your mind all at the same time. And all over that snake of a woman."

"For the record, I lost my virginity to Carol Parker when I was fourteen. You know that. Kate was just my first serious relationship."

"Po-tay-to, po-tah-to. I don't count Carol Parker because she was older, and that lasted all of thirty seconds," she said over her laughter.

"Shots fucking fired. I'll have you know my first time was not like most hormonal teenage boys. I went three rounds and stayed in control. I remember bragging about it to you, but you were completely uninterested."

"Yeah. I was fourteen. I didn't even know what you were talking about at the time. Anyway . . . this is all to say that Clara and I skied together for weeks, and she thought I had real talent."

Beebs came walking over, looking sheepish. "So, this is your girl, huh? You let me act like a jackass when you knew exactly who she was?"

"Eh, don't be so hard on yourself. You might be responsible for all of this starting up, because when you mentioned Sav was in town, I went straight to Whiskey Falls bar to see her." Savannah glanced over at me in surprise.

That part wasn't fake.

"So that means you snaked my girl. I had my eye on her first." He winked at her.

"You had your eye on me? You barely told me your name. We've got to teach you how to hit on a lady, Beebs," Savannah said, as her head fell back in laughter. She'd met all the guys a few days ago when she'd surprised me and brought us all cookies from Magnolia Beans to the firehouse.

She impressed the hell out of everyone.

"How did Rambo possibly land you?" the smartass said, and I just flashed him my cockiest smirk.

"I'm more appealing than you'd think," I said, as Savannah's hand moved over mine.

Cap came walking back over with Clara, and she and Savannah acted like long-lost friends. A few of the guys joined us, and we'd formed a half-circle on one side of the room.

"Since when do you attend social events?" Stinky asked, holding a small plate loaded with meatballs.

"He's trying to impress his girl." Bones tipped his head back and downed his flute of champagne.

"Hey, it happens to the best of us," Cap said. "It's good to see this guy smiling now and then."

I rolled my eyes as Stinky spoke over a mouthful of meatball. "Yeah. It's a hell of a lot better than that intimidating scowl you usually wear."

I flipped him the bird, and he waggled his brows.

It was good to see all the guys outside of the firehouse. We worked a lot, and we worked hard.

My phone vibrated, and I glanced down while Bones told some lengthy story about how he'd had to climb a tree yesterday to get Mr. Peters's cat down, and the cat scratched the shit out of his neck.

KING

Did anyone go to the fundraiser at dickhead Lenny's house?

RIVER

I'm not attending anything that involves Lenny and Kimber.

NASH

Same. Fuck that dude.

ROMEO

Demi is wiped out from the little monster she's carrying, so we're watching a movie.

Romeo's wife was pregnant and expecting their son in a few months.

I'm actually at the fundraiser now.

NASH

Well, this is unexpected. You hate that shit.

RIVER

Savannah went with him.

KING

Now it all makes sense.

ROMEO

The last man standing is going down.

KING

The bigger the asshole, the harder they fall.

Fuck off. You assholes told me to play the game. So I'm here.

NASH

With your girlfriend.

I scratched the back of my neck. It didn't feel right lying to them. I'd never lied to these guys. River knew the truth, but we'd agreed the fewer people that knew the better.

It's complicated.

RIVER

Don't overthink it. Just enjoy it, brother.

NASH

We're starting renovations out at the farmhouse tomorrow. I'm relieved to be done working on the steakhouse, which is officially opening this weekend. I have no desire to go there for a very long time.

KING

I'm much more invested in the farmhouse for Savvy. Not sure she should be staying out there while we're renovating the place.

RIVER

I noticed she went home with Hayes that night we were all at Whiskey Falls. I'm guessing that wasn't the last time she spent the night over there.

Let me know if you need me to drop off some tampons for you later. You must be menstruating.

KING

Someone sounds defensive.

ROMEO

No shame in saying you like her, brother. I always thought you two were more than friends.

Whatever. I've got to get back to the party. And now Savvy wants to throw a party for the firehouse and outdo Kimber's lame party.

NASH

Holy shit. Hayes is throwing a party?

KING

With his girlfriend.

ROMEO

I give him six months, and he's walking down the aisle.

RIVER

I don't think he'll wait that long. When you know, you know.

I tucked my phone into my back pocket and looked up to see all the guys huddled around Savannah. They were all laughing, and I just watched her.

My woman.

Fake or real—it didn't really matter at the moment.

She was here with me, and she felt like mine.

Maybe she'd always felt like mine.

12

Savannah

Renovations on the farmhouse were well underway, as was my fake relationship. It was not lost on me that out of the three relationships I'd had in my adult life, this one was by far the easiest.

Maybe it was because we knew it wasn't real and that it would have an expiration date.

I was having a great time with this. Even the big grump didn't seem to mind it. And today was the day.

He'd been at the firehouse the last three days, and we'd come up with our plan. I had six days left to tie the knot, and we figured today was as good a day as any for a fake wedding. Nash and Kingston had started the renovations at the farmhouse, and I'd be moving into the guest room at Hayes's house today.

I'd refused to move in with him until we were officially married, which we'd joked about over the last few days, because the irony was not lost on either of us.

The marriage wasn't real, so why was I holding out?

He thought I should just move in while he was at the firehouse so I could at least take a hot bath at the end of the day. But I didn't want it to look any more suspicious than it already did.

"You sure you're okay not telling your parents?" Hayes

asked as we drove to the courthouse. We'd filed for a marriage license this morning, and now we were off to make it official.

"Yes. We're eloping. People do it all the time," I said, as he parked in the lot behind the building. "Harry's going to be pissed because I told him he could be ring bearer someday."

"I'm glad you two have a relationship. I know the way everything went down was hard, but you got a brother out of it."

"Touché, hubs. That was a very glass-half-full response for you." I chuckled. "Anyway, I'll just tell him that we eloped."

He turned to look at me. "Eloping is usually two people running off to some luxury beach to tie the knot before rolling naked in the sand."

"That's one thing I've never wanted to do." I shrugged as I turned to face him, because he wasn't in any hurry to get out of the truck.

"What? Elope?"

"No. Roll naked in the sand. I feel like it's one of those things that sounds really good in theory, but imagine the shower you'd need after." I chuckled.

He sighed. "This isn't really an elopement. So I just want to make sure you're okay with everything."

"Well, it's not really a wedding either, so I'm fine."

His brows pinched together. "What will you tell your parents?"

"I'll tell my dad that we just couldn't live another day without being husband and wife. He always loved you, and it'll make him happy. Cancer has softened him in that way—you know, emotionally. He's always all up in his feels now. He'll be an easy sell."

"And your mother?"

"My mother has become much less judgy now that she married my high school theater teacher and got knocked up." I gave him a knowing look before continuing. "A torrid affair will do that to you."

"All right. So, we're doing this."

"As long as you're okay with it?" I asked, because he seemed a little off today. "Are you having second thoughts?"

"Not at all. I said I'd do it, and I have no intentions of breaking my word."

"That's very honorable, though not very romantic," I said over my laughter. "So, why are you acting weird and hesitant?"

"I'm just thinking about the elephant in the room."

"I have no idea what you're talking about," I said, as I tried to hide my smile. "The communication in our marriage is already deteriorating, and we haven't even said 'I do' yet."

"Savannah, stop fucking around. We're about to get married. This isn't a fucking joke."

I startled at his words. "You aren't even the marrying type. And you know that this is all fake. So why are you making it complicated? What's the problem?"

He ran a hand down his face. "What do you want me to do when they say I should kiss the bride?"

My chest squeezed. He'd agreed to all of this for me, and we both knew it. Hayes didn't give a shit if he got that promotion or not. That's why I was determined to impress everyone at the firehouse, because I wanted this to benefit him, too.

"Are you disgusted at the thought of having to kiss me?" I asked.

His eyes widened. "Of course not. I just didn't think our first kiss should be at a courthouse in front of a few random people."

"Well, it's a little late to court me now, don't you think?" I chuckled, but he wasn't smiling at all, so I pulled myself together.

"Come here," he said, voice hard and commanding.

I glanced around before unbuckling my seat belt and scooting closer along the bench seat of his truck. Before I could process what was happening, he reached for me and pulled me onto his lap. One leg fell on each side of his thick thighs, and his hands found my hips.

This was unexpected, but I certainly wasn't in a hurry to move away.

"What are you doing?" I cleared my throat and glanced out the window. "No one is here. No one is watching. You don't need to put on a show."

His moss-green eyes locked with mine. "I'd like to kiss my wife before I agree to spend my life with her."

I quirked a brow. "You're being dramatic. It's only three months, Lover. And I'll move out in two and a half months and say that I need space."

"It's the principle, Shortcake. I know you'll find this hard to believe, but I'm not a complete asshole. I don't want your wedding day to be awkward as fuck for you."

I nodded as my teeth sank into my bottom lip, making every attempt to remain calm. I could feel his erection growing beneath my ass, where I was settled on his lap. My heart hammered against my chest. "Wow. My man is a real romantic."

I tried to be funny, but my voice was void of all humor.

He didn't laugh. Didn't smile. His eyes zeroed in on my mouth, and the way he was looking at me had the air catching in my lungs.

His large hands found each side of my face as he pulled me forward without hesitation. His calloused fingers skimmed along my jaw as his tongue swiped out and traced a line along my bottom lip.

"I'm going to kiss my wife now." It wasn't a question, but he was giving me a moment to pull back if I didn't want it.

But I couldn't move. I didn't want to.

His mouth covered mine. Powerful and determined. My lips parted without hesitation, and his tongue slipped inside. Slowly at first, as he explored my mouth.

And his hands, they were everywhere. One tangled in my hair as he tilted my head to the side, granting him better access.

His other hand was on my neck and jaw, like he wanted to touch as much of me as he could in this moment.

His lips were plump and soft, yet firm at the same time. The man could kiss. His mouth devoured mine, his tongue tangling with mine, as he took the kiss deeper, and I moaned.

My hips were moving of their own volition, and I desperately wanted to stop grinding against him, because this was just supposed to be a pre-wedding first kiss.

A *fake pre-wedding first kiss*.

Yet this felt different.

And I hated that I couldn't get enough. I moved up and down along his thick erection, and I could feel everything even through my jeans.

He was long and thick and hard.

It had been a while for me since I'd even kissed a man, so my body was reacting in the most embarrassing way, and I didn't even care.

We'd been hanging out so much and spending all this time together, and of course, Hayes was a beautiful man. Who wouldn't react?

It was normal to feel things. But obviously, we had a history, and I knew how this story would end.

Red flags were going off in my head, but my body was on fire.

Desire and want and need—they took over.

My fingers scratched along his hair, and our breaths were the only audible sound.

I ground against him, up and down. Faster and faster.

Desperate for release.

Desperate to feel something because it had been so long.

What am I doing?

My thoughts were spinning, and I knew I needed to get myself under control, and just as my body started to tingle, I abruptly stopped moving.

I pulled my mouth from his, and his eyes locked with mine once again. His lips were so freaking plump and perfect, and it infuriated me that I wanted to kiss him again.

This. Wasn't. Real.

He was my fake husband.

A man who'd agreed to marry me so that I could inherit millions of dollars.

I would not blur the lines. I would not be made a fool for a second time.

I wiped my hand over my mouth and calmed my breathing. "Well, we got that out of the way. Now, let's go get hitched."

He didn't say a word as I slid off his lap and back onto the passenger seat. He got out of the truck and came around to my side just as I stepped out and shut the door. I tried to move past him, but his big body blocked me, my back pressing up against the passenger door.

"You okay?" he asked.

"Of course. It was fine."

"It was fine?" He frowned. "You didn't act like it was fine when you were dry humping me like it was your day job."

I gaped at the bastard. "Well, you can't control your erection around me, so what's a girl to do when you pull her onto your lap with that gigantic thing between her legs?"

He smirked. "He does seem to like you."

"It was a kiss. A one and done. I know that's your specialty. Now, let's go seal the deal, Lover."

"Such a bossy little wife," he said, taking my hand in his and leading me toward the door of the courthouse.

The next hour was fairly uneventful. One other couple got married before us. Jonathan and Loraine. It was the second time they were marrying one another. They told us their whole love story on our way out of the courthouse. We learned about their own children, their children from the marriages they'd had after they'd divorced, and their grandchildren. It took them a while to find their way back to one another, but here they were.

I loved a good happily ever after.

I could tell that Hayes couldn't wrap his head around the fact that they would get married for a second time.

"What made you come to Magnolia Falls to get married?" I asked, because they'd told us that they weren't from here.

"We used to come here in the summers when our kids were young. And then life got busy, and we stopped coming. So, when we decided to get married again, we knew this was the place we wanted to do it," Loraine said.

"How about you two? I'm guessing it's your first marriage? Have you dated long?" Jonathan asked.

I thought about how to answer the question, because we were married, after all. We should have a story.

"We were childhood best friends, and then we lost touch for a long time," I said, my fingers intertwined with my husband's.

My husband.

Our wedding was pretty uneventful, and we'd bought a cheap ring online to use for the ceremony. Our first kiss as husband and wife was nothing like the kiss in the truck before the wedding. It was a quick peck, and we were done.

"Yep. She just up and left me with no goodbye," Hayes said, catching me completely off guard.

"That's not quite how I remember it, Lover." I chuckled, but it was forced. "He was not sitting at home crying over me leaving. He had a girlfriend at the time. We were just friends back then. Nothing more."

"Oh, but you know how friendship can turn into so much more. Obviously, there were feelings there if you ended up here today," Loraine said as we all walked outside to the parking lot.

The sun was shining, and most of the snow had melted. But winter wasn't over in Magnolia Falls, and spring was still a ways away.

"I guess you're right."

"So, you just left the poor guy without telling him where you were going?" Jonathan asked, and even though his voice was laced with humor, I didn't like the way Hayes had painted this picture.

"No," I said, as we paused at their car. I tried to keep my tone light and humorous, but I was fuming on the inside. "It wasn't quite like that. My husband knows why I left and why I didn't keep in touch."

Hayes glanced down at me, and there was a question in his gaze.

Is he for real?

He was not the victim.

It reminded me of all the reasons I'd despised him over the last decade.

This was why I should never have agreed to fake marry this man.

"My wife loves to think everyone can read minds," he said. "I don't have a clue why she left."

The bastard.

"Listen, this is what I've learned the older I get," Loraine said, clearly noticing that our fingers were no longer intertwined. He'd dropped my hand after I'd dug my nails into his palm when he started playing the victim. "The past is the past. The happiest marriages are the ones that focus on the present."

"Wise words from a wise lady," Jonathan said, but Hayes and I were too busy glaring at one another. "Now you two have a wonderful night. I'm taking my bride to a lovely dinner to celebrate."

We said our goodbyes, and my husband opened the passenger door for me. I climbed in, and when he attempted to pull my seat belt out for me, because apparently, he thought I needed his help with that all the time now, I smacked his hand away.

He glared at me and slammed the door before stalking over to the driver's side.

And we drove back to his house in silence.

Happy first day as a married couple.

13

Hayes

Our wedding night was spent not speaking to one another. Savannah was obviously pissed that I'd shared that she'd left town without saying goodbye.

Fuck that.

The truth hurts sometimes.

So, if she wanted to stalk around the house like a child for the next week, she could have at it. I wasn't going to apologize for telling the truth.

We'd gone the entire week without speaking in private, all while putting on a show of being newlyweds in public.

Everyone at the firehouse was stunned that we'd gotten married so quickly. The harder sell was my friends.

They were shooting endless questions at me, as were their significant others.

And I couldn't ask my wife how to field all these questions, because she wasn't speaking to me when we were at home. She'd been staying in the guest room on the other side of the house. She made dinner every night, and she was a damn good cook, but she took her plate to her bedroom because, apparently, she couldn't stand the sight of me.

We'd been to Whiskey Falls with everyone to celebrate our wedding, but they didn't grill her the way they'd grilled me. Or maybe she just handled the questions better than I did.

She never seemed uncomfortable with any of it in public.

I'd just spent the last three days at the firehouse, and tonight we were taking Cutler to dinner at The Golden Goose. He'd been the one that I felt the worst about, because he genuinely seemed hurt that I'd gotten married without him being there. My sister Saylor hadn't been happy that she wasn't invited, but she loved Savannah so damn much that she let it go because she said all that mattered at the end of the day was that I was happy.

Cutler didn't seem to share that sentiment.

"My pops says the farmhouse is looking so good," Cutler said. "And my Sunny said that you're getting famous from the social studies."

Savannah's head tipped back in laughter. Why did I love the sound of her laugh so much? Maybe it was because I'd barely seen her over the last three days, and she hadn't uttered more than three words to me since getting here today. She did stop by the firehouse to bring everyone little gift bags filled with chocolate-covered popcorn, so she was holding up her end of the bargain, even if she barely looked at me when she'd stopped by. She'd gotten pretty good at faking it in public, and she'd given me a big hug and giggled when I'd made a joke, but she still wouldn't look at me.

And I was about done being ignored by my wife.

Fake or not—it was bullshit.

"I bet she meant to say social media," Savannah said, as she and Cutler each reached for a french fry and dipped them in their ketchup at the same time before taking a bite and laughing.

"What does that mean to be famous on the media?" he asked, as he reached for his grilled cheese.

"I started building my social media a while back when I worked at this big design firm, and people who liked my style followed me. And then when I came here, I shared that I'd be renovating this old farmhouse. The first few posts I made were of the bathroom being gutted, and they went viral. So I'm having fun with it." She smiled at Cutler and then straightened her features when she looked at me.

For fuck's sake. This is ridiculous.

"How about you stop glaring at me," I said, as the words left my mouth before I could stop them.

Cutler's eyes widened, and he looked between us. "You mad at Uncle Hayes, Savvy? He can be a big grump sometimes. But he loves you. That's why he got married to you, right?"

Her gaze softened, and she cleared her throat. "Yes. But sometimes you can be mad at people you love, too."

"I was kind of mad at Uncle Hayes for getting married without me." Cutler shrugged.

"Well, that makes two of us that were mad on our wedding day." She smirked.

How did this turn on me again?

"Were you mad that he didn't invite me, too?" Cutler asked.

"I should actually take the blame for that, Beefcake. We were just so excited to get married, and I didn't have time to tell my dad or my brother, and so I felt bad having anyone there if we weren't including everyone."

Cutler's head tipped back in a fit of laughter. "You two must really love each other because you couldn't wait for your family to come to the wedding. So I'm not mad anymore. And you shouldn't be mad at my uncle because you just got married, right?"

"I couldn't agree more. We're newlyweds, after all." I quirked a brow, knowing I was pissing her off. But I'd rather have her angry at me than ignoring me.

"Then you shouldn't have said what you said on our wedding day."

Why was she so hung up on this?

"Oh, man, what did you say to my girl, Uncle Hayes?"

"We met another couple who also got married on the same day, and they asked about our story. All I said was that she left me and didn't keep in touch, and she got mad. But sometimes the truth hurts." I shrugged, because I wasn't going to sugarcoat it just because she didn't like the story anymore.

"Are you kidding me with this right now?" Savannah gave me a death glare and then bit off the corner of her grilled cheese and tossed it back down on her plate.

"Did you leave without saying goodbye?" Cutler asked.

"Well, I tried to say goodbye. I called. I texted. And then I went over to his house to tell him I was leaving, and let's just say, that was all the goodbye necessary."

What the fuck did that even mean?

"Funny. I never got a message or a text, so maybe your memory is foggy." I took a sip of my water.

"My memory is never foggy," she said, and then she glanced at Cutler, and I could see the anger dissipate when she looked at him. "So, Loraine, that lady we met on our wedding day, gave some sound advice about marriage, and maybe I should take it."

"What did she say?" Cutler asked, because the little guy was always curious.

"She said to leave the past in the past and focus on the present and the future."

"What do you think of that, Uncle Hayes?" he asked.

"Well, I think I'd take her advice with a grain of salt. She married the same man twice, and she's five minutes into her new marriage and throwing out advice like she's an expert." I leaned back in the booth and crossed my arms over my chest. "Maybe dealing with the past is better than ignoring it."

Savannah's eyes were wild and angry as she shook her head at me. "Says the man who hasn't had a relationship in a long time."

"Isn't being married a relationship?" Cutler asked, and I barked out a laugh.

"Yes. It is. So, what else do you have to throw at me?" I smirked.

116

She rolled her eyes. "Fine, dear husband. If you claim you were so sad that I left without saying goodbye, why didn't you reach out?"

"I did. You blocked me, remember?" I said.

"Oh, man, you blocked my uncle? What does that mean?" Cutler asked.

"I didn't want to take his calls because we both needed to go our separate ways. I just don't know why he's acting like he was so hurt by it. He probably didn't give it a second thought back then." Her gaze locked with mine.

"Were you really sad?" Cutler asked. The little dude should consider being a therapist in the future, because this was the most we'd spoken in a week.

"Yes. I actually was."

"I don't believe you," Savannah whispered, eyes wet with emotion, and it made my fucking chest squeeze to see her hurting.

Even if I was pissed at her.

I still couldn't stand to see her upset.

"I'll prove it to you when we get home. I've got something to show you."

"You made my girl a special gift?" Cutler chuckled. "Man, my uncles know how to treat their girls."

Savannah was quiet for a few beats, and then she turned her attention back to the little guy beside her. "I'm looking forward to riding with you guys this weekend again."

"Oh, man." My godson turned to me and smiled. There was a little drip of ketchup on the corner of his mouth, and just as I reached for my napkin to clean him up, Savannah beat me to it. "You should see Savvy on a horse. She's so fast, and I like riding with all my girls. Poor Demi can't ride anymore because she's got the baby in her tummy. Do you think you guys will have a baby someday, too?"

The word was out of my mouth before I could stop it. "No."

"Yes. I'd like to have a big family," Savannah said at the exact same time, and we both stopped talking immediately.

I knew that Cutler was the closest I'd ever come to being a father.

I'd had too many bad examples in my life, and I knew how easy it was to fuck a kid up if you didn't step up to the plate. I'd never take that risk.

"Oh, man, Uncle Hayes. You got married, and it sounds like your wife wants to have babies."

Yeah, probably something we should have discussed, even if we knew this would be over in three months. We should at least be on the same page right now.

But that wasn't going to happen if we couldn't get past this dumbass argument.

We weren't married for real.

Sure, we'd had an epic make-out session in the car, and I knew she'd been on the brink of coming, but she'd pulled back.

Just like she was doing now.

"Well, I guess my wife and I have a lot to discuss tonight, don't we?"

Savannah sighed and changed the subject. She and Cutler agreed to share a milkshake, and I just listened as they talked and laughed for the next hour. There was a reason that she wanted to be a mother, and it was probably because she knew she'd be damn good at it.

Any kid would be lucky to have Savannah Abbott as a mother.

Or . . . at the moment, Savannah Woodson.

She'd agreed to take my name, as we thought it would make things more believable to get her driver's license changed and go through all the normal steps a newly married couple would go through.

After we took Cutler home, we made our way back to my place, and she padded down the hallway to her bedroom without saying a word.

So much for making progress.

I took a shower and slipped into my gray joggers and a tee before going into my closet and finding the box on the top shelf. I pulled out the envelope on the top of the pile in the box and thought it over.

What did I have to lose? We weren't speaking at the moment, and after we staged our fake divorce, she'd be selling the farmhouse and moving out of Magnolia Falls.

So why not at least put this shit to rest.

I made my way down the long hallway to her room and knocked on the door.

"Come in," she called from the other side.

I stood in the doorway, and my gaze traveled over every inch of her where she lay on her stomach on the bed, reading a book.

"Hey," I said.

"Hello, husband."

"Listen, Sav, I'm not a dude who wants to talk about every little thing; you know that."

"I do."

"But this shit that you're carrying—this anger toward me, I don't know what it's about." I crossed one ankle over the other as I leaned against the door frame. "That's the honest truth."

She pushed to sit up, legs hanging over the side of the bed now. "It doesn't matter. None of this is real anyway. I think it's just being back here—it's bringing up all these memories that I thought I'd tucked away."

"This marriage is the only thing that isn't real. Our history. Our friendship. That was all fucking real." I stepped forward into the room and tossed the letter onto the bed beside her. "I never got a text or a message from you the day that you left. You blocked my number on your phone, so I wrote to you after you left. The letters got returned. But I did try, Sav."

She looked up at me, honey-brown eyes with pops of amber and gold, wet with emotion. "Why? Why did you care that I left?"

I shook my head in disbelief. "How the fuck can you ask me that? You were my best friend. The guys are like brothers to me, you know that. But you and me, Sav, we were always different."

She swiped at the single tear running down her cheek. "I'm sorry for being an asshole at dinner. Beefcake deserves better." Her lips turned up in the corners, and I barked out a laugh.

"So, the apology is only for Beefcake, huh?"

She ignored the question and reached for the envelope beside her. "You hate writing. How many essays did I have to write for you in middle school and high school?"

"I still hate it. But I wrote to you. It's probably a bunch of chicken scratch, but I wanted you to know that I wrote you. That I was surprised you left without saying goodbye. That I missed you." I cleared my throat. I didn't like talking about this kind of shit. But everything had always been different with Savannah.

"I didn't leave without saying goodbye, Hayes. You just weren't home when I came over." She shrugged. "But I called. And I texted."

"I never got the messages, Sav. And then you just blocked me? That was fucked up."

She pushed to her feet and stormed toward me. "That was not fucked up. You are the one who fucked up. You are the reason I blocked you. You are the reason I didn't stay in touch."

"Fine. Just read the fucking letter. We can't pretend to be married with you hating me. We're supposed to be newlyweds."

"I can be a damn good actress when I need to be." She walked back to the bed and tore open the envelope.

"Yeah. Apparently, you've always been a good actress. You can turn it on and off whenever the fuck you want to."

"Takes one to know one," she said.

And when she pulled the letter out of the envelope, I turned for the door.

Drudging up the past wasn't something I wanted to do.

But it was the only way we could move forward.

14

Savannah

He left the room, and I was grateful that he was gone. I glanced at the envelope again and recognized the address.

My mother's address in the city.

It was the apartment she'd moved into with her lover.

My teacher.

Why would she have returned the letters to Hayes?

Probably because it was months before I'd agreed to see her after we'd moved. We'd had a horrible fight that day my father and I had packed up the car and left. I'd told her that she'd ruined everything. She'd broken my father's heart. She'd made me the laughing stock at my high school. Everyone in town knew what they'd done.

So, we hadn't been on the best of terms back then.

Not that things were perfect today, but we were better.

Civil.

Sometimes friendly.

I unfolded the notebook paper, and even his handwriting was strangely comforting to me.

Familiar.

Hayes Woodson had always felt like my home.

Until my home was shattered, and he'd turned on me like everyone else. I swiped at the tear rolling down my cheek and sucked in a deep breath.

Sav,

I don't know what the fuck is happening. I know you're going through a lot right now, but I can't believe you moved without talking to me. So fucking much has happened, and I don't know how to reach you, and I'm losing my shit. Barry and my mom had a fight. Saylor got hurt. It was bad. She went to the hospital, and I lost my shit on him. They held me for a few hours down at the police station.

Where the fuck are you, Sav? I've called and texted, and it looks like you blocked me. Your mom said you and your dad moved to the city? How the hell is that possible? I don't know what's going on, but I'm here. I'm staying with Nash and his dad. Saylor is with King. Jesus Christ, everything has gone to shit. Romeo and River got sent to juvie. I need to fill you in. Everything is a mess. I know you're upset about your mom's affair. It's been a rough couple of weeks for you, and I'm so sorry if I wasn't there for you when you needed me. I don't know why you and your dad took off. How could you move without telling me? I would walk through fucking fire for you. You know that. Please call me.

P & C, Hayes

I looked down at my wrist as the tears fell onto the paper. I ran my thumb over the tiny orange carrot tattoo on the inside of my wrist.

Peas and carrots.

That's what we once were.

I tossed the paper beside me on the bed and fell back. I squeezed my eyes closed and tried to remember that last day.

The day that everything changed.

* * *

"I'm sorry. I never meant to hurt you," my mother said when I came through the door, before anyone realized that I was there.

I'd gone down to my favorite place on the water after school to hide out until well after dark. I'd needed to quiet my thoughts. Mr. Jones was the most popular teacher at our school, and his wife, Mrs. Jones, was also very well-liked.

But I was now wearing a scarlet letter. One that belonged to my mother.

Her affair with Mr. Jones was all anyone could talk about, and the last two weeks since the news broke had been unbearable.

A living hell.

Someone had spray painted the word 'whore' on my locker. There were sticky notes that said things like: *Like mother, like daughter.*

I was somehow a home-wrecker now.

Mrs. Jones was my math teacher, so spending ninety minutes in class with her three days a week was a real joy.

She despised me. Everyone despised me.

Well, aside from my father, Hayes, Abe, and Lily.

At least that's how it felt.

And coming home to yet another fight was just icing on the cake at this point.

"You never meant to hurt me? That's your defense?" My father's voice was even and calm, but I heard the pain. I moved to the hallway so they wouldn't know I was there.

Had I ever wanted to disappear this badly before?

I hadn't eaten much in days, and nothing about my life was normal anymore.

"Billy, you know I can't handle things the way that you do. Keeping your cancer a secret, it's too much for me."

Keeping your cancer a secret? What the hell was she talking about?

"So, you went off and fucked your daughter's married teacher? That's how you cope with things, Delila? When I'm at my lowest, you turn your back on me?"

"I didn't expect to fall in love," she said over her sobs.

Oh. My. God. She was in love now? This was a never-ending nightmare.

"Well, who knew? Your husband finds out he has cancer, and when he needs you most, what do you do? You fuck another man and then you fall in love with him? That's about as low as it gets. I'm not going to lie. You've destroyed our family. Look what you've done to our daughter," he hissed, and I'd never heard my father sound so angry before. "Hayes got sent home from school two days ago, because he got in yet another fight trying to defend her from the hell she's taking at school."

I swiped at the tear running down my cheek. Hayes had punched Kory Langers in the face for making some vulgar comment about me spreading my legs just like my mother does. So he'd knocked him out and had been sent home from school. His football coach was not happy with him, and I felt like everything was crumbling around me.

My mother sobbed, and I leaned against the wall in the hallway and squeezed my eyes closed. My father had cancer? My mother was in love with another man?

"I'm sorry," she said over her cries.

"You're sorry? I wanted to tell Savvy about the cancer months ago, and you convinced me not to. You said you'd stand by me, and we'd get through it together. I begged you to move to the city so I could start more aggressive treatment. And you insisted we stay here. Was that all so you could be with your lover?" he shouted, and my eyes sprung open at the sound of the anger in his voice.

"I didn't want to uproot Savvy's life!" She'd stopped sobbing now, and her voice was crystal clear. My mom had always had a gift for theatrics.

"Really? Well, how's that going, Delila? She's being tortured at school. She has to sit in a classroom with your lover's wife and bear all the anger from irrational teenagers who don't have a fucking clue that she's an innocent victim."

"You know what, Billy? You and Savannah are not the only two people going through it. I've also been judged by everyone in this town," Mom said.

"Do you hear yourself? You are the one who did the crime. You are supposed to have consequences. Our daughter is not. I am not," he hissed.

"Billy," she sobbed. "I have said that I'm sorry every day for the last two weeks. What do you want from me?"

"What do I want? I don't know, Delila. Maybe a wife who's faithful. A wife who doesn't make me and our daughter the laughing stock of the town we live in. A wife who makes my survival and recovery her priority. A wife who will fight for our family!" he shouted.

"I can't fight for our family, Billy!"

"Of course you can't. You've never made me or Savvy a priority," my father said, and I used my hand to cover my mouth to muffle the sob that threatened to escape.

"I would if I could," she cried.

"You would if you could? That's such bullshit. You really think he's going to leave his wife for you? You're going to risk it all for a fling?" My father's voice cracked on the last word.

"He's leaving her." Her voice was eerily calm now. "I'm pregnant with his child."

Pregnant.

My legs went weak, and I slid down the wall, falling until my ass hit the floor.

This nightmare would never end.

The sound of glass shattering against a wall startled me, but I just stayed where I was. I couldn't move.

I couldn't think.

My father shouted for my mother to get out and said he'd be gone in the morning.

I tried to tune them out until I heard the front door slamming shut.

"Savvy, I'm sorry you had to hear that." My father's voice pulled me from my daze as he stood at the end of the hallway, looking at me. "We shouldn't be putting this affair on you. And you should have been told about the pregnancy privately. I'm sorry."

"Dad," I said, as a sob tore through me, and I pushed to my feet. "I don't care about any of that. You have cancer?"

He wrapped his arms around me and held me close. "I do. It's progressing, and I need to get my health under control."

"I heard you say that you'd be gone in the morning. Where are you going?"

"I wanted to talk to you about that, and I wish it could have happened differently. But I found an apartment in the city. I was hoping it would be the three of us getting a fresh start there, but after tonight, that's not going to happen, Savvy. I can't be here and fight this disease and deal with the fallout from the affair. I want the best for you, and I just don't think it's here anymore."

I pulled back and nodded. "I want to go with you. I want you to be okay."

I didn't know what would happen to my mother, but I knew I needed to leave with my father.

"Me, too. So, pack your things, and we'll leave in the morning. I'll hire movers to come get the rest of our things next week. I can't be here anymore." His eyes were so tired, but he didn't look sick.

How could I have not known? Not noticed? I'd been so caught up in my own drama, and now, none of it mattered.

"Okay. I'll pack my things and be ready to go in the morning."

He kissed the top of my head, and I went to my room and started packing. I checked my phone, and there were a slew of texts from Hayes, asking where the hell I was. I'd been MIA for hours, and we never went long without speaking.

I called him immediately, and it went straight to voicemail.

"It's me." I could barely speak over my sobs. "I need to see you. I'm leaving in the morning. My dad has cancer. My mom is in love with Mr. Jones, and they're having a baby. My life is a shit show, Woody. I need you."

I ended the call and finished packing.

I curled up on my bed, still in my clothes, and let sleep take me.

"You're actually moving?" My mother's voice woke me from a sound sleep, and I jumped up, looking down to see that I was still in yesterday's clothing. When did she come home? It sounded like she was in the kitchen, and I peeked out of my bedroom to look down the hallway.

"Savvy wants to come with me. She doesn't want to be here anymore either. It's too much. I'm asking you to let us go and not make this about you, Delila."

I didn't wait to hear her reply before hurrying to clean myself up.

My mother met me in my bathroom as I washed my face.

"I know I've made a mess of things, and I'm sorry. I'm going to make this right, Savannah. I'll talk to Ben. He can find a job in the city, too. We'll all get a fresh start there, okay?" she asked.

I couldn't look at her. Couldn't speak to her. The affair had been brutal, and now she was having a baby with another man. But none of that mattered to me at the moment.

My father was sick, and she'd put him through hell. Some things were just not forgivable.

She followed me out as I wheeled my suitcase to the front entryway. My father was standing nearby, tossing a few things into a grocery bag.

"I need to run next door and tell Hayes that I'm leaving."

He nodded, and my mother tried to move in front of me, but I sidestepped her.

"When I was leaving late last night, there was a squad car over there. They didn't have their siren on, but something must have happened with Barry again."

Hayes's stepdad was the worst.

"And you didn't think to tell me? What is wrong with you, Mom?" I whipped the door open and stormed outside.

"I have my own stuff going on, too, if you haven't noticed!" she shouted, before I slammed the front door behind me.

I jogged next door and hurried up the steps, just as their front door opened, and Kate stepped outside with a backpack on her shoulder. She and Hayes were dating, and I couldn't stand her. She'd made my life a living hell these past few weeks.

"Oh, wow. You look terrible," she said, and the corners of her lips turned up.

"Thanks for that. Where's Hayes?"

"He's not here. Some shit went down last night, and he's dealing with that."

"What happened?" I asked.

"Not my story to tell. And you have plenty going on in your own life, don't you, Bad Abbott?"

Bad. Fucking. Abbott.

It was the best her pea-sized brain could come up with.

"You do know that your little nickname makes no sense."

"Oh, you're clearly slow to the game. It's a play on words.

Bad Apple. Bad Abbott," she said as she pulled the door closed and stood in front of me.

"I didn't say that I didn't understand it. I said it makes no sense. It's stupid. And you're just a sad, mean girl who has nothing better to do than kick someone when they're down. I was hoping it would blow over with you, but I think it's time that I tell my best friend how horrible you've been to me." I crossed my arms over my chest and glared at her. Why the hell had I kept my mouth closed about it, anyway? I just knew if I said something, he would freak out, and she would most likely take it out on me even more. I wanted it all to stop.

It was too much right now.

I turned around to leave, and she grabbed my arm.

"Don't threaten me. You're no different than your mother. The Abbott never falls far from the tree," she said with a chuckle. She was really running with this whole apple analogy.

I shook her hand off my arm and glared at her. "It's not a threat. It's a promise."

"Do you know that Hayes and I sit around laughing about you?"

"No one believes you, Kate. You can go home now. I'm leaving," I hissed.

"Who do you think he called when he needed someone this morning? Not you. He called me. We're together, and you can't stand that, can you?"

I pinched the bridge of my nose. "I don't care. I don't have time for this."

"He's mortified that everyone thinks you two are best friends, especially after what your mother did. He doesn't know how to get rid of you. His coach is pissed that he got sent home from school for defending you. He's over it, Savannah. He's moved on, and you just keep on clinging to him. It's desperate and sad." She smirked as she looked down at her phone.

"You're pathetic and weak," I said, raising a brow. "You're

threatened by my friendship with him. You've been trying to come between us since the day you started dating him. What are you so afraid of?"

A maniacal laugh left her mouth, and she started reading something on her phone. "Sometimes I feel like my life would be easier without her in it. But I don't know how to walk away." She paused and turned the phone so we could both see the screen before she continued reading. "I know it's hard, Hayes, but sometimes you outgrow people."

"You're evil," I said, feeling my breath hitch in my throat.

She shoved the phone toward me. "Read it. Read what your best friend thinks of you."

HAYES

> I feel like a dick saying this, but I'm disappointed in the person she's become. I feel like all I do is take care of her. I just don't want to do it anymore.

> And you shouldn't. Sometimes you have to walk away from people. It doesn't mean that you don't care about them. It just means that you're putting yourself first.

I backed up. I didn't want to see any more. I shook my head and tried hard to hold in the tears until I got home. I would not cry in front of this evil girl.

And she'd always been so good at putting on a show. She'd act sugary sweet in front of people, but I'd seen her true colors many times.

And she'd clearly poisoned Hayes against me. What else could it be?

130

His words stung. He was the one person that always had my back. But clearly, that had changed.

"He's been trying to put distance there between you guys for quite a while. We sit around laughing at how needy you are." And then she changed her voice, in her best attempt at mimicking me in the worst way. "And now your dad has cancer, and your mom is knocked up by Mr. Jones. It's mortifying. He doesn't want to deal with your whiney shit anymore. Go find yourself your own boyfriend and grow the hell up."

I could feel the blood draining from my face.

He'd told her about my dad?

About my mom?

A heavy weight sat on my chest, and it was difficult to take a breath.

He'd laughed at me. He'd told his bitchy girlfriend my deepest secrets.

He wanted distance.

No problem. That's exactly what he would get.

15

Hayes

I was exhausted from my shift at the firehouse, and I'd climbed into bed after waiting out in the family room to see if Savannah would want to talk after I gave her the letter. I hadn't heard anything from her, so I'd decided to go to bed. It was going to be a long couple of months living with someone who wouldn't speak to me. We'd been fine up until our wedding day when I'd brought up her leaving.

I was the one who should be pissed, not her.

But I'd given her the letter in hopes she'd understand that I'd been hurt that she'd left.

And I didn't let people hurt me often.

But Savannah had always had the power to hurt me, because she'd implanted herself in the center of my fucking heart from as early as I could remember.

"Woody?" Her voice was a whisper from my doorway, and I sat up. The room was completely dark, aside from the little bit of light from the moon peeking in through the blinds.

"Hey. Are you okay?"

"Yeah. I just wanted to ask you something."

"Okay." I rubbed my eyes and glanced at my phone on the nightstand to see that it was nearly two o'clock in the morning.

I could see her silhouette moving toward the bed, and she came to sit on the side next to me. "I read your letter."

A groggy chuckle escaped my lips. "It wasn't a long letter. It shouldn't have taken that long."

"I was processing."

"There's not a lot to process, Sav. You left. I missed you. I wrote you a few letters."

"There are more letters?"

I cleared my throat, deciding how real I wanted to be. But we'd gone so long without seeing one another, so I decided to lay it on the line. "There are fifty-two letters."

"Hayes."

"Savannah," I said, mimicking her serious tone.

"Don't mess with me."

"I'm not messing with you. I wrote you once a week for a year. I guess I kept hoping that at some point you wouldn't return one, and you'd actually read it," I admitted.

"I don't understand. Why would you try so hard to reach me when you were dying to get rid of me?"

"Why would you think I was dying to get rid of you?"

"I called you that night. The night before I moved," she whispered. "I told you about my dad."

I pushed back so I was leaning against the headboard and placed my finger and thumb beneath her chin, turning her to face me. "I never got a call from you. I heard about you moving from your mother when I went over to your house the next day. She told me you'd moved and acted like I was the enemy and slammed the door in my face."

"That's because I told her that you wanted nothing to do with me because she'd made a mess of everything."

"What the fuck are you talking about, Sav? None of this is

making sense. Why would it affect my friendship with you if your mother had an affair? I didn't give a shit then, and I don't give a shit now. That has nothing to do with you. And do you honestly think I wouldn't have come immediately if you told me that your father had cancer?" I was pissed now. None of this made any fucking sense.

She started shaking her head, tears streaming down her face. "I saw the texts. I saw what you wrote about me."

"I thought you said I didn't respond to you?" I was starting to lose my patience with this.

"Kate," she said, her voice sounding almost frantic now. "I went to your house that morning before I left. You hadn't responded to my messages about my dad being sick, about my mom being pregnant—about me moving."

"You saw Kate the day that you left?" My thumb stroked along her jaw.

"Yes. She was at your house, and she came out the door just as I was about to knock. She told me that something had happened with you, but that you called her and not me because you no longer wanted to deal with me."

My chest was pounding because this was irrational behavior, even for Kate.

"I didn't call her. She'd called Nash to find out where I was because she couldn't reach me. He told her some shit had gone down, and I didn't have my phone. Apparently, she went to get it from my house because she showed up at the hospital where we were all waiting for Saylor to get released, and she brought it to me."

Savannah shook her head. "So you never told her about my dad having cancer or my mom being pregnant?"

"Of course not. I didn't know about them either. I found out about your mom later through the grapevine, and I didn't know about your dad until now. Why would you believe that I'd do that?"

"I don't know." She threw her hands in the air. "You'd been a little distant since you'd started dating that heathen."

"Sav, I wasn't distant because of Kate. Hell, we weren't even all that serious back then. Barry was drinking a ton during those days leading up to everything that happened, and I didn't want to tell you about it because you were dealing with all that shit with your mom. So, I tried to handle it. And then everything went down with River and Romeo right then, too, and it was a lot."

"I know. So I thought you just didn't want to deal with me." She squeezed her eyes closed. "Kate said you two would laugh about me. About the problems going on with my family. I was already dealing with all the name-calling at school, and I think I just felt really alone."

"But you know me. You fucking *know* me." I shook my head in disbelief.

"She showed me the text messages, Hayes. Your name was at the top. She couldn't have made that up."

"Made what up? I never texted anything bad about you. What did the messages say?" I asked, rubbing a hand down my face.

She was standing now, pacing in little circles as she tried to recall everything from all those years ago.

"They said that you wondered if your life would be easier without me in it. That you were disappointed in the person I'd become, and you didn't know how to walk away from me. And then she told me that you knew about my dad's cancer and my mom being pregnant."

"I would never have written that. You saw your name on those messages?" I asked, not hiding my frustration. I was wracking my brain.

"Well, I don't think there was a name on them, but she said they were about me."

I stopped to think back to that time. "Fuck me."

135

"What?"

"I was going through a hard time with my mom back then. Barry was getting drunk every day, and I'd told you that he'd gotten violent a few times, breaking things at the house and shouting at everyone like the asshole lunatic that he was. I wanted to get Saylor out of there. You knew all of that, Sav. Those messages weren't about you. I'm guessing they were about my mother. Kate had been over when a fight broke out between my mom and Barry, and I'd been angry. So I probably texted her and vented about my mom. You know I struggled with my relationship with her because of what she was exposing Saylor to. My disappointment wasn't a secret."

"Oh, my God," she whispered as the tears started rolling down her cheeks. "I freaking fell for it. She knew exactly how to play me. And I was in such a bad place, and she knew it."

"She's the fucking devil." I scrubbed a hand down my face. "So, we lost over ten years for nothing?"

"It's sad that she could make me doubt myself—doubt you that easily." She shook her head and swiped at her cheeks.

"Hey, you were in a really bad place at the time. We both were. Hell, I've questioned myself numerous times that I almost married the woman," I admitted.

Because what the fuck did that say about me?

"I think it all has a lot to do with what was going on in your life at the time, you know?" She reached for my hand, intertwining her fingers with mine. "You were dealing with a lot. Your dad had left and completely abandoned you and Saylor. Your mom remarried a total douchebag. You were doing everything you could to protect your sister. So, I don't know, maybe you didn't feel deserving of more than what Kate had to offer, because you were sort of drowning in all that negativity. And she pursued you hard. She wanted to date you, and she made it happen."

"I was just a dumbass who didn't know better. She was all

over me, and I probably liked the attention. I'm different now. I won't make that mistake again."

"I get that. But completely closing yourself off isn't good either, Woody." Her gaze softened, and she wrapped her arms around me and rested her cheek on my chest, hugging me tight. "I'm sorry for believing the worst in you. I knew you. I knew better. I'm sorry."

"Hey," I said, tipping her chin up so she was looking at me. "You aren't the one who did this. I'm the asshole who brought the devil into our lives."

"I always hated Kate," she said, her teeth sinking into her bottom lip, eyes remorseful, like she'd been feeling bad about it. "For the longest time, I worried I was jealous, you know, just that someone had come in and taken my best friend from me. It's not rational, but it happens, right? And people loved her—hell, she was the most popular girl in our class, even though she was a complete bitch to a lot of people behind closed doors."

"Kate is a master manipulator. It took me a long time to see it. She knows how to get what she wants. She knows how to work people, work the system, and that can be dangerous." I shook my head. "She never told me you came by the house that morning. She obviously listened to the message from you and deleted your voicemail and texts. She knew I was freaking out that I couldn't find you. Nash and King even went out to talk to Abe that next day to figure out where you were. And she just sat there with me that whole day, not saying a word. Watching me call you and text you over and over. She's the one who guessed that you must have blocked me after you hadn't responded to all the messages."

"Don't beat yourself up. Most people don't see her for who she is."

"You did."

"Yeah, I like to think I'm a pretty good judge of character.

That's why I took it so hard when I thought you weren't who I thought you were. Who I knew you were." Her voice started to quake. "And my mom had completely stunned me by falling in love with another man and starting a new life without me and Dad. So, I doubted myself about everything and everyone."

"It's going to sound crazy, so take this for what it is," I said, using the pad of my thumb to swipe away her tears.

"Tell me."

"Losing you was tougher on me than finding Kate in bed with Lenny. She was my fiancée, so that was a bit alarming. After you left, I think I really changed a lot, in a way I can't explain."

"Try," she whispered. "Because I changed, too, and it helps to know that I wasn't alone."

"Well, I wasn't a stranger to people leaving, people letting me down. My father taking off and starting a new family taught me at a young age that I couldn't trust people. My mother allowing a lot of bad shit to happen in our home meant that I could never trust her. My ride-or-die crew are my brothers, and I know they have my back. It's a brotherhood that took me a long time to fully invest in and trust, and I do. I would walk through fire for any one of them. And Saylor, man, she's just good to her core, and all I ever wanted to do was protect her from the shit going on around us. I would give my life for hers, and she knows it." I paused and looked away for a few beats before looking back at Savannah. "But you, Shortcake, you were always different. You were a part of me in a way that I can't even explain. I would do anything for you, but I also trusted that you would do anything for me. It went both ways. I leaned on you, I told you everything, shared my hopes and my fears, which I don't usually do. So losing you—it hardened me in a lot of ways."

"I get that. It was the same for me. I just put all my energy and focus into my father. Into the things that I could control. I tried hard to block out how much it hurt. You were my person, and I was really lost without you for a long time, Hayes. I grieved the loss of our friendship in the most painful way," she said, over a sob.

I wrapped her up in my arms and kissed the top of her head.

"This is the thing about you and me, Sav. We may have spent those years apart, but we never lost this connection. It's too strong. That's why when the fake marriage idea came up, I didn't hesitate. Because it's you. I have no fucking desire to ever be married. I don't want that life. I don't want to care about anyone that way. I'm not looking for a fairy tale. But if there's something that I could ever do for you—I wouldn't think twice. P and C, right?"

She traced her thumb over the little green pea inked on my wrist before pressing her wrist against mine, our tattoos meeting as our skin touched. It's something we used to do all the time. "Peas and carrots forever."

"And there is no one on the planet I would ever agree to that ridiculous saying for, or to getting this lame-ass green pea tattoo with, other than you." I barked out a laugh. We'd gotten the tattoos on her fifteenth birthday at some back-alley tattoo shop that didn't question our age, because Savannah thought a tattoo would make her look like a badass. But a tiny carrot on her wrist only got her grounded by her parents, and no one else seemed to notice.

But we always knew they were there.

A constant reminder of what we had in one another.

She chuckled. "I still think they are the coolest tattoos."

"Well, clearly, I'd do anything for you, but there is nothing cool about these tattoos, Shortcake."

Her lips turned up in the corners. "I'm glad we talked."

"Yeah, me, too."

"These are probably the most words you've ever used at one time." Her voice was all tease.

I moved quickly, flipping her onto her back and tickling her. "You like giving me shit, don't you?"

"It's my wifely duty." She laughed, and I held her gaze for a few beats. Damn, she had the most kissable lips I'd ever seen. Her tongue swiped out slowly along her bottom lip, and my dick sprung to life because he had a mind of his own. She quickly pushed me back and scrambled to her feet, readjusting her tank top back in place.

"Don't get weird. I can't control it, and you are my wife, right?" I laughed as I moved to sit back against the headboard.

"I finally don't hate you. Let's not complicate things." She raised a brow and smiled at me.

"We're newlyweds who sleep in separate rooms. I'd say things are already complicated."

"Goodnight, husband." She walked toward the door.

"Sweet dreams, wife."

And I didn't know why, but I felt the loss of her the minute she stepped out of the room.

16

Savannah

I'd spent the morning out at the farmhouse, overseeing the renovations and filming online content. My social media was blowing up, and I'd even gotten messages from a few interior design firms asking if I was interested in coming to work for them.

I'd spent hours at the tile store last week, choosing just the right tiles for the kitchen and bathrooms. I wanted to keep the character of the older home, but modernize it at the same time.

I called this aesthetic coastal-farmhouse-chic, and my hashtag had even gone viral.

Abe would have gotten a kick out of the fact that I was making a name for myself while renovating his and Lily's house.

Everything would be light and airy, as opposed to all the dark woods and finishes that they'd had. I was maximizing every single penny, as I only had a deposit to give to King and Nash, but they didn't seem concerned at all. But they also didn't know that my inheritance was dependent upon my marriage, which they didn't know was fake.

In their eyes, I was Hayes's wife, and they'd do anything for me.

So, I'd saved all the cabinets that we'd torn out during demolition, and I'd listed them online, along with the old appliances and some of the furnishings. They weren't selling for a lot of money, but a couple hundred bucks here and there would help.

King and Nash had brought a crew out to sand down the original floors throughout the home and stain them in a lighter color. Salvaging the floors had saved us a ton of money, and the lighter stain brightened the whole place up.

I'd told them that I had to get home, and they'd both teased me about the fact that I was getting Hayes to throw a party tonight for the guys at the firehouse.

Saylor, Demi, Ruby, Emerson, and Peyton had offered to come over and help me decorate the house. It was Saturday, so it was really generous that they were willing to help me on their day off.

When I arrived at the house, Hayes was in the kitchen wearing nothing but a pair of gray joggers. His back was to me, and I took in the Ride or Die tattoo inked across his chiseled muscles. My eyes trailed down his wide-set shoulders to his narrow waist. The man was thick and strong, and my mouth watered at the sight of him.

"You going to speak or just stand there staring, Shortcake?" His voice was gruff and sleepy, which didn't surprise me, seeing as he'd just gotten home from the firehouse.

"How was your shift?"

He turned around, crossing his legs at the ankles, and his chest was on full display.

"Long. We had a few medical calls, and then we had to go out to the Kramer house because Sally put banana bread in the oven to warm up and surprise her mom, but she forgot about it. She also forgot to take off the wrapping, and the paper caught on fire and set off all the smoke detectors. They were able to get the fire out, but it did some damage to the kitchen."

The Kramers were the sweetest family, and their ten-year-old daughter, Sally, was hilarious. I'd run into them a few times at Magnolia Beans, and that little girl was definitely going to take over the world someday with her drive and determination.

"I'm glad everything was okay."

"Yeah, me, too. How was your night?" he asked, even though we'd texted several times before I'd gone to sleep.

"Good. Uneventful. I just met King and Nash out at the house, and things are really progressing," I said, moving to the counter to pour myself a cup of coffee. "Is it going to make it hard to sleep if the girls are here to help me start setting up for the party? I know you need to sleep."

"Nah. Not at all. I can sleep through anything. The guys are all excited to come over tonight. Apparently, most of them have never been invited over. I've never been much of a party thrower."

"You don't say?" I chuckled.

"It's definitely not my thing."

"That's what your wife is for." I waggled my brows.

His tongue swiped out and moved along his bottom lip, as his eyes slowly raked over me from my head down to my toes. I squeezed my thighs together in response.

Why does my fake husband have to be so sexy?

"You're really going all out for this, huh?" he asked, as his gaze moved to the pile of bags and boxes filled with décor that I'd ordered for tonight. "Kimber's going to shit herself if your party is better than hers."

"It isn't hard to compete with Kimber. Her party was horribly boring. We've got karaoke, two food trucks, dancing, and the best part of all…" I said, moving to stand in front of him, because when Hayes was around, I wanted to be close to him. Touching him. Breathing him in. "It's just the firefighters and their significant others. We aren't inviting people and asking for money. It's a party. It should be fun."

"You never do anything half-assed, do you?" he asked, as the corners of his lips turned up.

"If fun were an Olympic sport, I'd for sure get the gold medal."

He didn't laugh; he just stared at me. It was this look of adoration that had my chest squeezing. "Thanks for doing this, Sav. It means a lot. I've never been good at playing the game."

"Are you kidding? I live for this stuff. But I'm not happy about you paying for it." We'd had an argument when he'd seen all the things I'd ordered. He'd demanded receipts and reimbursed me for everything.

"I've never thrown a party. The least I could do is pay for it. I just don't want to plan it. And maybe I'm an old-fashioned husband, but I don't want my woman paying for anything." He tapped me on the nose playfully, but I knew Hayes well enough to know he was chivalrous that way.

Hell, that's why Kate sank her claws into him. Hayes Woodson was the whole package—he was the only one who didn't know it.

"If you want this to be believable, don't act like a caveman. I'm a modern woman."

His hand moved to my hip, and he leaned forward and kissed the top of my head. "My wife is a stubborn woman. I'm going to catch some sleep. I'll see you in a few hours. You hid everything in your bedroom for tonight, right? We don't want anyone getting suspicious and finding out that we're sleeping in separate bedrooms."

"Yep. It's all shoved in my closet. There are no signs of life in the guest room." I chuckled as he made his way down the hall.

And I watched him move toward his bedroom.

His walk was so manly, the way his strong arms moved beside him. His legs were thick and long as they strode away.

The knock on the door pulled me from my Hayes daze, and I hurried to the entryway. When I pulled the door open, Peyton was holding two bottles of champagne in her hands, and Ruby, Emerson, a very pregnant Demi, and Saylor were standing behind her.

"Party's here!" she shouted as she stepped past me.

"Well, we've also got muffins," Demi said as she shook the pastry box in her hand and waddled through the door in the most adorable way. Her body looked exactly the same, aside from a ginormous protruding belly. From the back, you'd never know she was preggers, but then she'd turn around, and it was impossible to miss.

"I've got the flowers to make the arrangements," Ruby said, because she'd volunteered to pick up the flowers from Janelle at Magnolia Blooms, but we'd decided to put them together ourselves.

"I brought unicorn Krispies because Cutler insisted that you try them," Emerson said.

Saylor came in last and kissed my cheek. "And I have the orange juice. Let's get this place decorated."

We spent the next three hours covering every inch of the family room, living room, and kitchen in red and white Valentine décor. We made floral arrangements and set them all around the house. Everything looked perfect. Even better than I'd expected.

"Damn, it looks like Cupid puked in here," Ruby said over her laughter. "You've even got red and white pillows on the couches. Hayes is going to be stunned when he wakes up. You didn't miss a thing."

"Have you seen her Instagram? This is why people follow her. The girl can decorate and design a house like nobody's business," Peyton said.

"I had no idea what a big following you had until Demi showed me this week," Saylor said. "It's amazing. My brother is going to love it. I'm glad you guys were able to put that mess from the past behind you after all these years."

"I still can't get over everything with Kate." Demi shook her head in disbelief.

I'd filled them in on what we'd uncovered and why we hadn't spoken in all those years. They were all stunned to learn just how devious the woman was, especially considering she was just a teenager back then. But Kate had always been spoiled and self-entitled, and she was probably still evil to the people who had to deal with her today.

"You know, that's why people get so mad at a miscommunication trope." Saylor tipped her head back as she drank the last bit of her mimosa.

"What the hell is a miscommunication trope?" Ruby grumped. "I swear you make this shit up."

Saylor owned a romance bookstore, and it had become one of my favorite places to visit since I'd returned home.

"Um . . . that's a hard no. It's real. Both in fiction and, apparently, in real life. People can really fuck things up if they want to," Peyton said.

"Don't worry," Saylor said. "The miscommunication trope is just a small part of your story with Hayes. Your journey to making it down the aisle together. You've got so many good tropes going for you. Best friends to lovers and second-chance romance."

"Don't forget the shotgun wedding. That's got to be a trope." Peyton refilled her glass with bubbly.

"Excuse me. A shotgun wedding implies that I'm pregnant, and that is definitely not the case." I quirked a brow.

"Correct. We all know that my brother does not want kids," Saylor said, as if she were discussing the weather.

"Oh, I forgot about that. You don't want kids either?" Demi asked, completely lacking any judgment at all, as if she were just curious.

"You know, we haven't really discussed that. We were just so excited to get married, and we're working all of these things out now." I shrugged.

They all shared a look, but then they smiled and nodded. But Ruby was watching me with a knowing look.

One that told me she wasn't completely sold on our insta-love story and the rush to get married.

She'd been the only one outside of River who knew about the stipulation in the inheritance contract.

We'd have to step up our game and get our story straight.

We were already too far into this to change things.

There was no turning back now.

17

Hayes

"Hayes, are you up?" Sav's voice was sexy as hell, and I looked up to see her crawl onto the bed.

"Hey, what are you doing in here?"

"Can't a girl come see her husband?" she asked, as her hand stroked my dick right over the joggers I was wearing.

"Of course, she can."

"I was just missing you and wanted to see if you were up. And clearly, part of you is," she said, her teeth sinking into that pouty bottom lip.

She continued stroking me, and I groaned.

I wanted more.

I wanted her.

"What are you doing, baby?" My voice was gruff.

"What? We're married, right? I wanted to come in here and wake my husband up properly. Do you have a problem with that?"

"Never. What did you have in mind?"

Before the words were out, she was reaching for the waistband of my sweats and tugging them down. I wasn't wearing boxers, and she smiled up at me as my dick stood straight up, pointing at her like he'd been looking for her his entire life.

"I've been dying to taste you, Hayes," she whispered.

"You won't get an argument here," I said, as her hand wrapped around my cock and stroked up and down a few times. "I've been dying to taste you, too. It's all I fucking think about," I said, my voice barely recognizable.

"Tell me more," she whispered, before she leaned down and flicked the tip of my dick with her tongue and then circled the head.

"I think about how badly I want to bury my head between your thighs. How sweet you'll taste. I think about licking you and tasting you until you come on my lips. How desperate I am to see you go over the edge just one fucking time, Sav. To taste every fucking inch of you."

"Well, you're going to have to wait your turn, because I asked first, and we know how chivalrous my husband is." Her heated gaze found mine, and then she dipped down, wrapping her sweet mouth around my dick.

She bobbed up and down, somehow taking me all the way in without gagging. Nothing had ever felt so good.

"Such a good girl, Sav. Just like that." My fingers tangled in her hair as I bucked up into her mouth.

Warm and sweet and perfect.

"Hayes, are you decent?" Her voice was further away now.

There was a knock on the door.

"Hello? Can I come in?"

My eyes shot open, and I realized I was alone. My own hand wrapped around my cock.

Fuck me.

"One second," I called out, jumping to my feet and tucking myself in before walking to the door and keeping my lower body behind the door so she wouldn't notice my raging boner. "Hey."

"Hey? Are you okay? You look flush." She put the back of her hand on my forehead.

"I'm fine. I was just waking up."

"All right. Food trucks are here, and everything is ready. I just came to make sure you were up."

"I'm up." *Literally and figuratively.* My gaze moved to the black sweater she was wearing, one side falling off her shoulder and exposing her tan skin, before I trailed down to the fitted jeans hugging her curves just right. "You look great."

"Yeah? I wasn't sure what to wear to our first work party as a married couple." She chuckled.

Goddamn, I wanted to pull her up against me and crash my mouth into hers.

That fucking dream was messing with my head.

"I think you pulled it off, Shortcake. Give me ten minutes. I'll grab a quick shower and be ready." I tried to keep my voice light, even though I felt anything but.

Her eyes flickered, and she nodded. Was she struggling as much as I was?

We'd just gotten back on track. I'd lost her for all those years, and I wasn't about to fuck it all up again.

I was the last guy who should cross the line. Especially with a girl that meant the world to me.

This would pass.

"Okay. I'll see you soon, husband."

I winked and closed the door. I made my way to the bathroom and turned on the water. I was in desperate need of relief, and it was hardly a crime to get off to thoughts of your wife, right?

Even if our marriage was based on a lie. I'd gone a while without sex, and I was human. She walked around this place looking like a fucking goddess.

I couldn't help myself.

* * *

150

I had my sixth or seventh slider and took a long pull from my beer bottle. I'd never seen anything like this.

My wife was a fucking rock star.

We had two food trucks, one with sliders and one with tacos and a dude running a karaoke machine in the living room, where people were singing and dancing.

Everyone was having a great time. And I couldn't take my eyes off of her.

My woman.

I didn't even have to fake it. We'd sang a few ridiculous karaoke songs together, and everyone was laughing their asses off. We'd been hand in hand earlier, and I fucking loved it.

I'd never been that guy who wanted to show off his woman. But damn, I was proud as hell that everyone thought she was my wife.

When was the last time I felt that kind of pride?

Savannah had gone off to grab some sparklers from the office that she'd gotten for everyone to take outside in the backyard. I noticed Kimber standing alone. She'd been pouting most of the night, and her husband was three sheets to the wind last I checked. He wasn't handling the fact that Cap and Clara had spent so much time talking with me and Savannah. He didn't hide his irritation, as he'd glared over at me a few times and then came over and tried to interrupt the conversation.

Clara hadn't missed a beat when she answered his question quickly and turned her attention back to my wife. Lenny had stalked off, and I saw him taking shots at the bar.

"I still think a fundraiser would have been smart. Kill two birds with one stone," Kimber said, as she moseyed over to me.

I glanced up to see Beebs and Stinky belting out the worst attempt at a Taylor Swift song, and I chuckled. All the guys were singing along and cheering them on.

"Savannah and I just wanted to have a party. There were no birds to kill tonight, Kimber." I arched a brow and continued scanning the room, noting there was no sign of Lenny. "Excuse me."

I walked away and made my way to my office to look for Savannah.

I heard her voice when I was a few feet away, and I didn't miss the irritation laced in her tone, which made me walk faster on instinct.

And then I heard him. That fucker must have followed her down the hallway.

"I'm good. You should get back out there. I've got this," Savannah said, and I paused outside the doorway for a moment.

"How is such a beautiful woman married to such an asshole?" Lenny's words slurred.

Just as I stepped forward, Savannah replied.

"You have some nerve coming into our home and disrespecting my husband like that. You can get the fuck out of here now." She didn't hide her disgust, and I fucking loved it.

"Oh, I just wasn't sure if the *Abbott* still fell far from the tree. If memory serves, your mother liked to mess around on your father, didn't she?" he said, and I saw red.

I stormed into the room before I could stop myself, and Savannah's eyes widened as Lenny slowly turned and startled when he saw me.

"Get the fuck away from *my wife*," I growled, as I moved across the room and stood beside her.

"Easy, buddy. I'm just seeing if she needs help to carry anything." He held his hands up. "I was just messing around and having a little fun."

"If you don't want a fist down your throat, I suggest you go get your wife and get the fuck out of my house." I stepped closer, and Savannah put a hand on my forearm, probably in an attempt to calm me down.

"Yeah, sure. This party seems to have slowed down anyway. Time to move the party to my house," he said.

Yeah, good luck with that. Your wife looks like she's had enough of your shit for one day.

"Hey, Lenny," Savannah said as he turned to leave the room.

"Yeah, beautiful. What can I do for you?"

"Well, for starters, never insult my husband again in my presence, or I'll be happy to show you my master karate skills." She held up a finger when he chuckled and started to interrupt. And then she moved closer to him, and I followed like a fucking shadow. "And the Abbott joke—it's run its course, don't you think? It's juvenile and stupid. And for the record, my last name is Woodson. So find some new material, asshole."

Let's fucking go.

Savannah Abbott-Woodson was a badass, and I was fucking here for it.

Lenny stormed out of the office.

"You all right, Shortcake?"

"Yes, of course. Did you doubt my mad skills?" she asked, getting into her best karate kid stance, and I laughed.

"Never. But I'd kill him if he touched you."

"Such a protective hubby," she said, moving closer, her hands on my chest. She smelled like peaches and vodka, and it turned me the hell on.

Her cheeks were a little flush, as she clearly had a slight buzz going.

She'd never been a big drinker, and that seemed to hold true. We were similar in that way. We both always wanted to be in control.

"Always when it comes to you. Fake or real, I've got you. You know that." I kept my voice low, my eyes landing on her mouth.

Those soft pink, plump lips that I thought about every fucking day.

"I do." She smiled, her honey-brown gaze locking with mine. "We lost a lot of time, didn't we?"

"We did. But we're here now, right?" I pushed the long, dark waves away from her pretty face.

"Yes. That's what matters. Thanks for everything you're doing for me," she whispered.

Damn. I wanted to kiss her so fucking bad I couldn't see straight.

What was this woman doing to me?

This. Is. Not. Real.

You've just missed her. She's your best friend.

Off-limits.

I wasn't about to risk losing her for another decade by crossing the line while knowing it couldn't go anywhere.

I wasn't that guy. And she deserved a hell of a lot better.

The most I had to offer was a fake marriage and some mind-blowing sex.

Some would consider that a great offer. But Savannah wasn't one who would.

She'd always wanted more for herself.

Hell, I wanted her to have everything she wanted.

"I'd do anything for you."

"I know you would. That's how I got you to do that Elton John and Kiki Dee duet with me." She chuckled as she turned to grab the box of sparklers.

"Don't remind me."

"Come on. Let's go pass out sparklers before everyone leaves."

And that's exactly what we did.

The guys were having a great time, and Cap yelled out, "Let's call it a night, boys! Don't make these young lovebirds kick you out. They're newlyweds. They don't want a bunch of firefighters passing out on their couch."

I chuckled as he clapped me on the shoulder and leaned in.

"I like this side of you, son. She's good for you. Don't fuck it up."

"I don't plan to." The lie slipped from my lips so easily, and I wondered how we'd pull all of this off when it came to an end.

"Come see me before your shift next week. I want to discuss a few things about my exit and what's to come."

I nodded. "All right. Sounds good."

Hopefully, it was good news. Because I had no intention of working for Lenny. Ever. It wouldn't happen.

The guys all made their way out, hugging Savannah one at a time, and each one of the assholes waggled their brows at me over her shoulder, which made me laugh.

Once everyone was gone, we closed the door, and she fell against it.

"That was a success."

"Yeah, aside from Lenny being a dickhead."

She chuckled just as someone knocked at the door. She tossed me a wink. "Someone must not want the party to end."

She pulled the door open, and I immediately moved forward and stepped in front of her, because I didn't recognize the middle-aged man standing on the other side.

"Can I help you?" My tone was hard because a stranger being here this late was never a good thing.

"Is Savannah Abbott-Woodson here?" He glanced over my shoulder at her.

"Yes. That's my wife."

"You've been served. Have a nice evening." He held the envelope in front of him, and I snatched it from his hand before slamming the door.

"What do you think it is?"

"No idea," I said, handing the envelope to her.

She tore it open and stared down at it. "Sheana Wilson is suing me for the inheritance and asking for a second look at

Abe's will. I should have expected this. She preyed on a lonely elderly man, and she walked away with a lot of money. But she clearly wants more."

"I'll call River. We'll figure this out. Don't worry about it. There's a will for a reason." I pulled out my phone and typed out a text to River.

"I already started the process for my dad to get into the trial."

"Sav," I said, my voice serious, and she turned to look at me, and I saw the concern in her honey-brown gaze. "We've got this. I promise."

And I didn't care what it took, it was a promise I intended to keep.

18

Savannah

There was a knock on my bedroom door. I hadn't slept much, as a million thoughts were going through my mind. What if Sheana had a fair legal argument? I'd started the renovations on the farmhouse, and most importantly, my father's health was dependent on this money. I also had a lot of anxiety about the fact that I'd pulled Hayes into this mess. What if we got caught? How would that affect him?

I pulled the door open, and he stood there wearing a pair of navy joggers and a white hoodie. "Did you get any sleep?"

"Not really." I shook my head. "What if she digs into our marriage? I'm so sorry for dragging you into this. I promise you I will take full responsibility."

"Hey, hey." He pulled me into a hug. "I'm not worried about that. We're allowed to get married. We have a history; we don't have to explain anything. River, Nash, and Emerson are on their way over now. We need to get ahead of this."

"How do we do that?" I asked.

The knock on the front door had us both walking toward the entryway, and River walked in first, with Nash and Emerson behind him. They'd brought coffee and muffins, and it still caught me off guard the way they all supported one another.

The way they were supporting me because I was Hayes's wife.

In theory, at least.

"Thanks for being here," I said, as we made our way to the kitchen.

"Ride or die, you know how this works," River said, and the three guys all gave one another a fist bump. "So, this area of expertise is not my specialty, and we need to bring in someone better suited to handle this. There's a lot of money at stake, and this needs to be handled correctly."

"What does that mean?" Hayes asked as I sat beside him at the large kitchen table. "Who do we know that can represent her?"

"You've met my brother," Emerson said, looking at Hayes first and then turning her attention to me. "I told you that I have a twin brother, Easton. He's an attorney, and he's handled cases like this. I phoned him this morning, and he's meeting us here in a little bit," Emerson said.

"He's coming here?" I asked, shaking my head in disbelief, as I knew her family lived in Rosewood River.

"Yeah. Emerson also has a brother who has access to a helicopter, so Easton will be here shortly. He's a brilliant trial attorney, and he'll be able to handle Sheana just fine." Nash took a sip of his coffee.

"I'm sure she's just trying to cash in one last time, but she doesn't have a leg to stand on. But I've never been involved in an inheritance lawsuit, and I want to make sure you get the best representation possible," River said. "Bert is a probate lawyer, so he reads the will, but he doesn't handle disputes. That's where Easton will come in."

Emerson glanced down at her phone and pushed to stand. "He's here. Let me go get him. I'll be right back."

"Thank you so much for doing this. It means the world to me," I said, feeling a lump form in my throat. It had been a very long time since I'd depended on anyone other than myself.

She smiled before heading toward the front door.

"It's going to be fine. I've heard Easton is a badass," Hayes said, his hand covering mine where it rested on the table.

"Hey," the man I assumed was Emerson's brother, Easton, said as he walked into the room. "I'm Easton Chadwick. Nice to meet you."

Nash made introductions, and Emerson handed her brother a coffee as he took the seat across from me. He was wearing a button-up and a pair of jeans, and he seemed like a casual guy until he spoke.

"I've got to be back in Rosewood River by noon, so let's get down to business. Did you bring me those copies of the will?" He directed his question to River now, who handed him a stack of papers. Easton glanced over the papers and then looked up at me and Hayes. "All right, River has filled me in on the basics. I'm going to give it to you straight, but what I need to know right now is if you would like to speak alone."

Hayes glanced over at me before looking back at Easton. "It's fine to speak freely. We're all family here."

"Sounds good." He took a sip of his coffee and then shot a look at Emerson. "Seriously? It's unsweetened?"

She smiled. "No. It has two pumps of sweetener instead of four. Mom said that Dr. Plume said your blood sugar is high."

He rolled his eyes and set his cup down. "Ignore her. I had my blood work done after a late night out with a lot of cocktails. It had nothing to do with the coffee."

We all chuckled, and Nash reminded Emerson how much sugar she put in her unicorn Krispies, which got a few more laughs.

"So, let's talk about this lawsuit." He cleared his throat, quickly scanned the contract again, and then set the papers down. "She's after the money. I looked into it, and I know the attorney that she hired. Mike Hardman, he's a slick attorney out of Los Angeles. The good news for you . . . I'm better at this whole law thing than he is."

"If you don't say so yourself," Emerson said, using her hand to cover her laughter. "There's a reason everyone in the legal world calls him a shark."

"A shark?" I asked.

"Yeah. He looks all casual in his jeans and cowboy boots, but the dude is a cutthroat attorney." Nash smirked.

"All right. Thanks for the ego boost. Anyway, back to the facts. She's going for the cash grab. He left you a lot of money, and you're the only thing standing in her way. She's Abe's ex-wife, and she's claiming that Abe made a verbal promise to her that he was going to leave everything to her."

"They never spoke again after they were divorced, and he was angry that he had to give her the money that he did to get her to leave," I said.

"I'm sure you're right, but that isn't going to stop her from shooting her shot. Obviously, she and her attorney think they have a case."

"Do they?" I asked.

"Well, that depends on a few things. If everything in that will is followed correctly, she can't do a damn thing about it. But my guess is that Sheana heard about Abe's passing from someone in town, and she found out that everything was left to you. It's a small town. I'm sure people talk, and she probably got wind that you got married shortly after you arrived back in Magnolia Falls. Maybe she was in contact with the probate attorney, and he filled her in on the stipulation regarding the inheritance."

"The stipulation?" Nash asked.

"The stipulation that Savannah had to be married within thirty days, which you pulled off just under the wire," he said, holding up his hands when Hayes started to argue. "I'm on your side. There is no judgment here. I'm pointing out the obvious. She wouldn't have filed a suit if she didn't think there was room to get in there and rock the boat."

"What kind of room?" I asked.

"Like I said, she's claiming that there was a verbal promise made to her by Abe that everything would be left to her, which clearly makes no sense, seeing as his will was recently updated within the last three months." Easton reached for his coffee.

"And if any of that were true, wouldn't she have attended his funeral? She didn't keep in touch with him, nor did she care about him at all," I said, my words shaking a bit as I spoke.

"Listen, her case is weak at best. The verbal agreement won't stand up in court, and her not attending his funeral looks bad for her. But she'll most likely try to prove that you only got married in order to get the inheritance and then push that she had a verbal agreement," he said, as if we were discussing the weather and not the fact that we'd broken the law. Emerson stared down at the table, and Nash shot Hayes a knowing look. They were clearly suspicious, too, now that they were hearing all the details—or maybe they already knew and they just weren't saying anything. "Savannah, Hayes, I don't need to know anything more than the fact that you're in love and married. I'm here to help you prepare for what might be coming. It may not be anything. She might just shoot her shot and try to get a cut of your money, which we will not let happen. She doesn't have a leg to stand on."

"Unless she proves that we're frauds?" Hayes hissed, as if he were completely offended at the idea.

We are frauds. It isn't that offensive.

"Correct. If she were to have a case there and have any proof of any wrongdoing, then the contract would be void, and she could technically go after the money with her verbal agreement defense. If I were a betting man, I'd say that's what they are doing. She had you served with the papers, so she's coming after you. But I have never seen a verbal agreement win in a courtroom over a signed legal document. She's definitely reaching here. But you still need to be prepared for what's coming."

"What do I do?" I asked, trying hard to hide the tremble from my voice.

"Let's just say that if she was onto something, you would need to do everything in your power to prove her wrong. They are most likely going to bring in people to investigate your lives. So, for example, if you are not sleeping in the same bedroom," he said, raising a brow before continuing. "This is real talk. We're on the same team. If you ran off to get married because you reunited and there were old feelings there—fan-fucking-tastic. But if it's anything else, and I don't want or need to know that, I'm not here to judge. But we need to prepare for the worst-case scenario. It's always better to be prepared."

"And what does that look like?" Hayes asked.

"They will hire people. They will contact people in your lives behind your backs. They'll offer money and try to catch you in a lie. Let's start with the basics. Do you have a cleaning woman?" he asked, looking between us.

"Yes. She's back tomorrow. She's been on vacation for the last two weeks," Hayes said, and I sucked in a breath because I didn't even know we had a cleaning woman.

"Perfect example. They'll try to get to her. They'll ask if you're sleeping in the same room. If you're affectionate in front of her. For all I know, they'll have people looking in your windows. Snooping around your workplace. Landscapers. Employees. They'll try everything." He cracked his knuckles, his gaze moving from Hayes to me. "You just make sure you are sleeping in the same room and there is not a single reason for them to doubt that this is real. There should not be clothing hidden in a guest room closet. The only bed that looks slept in is in your bedroom. That you share. Trust me, people get crazy over money, and they will snoop around and try to find things you wouldn't even think of."

"That's not a problem," Hayes said. "But I'm gone three nights a week when I have my shifts at the firehouse."

"It's your job; they can't argue that. Savannah should be seen at the firehouse, and you need to be seen out around town often, as well," Easton said. "If you don't give them any reason to question you, they can't do a damn thing. I'm here to tell you what to do to protect yourself. If you listen to me, you'll be fine."

I nodded. There was a huge knot in my stomach, and my hands were sweating.

"They'll go to your parents, as well, so just make sure everyone is thrilled about the marriage." He glanced at his sister, who'd just reached for a muffin, and she chuckled before handing it to him.

"Oh, I haven't told my parents." I needed to be straight with him in case he was right.

The room fell silent, aside from Hayes, who spoke up immediately. "We got married fast, and she was afraid her parents wouldn't approve of us tying the knot without them. We were planning a trip to see them for the weekend and tell them in person soon." He squeezed my hand because we both knew we had no intention of going to tell them in person.

"My dad has cancer." The words were out of my mouth before I could stop them. "I didn't want him to have to travel here. And we didn't want to wait to get married."

Something crossed Easton's gaze, and I couldn't quite read it. But there was an understanding there, and he nodded. "Tell your parents today or by the end of the weekend. You can get on FaceTime or Zoom and do it face-to-face. If you want to plan a trip there soon, that's fine. But they need to know as soon as possible, or it will look suspicious. They could reach out to them; we just don't know. So, let's get ahead of this and get that taken care of immediately. How about your parents, Hayes?"

"My father and I haven't spoken in years, so there would be no reason to tell him. My mother knows, and she is thrilled about me and Sav getting married, as is my sister. Our friends are also happy about it," Hayes said.

"Good. So, Savannah calls her parents sooner rather than later and checks that off the list. You—er, continue staying in the same bedroom, even if you have an argument. There is no room for openings here. And absolutely no room for any indiscretions." He gathered all the papers and slipped them into his briefcase. "I'm going to read over these later today, and I'll be in touch with any questions."

"You don't have to worry about either of us having indiscretions. We're ridiculously happy," Hayes hissed, and everyone chuckled.

"Thanks for helping us," I said, my voice quiet.

"Hey, Savannah, listen . . . Abe wanted you to have the money and the house. I have no idea why he put in such a ridiculous clause, but I'm happy that you two found your way back to one another." Easton smirked. "If he wanted Sheana to have the money, he would have left it to her. So don't worry. It'll all be fine."

I nodded, and Hayes squeezed my hand the slightest bit. Most wouldn't have noticed, but I did. He could tell that I was spiraling. He wanted me to believe that everything would be okay.

But would it?

Hayes had agreed to help me. He wasn't having sex with other women in an effort to protect this secret, and now he'd be under a magnifying glass even more. And I'd have to move into his bedroom.

This was a complete mess.

We exchanged phone numbers with Easton, and he explained more about what to expect and continued to tell us how important it was to make sure everyone we interacted with knew that we were blissfully in love.

Hayes assured him that there was nothing to worry about because my fake husband was going to do whatever he could to protect this secret.

My secret.

"All right, I've got a client to meet in an hour, so I need to get out of here. I'll be in touch."

We said our goodbyes, and he was out the door.

"Don't worry. He's the best. You're in good hands," Nash said.

"I—er, I'm sorry for complicating everyone's life, especially yours," I said, shaking my head as I looked at Hayes. It was obvious that Nash and Emerson were suspicious that something was up, as I'm sure all of Hayes's close friends were.

The man didn't even do relationships.

Did we really think they wouldn't find it odd that he'd gotten married in a couple of weeks?

This was all supposed to be simple, but now it all felt very complicated.

"Savvy," Emerson said, and I turned to look at her. "We aren't here to judge. We support you both, no matter what."

"Agreed." Nash nodded.

"We're married. We're happy. That's all anyone needs to know. That's all that fucking matters." Hayes pushed to his feet and tossed his empty coffee cup into the garbage can. "And you're getting that money. And your dad is going to get into that trial, and he's going to be okay. Because you deserve that, Sav. You're the best person I know. You're my wife, and you fucking deserve everything good."

Everyone gaped at the man who was usually short on words.

"I'll be damned. Our boy is a sap for his wife, and I'm here for it." River pushed to his feet. "Now, let's get out of their hair. They're newlyweds, after all."

Emerson whispered in my ear that she'd do some research about the trial for my father after I gave the short version about his illness. We all hugged goodbye, and then it was just me and Hayes standing in the entryway of his home.

Of our home.

I looked up at him, unsure of what to do next.

"Let's get your things moved out of the guest room. Tonight, you're sleeping in my bed. *Our* bed. Don't even try to argue with me, because we're doing this."

And he wouldn't get one argument from me.

My husband was calling the shots now.

19

Hayes

It had been a day. We were dealing with a lawsuit from a gold-digging asshole who'd already taken advantage of a really kind old man.

And this marriage we'd gotten into was going to be scrutinized.

Savannah was beating herself up that she'd dragged me into this, but what she didn't know was that I was happy to be here.

With her.

I'd missed her. All these years we'd spent apart, something had been missing. And now she was back in my life, and I wanted to keep her right here.

We'd moved all her things into my room, cleaning up all signs that she'd spent any time in the guest room before Belinda arrived at the house this week to clean.

We were in such a gray area.

I was so fucking attracted to her, but so afraid to do anything that would run her off.

I was in unchartered territory.

I sat on the edge of the bed as the bathroom door opened. Savannah came out wearing her little sleep shorts and a tank

167

top. Her skin glistened, hair damp and long, and a drip of water ran from her shoulder toward her forearm, where her hair rested.

I had the sudden urge to lick it off.

Fuck. Now she was going to be in my bed. How the hell would I survive months of this?

"I could sleep in a sleeping bag on the floor. Who would know?" she asked, as she studied me.

"I thought I told you not to argue with me about this." My words were firm but not harsh. There was no humor there because I wasn't fucking around.

"Ahhh . . . my bossy husband is flexing again, huh?"

"I can flex any time you want, wife." I pushed to my feet, wearing only my briefs, and her eyes raked down my chest.

Her tongue swiped out to wet her lips, and she moved around me and climbed into bed. "It's not like we didn't sleep in the same bed dozens of times over the years, right?"

"Yep. It's not a big deal." I moved to turn off the light switch on the wall.

"Do you still need the side closest to the door?"

I flipped out the light and moved toward the bed. "Yes."

The room was dark. Quiet. I slipped in beside her beneath the covers.

"Why did you always insist on that side, even when you knew that was the side I slept on in my room?"

She'd texted me a few times when her parents would have these brutal screaming fights, and I'd sneak out of my house and in through her bedroom window.

Because when Savannah needed me, I was always there.

And vice versa.

"Because if anyone ever came into your room, they'd have to go through me to get to you," I said honestly. I'd lived with a man who was violent during my teenage years, so I assumed it was just my instincts wanting to keep her safe.

She rolled onto her side, moving closer to me, and her leg brushed against mine.

"You're so warm," she whispered. Vanilla and lavender flooded my system, and I reached for her hip and tugged her closer.

Flush against my body.

"You're cold. Let me warm you up." My voice was gruff, and I did my best to control my breathing.

Stay in control.

"You were always so hot all the time. I swear your body temperature is not normal," she whispered, but she didn't pull back. Her fingers traced along the muscles of my bicep.

"Maybe I'm just hot around you. Did you ever think of that?"

"Are you flirting with me, husband? You know you don't need to do that. I'm in this. There's no wooing necessary." She chuckled, but I knew her. She was nervous.

"This isn't about wooing you. We're married."

"Fake married."

"You don't have to keep saying that, you know? I'm aware of our arrangement. I find it offensive that you keep reminding me," I grumped.

Her hand moved to my cheek. "I'm sorry. I was just kidding. Maybe I'm just reminding myself so I don't forget. Things are—complicated."

Her words made my chest squeeze.

"I get that."

"So, tell me . . . why are you always so hot when you're around me?" Her voice was all tease now.

"Not sure, Shortcake. I probably always had a crush on you."

"Hayes."

"Savannah." I mimicked her serious tone.

"You did not. You slept in my bed many times. We were

169

always together. You never made a move. And we all know it wasn't because of lack of experience. When you liked a girl, you always went after her. So don't bullshit me."

"I'm not bullshitting you, Sav. I'm being honest. I did have a crush on you. And we spent a lot of years apart, so I guess—I don't know. Who knows when you'll leave me high and dry and get the hell out of town? I'm just putting it all out there because what do we have to lose?"

She was quiet for what felt like minutes.

"So then, why didn't you ever make a move?" she whispered.

It was a great fucking question. I'd thought about it more times than I could count over the years.

"Not sure."

"Try."

I thought it over. "Well, I'm trying to think of the best way to explain it. Do you remember that sandcastle competition you talked me into that summer before you left, down at the lake?"

"The one where we dominated and won the five-hundred-dollar grand prize?" she said.

"Yes. The one you made me assist you with for seven fucking hours. And you didn't allow breaks for food and water, if memory serves." I barked out a laugh, my hand stroking her hair away from her face.

"Of course, I remember. We made the front page of the *Magnolia Falls Chronicles*."

"Because everyone else in town was building a basic sandcastle. You built a gigantic farmhouse masterpiece out of sand." I couldn't help but smile at the memory. She'd drawn out her plan, and I'd told her she was crazy. It was too big. Too complicated. But that's the thing about Savannah Abbott. She never throws in the towel. She was always determined to master everything she tried.

"And this compares to your supposed crush, how?" She didn't hide her sarcasm.

"Do you remember how much time we spent building that front porch out of sand, and then at the very end, you were torn about adding chairs that we made out of sticks that would sit on the porch?"

"Yes," she said, as her chest pounded against mine.

"But then we both decided that it was already perfect just how it was, and we didn't want to risk ruining it by messing with it."

"Correct. It was the right call."

I cleared my throat. "That's how I felt when I looked at you. Like you were perfect. My favorite person. My best friend. And I was a lost kid, you know? Getting into fights and getting into trouble. I never wanted to do anything to mess up the best thing I had going for me. So, I tended to date people that weren't very good for me. Because I think I probably felt more comfortable in volatile situations where there was nothing to lose, you know?"

She was quiet, and then she sniffed a few times. "You were my favorite person, too. And you've grown into such an impressive man."

"Sav, don't do that."

"Do what?"

"Make me into someone I'm not. I'm closed off. Unfriendly. Far from impressive."

"That's not what I see when I look at you," she whispered. "I see a man who would do anything to protect his sister because he loves her so fiercely. A man who would walk through fire for his friends. A man who takes his responsibility as a godfather to Cutler very seriously, hence the endless supply of chocolate milk in the refrigerator. A man who was willing to marry a woman he hadn't seen in over a decade because she needed him. Even after she left him and was quick to believe the worst in him. A man with a huge heart that he hides behind all these sexy muscles," she said, with a little chuckle.

I didn't respond. I was still processing her words, which was difficult with her pressed against me.

"What are you thinking about?"

"Honestly, with your hot little body rubbing up against mine, I'm thinking about that kiss we shared. It's all I fucking think about most nights when I get into bed."

"I think about it, too."

"Yeah? What do you think that means?" I asked, my fingers tracing along the sliver of silky skin between the waistband of her sleep shorts and the hem of her tank top.

"I think it means you're attracted to your wife, and I'm attracted to my husband," she whispered.

"It would complicate things because I don't know that a kiss will be enough," I admitted. I wanted her. More than I'd ever wanted anyone or anything.

"I'm not a sandcastle, Hayes. You're not going to break me. I want you."

I want you.

That was all that I needed to hear.

My mouth crashed into hers, hand tangled in her hair, tilting her head to grant me better access. Her lips parted, inviting me in, and I explored that sweet mouth like my life depended on it.

Her hips started grinding up against mine, and my dick throbbed against my briefs. My hand moved up her back beneath her tank top, pressing her against me as I stroked her skin.

Breaths and moans surrounded us, and our tongues tangled as she ground up and down my cock, with only a little bit of cotton between us. And fuck, did I want this woman.

She moved faster.

Harder.

She was close.

Her head fell back as our lips lost contact, and she panted and dug her nails into my shoulders.

I gripped her hip on one side and helped her ride me harder, knowing what she needed.

"Come for me now, Sav," I demanded.

And that's exactly what she did. She went right over the edge on a gasp, and I fucking loved the way her body shook and trembled in my arms. I continued moving her up and down so she could ride out every last bit of pleasure.

And damn if it wasn't the hottest thing I'd ever seen.

Her breathing slowed, and her gaze locked with mine in the bit of moonlight peeking through the blinds.

"You're fucking beautiful," I said. I'd never been an emotional man. That was a complaint of Kate's, and she'd been right about that. I didn't feel things or get overwhelmed by emotions the way others did.

But seeing Savannah fall apart like that—it fucking did something to me.

Her hand moved to my erection, which was now hard as a rock.

"How about you let me make you feel good."

I wrapped my hand around her wrist to stop the movement. "I want that, but I need something first."

"Tell me," she said, her voice raspy and sated.

"I need to taste my wife right fucking now. I need to bury my face between your thighs and feel you come on my lips. I've thought about it so many times, Sav."

"How about we do it together? You taste me and I taste you. You aren't the only one who's thought about it."

Fuck me.

I nodded slowly, as her teeth sank into her bottom lip, and I nearly came right there.

"Clothes off. Now." I pushed up on my knees as she raised her arms over her head, and I pulled her tank top off, tracing my thumbs over her perfect tits. "I could spend hours licking and sucking these beautiful tits. Do you know that? Someone should make a sandcastle of your breasts. That's how perfect they are."

A sexy little laugh escaped her lips as her long hair fell all around her shoulders. "You're ridiculous."

I reached for the waistband of her shorts and pulled them down her thighs. I sucked in a breath when I took her in, lying there bare for me.

This is happening.

I wanted to memorize every gorgeous inch of her, so if she disappeared again, I could remember everything. I'd be prepared this time.

And then she rolled over, pressing up on her knees as she pushed me to lie flat on my back. She tugged my briefs down and gasped when my dick sprung straight up.

Eager and ready.

She raked her gaze over my body until her eyes found mine. "Now, do your husband a solid, and sit on my face. I want you to smother me. I want you to come so hard, you can't think of anything but my mouth on your pussy."

She smiled, a dark blush covering her cheeks, before she leaned down and kissed me hard one last time.

And then she moved, straddling my face and resting all that sweetness against my lips.

I gripped her hips, and my tongue swiped along her seam, causing her to yelp. But I held her right there. And I licked and sucked and teased her as she bent forward and wrapped her hand around my cock. I loved the way she rocked against me, all needy and desperate.

I pulled her closer, and my tongue slipped inside her, just as her mouth covered my dick.

And we found our perfect rhythm. My tongue slid in and out of her tight, wet pussy, as her lips slid up and down my throbbing cock.

I will not come first.

No fucking way.

She moaned as her tongue swirled around my dick, and she sucked harder. Faster.

I moved the pad of my thumb to her clit as my tongue devoured her. And she ground against me.

I knew she was close.

Her thighs tightened around my face, and her fingers dug into my thighs.

Harder.

Faster.

I didn't let up.

She cried out my name with my dick in her mouth and her pussy on my lips. And that's all it took.

I reached for her head in warning, letting her know I was going to come, but she stayed right there.

I unloaded into her mouth as a guttural sound left my lips, and she continued rocking against me.

And nothing had ever felt better.

20

Savannah

I fell forward, completely sated. My body felt like it was floating on air. Hayes maneuvered me like I weighed nothing, adjusting my body so I settled against him, my head on his chest.

Both of us were still panting. He wrapped an arm around my shoulder, keeping me close.

"You okay?" he asked, his voice laced with concern.

I pushed up onto my elbow to look at him. "Oh. My. Holy. Husband. We should have gotten fake married years ago."

His lips turned up in the corners. When Hayes smiled, there was something extra sexy about it. He didn't offer this to everyone, and you knew when he smiled at you that you were lucky. "That's the last time you call this fake, and I won't remind you again, woman."

My head tipped back in a chuckle. "Fine. Whatever we're doing, we should have done it years ago."

"You like my tongue on your puss—" he said, and I covered his mouth with my hand.

"You have the filthiest mouth, Woody. You're very . . . skilled."

"Wait till you see what I can do with my dick." He tugged me back down to lie on his chest.

"Well, the good news is that I was all worried about us staying in the same room, but this feels like a win-win. We pretend to be married, act like a real couple in every way, and give each other epic orgasms. It doesn't get much better than this."

"Careful, Shortcake. Don't get too caught up in the orgasms, or you might fall in love with me."

"Pfft . . . please. You're the one who had a crush on me when we were teenagers. And that intense growl of pleasure that escaped your mouth just a few minutes ago tells me that I know how to please my man. So, you're the one who needs to be careful," I said, my tone laced with humor. "And I know an unattainable man when I see one. Why do you think I was willing to do this whole marriage thing with you?"

"Why?"

"Well, there's no risk of anyone getting hurt. You haven't had a relationship since the heathen. That's a long time to be single."

He gripped my hair and turned my head so I was looking at him. "And what's your story? I don't see you with a boyfriend."

"Correct. I'm a girl with abandonment issues. My mother left my father and me for her lover, and she has a new family with him. And sure, we are all on good terms now, but that doesn't mean I forgot those painful years. Also, I thought my lifelong best friend betrayed me in the worst way, up until finding out recently that none of that was real. But those are some deep-rooted fears I have now. Obviously, I can't date a man who has commitment issues. So, yeah, I've been single for a long time, not because I don't want to get married, but because it needs to be the right man. A guy who makes me feel safe, but challenged and loved as well."

"Wow. You've put a lot of thought into this whole

relationship thing, yet you agreed to marry me in all of fifteen minutes in River's office, knowing what a horrible husband I would make?"

Why did he sound so wounded?

"My husband is such a caveman," I said with a laugh. "You've got such a tender heart beneath that very impressive body of yours."

"My heart is not tender, and stop evading the question."

"Yes. I've put a lot of thought into what I want. I will not be in a relationship like my parents had. I will not hitch my cart to a man who doesn't want me. I know how that story ends. And I've always wanted a big family because I hated being an only child, and a loveless marriage sucks for the kids. So, my children will live in a home that's filled with love. Safe and happy with lots of laughter and parents who are nauseatingly in love. That's probably why Abe put that ridiculous stipulation in the will."

"Why?"

"Because he thought I was being too picky."

"How often do you date?" he asked, his gaze filled with curiosity.

"Usually three times a week."

His eyes widened. "Three times a fucking week? Different dudes?"

"Yes. I live in the city. There are a ton of prospects. And guys swipe right a lot on me for some reason."

"Of course, they do. Look at you." He shifted me off of him and pushed to his feet, storming around the bed to get his briefs. I sat forward, pulling the covers over myself as I took in his toned ass before he covered it.

I was laughing again. "You sound jealous."

He crossed his arms over his chest. "And you just date them once? No repeat dates?"

I rolled my eyes, unsure of why we were talking about this, but

Hayes and I had always talked about everything. "Usually once. I don't let them pick me up. We normally meet at a restaurant for dinner or happy hour. Occasionally, I get asked to go to a football or a hockey game. But I always drive my own car."

"The piece-of-shit clunker you call a car?" he grumped.

"Don't insult Big Red. You sound jealous of a car now, too, and it's unbecoming." I smiled, and his mouth twitched. "That's usually it. I think I did a second date with two guys over the last year, and the rest have all been one and done."

"I thought you said you haven't had sex in a while?" he pressed, because he was clearly a nosy bastard.

"I haven't. My last serious relationship was two years ago. Haven't been with anyone since."

He gaped at me. "What about your five million dates? You didn't sleep with one of them?"

"No. I'm not having sex with someone that I don't think I'd actually date. So the one and dones get a kiss, if they're lucky." I shrugged.

"Poor bastards." He chuckled, but for whatever reason, he looked thrilled by the news. Like he enjoyed the idea of me torturing these men. "What about the two dudes who got second dates?"

"They got a good make-out sesh. A little under-the-sweater action. That's it."

"Yet you let me give you two orgasms and go down on you?" He quirked a brow.

"You're my husband." I sighed. "Listen, don't question the rules. I make them up as I go. But since we're being so open about things, how often do you date?"

"I don't. I go to a bar and leave with a woman. There's no make-out sesh or whatever the fuck you called it. If I go to her home, we usually fuck. Aside from Trish Windsor, who crossed a line, so I got the fuck out of there."

"What did she do?"

"She tried to cuff me to her bed."

"And you didn't like that?" I asked, completely mesmerized by the conversation.

"I don't get cuffed. I'd be happy to tie up a woman if that was her thing, but I'm not trusting some woman I barely know to lock me to her bed. What if she never uncuffs me? Makes me her sex prisoner? Not fucking happening."

My head fell back in laughter. "I can't believe she wanted to cuff you to her bed. And why do you always go to the woman's house? You don't bring ladies here?"

"No. Because if I'm already at home, I can't leave if I need the night to end."

"Yet you've agreed to me sleeping in your bed for the next few months."

"You're my wife." He quirked a brow. "And two years is a long time to go without sex, Shortcake. If you need me to remedy that for you, just say the word."

"I mean, we should consummate this marriage eventually, right?" I crawled across the mattress and found my clothing, pulling my jammies back on. This had been an eventful evening, and I should probably pump the brakes.

He climbed back onto the bed and patted his hand against the mattress beside him. "How about this? We take it one day at a time. If you want me to bury my face between your thighs every fucking morning and every fucking night and do nothing more, I'd be a very content husband with that arrangement. We don't ever have to have sex if it complicates things for you."

"Damn. I don't want to be cocky, but I feel like I must have one magical vagina covered in pixie dust if you're willing to . . . *go downtown* every single day until I divorce you and get back to the single life."

"No doubt about it. You've got an award-winning pussy, Shortcake."

We were both laughing hysterically now, and I rolled onto my side to face him. Just the way we'd started before all the orgasms.

It was quiet now, and the room was dark.

"I missed you, Hayes," I said the words so softly I wasn't sure he'd even heard me.

But then he tugged me closer, wrapped his arms around me, and kissed the top of my head.

He'd definitely heard me.

And I knew he missed me, too.

Exhaustion took me, and I slept for what felt like days, but in reality, I woke with the sun the following morning.

I stretched my arms over my head and blinked a few times as I processed where I was.

I sprung forward and looked beside me. No Hayes. Had he freaked out after what happened between us?

I padded to the bathroom to brush my teeth, tied my hair in a messy knot on top of my head, and made my way down the hallway toward the kitchen and family room.

"Husband? Are you up?" I called out when I heard the sound of pots and pans moving in the kitchen.

"I am. I've already worked out, and now I'm scrambling us some eggs." He stood at the stovetop, his back to me, wearing a pair of basketball shorts and no shirt.

Damn. This man's body could be a piece of artwork.

He glanced over his shoulder and smirked, like he knew what I was doing.

I moved around him and reached for a coffee mug in the cabinet, and I could feel his eyes on me.

My husband and I were playing a dangerous game of attraction.

I filled my mug with coffee and topped his off as it sat on the counter beside him. And then I intentionally brushed my body against his as I walked past.

"You know you can use your words and ask for what you want," he said, as he plated the eggs.

"What are you talking about?" I pulled out the barstool and sat down, and he took the seat beside mine, setting both plates in front of us.

"I'm just saying, we're married. If we want something, all we have to do is ask for it. Marriage is about pleasing your partner, right?"

"Agreed. That's a great plan. And thank you for the eggs. What can I do for you this morning?" I asked, forking some scrambled eggs and groaning after I swallowed.

"I'd like to hear you groan again like you're doing right now, but I'd like to be the reason you're groaning instead of those eggs." He smirked. "But first, we FaceTime your parents and rip that bandage off. They need to know that you're my wife before I give you any more orgasms."

"For a man who doesn't even do relationships, you sure have a lot of rules about this marriage," I said, taking another bite of eggs and purposely groaning extra loud because I knew it was getting under his skin.

"Deal with it. You're the one who agreed to marry me. And if you have any requests, I'm all ears."

"Anything I want?" I asked as I sipped my coffee.

"Sure. It's all part of the deal."

"Great. We'll call my parents, and then you can make me groan however you'd like, preferably in the shower because oddly enough, I've never taken a shower with a man, and I figure this marriage is a good time to knock things off the list. And for my request, I'd like to read another letter."

He squeezed his eyes closed, and I cinched my brows with confusion before looking down to see his tented shorts, and I covered my laughter with my hand.

"You've never showered with a man?"

"No. I tend to shower alone. But I want the letter, so if I have to save the shower for later, I'll take the letter."

He thought it over before pushing to his feet. "You can have both after we make the calls."

He reached for my plate, but I grabbed it from him. "You cooked. I'll do the dishes."

"Fine." He jogged down the hallway and came running back wearing a T-shirt now and holding my laptop.

"What are you doing?" I asked, as I finished loading the dishwasher.

"Getting your Zoom set up." He clapped his hands together. "Chop chop, woman."

I moseyed over to the dining room, where he had my computer opened and ready for me to log in. I sent both of my parents a text asking if we could hop on a quick Zoom call, and my father answered immediately, so I sent him the link.

"You're in such a hurry," I said, as I clicked on the link and waited for Dad to sign in.

Hayes leaned close to my ear. "The thought of making you come in the shower is all I can think of."

My breaths were coming faster now as the screen opened, and Hayes chuckled when my father came into view, and then he completely changed his disposition. "Mr. Abbott, it's so good to see you."

My husband can be a smug bastard when he wants to be.

Nadia was sitting beside him, and I introduced her to Hayes. He'd heard me speak about her plenty of times over the last few weeks.

"I love to see you two hanging out again after all these years apart," my father said.

Well, this is going to be awkward.

"About that, Dad." I cleared my throat, and Hayes found my hand beneath the table and gave me a look that made it clear that he wanted to explain.

"Mr. Abbott, I apologize that I didn't come to you first. I owed you that respect, but we just got carried away."

I dug my nails into his hand because I was going to be the one to say it. He could apologize all he wanted, but I needed to tear this bandage off. "We got married. We just—" I shook my head and shrugged. "We couldn't wait."

"We couldn't wait one more minute. And we didn't want anyone to try to talk us out of it," Hayes added. "We're ridiculously in love."

My father's eyes doubled in size, and his mouth fell open. "You two got married?"

"Married?" Nadia parroted.

"We did," I said. "I'm sorry I didn't tell you. I didn't want a big wedding or anything fancy, but I should have told you."

"Well, we'll just have to throw a big reception," Nadia said, leaning against my father's shoulder, as he swiped at the single tear coming down his cheek.

I sucked in a breath, preparing for him to be angry.

"I always knew you two belonged together. I couldn't be happier." Dad chuckled, his entire demeanor lighter now. "Now, just give me some grandbabies while I'm still around to enjoy them."

A heaviness settled in my chest. Lying to my father didn't feel good, even if he was the reason that I'd been willing to do any of this.

I couldn't speak because he was hoping for something that Hayes and I would never give him.

But then the man beside me surprised the hell out of everyone. "Give us a little time, but we're working on it."

My father beamed, and I dug my nails into Hayes's palm. He was going too far.

More laughter from my father, and we chatted for the next half hour, him asking Hayes endless questions before we finally said our goodbyes.

When I closed my computer screen, I turned to look at him. "You shouldn't have said that."

"Why?"

"Because it's a lie." I raised a brow. "We're not trying to have a baby."

"We're also not married for real. So we're already in this. And it made him happy."

"And what happens when this all ends and he's upset?"

"He'll be receiving the best treatment money can buy, and he won't give a shit if our relationship implodes. You can tell him that I was sterile."

"It's believable. You can be a little cold." I smirked.

He moved so quickly that I squealed as he tugged me onto his lap. "One more call, Shortcake, and then I'm carrying you to the shower."

"Don't forget about the letter."

"Sure. A little reading material after an orgasm sounds great," he grumped, and I looked down at my phone to see a message from my mom that she was ready to chat, and Harry was there, too.

"Okay, let's do this."

"Hello, Savannah. You look well," my mother said, as her face came into view.

"Hi, Savvy. I miss you!" Harry shouted.

"Harry, you don't need to shout, sweetheart. You can use a regular voice. An inside voice." My mom had never been patient with me, but she was so different with Harry. She wanted to talk everything out. I was grateful she wasn't that way with me, even if she appeared to be trying harder this time around. I just found it to be very annoying.

"Hey, buddy. I miss you, too. I wanted to introduce you to someone." I smiled and leaned my head against Hayes's shoulder.

"Is that Hayes Woodson?" My mother gasped, her tone extra snarky. "The boy you got your first tattoo with?"

"Wow. Nice to see you, too, Mrs. Jones."

I was ready to pull off the bandage because her judgy eyes were infuriating me. For a woman who'd made her fair share of mistakes, she never cut anyone any slack. No one got a pass from Delila Jones. And I had zero tolerance for it.

"Oh, baby. Drop the formalities. You can call her Mom." I chuckled. "Mom. Har. Say hello to my husband." I held up my hand and shook my hand in front of the screen, flashing my wedding ring.

"Husband?" my mom said. "You got married?"

"I sure did."

"Yes, we're married." Hayes squeezed my hand so tight I nearly squealed. "We just couldn't wait another minute."

"Cool. I always wanted a brother." Harry fist pumped the ceiling.

"Glad to hear it, Harry. I've heard lots about you."

"How did this happen? You lost contact years ago," she said, and she started scratching at her neck. It was her tell when she was nervous.

"Yes. Well, I think the fact that he'd written me all those letters, which had been returned to him so many years ago, caught us both by surprise. Ya know, *Mom*?" I arched a brow.

"Oh, yes, the letters. I just knew you two weren't speaking at the time, so I didn't want to cause you any more pain, Savannah."

"Don't give it a thought, Mom," Hayes said, in a sugary sweet voice, one I'd never heard from him. "I think it's what really sealed the deal for me all these years later. She loved that I saved them. So, thank you for torturing us both for the last decade."

My mother just stared at the screen. "Sure. I'm glad it all worked out. I'm—er, happy for you both. You always had such an interesting friendship. We'll have to have dinner the next time you're in the city. We're heading out to meet Ben to play some pickleball, so we've got to get going."

This is why I hated calling her. There just wasn't anything there between us, and it made me feel bad when the reality that we were more like acquaintances was so apparent every time we spoke.

"I can't wait to see you, Savvy. And I can't wait to hang out with my new brother, Hayes." Harry waved at the camera.

"Bye, Har. I love you."

"Love you, too," he said, as my mother ended the call.

"She's just as charming as I remember." Hayes turned to face me, oozing sarcasm, per usual. "You all right?"

"Yes. I'm good."

"Good? That doesn't sound good." He moved so fast I barely had a minute to process what was happening before I was tossed over his shoulder as he ran down the hall. "I think your first shower with a well-hung man ought to cheer you up."

I slapped his ass and laughed.

But he was right.

A shower with a well-hung man definitely cheered me up.

21

Hayes

"Married life looks good on you," Cap said, as he clapped me on the shoulder and then moved around his desk to sit across from me.

"Thanks."

"Was that Priscilla Larson I saw upstairs bringing you cookies?"

I laughed. "Yeah. She hasn't missed a year yet. I keep waiting for those grumpy teenage years to kick in and for her to realize she doesn't need to thank me year after year."

"You saved her life, Hayes. That's not something anyone forgets."

I cleared my throat and nodded. "Thank you."

"So, I wanted to talk to you about this position and make sure you know what you're up against."

I was just coming off a three-day shift, and I was tired, but I perked up at the mention of the promotion.

"I'm assuming I'm up against Lenny." I leaned back in the chair, stretching my legs and crossing them at my ankles. "Even though I think he'd be a terrible leader, I understand why we'd both be considered for the position, as we're both lieutenants."

"Lenny isn't in the running. Not really. I mean, he's applied for the position, of course, but he's never had my support. It's always been you I saw filling my shoes. The job is yours if you want it."

I wasn't expecting that.

"What do you mean? We're both lieutenants. We both want to be captain. Everyone knows we've been competing for the same position."

"At the end of the day, I've spent a lot of time with both of you. I know what's best for this firehouse, and I'm not shy about it." He leaned forward, folding his hands together and resting them on his desk. "Lenny isn't a bad guy. He's a decent lieutenant. He's a better firefighter than people think he is, and the reason they feel that way is mostly because he's gotten lazy. But he's capable, and that's why he's still here. But he's never been in the running for *this* position."

"Well, that's news to me. He's been campaigning with Kimber for quite some time."

He chuckled. "I'm more than aware of what he's been doing. But having a wife who throws fundraisers doesn't make one a fire captain. You've always been the only one in this house who has been considered. We've got some applicants from out of town, but you're the guy we want. Always have been."

"You're serious?"

"Do I strike you as a joker?" He smirked. We were similar in many ways. We were both quieter and focused on the job.

I rubbed my hands together. "I don't know what to say. I wasn't expecting this."

"You thought that I'd promote Lenny because his wife likes to throw parties?"

"I think everyone did." I shrugged. "We all know that a family environment is important to you."

"Creating a family environment does not happen because

someone threw a few parties. Creating this connection with the guys comes from being there. Modeling the behavior you want to instill. Showing up when they struggle or when there are challenges. Leading by example, and that's exactly what you do, Hayes. What you've always done. Every damn day that you come to work, you show up. You work hard. The guys respect it. The way you've taken Stinky, Beebs, and Bones under your wing and taught them the right way to fight fires. The right way to show up for your family here at the firehouse. That's what matters."

I ran a hand down my face. I wasn't used to being caught off guard, but I hadn't expected this.

"Thank you. It means a lot."

"I know it does." He smirked. "And it's great that you and Savannah found your way together. I like seeing you like this."

I quirked a brow. "Like what?"

"You know, there's an occasional smile on your face." He barked out a laugh. "It has nothing to do with you as a firefighter, Hayes. I wouldn't give a shit if you stayed single your entire life—I care about how you do the job. But as a friend. As a man who's watched you grow up and looks at you like a son. I like that you have something, some*one* to go home to. And I can tell that you like it, too."

"When did you turn into such a sappy dude?" I shook my head and used my hand to cover my laugh.

"Apparently, the older I get, the sappier I become." He reached for his coffee and took a sip before returning his mug to the desk. "So, what I want to talk to you about is the part of the job you might not like."

"Which is?"

"You're going to be a fucking babysitter sometimes. You're going to break up fights and have to ride the guys when they slack. You can't just call them assholes and shut down. You're going to have to check your temper at the door and be the guy everyone turns to with all their problems, even when you don't feel like it. And trust me, there's always something."

"All right. I can handle that."

"I know you can. That's why you're here."

"And what happens with Lenny?" I asked, knowing that he wouldn't take it well.

"Listen, if Lenny were being promoted, I know that you'd leave. Because you know that he wouldn't lead this house the way it needs to be led. But I think he knows you're the man for the job. I think he'll accept it."

"Pffft." I quirked a brow. "I think you're underestimating how much we despise one another."

"Well, that'll be up to him. Can you handle being his boss without being an asshole to him? Or at least no more of an asshole than you are to anyone else?"

"Yeah. If he does his job, I wouldn't have a problem with him. Hell, if he leaves me alone now, we won't have an issue. But it's usually him fucking with me. Trying to goad me, you know?"

"So don't bite. He's going to be offended at first. And, at the end of the day, this house would survive just fine without Lenny. It would not survive without you. So if he decides to leave, we'll throw him a party and wish him well. But it will be his decision."

"Is this official? Or is there still some red tape to get through?"

"No. The job is yours, Hayes. We're announcing it the minute you accept. Obviously, I'm not leaving just yet, but I'll start training you over the next few weeks." He pushed to his feet, and I did the same.

He extended an arm, and my hand wrapped around his. "Thank you, Cap. It means a lot to me."

"Do you need to discuss this with Savannah? Or do you need some time to decide if this is what you want?"

"Nope. I've always known what I want. She supports that. She wanted this for me. This firehouse is my home. These guys are my family. I'd be honored to walk in your shoes, and I'll do my best to make you proud."

His lips turned up in the corners, and he clapped me on the shoulder hard. "Already there, son."

He led me out of his office toward the kitchen, where Biscuit stood at the stove, pushing around some eggs in a pan.

"Listen up," Cap said, loud enough to get everyone's attention. The guys all went quiet, and Cap informed them that I'd be taking his position when he retired in a few weeks.

The entire table erupted in cheers and whistles and celebration. I wouldn't have guessed they'd be this excited. No one wanted Cap to retire, including me. But if he weren't the one here leading these guys, I knew I wanted it to be me.

"What's going on in here?" Lenny said. He tugged his coat off and walked into the kitchen, as he'd be starting his shift right when I was leaving.

My gaze locked with Cap's, and then he turned to Lenny and said the words I knew my nemesis would hate. "Rambo here is going to be the next captain of this firehouse. Everyone is just congratulating him now."

Lenny narrowed his gaze, and I saw the anger, but he straightened his face and forced a smile. "Congrats, man. That's great."

I nodded. "Yeah, thank you. I'm going to head out."

I held up my hand as Cap sat there answering all the questions the guys were firing at him about who could move into my current position. I laughed as I made my way down the hallway and found my coat, sliding one arm at a time into the sleeves.

"So, let me guess . . . your wife is some sort of ridiculous fucking social media star, and now you get the job? Way to play fair, Hayes." Lenny was standing there, just as angry as I'd expected him to be.

I reached for my zipper and took my time answering because he wanted to pick a fight right now. He wanted me to get angry, and then he'd play the victim. But he wouldn't get that from me.

Yeah, Savannah's farmhouse renovation had blown up on social media, and she'd gotten millions of views. Everyone in town was talking about how talented she was, and she'd received offers from several design firms in the city, interested in having her come work for them when she wrapped up this project.

She was leaving.

We both knew it.

But I'd stopped thinking about that because I was having a good time with our situation.

I turned, keeping my cool but stepping closer to him. Shoulders set, eyes locked with his. "How about you and I agree that you don't speak about my wife? You don't think about her. You don't talk about her. And we won't have a problem."

He smiled just enough to let me know he was enjoying himself. "Wow. Looks like everyone has a kryptonite, and I sure have found yours."

I took a step back and moved toward the door. I wouldn't engage with this asshole. Today was a good day, and I was not going to let Lenny fucking Davis change that.

"Have a good shift."

I hopped into my truck and tried calling Savvy, but it went to voicemail.

I sent the guys a text.

> I got the job.

RIVER

> Let's fucking go.

193

KING

Are you the new fire captain or a house husband? Your wife had a reporter out at the house earlier today. She's becoming quite the local celebrity.

Fire captain, dickhead.

But I couldn't help but smile at all the good things that were happening for Savannah. She fucking deserved it. She worked hard. And when it came to her passion for design, she didn't have to overthink it. She just got on camera and shared her work, and people fucking loved it.

Loved her.

I understood it.

Because I was crazy about her, too.

NASH

Congrats, brother.

ROMEO

Happy for you. You deserve it. How did Lenny take the news?

As expected. He'll cool down eventually.

KING

Does this mean I can pull all the fire alarms everywhere I go, and I won't get arrested?

I'll be the first one to call you in and do a citizen's arrest. How about you start calling me, Captain.

KING

Captain dick banana?

NASH

Have you told Savvy yet? She was bragging about you today at the house.

KING

Don't get a big head. She wasn't bragging about your . . . dick banana. She was telling the reporter all about your fire skills.

RIVER

Are you putting out a lot of fires at home? 😂

ROMEO

Hey, she loves her husband. No fault there.

KING

Well, she put me in her video today. I bet this one blows up the internet.

NASH

You were pretending to tile the backsplash on camera with your shirt off. I don't see that one going viral.

ROMEO

No one would love to go viral more than King.

KING

Have you seen my six-pack?

No one gives a shit about your six-pack.

KING

I think your sister would disagree. 😉

RIVER

So, when do you take over at the firehouse?

A couple of weeks.

RIVER

Look at you, Hayes. Everything is falling into place for you. You got the job. You got the girl.

KING

You've got the best friends anyone could ask for.

NASH

Six-packs and all.

I hate to interrupt this riveting conversation, but I need to go find my wife and tell her the news.

NASH

We left a half hour ago, and she was heading home. Happy for you, brother.

KING

By the way, are you sure you two want to sell that farmhouse? I think she loves it there, brother. Maybe you should think about keeping it, Captain. 😉

I set my phone on the center console and started driving toward our house. It was our house now, wasn't it? It didn't matter that this relationship wasn't real—she'd been the first person I'd wanted to tell the news to. The first person that I wanted to see.

I didn't know what we were anymore. It had been a few weeks of sleeping in the same bed, making out like teenagers, showering together—we'd traded more orgasms than one could imagine, but we hadn't had sex. And I didn't even know why we were holding back anymore.

Even she'd suggested we just tear off the bandage.

It was me who was afraid to take that step. And it made no fucking sense.

We were both on the same page.

We were having fun.

We knew how this would end. We'd agreed we'd stay friends after our very amicable divorce, but right now, playing house was a lot of fucking fun.

Our attraction was impossible to miss. We wanted each other. We were two consenting adults.

She wanted it.

I wanted it.

And I was done holding back.

It was time for me and my wife to take things to the next level.

22

Savannah

I'd just finished uploading a bunch of content reels for social media, and even I was surprised by the way things had blown up for me with this house. I was making a design name for myself through this project, and I couldn't believe how many people were following along on the journey.

Abe would be so proud.

My chest squeezed at the thought.

I'd offered to make dinner, as Hayes did most of the cooking when he was home. But I knew he'd had a long couple of days at the firehouse, and we'd stopped feeling the need to go out and be seen so much, as everyone in town just believed we were a couple now.

Even Belinda, who had been here today to clean the house, would share how happy it made her to see Hayes and me together. She'd tell me how different he was now and how he never used to smile or speak much before I moved in.

So nothing about it felt fake anymore.

Sheana hadn't dropped her lawsuit, even though Easton had met with her attorney to try to put it to rest. He'd advised us to keep doing exactly what we'd been doing as far as sharing a bed and being affectionate when we were in public, but he didn't think we needed to go overboard otherwise.

And the truth was, we weren't even acting anymore.

When he wasn't working, we were together. He'd come to the farmhouse and hang out while I worked. I always stopped by the firehouse when he worked. We went out with friends, and we did normal things that a regular couple would do.

In fact, this fake relationship would go down in the books as the best relationship I'd ever had.

Hayes and I may have spent years apart, but he was still my best friend. That hadn't changed at all. And the fact that he gave me orgasms every night I spent in his bed only made things all the better.

But we hadn't had sex. And I wasn't the one stopping it. It was he who was holding back. Maybe he thought I'd get too attached if we crossed that final line. And maybe he was right.

But that didn't stop me from thinking about it . . . all the time.

I could separate sex and love.

Hell, I'd had sex with past boyfriends, and I'd been fine to end those relationships.

"Wife!" his deep voice barked as I heard the front door close behind him.

I laughed and turned to see him walk into the kitchen. He'd been growing his hair a little longer than normal, and his scruff looked like he hadn't shaved in the few days since he'd left. His eyes were hard, lips plump, and I couldn't read this mood of his.

I could normally decipher everything that Hayes was feeling.

But something was different.

"What's wrong?" I asked, setting the box of pasta on the counter and moving toward him. "Did something happen?"

"Yeah. You happened."

"*I* happened?" I raised a brow.

"Yeah. You happened." He nodded slowly, his tongue slipping out and moving along his bottom lip. "I got the job. And all I wanted to do was talk to you. See you."

"You got the job!" I squealed and lunged forward, wrapping my arms around his neck. "Does that mean I have to call you captain now?"

He chuckled as his green eyes moved along every inch of my face, like he was trying to memorize each line and curve. "You can call me whatever you want."

"So why do you seem so..." I paused and took a step back as I looked at him. "You seem so tense. Shouldn't we be celebrating?"

"I'm tense because I couldn't wait to get here and tell you."

"And that's a bad thing?"

He huffed out a breath. "I can't sleep in our bed another night without burying myself in you. It's all I fucking think about, Sav. How badly I want you. And I don't want to fuck up this friendship, because I've missed you so much, and I don't know how to deal with all of it. How to deal with the way I feel about you." It came out in a flustered burst of words, like he couldn't hold them in anymore.

I was stunned, because Hayes wasn't big on feelings, nor was he a man that liked to talk things out. So this was—unexpected.

I moved closer, taking his hands in mine. "So tell me, then. How do you feel about me?"

"It's complicated," he said, his gaze locking with mine. "I've been good on my own for a long time, and now you're here, and you're all I see. Maybe it was always you, and that's why nothing else ever worked when you were gone. Maybe you've been what's missing all along."

A lump formed in my throat, making it hard to breathe as I forced my voice to work. "You got your best friend back."

"You're more than my best friend, Sav. I like coming home

to you. I like knowing you're in my bed, even when I'm not there with you. Knowing that you're waiting for me. Knowing that everyone thinks you're mine. Because you are mine, *Savannah Woodson*. And I know you only married me because you had to, and I'm not the guy you'd choose in a different situation because I can't give you all the things that you want. But I fucking love you. And even if you divorce me in a few months, I'd still want to date you."

My jaw hung open, completely stunned by his words. "You want to date me, huh?"

He rolled his eyes. "I just said all that, and that's all you have to say?"

"I feel the same way, Hayes. I think about you when I'm not with you. And of course, I worry that I'm getting too attached, because I don't know how this ends. How we go back to being just friends."

"Why do we have to? Hell, I'd stay married to you if I knew you wanted that. I don't want this to end, Sav. Now that I've got you back, I don't want to let you go. Not now, not in another month, not in another year. I. Want. You. Whatever way I can have you."

A tear rolled down my cheek, and he swiped it away with the pad of his thumb. "You have me. We don't have to figure everything out right now. We did things backward, and that's probably made things confusing, but who cares? At the end of the day, we want to be together."

"What does that mean?"

"I think it means I'd like to date my husband." I laughed, and he tugged me closer. "So how about you stop holding out on me, and we don't overthink it. I love you. I want you. You love me. You want me. That's enough right now."

"Yeah? Because I can't lose you again, Sav."

"I can't lose you either." My voice cracked on the last word. He reached one hand beneath my knees and the other at the base of my neck, and he scooped me into his arms, cradling me against his chest.

"You couldn't lose me if you tried. I'm not going anywhere," he said, as he carried me down the hall.

I'd thought about this moment a million times. I'd imagined Hayes being assertive, being a little wild and controlling, as he'd proven to be up until now when he'd buried his head between my thighs, night after night. When he'd made me cry out his name—over and over.

But this was different. He set me on the bed like I was made of glass. His calloused fingers moved to the hem of my sweater and gently pulled it over my head and tossed it on the floor. He traced his fingers over my lavender lace bra, taking his time.

"I dream about these tits. About this body. About your perfect peach-shaped ass," he whispered, his gaze on mine now. "I've memorized the sounds you make when you come. The way your honey-brown eyes light up when I take you over the edge. The way your lips part when you gasp. The way your skin blushes when I touch you. The way you rub my earlobe when you kiss me, and scrape your nails along my scalp when you want more. I've memorized all of it, Sav."

I sucked in a breath, overwhelmed by his words. "Hayes."

"I know I don't deserve you. I know you want a family and the fairy tale with the white picket fence. And I can't give you that, baby. I'm not the right man for that life. But I can love you with everything I have, for as long as you want me to."

I couldn't breathe. Tears rolled down my cheeks, and I placed a hand on each side of his face. "I don't like white picket fences. I like open fields."

He barked out a laugh, and I chuckled. I'd always known how to make this man laugh, even though he was wound so tight, most people were intimidated by him. I wasn't. I knew who he was.

I knew the man beneath the gruff exterior that he showed everyone else.

"I love you, Hayes Woodson. And this is exactly where I want to be. So don't worry about the future right now. We'll always be okay, because we're Hayes and Sav, right? Peas and carrots." My voice shook. "So how about you just stay true to your word and love me with everything you have today?"

"I can do that."

"Show me how you feel about me," I whispered.

He didn't need to speak a word for me to know that was exactly what he would do. He took his time undressing me, peeling off my jeans and then my bra and panties. Kissing every inch of me as he did so.

My skin burned with desire as his lips moved down my body. I tugged at his sweater, wanting to feel his skin against mine. He pushed to stand and pulled off his sweater, his gaze not leaving mine. I sat forward as I watched him unbutton his jeans before reaching for the zipper. My mouth watered at the sight of him. My heart pounded at the way this strong, powerful man had just been vulnerable with me.

For me.

I loved him.

Loved him in a way I'd never loved anyone.

I wanted that to be enough.

And tonight, it was enough. He moved to his nightstand and opened the drawer.

"Have you ever been with anyone bare?" I asked.

His hand froze on the drawer pull, and he turned to look at me. "Never."

"Me either," I whispered. "But I'm on the pill. And I want to feel you. All of you."

His lips turned up in the corners the slightest bit. "Well, I can't say no to my wife, can I?"

"You haven't yet."

He climbed onto the bed, hovering above me as his long, thick erection rested against my lower stomach. His mouth covered mine, and our tongues tangled as my hands moved to his hair, urging him even closer.

His mouth pulled back, and his lips trailed down my jaw and neck as he nipped at my earlobe. He licked and sucked a trail along my collarbone and down to my chest. His tongue swirled around each hard peak, and I arched into him, spreading my legs wider so that he could settle between my thighs. I squirmed, desperate for more, as his lips found mine again.

"You sure about this?" he asked, his eyes so earnest it nearly broke me. He was so worried about hurting me. Had anyone ever cared for me the way that Hayes did?

"Yes. I want this. I want you."

"You have me, Sav." He shifted, and I felt the tip of his erection tease my entrance. "You've always had me."

I arched off the bed as he pushed forward the slightest bit, and I gasped. "I don't think it's going to fit."

I could hear the panic in my voice, and it was clear that he heard it, too.

"Hey, you're going to be fine."

Before I could process what was happening, he rolled us over and maneuvered me on top, one leg falling on each side, so I was straddling him. "You're going to set the pace. Take me inch by inch, baby. You can do this."

Damn. My husband is one sexy-ass man.

I nodded and sucked in a deep breath as I positioned myself just above him. I wrapped my hand around his erection, and I moved down.

Slowly.

Taking the tip first and then sliding down inch by inch. Gasping as he stretched me wide.

His hands were everywhere, rubbing along my arms, my neck, my hair, soothing and comforting, as I slid down further.

"Such a good fucking girl, taking me all the way in, Sav. I wish you could see how sexy you look when I'm filling you up like this."

I sighed as I took the last of him in, and my head fell back on a gasp as I adjusted to his size. He didn't move at all; he let me take control. His hand fisted my hair, and he forced my head up so I was looking at him.

Needing to know that I was okay.

"Hey," I whispered.

"Hey." That sexy smile stretched across his face. "You okay?"

"I'm really good, actually." My teeth sank into my bottom lip, and I moved up his shaft before sliding back down. Slowly at first. He hissed out a groan as his hands moved to my hips, holding me still for a minute.

"Goddamn, baby. You're fucking perfect. Now ride me until you come all over my cock."

"I love your filthy mouth, husband."

"And I love your tight pussy, wife."

Oh my.

We found our pace, our rhythm. Like we'd done this a million times. We moved together as one.

We weren't in a hurry, savoring every minute of this ecstasy.

My body tingled with anticipation, and his hands and lips were everywhere as my head fell back, and I gripped his thick thighs behind me. I met him thrust for thrust until white lights exploded behind my eyes, and I had no control of my body as I went over the edge.

I cried out his name, and he continued moving my hips as he thrust into me one more time.

And then another.

Then a guttural sound left his throat, and he followed me into oblivion.

23

Hayes

I have news.

RIVER

I think this is the first time in the history of our group text chain that Hayes has started the conversation.

ROMEO

What's up, brother?

I'm in love with my wife.

NASH

Are you just now realizing this?

I'm just now telling you assholes so you stop giving me a hard time. You were right.

KING

Boom. It's about fucking time, you clueless motherfucker.

I'll let that slide because I'm in agreement with you.

ROMEO

Sorry. I blacked out for a minute. Has Hayes been kidnapped? Does someone have his phone?

NASH

LOL. This is a lot to process. How about we ask him something no one else would know to make sure that it's him?

RIVER

What are King's three fears?

Everyone on the planet knows that by now. Bees. Clowns. White vans.

KING

Why the fuck would we go there? How about something that will make it more obvious that it's him?

ROMEO

I can't wait for this.

KING

I didn't sleep at all last night because I'm trying to put a baby in my wife.

I will come over there and put your fucking head in the toilet and flush until your perfectly coifed hair is covered in toilet water and you can't breathe. Do not talk about putting a baby in my sister again, motherfucker.

NASH

It's definitely him.

KING

So glad you're safe, brother. 😂

ROMEO

This is Hayes in love. He's softer already, isn't he?

Nothing soft about me, you dickheads.

RIVER

Well, I'm just happy you owned it, because Easton called this morning, and Sheana and her attorney are apparently in town, questioning locals about you two. So, it's great timing that you're in love with your wife. Be prepared. They'll be coming for us as his best friends.

ROMEO

Let them ask whatever they want. We've got nothing to hide.

NASH

People get crazy when money is involved. We've got your back, brother.

KING

Ride or die.

RIVER

Brothers till the end.

NASH

Loyalty always.

ROMEO

Forever my friend.

I shot a quick text to Savannah to let her know Sheana was in town with her attorney. She replied and said that Easton just phoned her to let her know.

She wasn't worried.

We had nothing to hide.

This may have started out fake, but it was anything but now.

I didn't know what the future held, but I knew that I loved my wife. That I wanted her and only her. I'd even agreed to give her five more letters from the box, and she'd tortured me by reading them aloud in bed after we'd had sex that first night.

And now that I'd had her, I couldn't get enough.

We were like two horny teens having sex for the first time. We didn't leave the house the next day, as we stayed in bed all day. We'd ordered food, which we ate between having sex in the bed and then followed it up with sex in the shower.

I was ravenous when it came to this woman. I'd never been like this, and I was done questioning it.

We were living in the moment.

So anyone who wanted to question our relationship could suck a dick.

I was crazy about her, and I wasn't hiding it.

Nor was I acting.

"Rambo, there are some people here to see you. I sent them to the den area to wait," Santa said. He was the oldest member of our crew, and I fucking loved the dude. He'd been the guy to take me under his wing and train me as a rookie.

"Who is it?"

"It's Abe's gold-digging ex and some guy in a fancy suit. They were trying to ask the guys questions, but I led them to the den and told everyone not to speak to them."

Here we go.

"Thanks." I clapped him on the shoulder and made my way out to the kitchen, just as Savannah walked in. She dropped in sometimes, and the timing couldn't be more perfect.

"Hey, hubs. I know you have one more night here, so I wanted to drop off some tortilla soup for everyone." She set the crock pot on the counter and pushed up onto her tiptoes to kiss me.

Like it was just so natural to do it.

There was an easiness about her that had been missing from my life all the years we'd been apart.

And now that I had it back, I realized how much I needed it.

Needed her.

My hand wrapped around the side of her neck, my thumb

tracing along her jaw. "Sheana and her attorney are here. Santa sent them to the den, so how about you come with me, and we do this together."

I saw the concern in her eyes, and I smiled. It was fine. We were fine.

"I'm sorry they came to your work. That's ridiculous. They can't harass us."

"Hey. I'm not upset. Don't let them get to you. That's what they want. They can ask whatever the fuck they want. We're together. We're happy. That's all that matters."

She nodded as my fingers intertwined with hers, and I led her down one more level to the den. We walked in, and they were both sitting on the couch whispering about something, when they turned to see us there.

"Oh. I didn't expect to see you here, Savannah. You were our next stop. It's fairly easy to find you since you've made the renovations to *my home* so public on your social media," Sheana said, pushing to her feet and walking our way. She extended her arm, and we both just stared at her.

This wasn't a visit we'd wanted, and we owed her nothing. Abe gave her a big, fat check when they divorced because he wanted her out of his life. Sheana wasn't named in the will and didn't attend the funeral or send a card, flowers, nothing.

Savannah moved past her, ignoring her hand, and she and I sat down on the love seat across from where her attorney sat.

"This is my husband's place of work, and there is no reason for you to be here bothering him," Savannah said, her hand still in mine as they rested on her denim-covered thigh.

"Hayes, Savannah, it's nice to meet you. I'm Mike Hardman." He motioned for Sheana to sit back down beside him. It was clear there was no love there between Sheana and Savannah. "We were just in the area and thought we'd pop in and see if you were available for a quick chat. We didn't expect both of you to be here."

"Right," I hissed. "Because you don't want this to be real. But my wife drops by all the time, and today is no different. She brought soup for me and the guys. But our attorney, Easton Chadwick, who you've been in contact with, said that he told you not to try to speak to us without him present. But you came anyway, thinking you'd catch us off guard."

"Well, if you have nothing to hide, why do you need an attorney?" Sheana said, folding her arms over her chest, and Mike shot her a warning look, which I assumed was his way of asking her to stay quiet.

"Because this feels like harassment," Savannah said.

"My client feels she's entitled to that house and the money that you were left, because Abe verbally made a promise to her. And we've learned that there were some interesting stipulations in that will, so we just want to make sure that you've followed the guidelines in the contract that Abe required of you. It's as simple as that. We just have a few questions, and if you have nothing to hide, that shouldn't be a problem," Mike said, and he had this shady-ass smirk on his face.

"It's ironic, really." Savannah looked directly at Sheana. "I mean, you married a man much older than you and stayed all of three months. You fully took advantage of him and left with a lot of money in your pockets. I don't believe for one minute that he made you a verbal promise, because there would be no reason that he didn't include you in the will. But I do know that you never checked in on him toward the end stages of his life. You didn't attend his funeral or even send your condolences. Yet you come back here after he dies and question me? I loved him. He was like a grandfather to me, and you knew that. I spoke to him every damn day. I've known him since I was a little girl. I'm renovating the farmhouse that belonged to Abe and *Lily* because it's what *he wanted*. What *they* wanted. You don't care about him or anything other than cashing in on his death. And that, Sheana, is disgusting."

The room fell silent, and Sheana pushed to her feet.

"Well, guess what? He isn't your grandfather. He owed you nothing. And you clung to him and Lily because your own family is a mess. Your father is a pathetic excuse for a man, from what I've heard. His wife blatantly cheated on him, and everyone in town knew about it. Abe felt sorry for you, and that's just sad. I married him. He was my husband. That house, that money, should be mine. And you ran off and married the first man willing to do it, probably bribing him with a cut of the money. I'll prove it, Savannah, you just wait."

"Sheana." Mike's tone was harsh, and she startled when he pushed to stand and moved toward her. "Stop talking. This isn't helping anyone."

Savannah kept her cool, but my free hand fisted at my side as I pushed to my feet, dropping her hand as she remained on the love seat.

"If you ever fucking speak to my wife that way again, you'll regret it." I reached for Savannah, and she stood. "I signed a prenup, you dumbass. Next time, do your homework. Abe wanted my wife to have that money, and she should do with it what she wants. If he wanted you to have it, he would have named you in the will. This conversation is over. Get the fuck out of my firehouse, or I'll call the police and have you both removed."

Sheana started to speak, and her attorney held up his hand to stop her. "We're leaving. Now."

They left the room, and I turned as Savannah stepped closer, and I wrapped my arms around her. "You okay?"

"Yes. I hate that woman, though. She's got no heart. Abe regretted marrying her immediately, and he was always resentful that she got the money that she did from him. She took advantage of a really good man who was lonely." Her shoulders shook, and I just held her there.

"I know. She's just shooting her shot. They have nothing, and I think her attorney just realized it."

She looked up at me, eyes wet with emotion. "I'm sorry for dragging you into this."

"You didn't drag me into anything. This is exactly where I want to be."

"You're a damn good husband." She smiled. "But since I'm home alone tonight, how about you let me have another letter to read?"

She was relentless about these letters. They made me look like a weak pussy, the way I whined about missing her and begged her to call me.

"Why are you so obsessed with those letters? It's just more of me wondering where you were."

"Not true. There's so much in those letters. I like hearing what was happening in your life after I left."

"Worst year of my life," I admitted. Savannah was gone. River and Romeo were sent away to juvie hall. My sister and I were almost sent to foster care and then lived apart, with me staying with Nash and his father and Saylor staying with River and Kingston's grandparents.

"I know. But it helps me understand what you were going through."

I groaned. "You haven't snooped at all since I've been gone?"

She knew they were in a box on the top shelf in my closet. But that wasn't Savannah's style. She wanted me to give them to her.

She took her wrist and turned mine over before pressing them together. "Peas and carrots, hubby. I wouldn't read them without you being okay with it."

"How'd I get so lucky to marry you?" I whispered against her ear.

"I didn't give you a choice," she said, as she pulled back and smiled up at me. "But maybe this was all part of our journey, huh?"

"Maybe it was, Shortcake."

Because I'd do it all again, if I ended up right here with her.

24

Savannah

"This is so cute," I said, as I stood on a step stool and held one end of the banner as Saylor held the other.

We were throwing Demi a baby shower at Saylor's bookstore, Love Ever After. It was attached to Magnolia Beans, Demi's coffee shop, and Peyton had been carrying over all sorts of pastries and getting things set up. Emerson loved to bake, and she brought in towers with cupcakes and unicorn Krispies. Ruby was placing linens on the tables that we'd rented for people to be able to sit at and eat. Janelle had brought all the florals over from Magnolia Blooms, and Midge had just arrived and was setting up little grilled cheese sandwiches and tomato soup in clear cups along the rectangular table on the back wall.

"Thank you for following my directions about wrapping the sandwiches in the cute wax paper that I ordered with the little boxing gloves on it." Peyton studied the sandwiches and then looked up at Midge.

"Well, you didn't give me much of a choice, did you? And I think pictures on wax paper that you're going to throw away is kind of stupid," Midge snipped. She owned The Golden

Goose diner, and I'd known the woman my entire life. She was hilarious and quirky, and I'd always liked her.

"Hey, it's a baby shower. We don't go to negative town. And we're all about the themes here." Peyton put her hands on her hips.

"We're also all about the love here," Saylor said. We both stood back to admire the banner we'd just hung that read: *Celebrating our little Golden Boy!*

It was a boxer-themed baby shower because Romeo was a fighter, even though he no longer did it professionally.

"These tattoos are hilarious," Ruby said, holding up the temporary tattoos we'd sprinkled on the tables for people to take.

Ride or die. Brothers till the end. Loyalty always. Forever my friend.

"It was Beefcake's idea," Emerson said. "He's always talking about how he's going to get a matching tattoo with all the guys, so he's convinced Romeo and Demi's little guy will get one with him, too."

"That's so cute. I love that they all have the same tattoo." I started placing the floral arrangements that Janelle had dropped off on the center of each table.

"How about you and that hot husband of yours?" Midge asked. "Are you guys going to have kids? I can't see Hayes with a baby. He's such a grump. But he's easy on the eyes."

"My brother would be a fabulous father. He just doesn't know it because he didn't grow up with a father, and he's got it set in his head that he'd fail at it," Saylor said, her gaze locking with mine, as if she knew the topic was something we didn't feel the same about.

"Well, River and I sure aren't in any hurry to have kids. We're enjoying our time together." Ruby bumped me with her shoulder and winked.

"Yeah, that's another grump for you." Midge chuckled.

"River and Hayes would probably get arrested for beating up any boy that had a crush on their daughters."

The thought made me smile.

I could see it. Hayes as a father. But I also didn't believe in forcing your desires on someone else. People should live their lives and be true to who they are. That's what I was determined to do. So I wouldn't convince a man who didn't want children that he'd be a good father. He'd have to decide that on his own.

And we weren't going that far into the future. We were living in the moment.

I'd never hold him back, and he'd never hold me back.

We loved each other too much to do that.

"No doubt about it," Peyton said. "But I'm guessing these two will be knocked up soon." She thrust her thumb at Emerson and Saylor.

"We're planning a wedding and very happy focusing on Cutler right now. But we would like to expand our family, for sure," Emerson said. "But we aren't in a hurry."

"King and I are definitely trying," Saylor said. Her cheeks flamed pink, which made us all laugh.

"Honey, you have nothing to be ashamed of. Sometimes I think that man is going to tear your clothes off in my diner. He's always looking at you like a man obsessed," Midge said, and we all broke out into a fit of laughter.

"How about you?" Ruby asked, directing her question to Peyton. "You and Slade sure seem to be inseparable lately."

"My man is hot as hell. I'd marry him today, but he's working on his sobriety, and I support that. We aren't in any hurry." Peyton placed the pretty blue and peach floral paper plates and napkins on the buffet table.

"That's a good plan," I said. "There's no rush."

"Says the girl who got married a few weeks after she arrived back in town." Midge whistled. "You snatched yourself the most eligible bachelor in Magnolia Falls. The man no one ever thought would get hitched."

"Hey, when you know, you know. Let's all cram into that photo booth and take some pictures before this starts," Ruby said.

Peyton had rented a movie theatre-style photo booth so that we could have fun photo strips to take home.

Midge refused to climb in with us, but the five of us managed to squeeze in there together.

There was a knock on the door, and Emerson hurried over to where Nash was standing, holding the cake she'd made. She couldn't fit it all in her car when she'd come this morning, so she'd had Nash bring it when he dropped off Cutler.

The cake was three tiers high and covered in white icing, with a large dark blue boxing glove made of fondant sitting on top. There were even white fondant laces on the glove. We all gasped at how professional and gorgeous it was.

"Damn, girl. If that whole doctor thing doesn't work out, you could make wedding cakes for a living," Peyton said, as she guided Nash over to the dessert table.

"My Sunny is the best doctor and the best baker and the best mama around," Cutler said, and I didn't miss the way Emerson's hand went to her chest as if she were overwhelmed by the sentiment.

They were the perfect example of a family that was meant to be together. Emerson had shared her story with me about how she'd almost married another man, but thankfully, she'd found out that he'd cheated on her with her best friend. She'd come to Magnolia Falls to hide out for a while, and she'd never left. She'd found her forever here.

Where she'd least expected it.

I felt that same pull with Hayes. Like he was what had been missing in my life for the longest time. Ever since I'd left this town, it had felt like there'd been this hole that I couldn't fill, and somehow he'd filled it.

But not everything good lasted forever, and I knew that better than anyone.

I had job offers in the city that I would have killed for a few months ago. I was having fun with the social media design stuff right now, but that was temporary.

Like my marriage was supposed to be.

My husband wanted to date me, not spend his life with me.

I wanted a family.

He didn't.

I shook it off when Cutler tugged at my hand. "Will you put this tattoo on me, Savvy?"

"Of course, I will. Will you put one on me next?" I asked, as I led him toward the restroom and held the disposable towel under some warm water and then pressed the tattoo to his little arm.

"Oh, man, that would be cool. None of the girls have that tattoo yet. You'll be the first." He chuckled as I held the warm cloth over the tattoo on his arm. "Uncle Hayes told me you were different."

"He did?" I asked, checking my phone timer to see how much longer he had to wait.

"Yep. Remember how I was real sad that I didn't get to go to your wedding?"

"I remember. You know how bad we feel about it, right?"

"That's okay, Savvy. You're my girl now. But Uncle Hayes, he explained it to me," Cutler said, as he looked down and gasped when I peeled back the paper so he could see the words temporarily inked on his arm. His eyes were wide, and he waggled his brows when he looked up at me. "You know, my uncle Hayes never thought he'd get married. But he said he couldn't wait one more second to marry you because you were different. He said you were always different."

"I don't know if that's a good thing." I chuckled as he held the warm cloth over my tattoo.

"Oh, it's a good thing. He told me that you were his best friend, and then you left, and he was real sad, Savvy. And that when he had the chance to marry you when you came back, he was afraid if he waited, you'd leave again. And he said losing you once was terrible." He threw his arms in the air. "Just terrible! But losing you twice would be too much. That's why I wasn't mad anymore. He'd waited for you, and you came back." He smiled up at me with his pink round cheeks and those chocolate eyes that could melt anyone's heart.

And his words melted mine.

"Well, who knew my husband was so sweet?" I said, my voice all tease as I pushed the lump in my throat away.

Cutler's head fell back in laughter. "Nobody calls Uncle Hayes sweet 'cept you and me. I know he loves you and me, Savvy. And we know Uncle Hayes can be sweet, right?"

"Yeah, we do," I said, as I peeled the paper away on my own arm, and we both admired our matching tattoos.

"I like you with my uncle."

"Me, too," I said, tapping the tip of his little nose.

"That means you're my girl forever."

"Yep. You're stuck with me, Beefcake."

I took his little hand in mine, and we made our way back out to the party.

"Okay, Demi's here," Peyton said, as she took one last look around the bookstore. It looked stunning. The dreamiest baby shower I'd seen.

The door opened, and Demi's mother and grandmother walked in beside Demi, and her mouth fell open as she took it all in.

"This is too cute. Look at all the details!" she shouted. "Thank you so much."

"Man, I can't wait to meet my new brother," Cutler said as he squeezed my hand. "I'm going to teach him everything I know."

"I'm sure you will." I smiled down at him.

People started rolling in, and we played games where we guessed the size of Demi's baby bump, filled out cards with advice and encouragement, and laughed and ate and had the best time.

I realized in this moment that I'd missed Magnolia Falls more than I'd ever realized. I'd left this town, my home, under such awful circumstances, and I'd allowed that to block out all the good memories that I'd had growing up here.

I knew how lucky Demi and Romeo's son would be to grow up in Magnolia Falls, surrounded by love and the magic of small-town life.

I'd never felt so confused about my future.

I'd spent the last ten years cursing this town and convincing myself that I hated this place, when, in reality, I loved it here.

Magnolia Falls is home.

I spent the next few hours chatting with everyone and moving from one table to the next. Once all the guests cleared out, we helped Demi get her car loaded with gifts and got the bookstore cleaned up and back to normal.

I hugged the girls goodbye and made my way home.

I turned down our street and saw the house in the distance.

And for whatever reason, I started jogging. My booties clacked against the pavement in a rhythmic sound.

Because suddenly, I couldn't wait to get there.

To him.

Home.

25

Hayes

I'd ordered takeout before lighting a few candles. I wanted to do something nice for her. Something that I should have done weeks ago.

I heard the door open and close, and I hurried to the entryway to meet her.

"Hey," Savannah said, pulling her coat off and looking around curiously. "It smells good in here."

"I ordered us a pizza and a salad."

"Wow. That was sweet. You seem like you're up to something." She chuckled.

"Come on, I have a little surprise for you."

I led her into the kitchen, where a few flickering candles sat on the counter. The box of letters was sitting on the coffee table near the couch, and I'd set the food there with a bottle of wine.

"What's all this?" she asked, heading straight for the box of letters. "You're letting me read them all?"

"The box is yours. You can read them whenever you want." I sat down on the leather couch, and she sat beside me.

"Thank you. I thought you liked torturing me by giving me one every couple of days."

"Well, I wanted to talk to you about something, and these sort of tie into the whole thing."

She ran her fingers along the top of the box and looked up at me. "Is this where you tell me that you don't want to have your wagon hitched to mine anymore, and this is my parting gift?"

Her tone was light and laced with humor, but I also noticed the way her voice shook a little. We were in limbo. I needed to show her that I was trying. I wanted to fight for us, but I didn't know how.

"Nope. This is me telling you that I'm crazy about you. It doesn't matter where you are, because you live here, Sav. Right fucking here." I reached for her hand and placed it over my heart. "I know I'm not good at this. I know I'll probably fuck it all up. But I love you. So giving you these letters is my way of showing you all of me. There's shit in there that I don't want to remember, but maybe it'll show you why I am the way that I am."

She lunged forward and hugged me. My arms came around her, wanting to keep her close. "I love you exactly the way you are, Hayes."

"I know you do. But that's not what I'm talking about."

She pulled back, blinking several times to try to keep the tears at bay. "What are you talking about?"

"I'm talking about a life together. I want you to stay here. With me. I can back you in opening your own business right here in Magnolia Falls."

She didn't speak as I reached into the pocket of my flannel shirt and pulled out the little black box I'd hidden there. I opened it up, and there was a platinum band with a princess-cut diamond sitting on top. Classic and beautiful, just like her.

"Hayes," she whispered. "What is this?"

"That ring you're wearing isn't worthy of you." I chuckled, because we'd gotten it off of Amazon for twenty bucks, because we just needed something to look the part for appearance's sake.

"I want my ring on your finger. I know we want different things, but maybe none of that matters as much as we think it does. Maybe all that matters is you and me. Because when I'm with you, I'm happier than I've ever been. And I know it's selfish to ask you to be with me when someone else can give you everything you want. But I'm a selfish man when it comes to you. I don't want to let you go." My voice shook, which startled me. I wasn't used to being vulnerable, but I knew it was necessary. I didn't want her to move. I didn't want her to leave Magnolia Falls.

I don't want her to leave me.

"Are you doing this because you don't want to lose me as a friend again?" she asked. "Because things are different now. We're not going to lose touch this time. You're stuck with me," she said, as the tears streamed down her pretty face.

"I'm not doing this because I'm afraid we'll lose touch. I'm doing this because I can't live without you. I don't want to be friends who hook up. *I want you to be mine.* I want to grow old with you. I want to watch you chase your dreams and support you every step of the way. I want you, Sav. I want us." I used the pads of my thumbs to swipe the falling tears away. "I want a life with you."

She nodded, blinking a few times as the tears continued to fall. "I thought you never wanted to be married for real? Never wanted forever with anyone?"

"I thought so, too." I shrugged. "But then you came back to town like a blazing wildfire and brought me back to life. Setting my world on fire. And I know without question that we belong together. We might not be perfect, and things might get messy, but I'll fight for us every goddamn day if you take this chance with me."

"I'll take that chance with you," she whispered. "Because you are all I want, Hayes Woodson. You are all I need. You are enough."

Those were words I never thought I'd hear.

She took the fake ring off her finger, and I slipped the new ring on in its place.

There was an elephant in the room that we'd clearly decided not to discuss.

She wanted a family.

I wanted her.

At the end of the day, we'd figure it out.

I hoped that after reading the letters, she'd understand why I was the way that I was.

My intense fear of failing when it came to the people that I loved.

And right now, I just needed her to know that I was all in.

She stared down at her hand and smiled. "It's gorgeous."

"You're gorgeous, Shortcake."

"I need you to know that if it's just you and me for the rest of this lifetime, I can live with that, Hayes. I just needed to know that you felt the same way. *You* are my family, and that's enough for me." Her voice wobbled, and I knew what she was saying.

She'd give up her dream of a family for me.

And I was the selfish prick who was going to let her do it.

Because I loved her that much.

"We don't need to decide anything today. All we need to know is that we're going to make this work. Whatever it takes. And I think it will help if you read the letters." I tucked her long hair behind her ear, and she nodded.

I tugged her down and kissed her hard, my tongue exploring and claiming her the way I was desperate to do.

When I pulled back, she was smiling at me.

"I couldn't wait to get home today, but you surprised me, and I know you hate surprises, so thank you." She sighed. "So, I'm staying in Magnolia Falls. We're really doing this."

"Fuck yeah, we are. If you want this, Sav, I will be by your side. However you need me."

226

She nodded, her teeth sinking into her bottom lip. "I want this."

"That's all I need to hear." I tipped her back and tickled her as her laughter filled the air around us.

When I paused to look at her, a loud rumble came from her stomach, which made her laugh harder.

"Sorry. I didn't eat much at the shower, so I think I'm hungry."

I tugged her forward to sit and reached for a plate, filling it with salad and a slice of pizza. "Start with this. You need to eat, woman. You've been pushing too hard lately."

She'd been working long hours at the house, and she spent hours a day on the phone with the doctors in Dallas, getting things moving for her father.

"I got a call today," she said after she finished chewing. "From Dr. Dorsey."

"What did he say?"

"Dad's approved. He'll go to Dallas as soon as the next spot opens up. It's just a waiting game now. The spot is his." Her eyes were wet with emotion again. "It's his chance at a life."

"Holy shit. That's amazing. You got him in. Why didn't you tell me right away?"

"I was going to, but then you were all mysterious when I walked through the door." She laughed. "And then you sort of proposed again, which was slightly distracting."

"Looks like all good things are happening, huh? Have you told your father yet?"

"Nope. But he'll do it. He knows it's his best shot. I've been sending him material about it every day. Nadia and I are in constant contact, and she's keeping him updated as well. He agreed if he got the spot, he'd take it."

"Does he know you're paying for it?" I asked, because her father was a proud man. I knew he'd struggle with that side of things.

"He knows that his insurance is going to pay a portion, and the program covers a certain amount for each patient selected for the trial. But he knows that doesn't come close to covering it. He's aware that I have my inheritance check coming next week, but he doesn't know the cost of the trial, and honestly, neither do I. So I'm just going to set it all aside, and whatever it costs, we'll make it happen."

"That's a good plan. I did want to talk to you about something."

"What is it?"

"Are you sure you want to sell the farmhouse? I know how much you love that place. And you've made it your own. We could sell this place and keep that one if you want. I want you to be happy, Sav."

"You said it yourself. It's too much house. It's massive and has all that land. I think a family should live there and enjoy it." She smiled.

A family she knows I have no intention of giving her.

"I just know that you've poured your heart into that place," I said. "We don't need the money. I'll be getting a raise with this new position, and this house is paid off."

"I could use the money from the sale of the farmhouse to start my own business. I want to set the inheritance money aside for my father's treatment. The trial could very well use it all up and then some. So the house money could be something I use to get on my feet."

"You don't need to get on your feet. That's what I'm for."

"Hayes." Her eyes were hard now.

"Savannah."

"I'm doing this. I'm fighting for us. But I'm still me. I love my work, and if I'm not going to take those job offers that have come up, I'll need to start my own business here in Magnolia Falls, which is going to cost some money until I get things up and running. The farmhouse will make that all possible.

Renting a space is going to be expensive, and I have no money coming in yet."

I sighed. She was giving it all up for me.

And what the fuck was I doing for her?

"I just want to help you. I want to be a team. You aren't in this alone."

"I know that." She held up her hand and then reached for the box of letters and tapped it. "You've given me more than you realize."

I just hope it will be enough.

We spent the next hour eating and talking about our future.

When she'd gone to the bathroom, I'd texted the guys to ask them to put out some feelers about office space for her downtown.

It was the least I could do.

They'd responded quickly and said they'd be on the lookout and keep me posted.

There was a knock on the door, and I pushed to my feet just as Savannah came back.

"Who could that be? It's late," she said, falling in stride beside me.

I pulled the door open and startled at the sight of her.

Kate fucking Campbell stood on the other side.

And just like that, our perfect evening just got shot to shit.

26

Savannah

"Hey, y'all. Looks like the rumors are true, huh?" Kate "The Devil" Campbell stood on our doorstep.

Have I mentioned I despised this woman?

"What the fuck are you doing here?" Hayes growled, pulling me close and wrapping an arm around my shoulder.

"What? I can't just pop in and see how you're doing?" she asked, her eyes scanning over me from head to toe, before stopping at where my hand sat on my hip as she zeroed in on my ring.

"No. It's late. We haven't talked in years. Why are you here?" He didn't hide his irritation.

"I'm in town to see an old friend, and I ran into Lenny at Whiskey Falls. He told me you two got married, and I thought he was messing with me. I just wanted to see with my own eyes." She smirked before glaring at me. "I knew you always wanted him. You just had to wait it out for a decade."

My hands fisted at my sides. "You know nothing about me. Never have, never will."

"I heard Abe's ex-wife wondered if this marriage was even real. People do desperate things for money all the time. Hayes always did feel sorry for you."

Before I could get a word out, Hayes stepped forward, shifting his shoulder in front of me now, almost as if he were trying to shield me from all that evil. "Listen to me loud and clear, Kate. Savannah is my wife. She's the only woman I've ever truly loved. I just never thought I was worthy of her until she came back and proved me wrong. So you can turn your ass around and get the fuck off our property. You got me?"

Kate sputtered a few times as she took a step back and finally formed a sentence. "He's never going to give you what you need. He has no emotions. You'll stray, just like I did."

"After having him in my bed all these months, straying is the last thing I'd consider doing. But thanks for the concern," I said, thinking of all the hell this woman had put me through. I stepped up beside Hayes, and she was still staring at us with her mouth hanging open. "Hey, Kate?"

"Yes?" she hissed.

"Eat a dick." I slammed the door in her face.

Hayes's head fell back in laughter. "Damn, woman. That was badass."

"It felt pretty damn good." I shrugged. "Why do you think she came here?"

"She comes into town every now and then, from what I've heard. She's a miserable human being, so I'm guessing she and Lenny probably still stay in touch, because they're both pieces of shit. He probably told her I was married, and she had to come back and see it with her own eyes. I'd say we handled that well."

I nodded. "She clearly hasn't changed a bit."

"She never will." He studied me. "You look tired, Shortcake. Let's go to bed."

I nodded, and we stopped in the kitchen to put the food away and made our way to the bedroom. I was too tired to even wash my face tonight.

I'd been staying up late researching everything I could about my father's treatment, and I'd usually get to the farmhouse first thing in the morning to meet the guys and oversee the renovations.

I knew I needed to sleep. Hayes pulled me into his arms, and my head rested against his chest. I loved falling asleep to the sound of his heart beating.

"Thanks for bringing me back to life, Sav," he said, his voice quiet and calming.

"I wish I'd come back and found you sooner."

"It didn't matter when you came. I was always yours." He kissed the top of my head. "I'm going to do my best to be the husband that you deserve."

"You already are," I whispered.

And that was the last thing I remembered before sleep took me.

When I woke up the next morning, I reached for Hayes, but he wasn't there. I found a piece of paper on his pillow, and I sat up, blinking a few times as I adjusted to the sunlight flooding the room.

Sav,
  I knew you needed the sleep, so I didn't wake you. I'm heading to the firehouse. Call me when you wake up. Love you. H

I looked at the time on my phone and hurried out of bed. I was already late, and the guys would have started an hour ago. I brushed my teeth, got dressed, piled my hair into a messy knot on top of my head, and grabbed the box of letters.

I was dying to read them.

When I got to the house, things were well underway. The French doors were being put in, and the landscape in the front yard was getting a nice refresh for curb appeal purposes, which would be important when we listed it. The place was coming together.

I couldn't believe how quickly they'd gotten things done. But the bones had been there; it was all cosmetic. This house would sell for a small fortune once it was decorated and staged. I'd been finding furniture pieces everywhere and storing them in the garage, bringing them in as each room was completed. All the bedrooms were put together because all they'd required was a fresh coat of paint and the staining of the floors. I'd added area rugs, curtains, furniture, and décor. Each room had a unique vibe, and I loved the way this house was coming together.

"Hey, you all right?" Kingston asked as he pulled me in for a hug.

"Yes. I just overslept."

"You look tired, Savvy. You're working too hard," he said, handing me a donut and an iced tea from Magnolia Beans.

"I'm fine."

"Hey, you're here," Nash said. "We'll have these French doors in by lunchtime."

"Great. I'm going to go do some work upstairs in the bedroom. I'll check back in with you guys in a few hours."

"Sounds good." Nash patted my shoulder before one of the guys on his crew called his name.

I took my box and made my way upstairs. I set it on the bed and pulled off the lid. I'd read the first seven letters that he'd written me, and I'd been dying for more.

I pulled out the next one in the box.

I'd wondered what would have happened if these letters had made their way to me all those years ago. Would things have turned out differently? Would we not have lost a decade of time?

I unfolded the notebook paper.

Sav,

It's been two months today since you left. I don't know what the fuck is going on, but I'm struggling. I know I told you that Saylor is staying at the Pierces', and I'm staying with Nash and his dad. Romeo and River are stuck in that shithole of a place, and we can't see them. But they write us letters. So, I'm going to keep writing you until you decide to read one and write me back.

I can't believe my dad wouldn't even step up knowing that Saylor and I were going to be put into foster care. He's got all this money, Sav, and he can't be bothered. Who does that? And my mom, she's staying with that bastard. He put Saylor in the hospital, and she's still with him. She lost her kids, and she's still fucking with him.

I don't know how they can call themselves parents. I hate them for doing this to Saylor. I know she's freaking out because we've never been separated. Thankfully, I get to see her every day, and I know King's looking out for her. I promised her I'll get us our own place as soon as I graduate. I've got to get her out of that house.

Mark my words . . . I will never be selfish like my parents. I'll do whatever it takes to look out for Saylor. How do these assholes get to call themselves parents?

Please tell me that you're okay. I don't understand why you left. I'm dying without you, Sav. You're the only one who truly knows me. I need you. Please call me. Peas and carrots forever, right? I've got the tat to prove it. I miss you.

Hayes

My heart was heavy, because I could feel his pain through his words. I opened the next dozen letters, and every single one asked the same thing. When was I coming home? Why hadn't I called him? I could feel his pain bleeding through the ink on the paper. And then I opened the next one, and I fought the tears as I read his words.

Sav,

It's been five months since we spoke. I'm fucking miserable. I can't sleep because I'm constantly worried about you. Saylor is doing well, and I think living with the Pierces has actually been good for her. She and Pearl have bonded. They garden together every day, and that's been good for her to have some stability. But I worry about you. I heard Ben Jones left his wife and moved to the city with your mom. I'm sure this is awful for you, as you're probably going back and forth between your father's house and your mother's house. What the hell is wrong with our fucking parents, Sav? They're all so fucking selfish, and they don't realize the way it affects us. We're the ones who pay the price for their fucked-up choices.

I swear, Sav, I'm never having kids. Any dumb fuck can have a kid nowadays, and they don't have a clue the damage they could do. I hate my parents for what they did to me and Saylor, and I hate your parents for taking you away from me.

I'm not okay, Sav. It's like someone has cut out half of my heart since you left. I can't talk to Kate, and she's constantly bitching at me for being grumpy. You'd hate me now . . . I'm grumpier than I used to be, which is hard to believe.

I always thought I looked out for you, but the reality is you were the one looking out for me. Talking me down from my anger. Keeping me in check. You're my North Star, Shortcake. And without you, I'm lost.

I'm so fucking lost, Sav. Please call me. I'll come to you wherever you are. I'll borrow a car and come see you. Please. I can't do this life without you. Peas and carrots.

Hayes

Tears ran down my face as I folded up the letter and reached for the next. It was painful to realize that he'd suffered as much as I had. For some reason, I'd imagined him running around with his hot girlfriend and hanging out with the guys, living his best life, while I'd been drowning in chemo appointments with my father and my mother was pregnant and completely focused on her new family. I was just surviving back then, trying to adjust to a life in a big city where I knew no one.

But he'd suffered just like I had.

And it had hardened him in a way, too.

I read a few more letters and reached for one more when there was a knock on the door.

"Come in," I said, swiping my face clean and straightening my features.

"Hey, everything okay?" King asked, his gaze filled with concern as he stood in the doorway.

"Yeah, of course. Just going through some old things from the past."

"Are those the letters from Hayes?" he asked, glancing over his shoulder as if he wanted to make sure no one was listening.

"You know about the letters?"

"Saylor told me she found a box of returned letters to you when they moved into that apartment after high school graduation. Did you know he took custody of her and gave up his football scholarship?"

I nodded. "Yes. He told me."

"He doesn't know I know about the letters, so don't mention it. He'd be embarrassed. He's a proud man, Sav."

I nodded. "I won't say a word."

"I'm impressed he gave them to you. That's huge. He's different with you, you know?"

"What do you mean?"

He leaned against the door frame and studied me. "It's like he's been missing a part of himself all these years, and you were what was missing. We all see the way you've brought him back to life."

A lump formed in my throat. "Thank you. I think we were both missing a piece of ourselves, because he's brought me back to life, too."

"I'm glad you two found your way back to one another," he said, as someone shouted his name. "All right, how about you give us ten minutes and then come check out the French doors?"

"You got it." I smiled as he closed the door, and I opened the next letter.

Sav,

Six fucking months. I can't believe I'm still writing you letters when you don't even open them or read them. But somehow, it helps to write to you. It makes me feel close to you. I want to hate you for leaving me. I try to hate you, Sav, but I can't. Kate's trying to fill your shoes, but I can't talk to her. Not the way I talked to you. And she's a cold person, so I don't trust her. A part of me feels like maybe that's what I deserve. Someone who I can't hurt because sometimes I think she doesn't have actual feelings. I don't have to worry with her. Maybe we deserve each other.

My mother is still with Barry. She's a horrible example for Saylor. She married two men that have shit on her children. How will I ever forgive her or respect her after all that's happened? She had the audacity to tell me that someday I'd understand how difficult it is to do the right thing when I have kids of my own. Sav, I laughed in her face. I'm never having kids. I'm never going to do to anyone what my parents have done to me and Saylor.

Tell me how you're doing. Please. I need to know you're okay. Why won't you speak to me? What did I do to make you leave and cut me out of your life? I know I'm not an easy guy to be around. I get that. But you were the one person who appreciated me for who I am. I miss you. I'm not giving up on you, Sav. Peas and carrots. I've got the tattoo to remind me of you every day. Of us. Please call me.

Hayes

I folded up the paper and set it back in the box, lying back on the bed and processing what I'd read.

He had a lot of anger toward his parents, and rightfully so. He'd needed me, and I hadn't been there.

But we'd found our way back to one another, and I wouldn't allow anything to come between us again.

27

Hayes

"Why are we having my mother over for dinner?" I asked, as I wrapped my arms around Savannah's waist, her back to my chest. I kissed her neck and nipped at her earlobe as she continued stirring the pasta sauce.

This house was no longer just a bachelor pad where I crashed when I was home. She'd changed everything about it. It smelled good. There were colorful pillows on the couch and curtains on the windows.

It was a home now.

The transformation reminded me a little of myself. I was no longer a shell of a man. I was different in a way, too, as if she'd put colorful pillows and curtains on my soul.

Savannah Woodson had a gift for bringing everyone around her to life.

"Because I went over to see her with Saylor, and she mentioned that she hadn't seen you in a while," she said, as she turned in my arms and held the spoon up over her palm to let me sample it.

I groaned as the warm sauce hit my tongue. "Damn, baby. That's delicious."

"Right? It's Lily's recipe," she said, waggling her brows. "She taught me how to make this sauce my freshman year in high school."

"It's damn good. But I liked it better when I came home a few days ago and found you cooking in this same apron with nothing beneath it." I ran the pad of my thumb over her bottom lip.

"Hey, every day can't be Christmas," she said with a sexy-ass smirk on her face. "Your mom's coming over, and I think she might find it startling to find me in an apron with nothing underneath."

"She'd be fine with it." I smirked.

"She misses you. She's not with Barry anymore, and he's been gone for a few months. She made mistakes, but it's not too late to have a relationship with her. You can choose what that looks like, but she deserves a chance, doesn't she?"

"This is because of those damn letters, isn't it?" I grumped.

She'd been reading a few letters every day, and then we'd talk about them. About the year from hell that I'd had all those years ago.

The worst time of my life. A time when I'd invited Kate into my world even more because . . . she was there. And I was a dumbass teenager who was struggling.

"It's because life is about healing, Hayes. And you and me, together, we're healing."

How did she do that? Every fucking time? I couldn't even be mad around this woman because she made too much fucking sense. And she was good to her core, so it was hard to fault her for trying to make my life better.

"I'm healed as long as I have you. That's all that matters to me." It was the fucking truth.

"Hayes."

"Sav." I mimicked her serious tone.

"It's dinner. It's family. You make an effort because sometimes people are worth making an effort for."

I sighed. "I'll do it for you."

"I'm fine with that." She chuckled and turned back around to stir the sauce.

The doorbell rang, and she shot me a look without speaking a word.

Lose the attitude and answer the door.

My wife and I didn't need words. Never had.

I walked toward the entryway and pulled the door open. There was no more snow on the ground in Magnolia Falls, but the evenings were still chilly.

"There's my handsome son," my mother said with a big smile on her face, like we were the best of friends. She held up a pie, and I took it before opening the door wider and inviting her in.

"Hey, Mom. Thanks for coming." I cleared my throat.

"Wow. Look at this place. Savannah has done wonders to warm it up. And it smells so good." She rubbed her hands together and followed me into the kitchen.

"Stella, it's so nice to see you," Savannah said, as she came around the island and wrapped her arms around my mother like she was her favorite person on the planet.

"Thank you so much for the invite."

"Of course. Would you like a glass of wine?"

"I'd love one," Mom said, and I grabbed the bottle of chardonnay that Savannah had set out before handing her a glass.

Savannah was sticking to her tea, and I opened a beer. I needed to take the edge off.

We made some small talk before heading to the table. There were place mats and plates and napkins and flowers all set out. I didn't know when my girl did half the shit that she did. She was always going. Working at the farmhouse, on the phone with doctors about her father's treatment, getting things set up for her new business, cooking for the guys at the firehouse, spending time with the girls, and fixing up our home.

I'd never known anyone who worked as hard as she did. She

gave a lot of herself to the people that she loved, and here I was being annoyed that I had to have dinner with my mother.

"So, Hayes, you're taking over as captain soon, right?"

"Yep. In two weeks."

"That's incredible. Did you ever think you'd be captain of a firehouse? And you're still so young."

I thought it over as I twirled the pasta noodles around my fork. "Not really. I never thought I'd be a firefighter, honestly."

She paused, and her gaze locked with mine. "You always wanted to be a veterinarian when you were young, didn't you?"

I shrugged. "Yeah. I liked animals more than people back then."

Savannah laughed. "You really did. That's why I was surprised you didn't have any animals of your own by now."

"I agree. You used to beg me to get a dog. It went on for years. But your dad was allergic to most animals, and then Barry just refused to consider bringing in another mouth to feed."

I cleared my throat and bit my tongue because the topic still pissed me off. It was a small request. Saylor and I had begged her for a dog, and she'd always had an excuse.

Dad is allergic.

They cost too much money.

They're too much work.

Barry won't allow it.

You can get one when you're older.

"Yep. I remember."

"Well, seeing as you don't have a dog now, you've probably realized that they aren't worth the work. It's so much responsibility to have a dog."

Was she for fucking real? This is why I couldn't talk to this woman. She didn't have a clue about responsibilities.

My gaze locked with Savannah's. Her honey-brown eyes were filled with empathy, urging me not to shut down.

Talk to her.

"That's not the reason I don't have a dog, Mom." I cleared

my throat. "I don't have a dog because I'm a firefighter, and I'm gone three to four nights a week, so it wouldn't be fair to the dog. Being responsible has never been my problem. I'm sure you can agree with that."

The table grew quiet, but when I looked up, I found my wife smiling at me. Her eyes were wet with emotion. She wanted me to open up. She'd felt like I'd done that in the letters I'd written, but the past was in the past, and I had no need to talk about what happened back then. I'd moved on. We all had.

"I know you're a responsible man, Hayes. I know that I fell apart when your father left us when you were young. I know that marrying Barry was a huge mistake. I was not there for you and Saylor when you needed me. And I'm really sorry about that." She took a sip of her wine, and I wanted the conversation to end. I didn't want to go there. I didn't want to dig shit up that couldn't be changed. But she wasn't done. "You didn't want to be a firefighter right out of high school. But you did it for our family."

"I did it for my sister," I said, my tone harsh. "You had us in a home that wasn't safe, Mom. I couldn't leave and go to college, knowing that Saylor wasn't safe. So I did what I needed to do because you didn't step up. You were our mother. It was your job."

Her head tilted to the side, eyes softer than normal, but she didn't look offended. "Yes. It was my job. And I failed. I failed you. I failed Saylor. And honestly, I failed myself. But I've made changes now, and all I can do is move forward. I can't change the past, Hayes. But I can change what I do moving forward, and that's why I'm here."

We'd never talked about what happened all those years ago. Not in all this time. So hearing her say that she'd failed us, failed herself, meant something.

"I appreciate that."

"Do you wish you could go back to college now?" she asked, and she seemed genuinely interested.

"No. I would have hated college." I chuckled, and Savannah covered her smile with her hand. "I actually think being a firefighter was my calling. I love what I do, Mom. I don't love how I got here. I don't love that I had to grow up so fast. But it's made me who I am, and I wouldn't change a thing."

She nodded. "I understand that. And according to John Cook, you're an amazing firefighter. He told me that you see things before anyone else does. Almost like you can predict where the fire is going before it even moves."

I finished chewing my food and quirked a brow. "Where'd you see John?"

"He and Clara came by the bookstore when I was working the other day. She was grabbing a few books, and he and I chatted."

My mother was working for my sister, and they'd been trying to repair their relationship as well.

"That was nice of him to say." I shrugged.

"It's not surprising. You've always been a leader. That's one thing I was always drawn to from the first time I met you when we were kids." Savannah forked some salad and popped it into her mouth.

"Oh, yeah? You liked that I always had an opinion, huh?"

"I liked that you knew who you were, and you never wavered," she said, and my mom looked between us.

"I always thought you two would end up together. You had a connection even when you were little kids. Like you spoke your own language." My mother smiled and shook her head.

"It's what I missed most when we were apart," Savannah said. "That I just had someone who understood me. Who had my back."

"Yeah, Hayes spiraled after you left." My mother's words had me turning to look at her like she had three heads.

"What are you talking about? I wasn't even living with you."

"I know. But you changed. You lost your safe place, I guess. It wasn't because you were staying with Nash and his father.

It wasn't because you were separated from Saylor. It wasn't because Romeo and River were sent away. It was because Savvy was your person, and she was gone."

"I think it was a mix of everything," I said.

"I don't think so." My mother reached for her wine. "Because you came back home eventually. Saylor came back home with you. Romeo and River came home. But you were never the same, Hayes. And I think it's because you two were one another's person, and you lost that. So, you spent time with that evil woman, Kate. Even agreeing to marry her, which was shocking. And I was just happy that she showed her true colors before you made that mistake."

I took a long pull from my beer. I didn't think my mother had even been paying attention back then. It surprised me to hear how observant she'd been. "You never liked Kate, that much I knew."

"No one liked Kate," Savannah said, shaking her head in disgust, and the table erupted in laughter.

"I didn't like Kate because I recognized the pattern." My mother folded her hands together, and her gaze locked with mine. "I'd been with two horrible men in my life because I thought I didn't deserve better. That's why I let you take custody of Saylor and get your own apartment when you were just eighteen."

"What are you talking about?" I asked. I'd been surprised all those years ago that she hadn't fought me on taking my sister out of that house.

"I knew you were making sacrifices, but I allowed it because I was in too deep. But I didn't want that for Saylor, and I knew you would provide a better home for her. A safer home for her. And I believe that you were with Kate because it's all you knew. You only knew ugliness and instability when it came to relationships. And Savannah had been the one person who'd always been a light in your life. And after she left, I worried so much about you."

Fuck me.

I glanced over at my wife. Her eyes were wet with emotion. She just smiled at me and then held up her wrist. "Peas and carrots, baby."

I chuckled. "How about we update these tattoos and call it what it is?"

"You two really were peas and carrots."

"What would you call it now?" Savannah asked me.

"Something I never thought I believed in. But it's the truth. We're soul mates. It didn't matter if we were living near or far. We belonged together."

"Soul mates does sound slightly more romantic than peas and carrots." She chuckled.

My mother sighed. "Life is a journey. And the road is bumpy. But if you're willing to go through the rough spots, you can come out okay on the other side."

I looked over at her. "Is that what you did? You came out on the other side?"

"I hope so. I know it took me a long time to get here, but I'm trying. And I'd like to have a relationship with my son and my daughter-in-law, so I'm going to just keep trying." She shrugged.

I thought over her words. I never thought I would want to work on things with my mother. I was used to being let down by people. Used to putting up my walls.

But maybe Savannah was right.

Maybe some people deserved a second chance.

"Keep trying, Mom. It's nice to see this side of you."

Savannah clapped her hands together in celebration.

My mother laughed, and I rolled my eyes.

But I was happy, even if I pretended to be annoyed.

I never planned on being happy.

But here I was.

Living it.

28

Savannah

"You know he hates surprises, right?" River asked, as he stood in the kitchen of the farmhouse that was nearly finished being renovated.

"Yep. But he'll like this one, even if he pretends he doesn't," I said, as I guided everyone toward the kitchen. "He'll be here in five minutes."

I could not wait for Hayes to get here. He'd never cared for his birthday when he was growing up. Usually, he and I would go hang out on the lake. We'd take the old canoe that we'd found and tried to clean up, and we'd float around in the water. His mother didn't do the birthday thing, and he'd never cared.

He always made my birthday special, just like he did when it was Saylor's birthday.

But he didn't want to celebrate his own.

So, I'd get him his favorite cupcake and sing him "Happy Birthday," and we'd just sit in the boat and talk and laugh.

But this was our first birthday together as a married couple.

I still couldn't wrap my head around the fact that we were a married couple.

For real.

It wasn't fake. It wasn't for any other reason than we just wanted to be together.

"This was really sweet of you to do for my brother," Saylor said, wrapping an arm over my shoulder.

"He'll pretend to hate it, but we both know he'll love every second."

"And you have his surprise in the laundry room?" Ruby chuckled, as she walked up.

"Yep. I can't wait to give it to him."

"I just came out of there. He's going to freak out," Demi said, as she had both hands on her lower back and arched her baby bump toward us.

"I hope so," I said. "And you look like you're ready to burst."

"Any day now." She shrugged.

"I'm glad you were able to waddle your big belly here for the party. And I love that you've softened the big grump, Sav," Peyton said to her bestie, before turning her attention back to me. "I never even knew Hayes had teeth before Savvy came back to town."

That had everyone laughing, and I looked down at my phone to see the Nest camera go off. "He's here."

I had all the lights off, and everyone grew quiet as I heard the door open and close.

"Sav? You here?"

"Yep. I'm in the kitchen," I called out, trying to contain my excitement.

"Why is it so dark?" he grumped, just as he flipped on the lights to see us all gathered there.

"Surprise!" we shouted, and he just stood there, gaping at us.

"I hate surprises," he said, with a sexy smirk on his face as he moved toward me. He tugged me close, lifting me off the floor as my legs came around his waist. "But I love everything you do."

Everyone whistled and cheered, and he set me back down on my feet as he made his way around the group, getting hugs and birthday wishes from all his friends.

We had the French doors open to the backyard, and the cool breeze floated around us. There were acres of green grass and large trees, and it looked like something you'd see in a painting.

Everyone started eating and drinking, and Hayes made his way over to me and wrapped his arms around me, my back pressed to his chest. "Thank you, baby."

I turned in his arms. "You aren't going to tell me how much you hate this?"

"I mean. I'd rather have you all alone, but I can deal with it for a few hours."

"You know we can hear you, right?" Kingston barked out a laugh.

"We all know the dude hates parties," Nash said as Cutler stood beside him.

"Not anymore. My uncle likes anything our girl Savvy does." Cutler beamed. He was wearing a white tee, a black leather coat, and a pair of jeans and boots. His hair was slicked back with extra gel, and he was the cutest little guy I'd ever laid eyes on.

"You know it, little dude." Hayes high-fived him.

Ruby got the music going, and everyone was having a great time and walking around to see the latest updates at the farmhouse.

"Hey, I want to give you your gift. Will you come with me?" I asked, as I took his hand and led him toward the laundry room.

"Oh, does this mean I get to drop to my knees and bury my face between your thighs in the laundry room? Because I'm here for it," he whispered in my ear.

"No. We're having a party. But I'm all yours later."

"Fine. What do you have hiding in here?" I opened the door and pulled him inside.

He just stood there, gaping at the cute chocolate lab sitting in the corner of the room. He was a puppy, so he was still pretty small, but he was adorable.

"Sav," he whispered. "What is this?"

"It's a dog." I laughed and shook my head.

"I know it's a dog. But why is he wearing a blue bow and sitting in the laundry room?"

"He's your birthday gift."

"No fucking way. You got me a dog?"

"Yep." I turned to face him. "You have a wife now, so when you're away at the firehouse, he'll be with me. He'll be part of our little family. Saylor already agreed to watch him when I go to Dallas and you have a shift."

His gaze softened, and there was so much emotion there.

"Our family," he whispered.

The pup trotted over and started biting at Hayes's ankles as he bounced around, squeaking and attempting to bark.

"He's fucking cute." He bent down before completely sitting on the floor as the little guy climbed all over him.

"Happy Birthday, hubby. Cheers to many more." I went to sit beside him, and we stayed there for a few minutes before Saylor knocked on the door.

"Hey, we all want to meet your new addition," she called out through the door.

We made our way out, and everyone took turns holding our new pup, but Hayes kept taking him back, keeping him close.

He loved him already, and I hoped that this was the start of many more birthdays together that he allowed me to celebrate him.

His mom walked over and petted the top of the pup's head, as her son kept him in his arms.

"You got your dog after all," she said. "What are you going to name him?"

Hayes glanced over at me and then down at Cutler, who was standing there beside him. "Beefcake and I were just talking. Tell them what you came up with."

"Ride or die for all of my uncles is Rod, like my dad and

Uncle King's business. But a puppy needs a better name, so we think we should call him Roddy!" Cutler shouted.

"I like it." I petted the little pup on the back of his neck.

"Stop cradling him like a baby," River said. "He's a dog."

I laughed because seeing this big guy cradling this little puppy made my chest squeeze.

"Shhhh . . . he just fell asleep," Hayes hissed at River, and everyone laughed.

After a few minutes, I convinced him to put the dog in his crate so we could have cake.

We sang "Happy Birthday," and Hayes pretended to be annoyed, but I saw beneath it all. He loved it. The way his eyes kept finding mine, and his lips turned up just the slightest bit in the corners as everyone sang.

"Thank you," he said, and he blew out the candles before tugging them out of the cake and licking the icing off the bottom.

"You didn't make a wish," Kingston said.

"I forgot you two and your dandelions are all about the wishes. Maybe mine already came true." Hayes winked at me.

"Oh, boy." Demi's voice broke through the loud celebration, and we all turned to look at her. She stared down at the floor, which was covered in water. "I think we're having a baby, Golden Boy."

"Holy motherfucking shit balls!" Romeo shouted, running his hands all over her body like she'd just been in an accident. "Baby. Are you hurt?"

Emerson was at her side as Cutler gaped up at Romeo. "Uncle Ro must be scared because he just said all the bad words."

"It's all right. He's just nervous," Nash said, clapping Romeo on the shoulder.

"She's okay, but we need to get to the hospital right now. Looks like we're having a baby tonight," Emerson said.

"I'm so sorry about the mess." Demi stared down at the

water on the floor. "You guys stay here. I don't want to ruin the party. We'll keep you posted."

"Oh, hell no." Hayes picked up the cake and told King to grab the plates. "We're all going to the hospital. We can eat cake there."

Demi tried to argue that we didn't need to leave, but no one was having it. It was like a three-ring circus, the way everyone was frantically grabbing their keys.

"What about Roddy?" Cutler asked, and Hayes and I came to a stop as we glanced at him in his crate.

"I've got him. You go. I can hang here or bring him to your house and sit with him there," Stella said, surprising everyone.

Hayes leaned over and kissed her cheek. "Thanks, Mom. There's a key under the orange flowerpot in the backyard. You can take him to our house, and we'll meet you back there after."

"You got it. Go." She hurried us out the door.

Peyton and Slade had insisted on driving Romeo's truck, and Emerson piled in with them just in case there were any issues, and we all followed them to the hospital like a large caravan.

"I can't believe they're having a baby tonight. On your birthday," I said, as we drove the short distance to the hospital.

"You think she's okay? She's not due for another week, right? Is that fine? Is it too early?" he asked, and I could hear the fear in his voice.

This was his family.

Our family.

"It's totally fine to be a few days early. The doctor told her last week it could happen any time."

"All right. That's good. I can't believe how calm she was. Romeo looked like he was about to pass out."

I chuckled as we pulled into the parking spot beside Kingston and Saylor. Ruby and River parked on the other side of us, and Nash and Cutler were beside them.

We all hustled into the waiting room, and Kingston had the cake and the plates with him.

Peyton and Slade were there, pacing in the waiting room. Slade was on the phone with his parents, and Peyton filled us in. "They took her back. Emerson went with them."

"Pops, is my Sunny going to deliver my new brother?" Cutler asked.

"I don't think she's going to deliver the baby, but I think she'll be in there with them to make sure everything goes well."

"Well, we've got more than one reason to eat cake, don't we?" Kingston asked, as he started cutting the cake on the little table in the waiting room and handing out slices.

"Looks like you're getting all the gifts this year, huh?" Saylor asked, settling on the other side of her brother as they both held their cake plates.

"Yeah. This is going to be hard to top." Hayes looked up at me, his gaze locked with mine.

"We both always wanted a dog, and now our pups can be besties," Saylor said with a laugh. "And having a new baby to celebrate, who happens to be born on your birthday, if they get that baby out before midnight. That's pretty special."

"No doubt about it. Life has been full of surprises lately." He set his plate down and patted his lap for me to come sit. "This one being the best of all."

Saylor smiled. "I'm happy for you guys. And it's nice to see Mom spending time with you."

We sat there talking, everyone anxious to hear about the baby, as the next few hours passed. Hayes had called his mom, and the puppy was doing just fine.

Nash had tried to take Cutler home, but he'd wanted to stay, and he'd fallen asleep on his father's lap in the waiting room.

It was just before midnight when Romeo came out, with Emerson right beside him. Demi's mom and dad were sitting with Romeo's mother and grandmother, as Peyton and Slade paced around the waiting room, and we all moved to our feet.

"She did it. We've got a healthy little boy. He's seven pounds, eight ounces and already looks like a little brute," Romeo said, and we all took turns hugging him.

"Congrats, brother." Hayes pulled him in for a hug, and everyone took turns doing the same.

"Does this little boy have a name yet?" Peyton asked.

Romeo looked between his friends. "Well, considering he was born on this guy's birthday, it only seemed fitting to carry on that legacy. But Demi and I wanted him to have a piece of the men who have been my brothers every step of the way."

"Did you name him Roddy like the puppy?" Cutler asked, rubbing his eyes as his father held him on his hip.

"No." Romeo chuckled and turned to look at my husband. "His name is Hayes Pierce Heart Knight. The little dude's got a lot to live up to. He's got your namesake in there, too, Beefcake. And I'm hoping you'll come up with a cool handle for him when he gets a little older."

They'd found a way to incorporate all the guys as well as Cutler.

"I'll come up with the best handle for my brother, Uncle Ro."

I looked over at Hayes, and he was standing there staring at Romeo, eyes wet with emotion, and I could see he was overwhelmed by the gesture.

"Honored that my son will share a birthday and a name with you, Hayes. If he's half the man you are, he'll be winning at life." Romeo pulled him in for one more hug before telling us all we could go down to the nursery and take a quick peek before we headed home.

And that's exactly what we did.

My husband just stared through the glass at that little boy, like he'd never seen anything more perfect.

29

Hayes

"Hey, thanks for hopping on a call with me," Easton said, as we sat at the kitchen table staring at the computer screen.

"Of course. Is everything okay?" Savannah asked.

"Yeah. I'd say it's damn good. That's why I wanted to do this face-to-face, even if it's just through a computer screen." He chuckled. "Sheana's case is closed, and she won't be pursuing a lawsuit any longer."

"That's great. What happened?" I asked.

"She's being sued by her current husband's family. He's some billionaire out of Texas, and he's in his late eighties."

"Sheana is married?" Savannah asked with a gasp. "I didn't know that."

"Neither did I. Apparently, she met the man while he was living in an elderly facility where she was working, and she claims they fell in love. They got married a few weeks ago. His family knew nothing about it and filed a complaint because the man is worth a whole lot more money than Abe was. She's making quite the name for herself with this scam, and at the moment, she's got more to deal with than she can handle. She probably figured out that claiming he made a verbal promise to her wasn't going to hold up in a court of law. Especially considering Abe had recently updated his will, and she hadn't been included. So, they dropped the suit against you."

"That's such good news. I hope someone stops her from doing this. It's so disgusting that she preys on the elderly," my wife said as Roddy walked over and tried to jump up for my attention.

"Sounds like she preys on rich and elderly men, in particular. There's a special place in hell for people who do that." I shrugged.

"Agreed. And her attorney has his work cut out for him trying to defend her now, with her current track record. There was one man in between Abe and husband number three, as well, and she inherited a couple hundred thousand from him after he passed away."

"That's horrible." Savannah patted Roddy on the head before looking back at the screen. "Thank you for handling everything for us."

"Of course. I heard Romeo and Demi had their baby a few days ago. Named him after you, Hayes?" Easton asked.

"Yeah. I still can't wrap my head around it. He's a cute little guy. Looks like the perfect mix of his parents." I nodded.

I held him the day after he was born. This little bundle of dark hair and dark eyes, so innocent and perfect. I remembered the day that Cutler was born like it was yesterday. I realized in that moment that I already had two kids that I loved as if they were my own. I wasn't going to get out of caring just because I didn't have a child of my own.

I already cared.

Too fucking much.

But I was learning that it was okay to care. You just had to keep showing up and being there.

I could do that.

"Congrats to all of you. Exciting times out in Magnolia

Falls. Hopefully, I'll see you guys when I come to visit next. We'll have to grab dinner."

"Yes. We'd love that. Thank you for everything, Easton." Savannah waved at the camera as we said our goodbyes.

She turned to look at me after she closed her computer. "You've got to leave for your shift soon, don't you, Captain?"

It was my first official shift as captain, and I was ready. "I do. Three days away from my wife is not going to be okay with me."

She climbed onto my lap, straddling me. Her fingers tangled in my hair as she leaned down and kissed me. "Maybe Roddy and I will come visit you if things are slow."

"I'll be counting on it." I tugged her down one last time and kissed her hard.

I couldn't be late for my first day as captain, and it killed me to slide her off my lap and push to my feet.

"You're meeting Sabrina out at the farmhouse, right?"

"Yep." She nodded. The house was done, and Savannah was determined to get it listed as soon as possible to have the money to open her new business. We hadn't found any office space downtown that would work yet, so we were still looking. All the money from Abe had been put into a savings account for her father's treatment. "We're getting it on the market today."

"I told you that we have plenty of money in savings when you find the right spot for the business."

"And I told you that I don't want to take that money out of your savings."

"*Our savings*. We're married, remember?"

"Ahhh . . . how can I forget when my husband is the fire captain? Do you have any idea how sexy you are?" She smiled up at me, and my hands landed on her perfectly round ass.

"You're killing me. I don't want to leave." I thrust toward her, letting her know how turned on I was. I wanted her to know the effect she had on me.

"Go to work, hubby. I'll stop by later."

"Just know that there's no rush to sell the farmhouse." I kissed the tip of her nose.

"I have to do things my own way sometimes, Hayes. I don't have income right now. I've put away all the money from Abe for my father, aside from the little bit I've used to live on up until now. The farmhouse is the money I want to use to start my interior design business."

"I know, baby. But you love that house. I don't want you to rush into selling it."

"Go to work, Captain." She raised a brow and smiled.

"All right. Call me later."

"I will."

I grabbed my keys and glanced over one last time to see my wife, who was now holding Roddy in her arms and cuddling him.

My family.

My whole world.

I shook it off and made it to the firehouse in less than five minutes, parking in the spot marked *Captain*.

I would have more flexibility in my schedule now, but I didn't want to do anything too drastic until I got the hang of things.

It was quiet when I walked in, and I dropped my duffle in the hallway and turned toward the kitchen, when everyone shouted all at once.

"Captain Rambo is here!"

I rolled my eyes and pulled up the chair at the head of the table where Cap had always sat. They'd decorated it like a throne, so I assumed that's where they wanted me.

Bones set a plate in front of me with about half a dozen giant pancakes stacked on top of one another with syrup and sprinkles all over it.

"You trying to kill me with all this sugar?" I teased.

"Oh, now that he's married, he's eating healthy and taking care of himself," Beebs said with a cocky smirk.

"Hey, I've got to stay fit for my woman." I winked, and the whole table erupted in laughter.

Beebs and Bones were cooking today, and Stinky, Stretch, Biscuit, and Santa piled food onto their plates and dove in.

"So what happens with Lenny? He didn't show up for his shift the last three days. What's up with that?" Santa asked. The man was always direct and asked the questions that everyone wanted to know but didn't always have the balls to ask.

"I don't know. He said he was sick. I've got to give him the benefit of the doubt right now. We'll see how it plays out. Either way, we're okay."

"You deserve this job, Hayes," Santa said, catching me by surprise. He didn't do the emotional shit, and it's why we'd always gotten along so well. "You were made for it."

I finished chewing and nodded. "Thank you. I'll do my best to fill Cap's shoes any way I can. But nothing changes here, all right? We're a team. I'm still going to be out there fighting fires right alongside you. I'm just going to be overseeing everything to make sure it runs smoothly."

"You mean you're going to fight fires and be a babysitter, too?" Biscuit said over a mouthful of pancakes.

"Dude. You just spit sprinkles all over me," Stretch groaned, which made everyone laugh some more.

"And he gets the king's suite now." Beebs took the chair beside me and waggled his brows.

"The king's suite? That's a bit dramatic, yeah?" I asked.

I would get my own room, and I would be lying if I said that wasn't a perk I was looking forward to. My own shower and a bed that wasn't next to a bunch of chatty-ass dudes.

"It means you can have the little missus stay over." Bones jumped to his feet when I flicked a piece of pancake at him, and his head fell back in a fit of laughter.

"All right, I'm going to head down to the office, and I'll call you guys in one at a time to go over the schedule for the month. So, if you have any requests, get them together before I call you in. I want to get this nailed down today."

"Damn. Santa was right. You are made for this," Beebs said, keeping his tone light, but his eyes were telling a different story.

He wasn't being funny. It was heartfelt, and it meant something to him. Meant something to me.

I nodded and grabbed my bag before jogging downstairs and dropping it in my new room. It wasn't fancy or big, but it was my own space, and I appreciated it.

The next few hours were filled with paperwork and meetings.

While the guys were doing some training drills, I was placing orders to keep our house well-stocked.

We had dinner, and I was surprised how quickly the day got away from me.

When the siren sounded, we were on our way to a small fire out at the Conley ranch. It didn't require all of us there, but you just never knew what you were walking into, so we all loaded up.

It had been a quick turnaround, and we were in and out of there in less than a half hour.

"Hey, congrats. You popped your captain cherry," Santa teased, as we made our way back to the firehouse.

I sent Savannah a text when we'd been on our way out to the fire, because I knew she worried, and I'd sent her one when we were heading back to the firehouse.

I had someone who counted on me now, and I didn't need her staying up late worrying.

"See you in the morning, Rambo," a few of the guys called out, and I held my hand up as I made my way downstairs and they made their way upstairs.

When I pushed the door open, I couldn't help but smile. My wife was sitting on my bed wearing a tan trench coat, golden-brown hair falling in waves around her shoulders.

"Hey. What are you doing here?"

"Well, I got a call from Dr. Dorsey. They have an opening. They want my dad there tomorrow morning. I booked my ticket to Dallas first thing in the morning. Roddy is going to stay with King and Saylor until you get off your shift. So I wanted to see you before I left."

I ran a hand over my face. "I wanted to go with you."

"It's your first week as captain. You need to be here. I'll be gone for a week or two, and I'll get Dad settled. He and Nadia flew out tonight. It'll give them time to get situated before he starts treatment tomorrow." She pushed to her feet and reached for the belt of her jacket, tugging it open to expose her gorgeous body in nothing but a pink lace bra and matching panties.

"Jesus. You're so fucking beautiful, baby." I tugged her closer, my arms coming around her as my hand slid down her back, and I gave her ass a squeeze.

"I've always wanted to have sex with you in a fire truck," she purred.

I tipped her chin up, eyes locking with mine. "Not a fucking chance that I'm letting any of those assholes see you naked. But how about I have my way with you in my new room? Does that work?"

"Ahhh . . . the captain's quarters," she said, stepping back and moving slowly across my room as she picked up my fire hat and put it on her head. She let the trench coat drop to the floor in a heap as her teeth sank into her bottom lip. She walked toward me and plucked the suspenders off my shoulders before unbuttoning my pants and tugging down my briefs. They fell to the floor, and she pushed me back onto the bed. She dropped to her knees and unlaced my boots, one at a time, and slipped them off and tossed them to the side.

"Goddamn, woman. You're too fucking sexy for your own good."

"That's because I can't stop thinking about my husband out there fighting fires and protecting people." She stood up, placed one leg on each side of me, and straddled me.

I reached for her hips and glided her lace-covered pussy right over my erection. Up and down, as she groaned. She found her rhythm and continued grinding along my shaft, teasing me, as I reached for her bra and tugged the cups to the side. My mouth came over one of her perfect tits first. I sucked and took turns moving from one to the next.

I was so turned on I couldn't see straight. Her breaths were coming hard and fast, and my hands moved between us as I found the lace waistband and tore it easily from her body. She gasped when I pulled the fabric between her legs and held it up for her to see. "I'll buy you a new pair, but I need to be inside you right now."

She smiled as she pushed up, lining the tip of my dick with her entrance, and slid down slowly.

"I needed this, Hayes," she whispered. "Needed you."

I buried myself inside her and groaned as I gripped her hips and slid her up and down my cock—and nothing had ever felt so fucking good.

"I'm yours, baby. Ride me until you come all over my dick."

"I intend to, Captain," she purred, as I tugged her mouth down to mine.

I drove into her over and over, needing to feel every inch of her.

Because Savannah Woodson had all of me.

She was mine, and I was hers.

And I wouldn't have it any other way.

30

Savannah

I'd arrived in Dallas and Ubered to the hospital where my father would be receiving treatment for the next few months. He and Nadia had already settled into the apartment, which was attached to the hospital. My father would stay at the hospital, and Nadia and I would stay in the apartment.

I'd paid the deposit for him to start treatment, and I was damn proud to be able to do this for him.

It was the first time in many years that I felt hopeful about my father's future.

There had been this dark cloud over us for many years.

I'd researched and educated myself every chance I had.

And it had led me here.

Nadia pulled me into her arms and hugged me. "Thanks for making this happen, sweetheart."

I smiled, trying hard not to cry, because that would just make my father worry.

But it was emotional being here.

Hope was a dangerous thing. It allowed you to believe, to imagine that things could be better—all while knowing there were no guarantees.

I said a silent thank-you to Abe and Lily for making this possible. For giving my father the chance, something he wouldn't have had without this money.

"Of course. I'm so happy they got you settled in the apartment already."

"Well, they wanted to start first thing this morning, so coming last night was a good decision," she said. "I've taken a leave from work, and we've got enough saved to cover rent on the apartment back home for a couple of months."

"And I have this money set aside to help with all the expenses while he's here. So whatever you need, I've got you, okay?" I sure as hell hoped I was right. I knew this could go up into the seven-figure price range, so I was afraid to make promises that I couldn't keep. But I also had time, because everything did not have to be paid upfront, and we could make payments when all was said and done if needed.

"Thank you, my love. Come meet Dr. Dorsey and see your dad."

I'd had several Zoom meetings with Dr. Dorsey, but I was looking forward to meeting him in person.

"There's my girl," my father said, and I startled a bit at how thin he looked. He'd hidden it well on our FaceTime calls. I straightened my face and gave him a hug.

"Hey, Daddy-O. I'm so glad you're here."

"Me, too," he said, his voice definitely making it clear how exhausted he was.

"It's nice to meet you in person, Savannah. I'm Grant Dorsey." He extended a hand, and I hugged him instead. This man had helped make this happen, and I'd be forever grateful. He chuckled and patted my shoulder.

I guessed he was in his late forties, with salt-and-pepper hair and kind eyes.

"Thank you for making this happen," I said.

"Don't thank me. You did all the hard work. He's a perfect

candidate, and you went through all the hoops necessary to be here." He'd agreed to keep the financial situation discreet, as my father would never be okay with me using all of Abe's inheritance to cover the cost of the treatment. Nadia, Dr. Dorsey, and I had agreed to keep the details to ourselves. Insurance would pay a small portion, the pharmaceutical company had agreed to cover some expenses, and I'd cover the rest.

There was nothing I wouldn't do to save my father's life.

At the end of the day, what else was there?

The people you loved were all that mattered.

So, we got down to business. They took endless amounts of blood and ran a ton of tests over the next few days.

They wanted every single number to be current so we'd know exactly where he was starting.

Where his baseline was.

We'd been warned that things would get worse before they got better.

Dad would be here at the hospital, while Nadia and I spent our days here and our evenings at the apartment.

Nadia would stay here full-time with my father, and I'd be going back and forth to Magnolia Falls. Hayes wanted to come here, and eventually, we'd figure out a schedule, but right now, he was needed at home, and I was needed here.

I was going to roll with whatever we needed to do.

The next few days had been grueling on my father. I'd fallen into a routine, and I appreciated that I could be here to see how all of this worked. That I could ask questions and take notes and be present when my father needed me most.

I couldn't believe that it was already dark again. The days were blurring together. I hadn't eaten much today, as my focus had been on my father.

Nadia went to the cafeteria to get us a couple of sandwiches, and Dr. Dorsey pulled me outside of the room to tell me the plan for the next several days.

There were a few more tests to do, and then they'd start his treatment slowly to see how he responded, and then amp it up if all went well.

"I'm going to have the nurse draw your blood this week, as well," he said as he jotted something down on his chart.

"*My* blood?"

He looked up, surprised by the question. "You're his only child. It's not common that children of parents with the disease have it, but as a safety precaution, I'd like to rule it out."

A heaviness settled on my chest at his words, because the thought of both of us having this disease was terrifying. My life had finally just started. I needed to be strong for my father. Be there for Hayes. Start my business.

Live my life.

But I nodded, because what choice did I have? "Okay, sure."

Nadia and I ate as my father started to doze off. She wanted to stay late and read her book beside him, so she gave me the keys to the apartment, as I wanted to call Hayes and speak to him. I'd missed several calls from him today, and we were used to speaking throughout the day.

"Hey, beautiful," he said, as he answered the phone. "How did today go?"

"It went pretty well. He's almost done with all the tests, and they may start treatment tomorrow or the next day. He looks really thin, and he's definitely tired," I said, as I walked across the enclosed bridgeway to the small apartments where family members stayed.

"Well, that's why he's there. He needs the treatment, and they can help him. Don't let the way he looks now scare you. It's just proof that he's where he needs to be."

I pushed inside the apartment, dropping to sit on the small pull-out couch. I nodded, even though he couldn't see me. "I know."

The words sounded like more of a squeak than actual words.

My phone rang while I was holding it to my ear, and I saw the FaceTime call from Hayes and answered it.

"Hey," I whispered, swiping at the tears.

"Hey, Sav." He smiled, and I didn't miss the concern in his eyes. "I wanted to see your face. You're not alone, okay? I'm here."

"I know you are. I'm fine. I just—he looks bad. And I miss you."

"I miss you, too. He's going to be okay. He's fighting the fight. That's all you can ask for."

Something about seeing his face calmed me. "Yeah. You're right. It was just a long day."

"I can come there tomorrow if you want me to."

"No. Don't be silly. You're back at the firehouse tomorrow. I'm fine. This is going to go on for months, and I'll come home once he finds his rhythm with the treatment. You can come back with me soon. But right now, there's not much to do." I didn't mention that they'd run my blood work, as well, because I knew Hayes well enough to know that he'd freak out and worry. "Tell me how Roddy's doing."

I wasn't worried.

I felt fine.

It wasn't a disease that was passed on genetically.

It was rare and highly unlikely that two family members would get it.

"All right. You just let me know. If you need me, I'm there." He leaned back on the couch and pulled our pup up so I could see him through the phone. "This guy chewed up my work boot a little bit, but otherwise, he's doing well. He misses his mama."

"Awww . . . how does he look bigger when I've only been gone a few days?"

"Maybe because he eats like a goddamn horse. He devours his food. And then he begs for more." Hayes laughed, and I finally felt relaxed for the first time today. "Tell me how your last shift went as captain. It's been so busy here; I feel like you haven't gotten to fill me in on everything." I leaned back on the couch as he told me about the calls they'd gone on and how proud he was of his guys.

"Have you heard anything from Lenny?" I asked.

"Nope. But I got a call from a firehouse in Thomas Creek asking about him. So obviously, he's got his feelers out." Hayes ran a hand down his face. "I get it. I'd have done the same thing."

"What did you tell the guy inquiring about him?"

"I said he was a hell of firefighter, because he can be when he wants to be. He's an asshole, but I'm not going to stand in the way of him getting a job."

"You're a good man, Hayes Woodson."

"Thank you, baby. I miss your face. I miss your body. I miss your laugh."

I chuckled. "I miss you, too. So much it hurts. Does Roddy like playing with Dandelion?"

"Yeah, we stopped by there today. He definitely likes playing with Dandelion. Winnie was over there, too, and the three of them ran wild in the yard." Dandelion was King and Saylor's dog, and Winnie was Emerson and Nash's dog.

"That sounds fun."

"You're exhausted, baby. Get some sleep," he said, and I could see the concern on his face.

"Okay. I love you."

"I love you, too. You sure you're okay?"

"Yeah. I'm good, I promise. Get some sleep."

"All right. If you need me, just call."

"Always," I said.

I ended the call and made my way to the shower. I let the water run down my head. I felt better already after talking to Hayes. He was right. My dad was exactly where he needed to be. And even though I missed my husband, I was exactly where I needed to be, too.

Before I climbed into bed, I went to my suitcase and pulled

out another letter. I'd brought a few with me, because for whatever reason, they made me feel close to my husband. The pile of unread letters was getting smaller. It was almost like reading a favorite book where you didn't want to finish too soon, but you couldn't wait to read more.

Hey Sav,

Seven fucking months and no word from you. Saylor and I have been back home for a couple of weeks now, and, of course, Barry is here. My mother is acting like we're one big happy family. It's completely crazy. This dude hurt Saylor, and now we have to fucking live here.

I could handle it if you were living next door, Sav. Or even if you just replied to one letter. One fucking letter. I'm losing my mind. I miss you. So much has happened, and I can't wrap my head around it.

All these firsts that I realized I'd never done without you. My first birthday without you has come and gone. I was sure you'd call. Kate threw a party for me at her parents' house, and she didn't invite the guys. So none of the people there were my friends. I hated every minute. I snuck out early and met the guys at Romeo's dad's gym, and we drank a beer in the alley. Kate didn't talk to me for three days, and I can't say I minded it.

But she's back now. She just shows up, you know? Maybe she's one of the few people who can actually tolerate me.

Anyway, I had my first football game. I realized it was the first time I've ever played a game where you weren't there. I've got my guys there, cheering for me. Kate's a cheerleader, so she's out there shouting her ass off for me. Yet I feel completely alone because you aren't here.

Fuck. I'm probably just tired. Tired of writing letters that you'll never read. I had some scouts out at the game,

*but I don't know if college is even an option anymore.
We'd always planned to go together. Do you remember
that, Sav? That plan that we had?*

*Truth is, I can't leave Saylor in this house alone. I'm
going to need to figure something out if I want to leave
Magnolia Falls to go to school.*

*The one person I usually talk this shit over with is you.
The only person I trust when it comes to these types of
decisions. Kate thinks college is stupid, so there you go.*

*Maybe college is stupid. I just don't know that I care
about much anymore.*

*I hope you read this. I still look at my stupid green pea
on my wrist and wonder if you remember what it means?*

*Because I'm starting to think you'll never come back,
and I'll never hear from you again.*

I'll keep trying for a while more.

*You've got to give me something, Sav. I'm losing faith
in us. Maybe I'm fucking crazy, and we never were as
close as I thought we were.*

Hayes

My heart ached as two tears dripped down onto the inked
paper, making it bleed. I couldn't wait to wrap my arms around
my husband and tell him that there hadn't been one day after I
left Magnolia Falls that I hadn't thought of him.

Because it was the truth.

* * *

The next few days were intense. We'd been here for ten days,
and my father had started treatment. He was dealing with all
the side effects that we were familiar with when it came to
chemo. This was a more intensive type of chemo, and he was
vomiting and nauseous and feeling horrible.

Nadia and I took turns sitting with him, and I went for walks outside when I needed to get out of the hospital. Emotionally, it was taxing watching someone you love suffer in this way.

I'd prepared for it, but it was definitely taking a toll.

I had just finished reading another chapter of my father's novel. He would sleep while I would read, and then we'd discuss it. It was a beautiful story, and I'd been emotional from the first page when I realized that he'd written a book about a young girl that fit me in every single description, but that he called fiction. Her relationship with her father mimicked ours, and it was about the young girl's journey to finding her own happiness. I set the book down and rubbed my eyes as he woke briefly and growled at me for water. He was moody and angry at the world, and that was fair. They'd prepared us for everything, which was why Nadia and I took shifts and breaks.

I missed Hayes. I missed my life in Magnolia Falls.

My phone rang, and it was my husband. He always knew when I was thinking of him.

We'd fallen asleep with our phones beside us the last few nights, because I'd had a hard time sleeping lately.

"Hey, baby," he said, his voice sounding tired.

"Are you feeling okay?" I held the phone up so I could see his handsome face. Three of the guys had gotten the stomach flu, and he'd had to pick up extra shifts to cover for them.

He was handling his new position as captain like a rock star. I hated that I wasn't there to bring him soup and support him right now.

"Yeah. Just tired. We had a bunch of calls today, and it's been busy."

"I wish I was there to bring you dinner."

"I wish I was there to sleep next to you. I don't sleep well without you," he said, his voice strained and exhausted.

We were both struggling being apart, and I knew I was here for at least another week.

He wasn't sleeping well.

And neither was I.

It was amazing that we'd lived for a decade apart, and now we couldn't handle being apart for a week or two.

I hated how much I needed him now.

"Me either."

"Even when I'm away at the firehouse, I just like knowing you're in our bed."

"Me, too."

"Tell me how your dad is doing today."

I spent the next twenty minutes filling him in on everything, and then I heard the siren go off in the background.

"I've got a call, baby. I'll phone you later or in the morning if it's too late."

"Okay. Be safe. I love you."

"I love you."

I ended the call and made my way back to my father's room just as Dr. Dorsey was coming out after his evening rounds.

"How's he doing?"

"He's miserable, but that's to be expected, and it's a good sign because it's doing what it's supposed to." He cleared his throat. "Do you have a minute to come to my office?"

My stomach dipped. Why would he need me to come to his office?

Was there more going on than I knew?

Was the cost of treatment more than we'd expected?

My mind raced as I followed him down the hallway to his office.

He closed the door and motioned for me to take the chair across from his desk as he made his way to the other side and sat down.

He typed something on his keyboard and woke up his monitor, and I folded my hands together nervously.

"Is it bad?"

"Well, I guess that depends on if you were expecting this."

"Expecting this? Does he have complications?" I rubbed my temples with my fingers because I just didn't know how much more I could handle.

"He doesn't have any complications, Savannah. At least not more than we'd prepared for, and I've already shared all of that with you."

"Okay. Then what is this about?" I asked, leaning forward, unable to hide the concern from my voice.

"This is about you." He turned his computer screen toward me. "You're pregnant."

You're pregnant?

"Pregnant? That's impossible. I'm on the pill. I can't be pregnant." Panic erupted beneath my skin. My heart raced. My palms were suddenly ridiculously sweaty.

"Well, one can get pregnant while taking birth control. Do you ever miss a day here and there? That increases your chances."

I hadn't been great about it with all that had been going on.

"I've probably missed a day or two. Or three," I winced.

Oh, my god. What had I done?

"Well, I'm not a gynecologist, but I can read the blood work. Your HCG levels are unusually high."

"What does that mean?"

"I can't say for certain, but it typically means that there's a chance you're having twins."

"Twins?" I could barely get the word out.

More than one baby.

Two babies.

There was a chance I was pregnant with two babies.

By a man who didn't want children.

My head was spinning. I couldn't process this.

I'd made a mess of everything.

Dr. Dorsey came around the desk and bent down to look

at me. "The good news is that your blood work was perfect otherwise."

Somehow that doesn't feel like a relief.

Because I may have just lost the love of my life.

And I didn't know how to do life without him anymore.

31

Hayes

"It's a great property. Nothing else like it in Magnolia Falls," Nash said as we walked toward the barn.

Cutler ran ahead of us, with Winnie and Roddy chasing after him. It was good to see him running around and feeling well, and the asthma medication they were using now seemed to be working much better. He hadn't had any attacks in months, but it didn't hurt that Emerson was a pediatrician and was on top of it.

"Yeah. I know how much Savannah loves it out here, so I wanted to get your perspective."

"Well, it's going to sell fast because it's unique. If you aren't sure about letting it go, you need to get it off the market right away." Nash paused in front of the barn and chuckled when he glanced over to see Cutler rolling on the ground with Roddy and Winnie watching them like she couldn't figure out what they were doing.

"He's feeling good, huh? No issues lately?"

"No. He's been great. But you just never know, so I'm always prepared, and I've always got his inhaler on me, just in case. It can sneak up out of nowhere."

I knew how seriously he and Emerson took it. We were all

aware of the asthma action plan and always had the inhaler on us when we had Cutler at our homes.

"Damn, brother. Parenting is not for the weak at heart."

"No question about that. You don't think you and Savvy will have kids? She's pretty fucking amazing with Cutler." He pulled the door to the barn open.

"She knows that kids aren't in my future. It kills me, though, because I know she wants a family, and all I can offer her is me and Roddy." I chuckled, but the truth of it was always with me.

When I closed my eyes, I could see us living here at the farmhouse. And every time I allowed myself a moment to think of the future, I would see a bunch of kids running around on the property. There were animals, laughter, and love.

Things I'd never had.

Things my sister never had.

"I just don't think I'm cut out for it. And failing at it—it's too risky, you know?" I scratched the back of my neck as I followed him into the barn.

"You really don't get it, do you?" he asked, as we both turned slowly to take in the enormous wide-open space in the barn.

"Don't get what?" I asked, as Cutler and the dogs came barreling inside.

"Hey, Cutler," Nash called out, and the little dude came running over.

"This place is cool, Pops."

"It is." Nash chuckled. "Tell Uncle Hayes here who I say is the best dad I know, next to Gramps."

Cutler smiled up at me. "Uncle Hayes is the best dad you know. When things are bad, you always think of him, and you know it's going to be okay."

What in the actual fuck are they talking about?

"You got it, kiddo." Nash ran a hand over the top of Cutler's head before he took off running after Winnie and Roddy again.

"Not sure what you mean, but I think we both know that I had a shit example when it comes to being a parent. Unfortunately, I know the risks. I know the outcome when you fuck up."

"Dude. Look in the fucking mirror. You don't fuck up. Ever. You're the most reliable guy I know. You may hate most of the world, but when you love, you love harder than anyone. You're fiercely protective of the people you care about, and it's impossible to miss." He knocked on the wall inside the barn and ran his hand down the wood. "This is well built."

I was still reeling from what he'd said, but I didn't respond. There was no question that I loved my people fiercely, but I was also a grumpy bastard who took a long time to warm up to people. I'd always been cautious when it came to trusting others.

"All right. I'm going to spell it out for you, because you clearly don't see it."

"I can't wait," I grumped, as I folded my arms over my chest.

"The reason I tell Cutler that you're the best dad I know is because you taught me at a young age what it meant to be a parent. From the minute I found out that I was going to be a father, and the moment I realized I'd be doing it alone, I thought of you. Of the way that you sacrificed and did whatever you needed to do to protect Saylor. You gave up a football scholarship, a chance to go away to college and be a selfish asshole. You got an apartment at eighteen years old so you could take custody of your younger sister. You gave her the life that you wanted her to have. You worked your ass off to make sure she went to college and had all the experiences you thought she deserved."

I blew out a breath. That was just what you did for the people you loved. "Your point?"

"My point is, you love to say you'd never have children because you wouldn't be cut out for fatherhood. But the truth is, you've already been a father. And a damn good one. Saylor always says that you were more of a parent to her than a brother. She attributes her success to the fact that you sacrificed so much to give her the future you thought she deserved. Your sister is kicking ass because she had a parent who supported her. And I've got news for you, asshole. That was not your mom or dad. That was all you. So, I think it's about time you owned the fact that you're already a father. And a damn good one."

His words hit me hard. Right in the center of my chest. That feeling like you might be having a heart attack and then you realize it's just all these feelings stirring around inside you.

"I should kick you right in the dick for pulling this shit this early in the morning," I hissed before clearing my throat to push the lump away.

He chuckled. "It's noon. You're a good man, Hayes Woodson. Just accept it and stop fighting it. That's why Savvy won't push you into anything you don't want."

"Why is that, ole wise one?"

"Because she's just like you. She's willing to sacrifice her own dreams for the man she loves. We all see it." He shrugged. "It's not my place to tell you what to do, brother. She wants to be with you, and you want to be with her. But missing out on something magical because you're afraid—that's not who you are. You're the bravest bastard I know."

"Fuck you," I said dryly, which made him laugh harder.

"Let it go, Hayes. The past. The anger. The fear that you're going to be left or fail or whatever the hell it is that you're wrestling with. You're better than that. You aren't your father. You aren't your mother. You're a really good guy. A man I trust my son with implicitly." He clapped me on the shoulder. "We all see it. Cutler sees it. Your wife fucking sees it. The only one who doesn't see it is you. So open your fucking eyes and let yourself be happy. You've earned it."

I looked away, trying hard to push away all these feelings that were swirling around. I pinched the bridge of my nose to stop my eyes from watering. "Damn seasonal allergies."

He barked out a laugh. "Yeah. I know, brother."

"All right. Let me process this."

"Wow. You're actually admitting to having feelings? This is a huge breakthrough." He quirked a brow.

"If you tell anyone, I'll make King shave your balls in your sleep." I moved toward the window to look at the clear view of the water in the distance.

This place would be fucking perfect for what I had in mind.

"It's our secret." He took out his tape measure and started measuring different areas and jotting down the measurements on his iPad.

"We've got to bring Sunny out here, Pops. She'll love it." Cutler turned to look at me. "Hey, Uncle Hayes, did you hear that I want to start calling my Sunny mama?"

I couldn't help but smile, because this kid was so honest and open; it always made my chest squeeze. "I think she'd love that. Did you tell her yet?"

"Nope. I'm going to tell her on Mother's Day. It's going to be the bestest surprise ever." He jumped up and then ran toward a pile of hay in the far-right corner and dove into it.

I turned to Nash. "Emerson was exactly what was missing from both of your lives, huh? She was everything you guys needed. And you and Cutler were exactly that for her."

"You know, for a grumpy fucker, you sure have a lot of insight into everything that's going on around you."

"Whatever. I just pay attention when it's the people I care about," I said, pulling out my phone and taking a picture of Cutler in the hay. I'd show it to Savannah later when I told her my plan. Right now, she had enough on her plate.

She'd been a little distant the last few days. She was quieter on our calls. Normally, I'd be concerned, but Ruby reminded me that Savannah was dealing with a lot, being there with her father.

My plan was to handle everything here. Come up with a plan to keep the farmhouse that I knew she loved.

279

Savannah was so busy doing everything for everyone, and she wasn't used to anyone doing the same for her.

I was here to show her that I was that man.

"You think it's doable?" I asked Nash as he jotted down a few more measurements.

"Everything is doable, brother. It's going to cost you, but King and I will get it done for as reasonable as possible—and at the end of the day, it's a really good investment." He looked up at me and smirked. "Investing in your future is a good thing. It means you see one. And this would be an awfully big house for just two people. But you already know that, don't you?"

I flipped him the bird, turning to look out the window at the big open space.

A perfect place to raise a family.

And for the first time in my life, I actually saw it.

Wanted it.

But I had a lot to figure out before I presented my plan to my wife.

So today was the start of putting this plan into action.

"Uncle Hayes!" Cutler shouted. "Come jump in the hay with me."

"Isn't hay an allergen? Should he be doing that?" I asked Nash.

He chuckled. "Those are the words of a father, you dicknugget. But Cutler isn't afraid of living and having fun. So go jump in the hay with the boy. I've got the inhaler in my pocket if we need it."

"Damn. Emerson is rubbing off on you. You aren't nearly as uptight as you used to be," I said with a laugh as I jogged over to my favorite little dude and dove into the hay beside him.

Laughter filled the barn, and I lay there on my back, imagining a life I'd never thought possible.

And it was right here in my grasp.

Or maybe I was already living it, and all of these other things would just make it all the better.

I pulled out my phone and sent a text to Savannah.

Thinking of you. I love you, baby.

I could see that she read the text, and the three little dots moved around the screen before they disappeared.

No message came through.

She was definitely struggling, and I wasn't sure what to do about it.

I dialed our realtor's number and sat forward.

"This is Sabrina," she said on the other end of the phone.

"Hey, Sabrina. It's Hayes Woodson. Can you meet me at my place in an hour? I think I want to list our other home, and I'd like to talk to you about the farmhouse."

"I was just about to call you and Savannah. We got an offer, and it's a good one," she said, and she didn't hide her excitement.

"Can you do me a favor?" I asked. I'd known her since elementary school, as we'd grown up together.

"Of course. Name it."

"Don't send the offer to my wife just yet. She's got a lot on her plate with her father, and I have a few things I'd like to discuss when I see you this afternoon."

"Okay. You've got forty-eight hours to respond to the offer, so we've got time."

I was grateful that Savannah had added me as a decision-maker on the listing, even though my name wasn't on the title of the home. As her husband, she'd asked that I be the first contact, knowing that things would be busy in Dallas.

And I had no intention of accepting this offer.

Because we weren't selling this home.

We were going to start our lives here.

I didn't have a doubt in my mind.

Everything was suddenly crystal clear.

32

Savannah

"So, there are two heartbeats. You're definitely having twins," Dr. Shaker said. Dr. Dorsey had referred me to a friend of his that had an office up the street as a courtesy.

My eyes watered because the thought of two little humans growing in my belly was overwhelming in the best way—and in the worst way. My emotions were all over the place.

I was thrilled about being a mother.

But I was terrified that it would cost me the man that I loved.

I hadn't wanted to talk to him about it until I knew for sure. Until I knew this wasn't a mistake.

I was pregnant.

With twins.

I was going to be a mother, and Hayes was going to be a father.

A tear ran down my cheek, and Dr. Shaker reached for a tissue and handed it to me as she cleaned the gel off of my stomach. I wasn't showing yet, but from the side view, it looked like I'd had a hearty lunch. No one would even know I was pregnant yet, but here we were.

I'd just heard two heartbeats.

I sat up and pulled my shirt down. "Thank you for doing this."

"Of course. I know it's a lot to process finding out you aren't carrying just one baby, you're carrying two. I'm sure it's hard being away from home and finding out the news, but Dr. Dorsey called in a favor, and I was happy to help," she said. She was tall with long red hair and absolutely stunning. I felt a comfort with her immediately.

"My husband and I haven't been married that long, so we weren't exactly planning on this," I said. "Being on the pill, I didn't even think it was possible."

She nodded, no judgment in her gaze. "It's a lot. Have you told him yet?"

"No. I'd rather do it in person." I fidgeted with my hands. I didn't even know how to have the conversation, if I were being honest. He'd made his feelings known upfront. I'd said I was okay with it. And now I was changing everything up.

Forcing his hand.

"Here you go," she said, as she handed me more tissue, and I realized tears were streaming down my face. "It's okay to be scared. It's okay to have doubts. Everything you are feeling is perfectly normal."

"Thank you." A sob escaped my throat. "I'm just—surprised and confused. I'm really happy, and then I feel guilty that I'm happy because this wasn't the plan. And then I'm really sad and then I feel guilty for being sad because I'm pregnant. With two babies. How lucky am I?" I blubbered. "But I came here to focus on my father, and I just got married, and we weren't planning on having kids, and now I'm pregnant with twins?"

I was full-on crying now in the examination room of a doctor I'd never met before today. And she did the most unexpected thing of all.

She wrapped her arms around me and hugged me.

"All of these feelings are valid, Savannah. It's okay to be happy and sad and confused and elated all at the same time. But I'm going to give you a little advice that my grandmother

283

told me a long time ago, and trust me when I tell you she is the wisest woman I know."

"Okay," I whimpered as she pulled back and sat down on her rolling stool, sliding right in front of me.

"There is no perfect time to be pregnant or to have a child. You'll never feel like you have enough money or enough time to bring a baby into the world. But that doesn't mean it isn't the right time, and I speak from experience."

"You have children?"

"I have three. Ask me how many kids I planned on having?"

"Two?" I swiped at the tears running down my cheeks.

"Nope. Zero. I wanted to start my practice and focus on my career. My husband was okay with it, as he's also a doctor, and though he'd wanted children, it wasn't a deal-breaker when I'd told him that I didn't."

I couldn't wrap my head around that. "You deliver babies all day, and you didn't want kids of your own?"

"Nope. I just never felt that need to have them, but I love bringing them into the world and watching that joy on my patients' faces." She shrugged. "And then I got pregnant with Benson. I was very overwhelmed when I first found out. I cried and wrestled with what to do. My husband supported me either way. But then I felt my son move, and I don't know, something changed in me. But I had a partner who supported me, one that I supported, as well. And we talked it out and decided that we would have one child. One would be plenty." She chuckled.

I laughed and shook my head. "And now you have three?"

"Yeah. Who knew I could love those little hellions so much?" She shook her head. "Three boys. And they're loud and messy and—fabulous. My point is, it's okay to be scared. It doesn't mean it's a bad thing. You have choices and options, and I'm happy to discuss them if you want."

"Thank you. I know that I want these babies. I just hope it's not at the expense of my marriage."

There. I said it.

That was my fear.

"Well, there's only one way to find out. Sometimes people surprise you, you know?"

"I know that Hayes loves me. He'd do anything for me. But I don't want him to do anything at the expense of his own happiness." My words broke on a sob again, and I was mortified that I was such a mess.

"You'll talk to him when you're ready. And I'm here if you need me." She wheeled back and pushed to her feet before scribbling her phone number down on the back of a business card. "You call me anytime, okay?"

"Thank you. I really appreciate you seeing me." I swiped at my face with the tissue before blowing my nose.

"Of course. We'll talk soon." She handed me the photos from the ultrasound and waved before leaving the room.

I stared down at the photos and pushed to my feet.

When I stepped onto the elevator, I pulled out my phone and saw the missed calls from Hayes, Saylor, Demi, Ruby, Peyton, and Emerson. My heart raced because though we all talked often, they didn't usually all call at the same time.

I went to listen to the voice messages just as a text message popped up.

HOT HUSBAND

> Hey. I've called a few times. I didn't want you to hear from anyone else. There was a fire early this morning, and I fell through some flooring that was no longer stable. I'm fine. I'm just getting checked out at the hospital, but you know how everyone likes to make things a big deal. How's your father this morning?

As soon as I was out of the building, I dropped onto a park bench to sit and pulled out my phone to FaceTime him. It had been days since I'd seen his face. I'd been avoiding it because I knew seeing him would make me more emotional.

He picked up immediately. His face was covered in soot, and his hair was disheveled.

"Hey, beautiful. I missed your face." His smile was forced, and a nurse handed him a bottle of water.

I nodded, fighting the tears that just wanted to fall all day long lately. No words came at first, and I just tried to breathe in and out and keep it together.

"Everything is okay, Sav. I'm right here."

"You're okay?" I squeaked and shook my head frantically. "I need you to be okay."

"I feel completely fine. A few scratches and bruises. Nothing that won't heal in a few days," he said.

"And a fractured wrist and a concussion," the nurse grumbled beside him.

"You have a broken wrist and a concussion?" I gasped and held my hand over my eyes to hide the tears.

It was all too much lately.

My father's suffering. My unexpected pregnancy with twins. And now Hayes was hurt, too?

In what universe did any of this feel fair?

"Savannah." His voice was hard, pulling me from my meltdown, and I dragged my hand away from my eyes.

"Yes."

"I. Am. Fine." He glared to the side, and I assumed it was aimed at the nurse. "Any time someone hits their head, they say it's a concussion."

I heard the nurse disagree with him, and he asked her if she could give him a moment.

"Baby. Look at me. I'm worried about you. I'm not worried about me. I'm a firefighter. Sometimes we fall. This wasn't that bad. I've had worse. But you've been distant. I know this is a lot with your dad, and I understand that, but we're a team. And when you're hurting, I'm hurting. So you need to talk to me and tell me what the fuck is going on."

I shook my head and shrugged. "It's just been a lot. I'm sorry I worried you. That's the last thing I want to do."

"I don't give a shit about that. I don't want you to shut me out. We did that a decade ago, and we lost a lot of time. That's not who we are. If you need me there, I will get my shifts covered. If you want to come home for a break, I will book you a flight right fucking now. But you have to tell me what you need." His green eyes locked with mine through the phone.

What do I need?

"I need time," I said, just above a whisper.

"Time? What the fuck does that even mean? Time for what? You're already in a different state. You aren't telling me shit about what's going on. And you need time?"

I nodded. Because it was the truth. I wasn't ready to tell him. Because telling him meant everything could end right now. And I couldn't handle that.

"I love you," I said, because he needed to hear it.

I needed to say it.

I loved him so much, and I was struggling to embrace what was happening in my life. Struggling to admit that I wanted something that he didn't. Something that could tear us apart.

"Okay. I'll give you time." He shrugged. "I'm here when you want to tell me what's going on."

We just stared at one another for the longest time before he spoke again. "I love you."

"I love you, too." I ended the call and sat on the park bench for the next hour, and I let it all out. I didn't care who saw me. And as people walked by, some didn't react, others gave me an empathetic smile, and a few looked annoyed to see a grown woman blubbering on a park bench in the middle of the day in a busy city.

And I didn't give two shits.

Because sometimes you just needed to let it all out.

I'd held everything in for such a long time, and ever since I'd come back to Magnolia Falls and found my way back to Hayes, I'd started facing all the things I'd been running from.

Finding Hayes had opened me up.

And now I was feeling everything.

I glanced down at the little carrot tattoo on my wrist and ran my thumb over it.

He was the other half of my soul, and I couldn't do life without him.

So I'd have to come clean.

And I'd just hope like hell that he'd pick me.

That he'd pick us.

I reached for my phone and looked at the group chat with the girls, who had all told me about the fire and Hayes being in the hospital. They'd been checking in daily, and I appreciated this new friendship I'd found with these amazing women.

> I just talked to him. Is he telling me the truth? Is he okay?

SAYLOR

> I'm here at the hospital, and he's fine. I promise. He's a stubborn ass and wants to go back to work, but they want him to take a few days off.

RUBY

> Who falls through a floor during a blazing fire and wants to go back to work? Stubborn is an understatement. But River is there at the hospital, as well,

and he said he seems good. I'll go check on him as soon as I get off work.

DEMI

Romeo said he's much more concerned about you than he is about himself. Are you doing okay? I miss you.

PEYTON

Of course, he misses his hot wife. What's not to miss? When are you coming home?

EMERSON

I just got to the hospital. He'll be okay in a few days. A fractured wrist and a mild concussion. He'll be good as new before you know it. How are you doing? I know it's a lot with your father, Savvy. It's never easy to watch someone you love suffer. We are here for you if you need us.

Saylor sent a picture of herself and Emerson smiling at the hospital, with a grumpy Hayes flipping the bird at the camera behind them. I chuckled. I knew he was okay by the look on his face.

RUBY

We need a bottomless mimosa brunch really bad. And now Demi can join in with us.

DEMI

I'm nursing. We don't need baby Hayes to be on the bubbly. He's already the gassiest baby on the planet.

I haven't gotten my daily photo of baby Hayes today. Please send one soon. Those photos get me through most days.

Demi sent a photo of baby Hayes in nothing but a diaper, lying on his back sleeping.

PEYTON

That kid is such a porker.

EMERSON

He's a healthy, happy baby.

SAYLOR

I just want to squeeze those chunky little thighs.

RUBY

And he always smells like baby powder and sunshine.

He's perfect. I love you guys.

RUBY

Love you. Mimosas the minute you're home.

There were no mimosas in my future. But I couldn't say that yet. I couldn't tell a soul the news that I was pregnant until I told my husband.

And this secret was killing me.

33

Hayes

KING

How's the head, Hayes? I can't believe you refused to stay with us while you recover. Your sister is worried about you. Have you always been such a stubborn ass?

RIVER

Is that a trick question? The dude is the most stubborn guy I know. This is no surprise.

NASH

I've been by his house a few times, and he's brooding. He literally didn't say more than two words when I was there.

ROMEO

I think Savvy's made him soft. He can't handle her being gone.

I can't handle her being gone? This is not about her being gone. I'm fine with her being there with her father. This is different. She asked for time. Tell me any situation where someone asking for time ended well.

KING

A medium rare steak that you would like to be well done. A bomb that you can't dismantle. When you're taking a shit, and you need to relax. When you're in a hot bath that you don't want to end. When a woman is on the brink of an orgasm and just needs a little more . . . time.

NASH

Wow. You just pulled those out of your ass?

KING

He asked the question. Time is not a bad thing. How about you stop pouting and just let her take a beat. Her dad is sick. It's a lot.

Fuck off, dicksnout. I know her dad is sick. I've offered to go there, and I check on him daily. Those examples are not someone's wife asking for time away from her husband. The writing is on the wall. This has nothing to do with her dad.

ROMEO

You sure about that?

Yeah. She talks to me about her dad all the time. Something changed. Hell, maybe she just got some "time" away from me and realized this marriage was a sham.

KING

That doesn't sound like Savvy.

RIVER

Agreed. This may have started as a sham, but it sure as fuck didn't end that way. I think you're overthinking this. I'm guessing she's just stressed about her dad. And she's selling the farmhouse, or at least she thinks she is. And she's starting a new business. That's a lot all at once.

ROMEO

Maybe you should tell her you aren't selling the farmhouse. That could cheer her up. Demi is sending her pictures of baby Hayes every day, and she said they're helping her get through the day.

Well, she's more responsive to Demi than she is to me. I barely get more than a few words response by text. She hasn't FaceTimed me in almost a week. Since the day she asked for space.

KING

Well, your face was covered in soot. It freaked me out, too. You looked like one of those creepy Halloween masks, with the guy who has no face.

RIVER

He had a little soot on his face, you drama queen. 👑

KING

We can agree to disagree. Maybe take a shower and send her a selfie so she remembers how good-looking her husband is.

NASH

Is it possible that you give the worst advice on the planet, King? This has nothing to do with his face.

RIVER

Agreed. I find Hayes to be very good-looking.

NASH

Same.

ROMEO

I named my kid after the dude, so obviously, I agree.

KING

Well, since we're sharing. I tasted Demi's breast milk yesterday. It's not for me.

What the actual fuck are you talking about?

KING

I went to see the baby. You know, the cuter, nicer Hayes. LOL. Anyway, she has breast milk in the refrigerator, and Romeo told me he tried it, so I wanted to see if I liked it.

RIVER

Of course, you did.

ROMEO

I was laughing my ass off because he got all quiet after. Like he'd seen Demi's boobs.

KING

I had to process the fact that I drank the milk that came from her teat.

NASH

You are one crazy fucker.

RIVER

Let's bring it back to Hayes. What can we do for you, brother?

You could not bring it back to Hayes.
That would make me happy.

ROMEO

Not possible. If you're in a bad place,
we're all in a bad place.

KING

Agreed. I don't thrive when one of us is
off. It kills my mood.

RIVER

Listen. Swallow your pride and call her.
Don't do a chickenshit text. Pick up the
goddamn phone and call your wife.

ROMEO

I agree with River on this one.

KING

You want me to call her and feel her out
for you?

No. I want you to not get involved. Can
you do that for me?

NASH

What are you going to do?

> I'm respecting her wishes and giving her time.

RIVER

> I don't think that's a good idea.

ROMEO

> I agree. Time is never anyone's friend.

KING

> Don't make me give you more examples of how time can be a good thing.

> I'm setting my phone down. Taking the dog out for a hike. I'm fine.

I got Roddy ready for a hike and managed to check my phone eight hundred fucking times while I was gone, hoping she'd call and tell me what the fuck was up. I was like a lame teenage girl with a crush.

Pathetic.

A weak pussy.

Savannah had me spun around the axle, and I didn't know what to do with it.

After I got home, I drank a big glass of water and dropped to sit at the table. Sabrina had called to tell me we'd received two offers on this house, which had shocked me. It had only been listed for a few days, but she'd shown it multiple times. She said that she'd emailed the offers to me.

My eyes widened as I took in the first one, which was a full-price offer. The second offer was a few thousand dollars under asking, but they'd made a cash offer.

I replied and asked her to check and make sure the first offer was someone who'd been prequalified, and she said they had.

I wanted to run it by Savannah, but she didn't even know I'd listed the house at this point.

While she wanted time, I was making plans.

Plans for our future.

Plans I intended to keep.

34

Savannah

I wasn't sleeping well, and I knew the only way things were going to get better was to talk to Hayes.

To rip off the bandage.

Avoiding the conversation, avoiding my husband, the man I loved, certainly wasn't working.

This just wasn't a conversation I could have over the phone.

I knew my pulling away had hurt him, and I felt sick about it. Saylor had been messaging me every day, and she'd let me know that Hayes was shutting down. She thought he was struggling with me being gone, but she didn't know the half of it.

I was an asshole.

A big, pregnant asshole.

What kind of mother would I be if I couldn't even have a conversation with my husband? Yes, it would be a difficult one, but running from it wasn't going to make things better.

I made my way into my father's room just as Dr. Dorsey stepped in behind me.

"How's everyone doing this morning?" he asked.

"I actually kept breakfast down, so that's a good thing." My father was sitting up, his bald head shiny from the cream that Nadia liked to rub on his head to keep the skin from flaking off.

"That's great news. But even better news is the latest numbers. Your body is responding to the combination of the two drugs being used together. These are the best numbers you've had since you were diagnosed, Billy."

My mouth fell open, and I clapped my hands together.

Good news.

How long had it been since we'd had good news? Yes, getting into the trial was huge, but it had been years since we'd had any positive feedback regarding my father's illness.

He was responding to the treatment.

He was freaking responding to the treatment.

He might actually be around to know his grandchildren.

I covered my face with my hands and cried.

But for the first time in a while, these were happy tears.

Nadia was on her feet, pulling me into her arms as tears streamed down her face.

"He's responding to the treatment," she said. "This is really happening, Savvy."

"Well, hot damn. I'm happy about the good news, but seeing my two girls all lit up like this would be reason enough for treatment," my father said.

"I don't want to give you false hope. We still have a ways to go. But yes, this is good news, and I think it's fine to celebrate that. The hope is that things just keep getting better, and at this point, there's no reason to believe that won't happen," Dr. Dorsey said.

"Thank you. Sometimes just having some good news is enough to help you keep fighting," I said.

"So, Dr. Dorsey, can you tell my daughter that she can go back to her life? You know she's newly married," Dad said. "She married the boy next door. I always knew they had a thing for each other."

"Oh, my gosh, Dad." I shook my head and chuckled. "Dr. Dorsey doesn't need all this information."

"Well, I wasn't done." My father raised a brow and smirked at me. "She's a very talented interior designer, and she's opening her own business back home. She can't be sitting in a hospital all day with me. She needs to be out there living her life."

"I agree. I've got things covered here, and I think you should just come back once a month for a visit. It's going to take time, Savvy. And you should be home with your husband, opening your business and calling us with all the exciting news every day," Nadia said. "Your father lives for those calls. They help him feel like he's out there living his life, too."

A lump formed in my throat, and I nodded as I took his hand. "You will be, Dad. I can feel it in my gut. You're going to get through this."

"I have to side with your family on this one, Savannah," Dr. Dorsey said. "You can come visit often. But sitting around watching him fight this disease is not going to help him get better. And as a parent myself, there's a lot of joy in seeing your children shine. So go out there and make your dad proud."

"I was actually coming to talk to you just now, because I booked a flight home today. But I'll come back in a week." I swiped at the tears falling down my cheeks.

"How about we meet in the middle, and you come back in two weeks?" Dad said.

"Well, I could come relieve Nadia sooner."

"Sweetheart, I don't have a life I want to live that doesn't include my fiancé right now. And I'm sure if Hayes was in this position, this is where you'd want to be. Where you'd need to be. But I've got this. He's stuck with me," Nadia said with a chuckle. My father was lucky to have found a woman who loved him so fiercely.

"Wait. Did you just say fiancé?" I gaped at them as Dr. Dorsey chuckled and excused himself from the room.

"Yep. He asked me last night. We've been talking about making it official for a while," she said, flashing me the ring.

"I didn't want to tie her down to a man who didn't have a future. I've had the ring with me for six months now. And last night, I felt like something was changing. And when you feel it, you act on it," Dad said.

I stared down at the ring and hugged Nadia before hugging my father. "I'm so happy for you both."

"Yeah, yeah, yeah. Get out of here and let us plan a wedding already, okay?" Dad said.

"Okay. Two weeks. And if for any reason you need to go home and want me here for a few days, just say the word. I'll be working for myself, so I can set my own schedule."

"Deal." Nadia wrapped her arms around me and kissed my cheek. "Your father is lucky to have a daughter who fought hard for him to get into this program. A daughter who never gave up on him. You are the reason that he hasn't thrown in the towel, Savvy."

I couldn't speak because I was overcome with emotion, so I just hugged her back.

"I'm so glad that he has you, Nadia. He's a lucky man."

The nurse walked into the room and interrupted us. "It's time to get started for the day. You've got some food in your stomach, so let's get things going. Dr. Dorsey wants to increase the amount of meds you're getting again today, and we'll see how you respond. Let's head down to the treatment room." She stepped out of the room, leaving the three of us alone.

"All right, baby girl. Get out of here. Grab your bags and head to the airport. Go home to your husband and start living this beautiful life you're creating for yourself. Nothing makes me happier," my father said.

I kissed his cheek as I rubbed my hand along his bald head. "I love you, Dad."

"I know you do. And I love you, too." He smiled and pointed at the door. "Go."

I gave Nadia one more hug before heading out of his room and toward the bridge that led to the apartment.

Suddenly, I couldn't get home quickly enough, and I was jogging.

I looked up at the other end to see a person come around the corner with a duffle bag thrown over his shoulder.

My eyes widened as I took him in. Tall. Broad shoulders. Beautiful green eyes. His overgrown scruff making it obvious he hadn't shaved in days.

Hayes Woodson.

My husband.

He'd come for me.

Before I realized what I was doing, I was sprinting down the bridge. His lips turned up in the corners as he dropped his duffle bag, just before I threw myself against him on a whoosh.

He wrapped his arms around me, one on my lower back and one on the back of my head, like he just wanted to keep me right there.

We just stood there hugging for the longest time before I pulled back to look at him. "Hey, husband."

"Hey, wife."

"What are you doing here?"

"I'm done giving you time, Sav. I missed you, so I booked a ticket and decided to come find you myself."

My eyes zoned in on his wrist to see the splint, and I ran my fingers gently along the fabric as I cringed that I'd just jumped on him. "Oh, my gosh. Did I hurt you?"

"Not from lunging into my arms. But not taking my calls, not telling me what's going on—yeah, you hurt me, baby." He quirked a brow, arms crossed over his chest.

I glanced around us, not seeing anyone in sight.

So I guess we were doing this right here.

304

"I booked a ticket home today. I was coming to talk to you. I was just going to get my bag and head to the airport."

"Well, here I am, Sav. How about you just tell me what's going on?" He cleared his throat. "Is this too much for you? The marriage? The life we're building? Me? Is it too much?"

"You think it's too much for me?" I shook my head in disbelief.

"I don't fucking know. Everything was good when you left, or at least I thought it was. And then you came here, and everything seemed fine, and then you went silent on me. Stopped calling. Your texts are short. You're treating me like a fucking acquaintance. So, if this is done, you're going to need to tell me right here. Right now. And then you're going to have to convince me that there's a reason we don't belong together, because I don't see it. I love you so fucking much, and it's killing me that you're pulling away."

This was the most vulnerable he'd ever been in all the years that I'd known him. My chest squeezed, and I took his hands in mine.

"I'm not pulling away."

"Don't lie to me. There's something going on, and I can feel it in my gut. So, we're not leaving here until you talk to me. I'm not losing another decade with you. Because I'm back home making plans for our future. A future that I want with you."

"I've been gone for two weeks. What kind of plans could you have made?" I laughed and blinked several times as I tried to see through my falling tears.

"Nope. I'm not giving you any more until you talk to me." He shrugged, his hands wrapped around mine, and his sage-green gaze was intense and unwavering as he looked down at me. "Tell me what's going on now."

"They wanted to run some tests on me—you know, check my blood work to make sure I wasn't showing any early signs of the disease."

"You're sick?" His eyes softened, and I didn't miss the concern. "You thought I wouldn't be there for you if you were sick? I'll move fucking mountains for you, Sav. We're in this together."

"Hayes, I'm not sick."

"Okay. So, what is it?" He threw his hands in the air in frustration.

Do it. Just say it. He's here. He has to know.

"I'm—" I looked away because the thought of seeing him disappointed would be the end of us. "I'm pregnant."

"You're pregnant?" he asked, and there was no fear in those words. He sounded . . . relieved. *Happy.*

I turned to look at him. "Yes. I'm having a baby. Our baby."

"That's why you haven't talked to me?"

"Well, you don't want kids, right? So I was stunned to find out I was pregnant, and then I panicked because I don't want to lose you."

"Baby, you would never lose me. And I'm sorry if I made you think that I would ever walk away from you or our child."

"But that doesn't change the fact that you don't want children, Hayes. And now I'm pregnant," I said. "So, where does that leave us?"

"It leaves us right fucking here. Exactly where we were when you left." He tugged me close, one hand moving to the side of my face. "Sav, I never thought I'd want to be married, and now I can't imagine a life where you aren't my wife. People change. You changed me. You made me want things I never thought possible. You carrying my baby doesn't make me feel anything other than happy. Excited about the future—with you. Growing our family together."

"You're serious?" I asked, my eyes searching his.

"I've actually been having some thoughts of my own. Thinking about a future with you that I hadn't imagined possible. And it doesn't fucking scare me, baby. The only thing that scares me is a future that doesn't have you in it."

I took his other hand and moved it to my stomach. "Well, I'm glad you feel that way, because apparently, there are two babies in here."

"Twins?" His smile widened, and he shook his head as loud laughter bellowed out. "That's so you, baby. You're such a rock star. And my sperm must be fan-fucking-tastic if I put two babies in you at the same time."

My head fell back on a chuckle. "Definitely not the reaction that I expected."

"I'm not always going to say the right thing or do the right thing, but I promise you, I'll always be there for you. For our children. And I may not have known that I wanted kids the way that you did, but now that we're having two, it feels right. We never do anything by the book anyway. We got married on false pretenses, and then we fell in love. We agreed we wouldn't have a family, and now we're having two babies. And guess what?" he said, using the pads of his thumbs to swipe the falling tears from my face.

"What?" The word sounded wobbly.

"We're going to be amazing parents. Because we live in a home filled with love. And that's all you need."

"Who are you, and what have you done with my grumpy husband?" I asked, as I smiled up at him.

"Nash and I had this talk, and he reminded me of something."

"What's that?"

"Well, the reason I didn't want kids was because I feared I would fail at it. Fail at being a father. I wouldn't want to put my kids through what I went through growing up. But he reminded me that I'd been more of a father to Saylor than I'd realized. I'd already proven I would be better at it than my parents were, because she's fucking amazing. So, I've got this, Sav. I'm going to do my best to be a good father to our children, and they're already winning because they'll have the best mom anyone could ask for."

"This is all I needed to hear," I said over the sobs escaping my throat. "I just wanted you to stay. To be here with us."

"I'm not going anywhere, baby." He pulled me close and wrapped his arms around me. "I love you, and I love our babies that are growing in your belly. I love the life we're building together. It's a life I never dreamed of, and that's all because of you."

"Me, too."

"This will be something positive for your father to fight for, too. Knowing he has grandchildren on the way. Old people live for that shit." He chuckled.

I looked up at him. "I haven't told him yet. I haven't told a soul. I wanted to tell you first, but I couldn't do it over the phone."

"Well, then, let's go tell him the good news, and then I'll book myself a ticket and take you home."

I nodded as he scooped up his duffle bag and intertwined our fingers.

"Let's go."

And we walked hand in hand down the bridgeway toward where my father was receiving treatment.

Today had ended up being filled with more good news than anyone had expected.

And that felt damn good.

35

Hayes

"I still can't believe we're moving in here. You made some awfully big decisions without me, Captain," she said, as we walked toward the barn.

"Well, that serves you right for not taking my calls." I chuckled before turning to look at her. "When Nash and I came out here to talk about a few things that I'm about to show you, I saw it, Sav."

"You saw what?"

"Our life here at this farmhouse. I saw us filling those bedrooms with a bunch of rug rats, and—" I scratched the back of my neck and looked out at the acres of green, "—I could see our family growing here. Before you even told me you were pregnant, I saw it. And it's a damn good life."

She tilted her head to the side and smiled. "It's a damn good life, hubby."

"Come on, let me show you my plan for the barn." I led her inside, where there was a rectangular table in the middle with the drawings that Nash and King had had drawn up by their architect.

"Don't tell me you want horses. You hate riding." She chuckled.

"Nope. If you want horses at some point, we've got plenty of land to build another barn. But this structure is sound, and right now, it fills a need for something more important." I stopped at the table and tapped on the drawings. "We'll add dry wall and a private drive and do a full renovation on this place. And that way, you'll have your business right here on our property."

Her eyes widened, and she studied the plans. "Oh, my gosh, you want to turn this into my office space? This is brilliant. I love it."

"I had the architect add in this little enclosed area over here after you told me about the babies. We can make a little nursery in here so when you're working, you can have the babies out here with you. And when I'm not at the firehouse, they'll be with me in the main house. And if you want to hire a nanny on the days you're working and I'm not around, that works, too. I just wanted you to have options."

She just stared at me as she shook her head. "Wow. You've thought of everything."

"I want you to know we're in this together."

"I know we are. And I love that you aren't assuming I'd stop working and that you took the time to think of all the different scenarios."

"Two kids are a lot, Shortcake."

"I know. There's two of us and two of them. They're going to keep us on our toes," she said, as she started walking the length of the space. "I definitely like the idea of having a nursery for them out here. Obviously, I'll take some time off to adjust to being a mom and enjoy a few months with them, but I think it would be fun to build a business that they're a part of. They can be out here when I'm working, and if it gets too hectic, we'll hire some help."

"I can't believe Saylor's pregnant, too." I chuckled. "Fucking King couldn't wait to tell me."

"I know. It's pretty cool that we'll be pregnant together and

raising these kids together. Cutler is going to be a busy guy."
She paused to glance out the window. "It's beautiful out here.
I'm so happy you didn't let me sell this place. And having the
office on the property will be perfect. How long did they say
the renovation would take?"

"Not too long. It's got good bones, and there's that little
bathroom in the back, so there was already plumbing out
here. You'll handle the design aspect, and they'll just get it
all finished and ready for business. They said a couple weeks
and they could have it ready for you, pending you don't pick
flooring or materials that are back-ordered."

"I can definitely work with that timeline. Hopefully, I'll find
clients fairly quickly, seeing as there isn't a design firm in town."

"You'll be fine, baby. There's no rush. We're good
financially, especially with this place being paid off. We've got
my income and the money from the other house once it closes.
It's a good nest egg."

"I also spoke to the billing department at the hospital in
Dallas, and I don't think the trial is going to be as much out
of pocket as I'd assumed. Turns out, Dad's insurance is paying
a decent chunk, and the trial itself covers a portion for the
patients selected, as well. I got the first bill, and it wasn't bad
at all. So we've got the inheritance to tuck away, too."

"Keep that money in an account for your father's treatment
for now. Let's get him better so he can watch his grandkids grow."

"He's still on cloud nine since we told him the news. I think
he's serious about moving back to Magnolia Falls after he
finishes the trial. Nadia said she'd love small-town life too,
and they want to be close to the babies."

"I think it's great," I said, as I pulled her into my arms.

"Hey, you beat us here," Nash said, as he and Kingston
strode toward us.

Kingston hugged her tight and spun her around. "Looking
good, little mama."

Nash hugged her next, and then we all stood around, looking at the design plans. The guys were just as excited as Savannah was.

"You know, Nash and I were talking, and we had this idea we wanted to run by you," Kingston said as he turned to face us.

"Sure. What is it?" Savannah asked.

"We were thinking we could partner up with you. We don't have a designer on our team, and with people going crazy about your design on this renovation out here, and our current client list being so backed up, we could do some good things together," Nash said.

"I would love that. And I'm ready to start now. I'll be going to Dallas twice a month on the weekends, but otherwise, I'm here and ready to go. I don't need this space to be done to start working. That house has more rooms than we know what to do with right now, so I can work out of one of the guest rooms."

"Well, you are pregnant with twins, so you don't need to be overdoing it either," I said, and everyone gaped at me.

"Oh, no, he didn't," Kingston whisper-shouted, which made everyone laugh.

"Hayes." My wife raised a brow at me.

"What? You have two humans growing in your belly."

"Uh, yeah, I'm quite aware. I'm a few weeks along. I plan to work through my pregnancy, so don't even think about going all caveman on me."

Kingston was laughing hysterically, and Nash just gave me an apologetic look. "Yeah, thanks for having my back, assholes."

"Okay, well, aside from that failed attempt at telling your wife she shouldn't work when the baby is the size of a pea, I think we have a partnership that will be great," Nash said.

"Hey, she's got two peas in there, buddy. She needs to be careful," I grumped.

Savannah shot me a warning look. "*She* can hear you. And she is just fine working. You're the one who fights fires for a living. Should I ask you not to do your job while I'm pregnant and after we have kids?"

"She makes a good point. We're going to let you dig yourself out of this one on your own, brother," Kingston said.

"Agreed. Savannah, we'll have a team up here tomorrow to start the renovations, and I'll bring over the plans for the house we're starting next week. It's the Windsor ranch, and his wife doesn't know what she wants as far as décor goes, and she told us to pick everything," Nash said.

"Yeah, that's always fun when you have to try to guess what they like." Kingston threw his arms in the air. "And then they hate what you pick and blame you."

"Well, it's always good to sit down with the client and show them a few different pictures to figure out what their style is. Even if they don't know what it is, you can find out a lot by what they do and don't like, then come up with an aesthetic that works before you order any materials," my wife said.

"Damn, look at our partner using all sorts of big words. You're going to make us look a whole lot smarter than we are." Kingston was laughing as he walked backward toward the door.

"I think this is going to be a really good partnership. We'll see you tomorrow." Nash turned to leave and then called out for me. "Hey, Hayes?"

"Yeah?"

"If you aren't out of the doghouse tomorrow, let me know. We can build you and Roddy matching houses for the backyard."

I flipped him the bird as my wife's head fell back in laughter.

I took her hand and led her toward the house, with our pup following behind us. "So, when do you want to move in?"

"I'm ready whenever you are. We can get the other house packed up pretty quickly. Whatever furniture we don't need from this house and the other house, I can store for when I want to stage projects or if we decide to flip a few houses."

"Look at you, Mrs. Woodson. Already talking like a businesswoman." I pulled the door open, and we stepped inside.

"It feels like home, doesn't it?" she asked.

"Yeah. But we need to christen every room to make it official."

"Well, how about we start with one room right now?" She waggled her brows. "Pregnancy hormones can make a woman very horny."

"How was I ever against knocking you up, woman?" I barked out a laugh and tossed her over my shoulder. "Where should we start?"

"You pick. I don't care where we go, as long as I'm with you." She smacked my ass, and I jogged down the hall toward the bedroom and set her down gently on the bed.

"Hayes, you don't have to treat me like I'm made of porcelain. I'm fine."

I hovered above her and leaned down, my nose rubbing against hers. "Have you ever loved someone so much that you just want to make sure nothing ever hurts them?"

She sucked in a breath, and her gaze softened. "Yes."

"When I look at you, I feel so much, and I'm not used to that. So I just want to protect you and love you, and if I could put you in a box and keep you safe there, I would do it. And if that makes me an asshole or a caveman, so be it."

"Okay, well, I love you, too. I get nervous every time you go to work. But guess what?"

"What?" I asked, knowing there was going to be a life lesson coming my way.

"I love you for the man you are. I love that you're passionate about your work. So I guess we both just have to learn to trust that everything will be fine. And keep in mind, women have been having babies for a long time, Hayes. I'm not the first or the last." She chuckled.

"But you're having two, and that's a lot for you to have to schlep around."

314

Her laughter filled the room around us, and I fucking loved it.

"It's a lot to schlep around. But we also get a two for one, right?" she said, with this silly smile on her face. "I only have to be pregnant once, and we get two babies out of the deal."

"That's true." I shrugged. "I'll back off. Just give me time to get used to it."

"Well, you've got a lifetime to get used to it. I'm not going anywhere."

"I like the sound of that. And seeing as you won't let me put you in a little box, how about I bury my head between your thighs and enjoy this one."

"Nice transition. Feel free to have your way with me, husband."

And that's exactly what I did.

Because pleasing my woman could be my day job.

And I'd never get enough.

* * *

KING

You out of the doghouse yet, Captain?

ROMEO

What did I miss? He just got her home. How is he already in the doghouse?

NASH

Because it's Hayes, and he has no filter. He tried to tell Savvy that she shouldn't work while she's pregnant.

RIVER

Ruby would cut off my balls if I pulled that shit.

KING

Is Ruby pregnant, too?

RIVER

No, you dinkledick. We aren't ready for that crazy shit yet. But if I ever told her what to do, pregnant or not pregnant . . . 🔪💀

KING

Seeing those two emojis together makes me very uncomfortable.

More than these? 🐛💀

KING

That's taking it too far. Welcome to the chat, you pussy-whipped fucker.

For the record, I am not in the doghouse. And I did not tell her not to work. I just know you two like to take on a lot of jobs, and I don't want her to be working too hard.

ROMEO

Yeah, Demi and I had that argument a few times. Good luck with that. We all fell for strong women, which means we can't tell them what to do.

NASH

How about that . . . All five of us are married now. Who'd have ever guessed it?

Not me. And I sure as shit wouldn't have guessed that King would marry my little sister.

ROMEO

Ride or die, brothers.

RIVER

Damn straight. Now you're all knocking up your women and starting families. Hayes is living in a farmhouse that is so fancy it could be featured on HGTV.

You did not just throw out that statement. Are you watching HGTV now? Let me know, and I'll drop off a box of tampons and some nail polish later.

RIVER

Ruby loves that channel. And who are you to talk? You carry that puppy around like it's a baby.

KING

I didn't want to bring this up, but Hayes had Roddy wearing booties when we he took him for a hike.

Protecting a dog's paw pads is called being a responsible pet owner.

NASH

These are not conversations I ever thought we'd be having.

ROMEO

I can't say I mind it. It's a lot better than the drama we grew up with. No one's getting arrested or put in prison.

RIVER

Damn straight, brother. We're living the lives we couldn't even dream of when we were teenagers.

KING

Good women. Good jobs. Good friends. I'd call that a damn good life.

Are you drunk?

KING

Nope. Just happy.

Yeah, brother. I think we all are.

Ain't that the fucking truth.

36

Savannah

I'd just arrived back from Dallas with Hayes. He'd worked his schedule so that he could take off the weekend and come with me. We'd gotten a hotel near the hospital and spent our days with my father and Nadia and our nights wrapped around one another.

It made the stress of this whole experience so much better with my husband by my side. My dad was four weeks into treatment, and to say he was responding well was an understatement.

His numbers were improving.

He was feeling better.

Eating better.

Sleeping better.

It was a small win, and one that I would take. He was improving, and there was hope in that. I knew it didn't mean that he would be cured overnight, but the hope was that eventually he would be in remission.

I wanted my father to be around to know my children.

He and Nadia were already looking at homes in Magnolia Falls. They planned to get married and move there when they left Dallas. I couldn't ask for more.

Life had a funny way of working out.

Hayes had dropped me off at The Golden Goose to meet the girls for lunch, and he was going to run a few errands.

"Hi, Midge," I said, as she walked me to the back where Demi, Ruby, Saylor, Emerson, and Peyton were sitting.

"Why didn't you bring that sexy husband of yours in with you?" she grumped.

"He'll be back to pick me up. I'm sure he'd be happy to come in and say hello," I said with a laugh as I slid into the booth.

"Hey," Peyton said. "Did you come straight from the airport?"

"Yep. Hayes dropped me off."

"Well, he loves doing that and keeping his eyes on you. He's been hilarious since you found out you were pregnant." Saylor chuckled, and we paused to place our orders with Letty.

"Please. I notice King is constantly at the bookstore ever since you found out you were pregnant," Demi said, and the table erupted in laughter.

"I've got to tell you, I'm scared to drink the water in Magnolia Falls lately. Two of you are pregnant, and I feel like Emerson is next. Peyt, you and me are the last ones holding out." Ruby reached for her Coke and took a sip before setting the glass back down.

"I think Nash and I are going to start trying after the wedding, but there's something that's more important right now." Emerson put her hands together, and we all leaned in because it sounded like she had some big news.

"Are you okay?" I asked.

"Yes. We're great. But my brother, Easton, is helping us start the discussion with Tara." Tara was Cutler's biological mother, and I'd heard the horrible stories about her from Hayes and the girls.

"What discussion?" Ruby asked.

"I want to adopt Cutler. He heard about adoption and what it was, and he came home and asked Nash and me about it. I've been looking into it ever since, and it just feels right, you know? Easton has reached out to Tara, and we'll see if she's even willing to consider it."

"Wow. That would be amazing," Demi said, her eyes wet with emotion.

"Yeah. So that's first and foremost, and then the wedding, and then we'll start trying for another baby."

"Damn. You've all got baby fever," Peyton said. "I've actually got news, but it sure as hell doesn't involve a screaming child, because, ewwww. No offense. I'm sure you'll all have great kids and your vaginas will bounce back just fine." More laughter erupted around the table as Letty set down our plates.

"What's your news?" Saylor asked, as she bit off the top of a french fry.

"Slade and I are moving in together." She shrugged. "I'm going to shack up with Demi's brother!"

I laughed, and Demi's entire face lit up. "He told me he was going to ask you."

"So I guess we really are sisters, huh?" Peyton said.

"Of course, we are. You didn't need to shack up with my brother to make that happen. But I'm glad you are. I love seeing you both so happy together."

"Look at us," Saylor said. "We're just a bunch of ridiculously happy women."

"Who'd have thought it?" Demi said, her voice laced with humor.

"Not me." Ruby shrugged. "I always thought being happy was overrated. But look at me. I am nauseatingly happy, aren't I?"

"You are. I'm embarrassed for you," Peyton said, bumping Ruby with her shoulder. "You smile all the time. What would your vampire family think of you?"

"Well, look at Hayes. He gave me a run for my money when it came to being a big grump, and then little Miss Sunshine came back to town, and he's a new man."

"He really is putty in your hands." Saylor beamed at me. "King said the renovations are coming along at the barn, and your office space will be ready in a few weeks."

"Yeah. We're still unpacking boxes from the move into the house, but we're pretty settled. And for now, I just work out of the house. It'll take some time to build the business up."

"Yeah, but you're already taking on a few projects with the guys, right?" Emerson asked.

"Yes. And I love it. It's so fun to help create people's dream homes or dream businesses, you know?"

"I can't wait to find out the sex of the baby so I can have you help me design the nursery," Saylor said.

"Yeah, I'm so excited about finding out the sex of the twins, too." I reached for my grilled cheese sandwich and took a bite. My appetite was pretty ravenous lately.

"I'm amazed at watching Demi nurse little Hayes, but how in the hell can someone nurse two babies at the same time?" Peyton gasped.

"From everything I've read, it's doable. But I'm just going in with the attitude that I will do the best I can. If it works, that would be wonderful. If it doesn't, I can pump, and we'll figure it out."

"I can't imagine having anyone on my boobs all day." Peyton shook her head in disbelief.

"You're feeding your baby. It's natural and beautiful." Demi chuckled.

"Oh, really. Look down at your shirt, girl. You're leaking. I don't know how beautiful that is on your cute blouse." Peyton sipped her soda, and I tried to hide my smile.

"I hope you and my brother have lots of babies, and I get to tease you about your leaking breasts someday." Demi smirked.

Peyton shivered dramatically. "I have such perky breasts. I'm not sure how I feel about that."

We spent the next hour talking about everything from babies to work to sex to home décor.

Girl talk was my favorite. I loved the bond I shared with these women, and there was nothing that we couldn't talk about.

I was grateful for the life I was building in Magnolia Falls.

* * *

"Why do you look so nervous?" I asked, as Hayes held my hand in his when we stepped off the elevator.

"I just want to make sure everything is okay."

I peeked up at my husband, this big, strong man beside me, who looked like he was about to pass out.

"Hayes," I said, coming to a stop as he turned to face me. "We're meeting our doctor, and it's just a checkup."

"Savannah." His tone was lacking all humor. "You are carrying two humans in your belly. One is a lot for most people. You have two. I want to make sure you're okay."

I sighed. He was ridiculously protective, but I couldn't fault him.

I worried every time he left for work.

When you loved someone so much that you couldn't imagine your world without them in it, you could behave irrationally at times.

"Okay."

He lifted my hand and pressed it to his lips before leading me down the hallway to the last door on the left.

I checked in and gave them my insurance information, and they called us back.

It was all very standard, with getting my weight and vitals and everything you did when you went to a regular doctor's appointment, yet my husband paced around the room the entire time.

The nurse chuckled. "First-time dad?"

"Yes. This is all new for us."

"I understand. It's normal to be nervous. I'm going to have you slip into this gown, with the opening in the front. You can hop up on the bed once you're changed. I'll step out of the room and give you some privacy."

"Okay, that sounds great." I pushed to my feet.

"You're going to love Dr. Shorting. She's wonderful. She'll be right in," she said, just before leaving the room.

"I think that's a good sign that her name is Dr. Shorting."

I chuckled. "You do? Why?"

"Because I call you Shortcake. So there you go."

I took off my clothes, and he put them on the chair while I slipped into the gown and hopped up onto the table. "I love you, Hayes Woodson."

"Love you, too, baby."

The door opened, and a woman who looked to be in her mid-forties, with shoulder-length brown hair and warm, brown eyes, walked in. She extended a hand to me first and then to Hayes. "Hey, I'm Dr. Shorting. It's nice to meet you, Mr. and Mrs. Woodson."

"It's great to meet you. You can call us Savannah and Hayes," I said.

She leaned her back against the counter and flipped through the file that she held in her hand. "So I've got a copy of your blood work that was done in Dallas, and I can see why they had reason to believe you were carrying more than one baby with how high your HCG levels were. I've got your ultrasound report here, as well, but I'd like to do my own now, just to see what's happening here first."

I nodded, and she guided me to lie back. Hayes moved beside me and took my hand. She opened my gown, exposing my belly, and poured the jelly-like substance onto me. She turned on the monitor and used a hand-held device, which she placed on my stomach. She rolled it around and studied the monitor.

The sound had me leaning up a bit to see the screen.

"There's the first heartbeat, and it sounds strong," she said, her voice calm and soothing. She continued moving her wand around and paused. "And here's the second heartbeat. You've definitely got two babies in there, and it looks like they each have their own placenta and amniotic sac, which will give them the best chance of growing well."

She pointed out their positioning and told us some technical stuff that I was trying to focus on, but I was just relieved that there were two heartbeats and all was still going well.

A part of me worried that I'd come here today and find out I was no longer pregnant. I was prepared for the rug to be pulled out from beneath my feet.

It's amazing that you can find something out and feel completely panicked in one moment, only to realize that it's everything that you wanted.

And now that Hayes was on board, this was everything I wanted.

Everything *we* wanted.

She printed out a few pictures, cleaned the gooey stuff from my stomach, and helped me sit up.

She went over all the things we'd need to be aware of. Twin pregnancies tended to be higher risk, so she'd be keeping a close eye on me and the babies. She said we'd have more ultrasounds done than you normally had with a single pregnancy. She guessed I was around ten to eleven weeks along, and everything was looking good thus far.

She asked a bunch of questions about how I was feeling as far as morning sickness and breast tenderness, and I shared that though my breasts were sore, I hadn't experienced any morning sickness yet. But I was definitely tired, which she assured me was completely normal.

"Do you have any questions for me?" she asked.

"I think you've covered everything on my end," I said, glancing at my husband, who looked like he was ready to burst. "But I think Hayes may have a few questions."

She smiled. "Of course. You can ask me anything."

"She's determined to work through her pregnancy. Do you think it's safe?" he asked.

"Yes. There's no reason for her to quit working, at least not right now. With Savannah carrying twins, we will be keeping a closer eye on her. So this first trimester I'd like to see you every two to three weeks. We'll do screenings at weeks twelve and sixteen. Your second trimester, I will ask to see you twice a month, and your final trimester, we'll meet weekly. So we can determine along the way how you're feeling and adjust your work schedule accordingly. Does that sound okay?" she asked, her eyes soft as she looked at Hayes, making it clear that she understood his concern.

"All right. And we have a dog. Should we get rid of him?" he asked, and I gasped.

"Get rid of Roddy? What are you talking about?"

"I love Roddy, but he's a puppy, and he likes to climb all over you." He shrugged.

Dr. Shorting chuckled. "You don't need to get rid of Roddy. But you can definitely insist that he doesn't jump up on you."

"Savannah's father is in a cancer trial in Dallas, and she travels there every couple of weeks. Is it safe for her to continue flying?"

"Yes, absolutely. You can still travel through your first and second trimesters comfortably. But you will have to listen to your body. If you're exhausted, then maybe you skip going that week. Does that make sense?"

"Yes," I said. "I can do that."

"Listen, Doc, I'm just worried about my wife. This woman right here…" Hayes said, motioning his hand from my head to my feet. "She's my whole world. And I need to know that she's getting the best care possible."

I covered my eyes with my hand because even though it was sweet, I was embarrassed that he was questioning her.

She chuckled, which had me relaxing. "I have a husband at home who is just like him."

"There's two of them in Magnolia Falls?" I asked, and Hayes rolled his eyes.

Dr. Shorting looked back at my husband. "I give you my word. I will take the best care of Savannah that I can. I'm going to give you my home number, and you can call me after hours if you have any issues. We're a team, and we're in this together, okay?" She extended her hand to Hayes, and he shook it before she turned to me and did the same.

She left the room, and I changed back into my clothing, and we stopped at the front desk to make our next appointment.

When we were on the elevator, I glanced up at him. "Get rid of Roddy? Are you serious?"

"I love that little fucker, but if he hurts you, he's gone."

I shook my head and laughed. "You're lucky I love you."

He reached for my hand, the corners of his lips turning up. "I'm the luckiest man on the planet. I don't doubt that for a minute."

And I knew I was the luckiest woman on the planet, too.

Because this man may be overbearing and protective, but he was all mine.

And I wouldn't have it any other way.

"Good, because there's something I want to do when we get home. And I'm hoping you're on board."

"Name it," he said as we drove toward the house.

"I saved the very last letter for us to read together."

He groaned. "I'm glad that it's the last one, at least."

I chuckled when he pulled into the driveway, and we made our way inside. I told him to meet me on the couch, and Roddy jumped up to sit beside him as I went down the hall to grab the last letter.

I sat down beside him and tore it open. "You never wanted to read these after all these years? Every single one was still sealed."

"I wrote them. Why would I need to read them?"

I laughed as I pulled out the last letter he'd written me and unfolded it.

"I'm going to read it aloud."

"Of course, you are. You love to torture me," he said, as his hand rested on my thigh, and our pup lay sprawled across his lap.

Sav, it's been one year today since you left. I said I'd write every week for a year, and if you didn't answer, I'd stop writing. So, this is the final letter I'm going to send, and I fully expect it to be returned.

I paused to look at him and smiled. "You gave it a good fight. I wouldn't have guessed you'd hang in that long."

"Yeah, well, there you go. I didn't give up easily," he grumped.

I looked back down at the paper. *Today I went out to see Abe. That's how desperate I am. I don't feel like myself, even after all this time. I didn't mention the letters to him. I just asked if he'd heard from you. He told me he had and that you seemed to be doing well. He's a loyal fucker, so he didn't give me much. But I'm not going to lie. It pissed me off. You talk to him all the time, and you won't even read my letters or pick up the damn phone and call me. I just don't get it.*

I sighed and glanced at him again. "I didn't know you went to see Abe."

"Yeah. I forgot about that. I was pretty desperate at the time. And then I remember feeling defeated because I imagined you were chained up somewhere all that time, unable to talk to me. But you were talking to him and Lily."

I squeezed his hand. "I'm sorry. But I love that you went to see him."

I looked back down at the paper in my hand and continued. *Abe told me not to give up on you, but he didn't tell me anything more. I started to leave, and he stopped me. He asked me if I was still dating Kate, and I said that I was but that I missed my best friend. And then I made some snide comment that you weren't a very good best friend if you could just up and leave me the way that you did, so maybe I needed to find some new friends.*

I sighed, because I could just picture him and Abe having this heart-to-heart. I looked back down at the words he'd written me all those years ago. *He asked me if I really felt that way about you. And I told him that I wanted to hate you but that I just couldn't seem to do it. I'm so pissed at you, Sav. But I can't hate you, no matter how hard I try. And you know that I don't normally struggle with hating people. It usually comes really easy for me.*

My head fell back on a laugh, and I kissed his cheek. "You do normally find it easy to hate someone, but I'm glad you didn't hate me."

He shrugged. "You're impossible to hate."

I looked back down and continued reading. *Abe thought it was funny. He was the only person I'd opened up to about you, and the old dude just laughed at me. But when I tried to leave again, he said he had one more question. He wanted to know what I would do if you came back today or in five years or in ten years. Would I forgive you and just be happy to see you, or would I turn my back on you? I didn't need to think about it for long. The answer was easy. Because even after everything, Sav, you're still my best friend. And there would never be a time that I wouldn't be happy to see you. Because my world is such a better place when you're in it.*

I sniffed a few times but kept my eyes trained on the letter. *So, I'm going to stop writing now, because it just feels like it's time. But just know that if you come back today or in five years or even in ten years, I'll be waiting for you. And that's the truth. I hope you find your way back to me, and I told Abe that. And the old fucker just smirked and told me only time would tell.*

I had to pause because the lump in my throat made it difficult to speak. I sighed before moving on to the final few sentences. *I miss you today, and I'll miss you in five years and in ten years. Because you're my favorite person on the planet, Savannah Abbott. Peas and carrots. Hayes.*

I just sat on the couch crying, and my husband wrapped his arms around me.

"Well, damn. I forgot about that conversation. I think that sneaky bastard knew I'd marry you." He laughed as his lips kissed my forehead.

"I think he probably knew you were my other half, and he hoped I'd come back here and figure it out."

And I closed my eyes and said a silent thank-you to Abe.

Because he'd helped me find my way home.

He'd helped me find my happily ever after.

Epilogue

Hayes

Nash and Emerson hosted their annual Fourth of July party, and everyone was there. We'd all teased Romeo for wearing some sort of sling across his chest with baby Hayes tucked inside. He was a damn good father, and I was proud as hell to see the man he'd become.

We'd all met when we were just kids, but seeing these guys as husbands and fathers—it was a good thing.

We'd beaten the odds.

When I'd passed on my football scholarship, I think a lot of people wrote me off and thought I'd just be some fuckup. But I'd put my head down and worked hard to become a firefighter, and now that I was captain, I fucking loved it. It was what I was meant to do.

I sipped my beer as I sat with the guys around the fire and glanced over at my wife. She was in her second trimester now, and her baby bump was cute as hell. She was growing every day, as were our children.

We were having two little girls.

Never in my wildest dreams could I have imagined I'd be a father to two little princesses.

But here we were. Filling our nursery with everything pink and frilly.

And I'd be lying if I said I wasn't loving every damn second.

My life had completely surpassed any expectation I'd ever had, and it was all because this woman had come back to town and turned my world upside down.

In the best way.

"Wait till you see the fireworks I have planned this year. Best ones yet. I went all out," Kingston said.

"You always go all out." Romeo chuckled as Demi walked over and kissed his cheek, scooping the baby up out of his arms.

"I'm going to go nurse him inside," she said.

"Do you want me to come sit with you?" he asked.

"Nope. I'm going to have a little quiet time with my boy." She smiled and walked inside the house.

"You guys are all so . . . married." Easton took a swig of his beer. He'd come to Magnolia Falls tonight after being at his parents' party this afternoon, apparently. Since the dude had access to his brother's helicopter, he'd left one party and made it to the next. He'd really helped me and Savvy out with our situation, and I liked him a lot.

River barked out a laugh. "Who'd have thought we'd all be married like this?"

"Not me," I said. "Never thought I was the marrying type."

"Yet here you are, with twin girls on the way," Easton said.

"I'm glad you came tonight. It means a lot." Nash took a long pull from his beer, and I studied him. He'd been quieter than normal.

"Something on your mind, brother?" Kingston asked.

Nash looked at Easton, and the corners of his lips turned up. "We're waiting to tell everyone when it's final, but I guess I never keep anything from you fuckers."

"What's going on?" I asked, glancing over to see Cutler sitting on Savannah's lap with his head back in a fit of laughter.

"Easton met with Tara about the idea of Emerson adopting Cutler," he said, and you could see all the emotion there, written all over his face.

"And what did she say?" Romeo asked as he leaned forward, resting his elbows on his knees.

"She said she wouldn't fight it." Easton glanced over at his sister before looking back at the fire.

"Let me guess. She wants money?" I asked.

"You know, I expected that, to be honest. But that's not how adoption works. I told her that I spoke to Cutler, which I did, and I shared that he'd started calling Emerson mama, and they'd like to make it official. I assured her that she'd be welcome to visit, and they wouldn't have an issue with her having lunch with him when she came to town. But I said that Cutler wants stability. He's surrounded by it now." Easton shrugged. "And she cried and said she knew she'd failed him."

"Turns out she has a heart underneath that selfish exterior," Nash said.

"I told her that it's never too late to do the right thing. Nash and Emmy are getting married. She's been a stable force in his life. And they'd like to make it official." Easton paused when the flames crackled around us before continuing. "She said she saw the way Emerson cared for Cutler when she was here. She wanted to do the unselfish thing for her son. So I needed to come tell my sister the news in person today. It's important to her."

"Damn. I did not see that coming," King said.

"Sometimes people do the right thing." I shrugged.

"I'm happy for you, brother. It's all working out," River said. "For all of us."

"How about you?" Easton directed his question to River. "You and Ruby going to follow suit and get pregnant with triplets?"

More laughter.

The twin jokes were never-ending.

The dude who swore he'd never have kids got a two-for-one special.

Get your shotgun ready. You've got two little princesses to protect.

Two teenage girls at the same time is your punishment for being a broody asshole all these years.

I didn't mind it. I found it funny. It was a reminder that we didn't always know what the future held. And that's what life was all about.

It was a journey, and I was grateful for the one I was on.

"We talk about it, but we're not there yet. My girl wants to save the world first. She's starting a foundation for the kids she works with, so get ready to help with the fundraising." River sipped his beer.

"What's her plan?" Easton asked.

"She wants to buy an old house here in town and fix it up, which means King and Nash and Savvy will be donating a shit-ton of time." River barked out a laugh. "Give these kids a place to go after they leave juvenile detention. They don't all have families waiting for them. She wants to offer another option outside of foster care."

"We've already told her we're all in. Whatever she needs," Kingston said.

"And you two will be offering up big muscles to help out," Nash said, looking at me and Romeo, and we nodded.

Hell, she wouldn't even need to ask.

"I'd be happy to contribute," Easton said. "I could talk to my firm, see if they'd make a donation."

"That would be great, man. Thank you. She's getting all the paperwork filled out now. Savvy offered to decorate the place, and she thought she could get a lot of the furniture donated from local stores," River said. "And Emerson offered free medical evaluations when they first arrive at the house.

334

Saylor is going to reach out to a bunch of bookstores to see if they'd donate age-appropriate books. And Demi said she'd do a weekly breakfast at the house donated by Magnolia Beans."

"Damn. You guys don't mess around here. You're all so quick to jump on board. I love it," Easton said.

"You've got a lot going on back home, too." Nash stretched his legs out in front of him, crossing them at the ankles. "You've expanded the office in Rosewood River, and you're running the show, right? You think that's your final hoop to jump through to make partner at the firm?"

Easton was a badass lawyer. Nash had told us stories about the way he'd made a name for himself in the courtroom.

"Yeah. I commute to the city for trials, but it's nice having an office outside of the city. The partners wanted to downsize the huge office space we had downtown, as a lot of people who work for the firm live outside the city anyway, so in reality, it was fiscally a good move to expand the office there."

"And this was your idea, right?" Nash smirked. "That has to earn you brownie points."

"We'll see. Charles Holloway's father founded the firm, and he likes to dangle the carrot over my head. Most of the partners are getting older now and will be retiring soon, so he needs to bring in some new blood." Easton shrugged.

"Sounds like you've got it in the bag," River said.

"We'll see. He just dropped some bullshit bomb on me this week that I'm not thrilled about."

"Yeah, Em told me that he's making you mentor his daughter?" Nash said, and he quickly covered his laugh with a cough.

"It's not fucking funny, dude. I've won more cases for our firm than any of the partners there, and now he wants to make me a babysitter?" Easton shook his head in disgust. "She just graduated from law school, so she has zero experience. He's clearly testing my patience. But I've got a high tolerance for bullshit."

"What will you do?" I asked.

"I will not be going easy on her just because her daddy is a founding partner. I'll make her work just like anyone else would have to. My guess is she'll be running for the door within a few weeks." He smirked. "If you can't handle the heat, get the fuck out of the kitchen, right?"

"Sounds like you've got a good plan in place," Kingston said.

"Always do." Easton pushed to his feet and asked who needed another beer before jogging into the house for refills.

We sat there shooting the shit for another hour before Kingston got the fireworks show up and ready. We all pulled our chairs down by the water, and Nash got the music going, and we watched the best light display we'd seen to date.

"Uncle Hayes, do you think the twins will like chocolate milk like I do?" Cutler asked, as he stood next to my chair where Savannah sat on my lap.

"I think they'll look up to you to tell them what's good and what's bad." I ran my hand over the top of his hair.

The kid who had truly taught all of us how to be a father. How to love fiercely. How to show up for the people you cared about.

This kid is all of ours.

And the thought that Emerson would officially get to be his mother was the way it should be. I knew he'd wanted it. Craved that maternal person in his life.

"I'm going to tell them everything. I'll teach baby Hayes and Uncle King and Aunt Saylor's little boy how to swim and play baseball. I'll teach the twins how to make unicorn Krispies like my mama does."

He'd started calling Emerson mama on Mother's Day, and every time he said it, I saw the way it affected her. She loved him as her own, and he felt that.

We all felt it.

"These kids are going to be lucky to have you to look up to," Kingston said, as he kissed Saylor's cheek where she sat on his lap.

"I'm the lucky one. I've got my pops and my mama. I've got the best uncles, and they found the best girls, and now our family just keeps getting bigger." He ran off when Emerson called for him from the house.

"For fuck's sake," River said, as he swiped at his eye. "Is it allergy season again?"

Kingston sniffed a few times, and Romeo cleared his throat and looked away. Nash glanced at me, and I blinked several times to stop myself from acting like a blubbering pussy.

Easton barked out a laugh. "You really are a bunch of sappy bastards."

Laughter erupted around us, and I just sat back with my arms wrapped around my girl, my daughters both growing in her belly, surrounded by my family.

After another hour of eating enough pastries to feed a small country, and more chatter around the fire, we all said our goodbyes.

Savannah and I had walked there, as we only lived a few blocks away. The sky was dark, but all the stars were out tonight. There were random pops and cracks from the fireworks going off nearby.

Savannah was going on about how excited she was to help Ruby with the foundation for the kids, and then she came to an abrupt stop.

"Are you okay?" I asked. "Are you too tired to walk home?"

She didn't say a word. She just reached for my hand and settled it on her lower belly. I stared at her, just as a little jolt landed on my palm.

"What the hell is that?"

"That's the first kick," she said. "Someone is up and ready to party."

I stood there staring down at my hand on her belly as another kick came.

"They must like the fireworks," I said, as my hand moved slowly back and forth over her sundress.

"I think they like the sound of your voice."

"Do you like the sound of Daddy's voice, girls?" I teased, just as another kick came.

I'll be damned.

Savannah chuckled. "I told you. Now, let's get home. I want to take a bath with my husband."

"Oh, yeah? Any chance I have to get you naked I'm going to take."

"It seems it happens daily, so I'm kind of a sure thing." She laughed as I scooped her up in my arms.

"You're the only sure thing I want, Shortcake."

"Good. Because you're stuck with me for life." Her head fell back in laughter as I cradled her against my chest and carried her up the steps to the front door.

"I'm going to hold you to it." I pushed the door open.

And I meant it.

I'd never believed in happily ever after until I started living it.

It had been the girl next door that had my heart all along.

And I was never letting go.

Acknowledgments

Greg, thanks for always supplying me endless book boyfriend inspiration. Love you forever!

Chase and Hannah, you have my whole heart. I'm so proud of you and love you both so much!

Willow, endlessly grateful for your friendship! Thank you for always supporting me and encouraging me and making me laugh! Love you so much!

Catherine, thank you for celebrating all the things with me, for listening, for making me laugh and for being such an amazing friend! Love you!

Kandi, you are such a bright light in my life. Thank you for being the biggest cheerleader and always helping me push through the challenging days. I would be lost without you. Love you!

Elizabeth O'Roark, so happy to be on this journey with you. Love you my sweet friend!

Pathi, I would not be doing what I love every single day if it wasn't for YOU! I am so thankful for your friendship, and for all the support and encouragement! I'd be lost without you! I love you so much!

Nat, I am SO INCREDIBLY thankful for you! Thank you for taking so much, and never hesitating to jump in where you are needed. Thank you for the daily encouragement, taking so much off my plate and going to signings with me so that

339

everything runs smoothly. I am forever grateful for you! Love you!

Nicole Moeslacher, thank you for making the most gorgeous cards for my PR boxes. I love you to the moon and back.

Nina, I'm just going to call you the DREAM MAKER from here on out. Thank you for believing in me and for making my wildest dreams come true. Your friendship means the world to me! I love you forever!

Kim Cermak, thank you for being YOU! There is just no other way to say it. You are one in a million. I am endlessly grateful to have you in my corner, but most importantly, to call you my friend. Love you!

Christine Miller, Kelley Beckham, Tiffany Bullard, Sarah Norris, Valentine Grinstead, Meagan Reynoso, Amy Dindia, Josette Ochoa and Ratula Roy, I am endlessly thankful for YOU!

Paige, first you saved me at the Gaylord when I was wandering and lost. And then we arranged the marriage of Louie and Penny! It doesn't get any better! I love you so much and I'm so grateful for your friendship!

Stephanie Hubenak, thank you for always reading my words early and cheering me on. The daily chats are my favorite. Love you so much!

Kelly Yates, thank you for the banana bread fire inspo! LOL! So thankful for you!! Love you!

Logan Chisolm, I absolutely adore you and am so grateful for your support and encouragement! Love you!

Kayla Compton, I am so happy to be working with you and so thankful for YOU! Love you! Xo

Doo, Annette, Abi, Meagan, Diana, Jennifer, Pathi, Natalie, and Caroline, thank you for being the BEST beta readers EVER! Your feedback means the world to me. I am so thankful for you!!

To all the talented, amazing people who turn my words

into a polished final book, I am endlessly grateful for you! Sue Grimshaw (Edits by Sue), Hang Le Design, Sarah Sentz (Enchanting Romance Designs), Emily Wittig Designs, Christine Estevez, Ellie McLove (My Brother's Editor), Jaime Ryter (The Ryter's Proof), Julie Deaton (Deaton Author Services), Kim and Katie at Lyric Audio Books, and the amazingly talented Madison Maltby, thank you for being so encouraging and supportive!

Crystal Eacker, thank you for your audio beta listening/ reading skills! I absolutely adore you!

Ashley Townsend and Erika Plum, I love the incredible swag that you create and I am so thankful for you both!!

Jennifer, thank you for being an endless support system. For running the Facebook group, posting, reviewing and doing whatever is needed for each release. Your friendship means the world to me! Love you!

Rachel Parker, so incredibly thankful for you and so happy to be on this journey with you! My forever release day good luck charm! Love you so much!

Natasha, Corinne and Lauren, thank you for pushing me every day and being the best support system! Love you!

Amy, I love sprinting with you so much! So grateful for your friendship! Love you!

Gianna Rose, Rachel Baldwin, Sarah Sentz, Ashley Anastasio, Kayla Compton, Tiara Cobillas, Tori Ann Harris and Erin O'Donnell, thank you for your friendship and your support. It means the world to me!

Mom, thank you for being my biggest cheerleader and reading everything that I write! Love you!

Dad, you really are the reason that I keep chasing my dreams!! Thank you for teaching me to never give up. Love you!

Sandy, thank you for reading and supporting me throughout this journey! Love you!

To the JKL WILLOWS . . . I am forever grateful to you for your support and encouragement, my sweet friends!! Love you!

To all the bloggers, bookstagrammers and ARC readers who have posted, shared, and supported me—I can't begin to tell you how much it means to me. I love seeing the graphics that you make and the gorgeous posts that you share. I am forever grateful for your support!

To all the readers who take the time to pick up my books and take a chance on my words . . . THANK YOU for helping to make my dreams come true!!

Obsessed with Magnolia Falls?

Continue your journey with the rest
of the series . . .

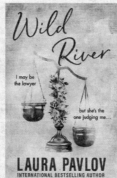

ONE PLACE. MANY STORIES

Bold, innovative and
empowering publishing.

FOLLOW US ON:

@HQStories